A SILENCE IN BILBAO

BOOKS BY MARGARET SHEDD

A SILENCE IN BILBAO

MALINCHE AND CORTÉS

THE HOSANNAH TREE

RUN

RETURN TO THE BEACH

INHERIT THE EARTH

HURRICANE CAYE

A SILENCE IN BILBAO

Margaret Shedd

DOUBLEDAY & COMPANY, INC.

GARDEN CITY, NEW YORK

1974

Excerpt from Eugene Vance's
READING THE SONG OF ROLAND © 1970.
By permission of Prentice-Hall, Inc.,
Englewood Cliffs, New Jersey.

Library of Congress Cataloging in Publication Data

Shedd, Margaret Cochran, 1900–
    A silence in Bilbao.

    I. Title.
PZ3.S5412Si   [PS3537.H515]   813'.5'2
ISBN: 0-385-00586-5
Library of Congress Catalog Card Number 73–15365

THIS BOOK
IS FOR THREE MEN NAMED JOHN

JUAN RULFO
A GREAT WRITER AND MY EVERLASTING FRIEND

JON BILBAO
WHOSE HELP IN ALL BASQUE MATTERS
HAS BEEN VITAL, INFORMED, UNSTINTED

JOHN D. JOHNSTON
NUMBER B25589, FOLSOM PRISON, CALIFORNIA

PIDO LA PAZ Y LA PALABRA

+*Escribo*
en defensa del reino
del hombre y su justicia. Pido
la paz
y la palabra. He dicho
"silencio"
"sombras" "vacío"
etc.
Digo
"del hombre y su justicia,"
"océano pacífico,"
     lo que me dejan.
                    Pido
la paz y la palabra.

BLAS DE OTERO

THE AUTHOR OFFERS GRATEFUL ACKNOWLEDGMENT

—to BLAS DE OTERO, the bilbaíno poet, for use of the lines *Pido la paz y la palabra.*

—to ANGELES ARRIEN, with affectionate gratitude, who not only loaned her name for one of the characters but read the manuscript through more than once and gave valuable counsel in large and small matters.

—to PEDRO DE BEITIA for the chance to study two Basque films, one made during the Spanish Civil War and one made recently in the French and Spanish Basque country.

—to the EMBASSY OF SPAIN in Washington, D.C., for the loan of many clippings and one book about the Burgos trial.

—to JOSE M. DE BARANDIARAN for the pleasure of his *Mitología Vasca* with its splendid insights.

—to ITXAROPENA GOIKOETXEA, for making available material on the Burgos trials and for the use on the book jacket of a detail from her painting *Burgos en Euzkadi.*

With all this help, and much more, the author still may have made mistakes. If so, these mistakes are her own.

This book is fiction. There was no way for the author to meet prisoners, court-martial Board members, inspectors, or bishops. Therefore, many characters and some events are extremely fictional.

A SILENCE IN BILBAO

1

He stood straight, overlooking the valley which opened below his small house. He did not move or shift his eyes. Behind him and the cabin rose the flank of the mountain, Anboto, a vast triangular rock abutment steadfastly gray in the dawn light. Around and approaching the crag's base there were beech trees and chestnuts whose branches moved in a rising ocean wind. Now the man put the tip of a makila he had in his right hand against a tree trunk. He turned his head, listening. Then he walked clear of the house and faced Anboto.

There was a mountain whisper, echo of sounds from a patch of blackberry bramble down the valley. Presently it came from a clearing under large trees. Anboto sent that back: men plainly walking. And now they were visible, although the one at the mountain foot did not turn toward them - three men, one lagging. Two were short and heavy, the one in the lead almost square, and both wore berets.

The third, taller man wore a cap. All of them were young. A flock of sheep drifted away from the path and the dog barked briefly and then went on with his herding duties. By the time the first two reached the house, the man up there had come back from facing Anboto and stood at his cabin door.

"We are Luku and Matai," said the square-cut man. "Here, Eagle, touch my hand." The name Eagle was said in English then and always.

"I know your step and Luku's, and I know your voices. Who's the other? Surely not a Basque? You must have worn him out on the mountain. Do you have to leave him down there among the sheep?" The Eagle, Arrano, laughed easily.

"He's an American. He's all right. I guarantee him. He's sitting on your sun rock looking at your valley. We'll tell you about him later." They didn't laugh.

The man below took off his cap and wiped his face and neck, then shook his head as if to enjoy the morning wind.

"There's hot coffee on the fire. I'll bring it." Arrano's blue eyes were not defiled nor the sockets scarred. His hands quickly found whatever they searched for. While he was in the house, Matai and Luku paced up and down. They could not leave off the changeless, unflagging mountaineer's pace. Matai, who had a fixed but true smile, put his hands over his eyes briefly. When Arrano gave them the coffee mugs both young men drank eagerly and ate from the bread loaf he had also brought with him.

Luku said, "Let me get a mug of coffee for the American and take it down to him. Have I permission to go into your house, Eagle?"

Eagle nodded and Luku went on the errand.

"How can you be sure of your Northamerican friend?" Arrano asked Matai.

"Ala! You have to believe in a man sometimes, even a

2

stranger. I've talked to him, Eagle, for hours and hours. There's nothing the matter with him except that he's an innocent."

"They can be dangerous."

"Not this one. He's become my friend. Basques can use a few American friends."

"Yes, I've known some good Americans and those were innocents too. But the bad ones are real fanfarristas."

"Not Paul. You'll see."

"What have you and Luku come up here to talk to me about?"

"Better to wait for Luku." As soon as Luku returned, Matai spoke. "Listen, Eagle, when did you last see Jon Arizeder?"

"I saw him two weeks ago Sunday."

"In Bilbao?"

"No, in Donostia. We went fishing in a boat someone loaned him. Why are you asking?"

"Did the gristapo see you together?"

"Probably. Why?"

"Eagle, I wish we were not the ones to tell you this, but we've carried the word like knapsacks of stone and we have to tell you." Matai swallowed and stopped.

Arrano turned his right side toward them, again seeming to look into the valley. He waited, perfectly still.

It was Luku who finally said, "Arrano, Jon Arizeder threw himself from the balcony of the pelota court . . . in Gernika. He fell almost at the feet of Franco . . ."

"What? What are you talking about? Jon Arizeder, my best friend?"

Matai spoke, "I know, you can hardly believe it. Neither could we when we saw it happen. He had set fire to himself. He dived from the balcony rail in flames. No one will ever forget the sight."

3

"The inaugural game in Gernika? Did Franco attend?"

"Right."

"I half understand now. But, no, I don't. Why do you suppose he did it?"

"We came to ask you why. You know him better than anyone. From what he said that day you were fishing, you must have some idea. Eagle, he looked like a meteor, his head its head."

"Did he kill himself?"

"He's still alive."

"Thank God. I thought you were saying he died. Where is he?"

"The police took him." Luku's deep voice said this hurriedly.

Arrano made a ferocious but truncated gesture, as if he intended to dig out his eyes, his hand angled like a hoe. Then he paced back and forth striking his thighs and finally he gave one great shout which came back on them from Anboto. "Tell me all of it. Last night? In Gernika? The arrogance of Franco to go there! No wonder Jon was insulted. In the new frontón? All right, tell me all of it, Matai."

"The frontón was full. Arizeder brought in two bottles of alcohol wrapped in a newspaper like bottles of wine. He poured it on himself in one of the toilets. That's what we heard afterwards. None of us saw him before the game. El Molinero had made his tenth score, and that silence after applause, you know how it is, and there was Arizeder. Pulling himself up on the balcony rail. At first you could hear the click clack of the ball, because the players hadn't seen him yet and had started again. He stood there. Then he dived, Eagle, he didn't jump. He was shouting Gora Euzkadi and something about Gernika. We could hear easily. Everybody was silent, even the informers in every third seat. He held them silent. And then there was another sound - the

4

flames, Eagle. He fell, plaust, about three meters from Franco and he knocked down two civil guards. If he had wanted to he could have struck Franco."

"I know that. Go on. So you went to him."

"As near as they would let us. He was unconscious. He lay there burning. His wristwatch had fallen off. Otherwise he wasn't disordered and his face was calm." Matai got into step with Arrano pacing.

Luku's voice was deep and gentle, "Eagle, why don't you sit down and rest a moment?" There was a rough-adzed chair in the doorway.

Arrano shook his head, "Not yet, dear friend. You, Luku, tell me what you saw."

"It was a bad thing, Eagle! The photographers rushed in. The Civil Guard had got hold of a blanket to put out the fire but they held back until Franco gave them the sign. The benighted old man stood up in his seat and looked for a long moment at Jon burning before he gave the sign. Chus! that man has no feeling."

"Except for revenge," said Arrano.

"Meantime the photographers took pictures. That's what I saw, Eagle."

"And Jon didn't speak again?"

"Not that we could hear. He lay there in the flames. His head wasn't burning. He was unconscious."

"How do you know he wasn't dead?"

"The loudspeaker kept saying he wasn't but of course that meant nothing. They called for a doctor, and Dr. Arriaga - I think you know him - went down. First they made him look at the guard who was hurt - at least he'd fallen down and one of his gaiters was half under Jon. Dr. Arriaga told us afterwards that Jon's neck was badly twisted and there was no way to be sure of the degree of burns but he was alive. The God-pissing loudspeaker went on and on

5

saying Franco was not hurt, that the madman had tried to jump down and kill the invincible leader but had failed . . ."

Matai interrupted, "Look, Eagle, we came to tell you this but also that Mascaró without doubt will be sending his men up here to arrest you, especially if they saw you together two Sundays ago."

"Mascaró? You mean Jon is in Mascaró's jail? I thought that little fat zipizopo, Bonavit, was in charge of the Bilbao district."

"Not since the Basauri prison break. They demoted him to Sevilla. And now he's back, but in Pamplona."

Luku said, "It was Matai who planned that Basauri break. It was his work, did you know it, Eagle?"

"I didn't know and I give you my congratulations, Matai. They say it was well done. Those nine are safe in France, is that right?"

"Safe until they decide to come back here. But it was the work of everyone, you know that, Luku. Why do you say it was mine? Anyway it's past and gone and what we have to do now is altogether another chosna. With Mascaró as storekeeper."

"In the name of heaven will you tell me whether Jon is in Mascaró's jail?"

"No, no, he's not in jail. We followed the ambulance to Bilbao - many Basques did - and we saw him taken to the Holy Saint Anne Hospital. But we also saw Mascaró take that lopsided face of his into the side door. Listen, Eagle, we can break him out. The nurses are mostly Basque and some of the doctors. Isa knows many of the nurses. Shall we do it?"

Arrano held his two hands toward the young men who stood side by side. He suddenly looked much older than they; nevertheless his pride gave him strong carriage and a clear voice. "Matai, let him alone until he knows he's alive. He knew what he was doing. He as much as said he was going to do something. I'm still not clear why he did this but I'm certain he knew just what he was doing. It goes without saying that he never intended to kill Franco."

Luku spoke, louder than before, "Eagle, maybe you should tell us quickly as much as you can about the day you spent with him. What happened?"

"For one thing we passed within a few meters of Franco and his guards. And by the way, it was not gristapo protecting the old man but Carlist red berets - I could tell by their voices while they were mauling the mushroom tortas we'd brought for lunch. No matter how much the old general likes to use red berets to prove the Basques love him, he better watch out." He crossed himself. "Ujuju! God prevent anyone from warning him."

"Don't get your hopes up, Eagle, you know there were three plainclothesmen to back up every red beret."

"Even so it would have been possible for Jon to shoot Franco. Yes it would. They looked in our lunch but they didn't search us. At a time like that I miss my eyes," and he used the hooking gesture. "Jon and I had a game we played through Franco's war, especially when we were prisoners in Santoña at the end. I don't know how many of you young ones know the half-whisper voice our grandfathers taught us. We also played it when we were with the maquis and had to talk French. You get tired of French. Whenever new men came into the maquis battalion we looked them over and told one another what we saw. So while the lunch paper rustled and the red berets gave orders in their dreadful kind of Spanish, I heard Jon say in the voice under his voice, 'Look straight ahead, Eagle.' Which I did, until somebody shouted, 'Don't stare at his Excellency like that.' So, Matai, maybe they would recognize me."

"It was a bad risk to use that voice in front of Carlists. Don't get careless, Eagle, you may yet have to cross the border between patrols. So you got into Jon's boat - was that the way it went?"

"Jon made me walk very fast, holding me tight by my left wrist, and when we were in the boat I asked him who I'd been staring at, and he said, who did I think? And I said, 'Well, blindness has given me one pleasure.' And I asked if he had a pistol. He didn't answer. So there we sat baiting our hooks and he finally said, 'It's not necessary for me to kill him. He's killing himself. He already wears the gleam of a long painful death and it's better so.' I told him I thought it would have been worth it, I mean both our deaths. He said, 'Oh certainly, as to that.' So why didn't he do it, I asked him. He said, 'I don't know exactly except that one must be prepared to abandon one's ethics and I'm not prepared.' And he changed the subject. He said, 'You know, my friend, you really do resemble an eagle. Who was it first gave that name to you?'" Arrano stopped and no one took his silence away from him.

But he went on. "I have to try to understand what Jon did, so let me talk myself out. We'll get a warning when Mascaró's men start up the mountain?"

"Yes, Gorka will give us the irrintzi."

Arrano sat down in the chair. "He and I both have the same given name and we were friends in school so naturally I got a nickname. And because of my sight I was often used as a lookout then. But it was a woman who turned the word into English. She was proud of her English. My little Eagle. Imagine." He laughed angrily. "I was startled when Jon asked me that question. He knew the woman had named me and he knew what she had cost me. We never talked about her. I suppose she's dead by now. I have never heard anything about her."

There was another pause before he went on, very fast now. Meanwhile he stretched his shoulders and arms. As if they

8

had asked him a question he answered, "Yes, the French woman. Those were the days I thought I was happy and had all I needed, in battle a friend like a brother and a beautiful woman at night . . . I found her after we had joined the Free French and were running our American spy service between Bilbao and Bayonne. We had several routes. One went through here where I live. She came with me once. I was arrested at a border crossing I thought was safe. She spoke by name to the Franco border guard, Melchor Mascaró, him and his half-and-half handsome face." He paused. "I saw at once they were lovers and she was calling him to attend her itch. Also she was about to receive a reward for delivering me to him and the Germans. She was one our game didn't find out when she joined the maquis battalion. While I was blindfolded and waiting - I thought to be shot - she said something about a blind eagle. It was a German who did it. At first I didn't know I was blind."

Matai said, "I'm listening to everything you say, Arrano, if you feel it's important to tell this now, and I had not known how it happened although I knew Mascaró had a hand in your blinding, but . . ."

Luku interrupted, "We must hear everything Eagle has to say. Afterwards we'll take you to the new cave. Isn't that the plan?" He turned to Matai who nodded.

Matai was the leader of the two but Luku, taller although in the same square mold as Matai, an apachao in the Basque language, was so different from Matai that they might have been matching but opposite parts of a Basque whole. Luku had two laughing sisters; that was one difference. Matai had only a stiff, shallow, well-ordered Falangist brother and a mother to match. Luku's mother was a wiry talkative catchall of love. Matai by no means had finished seeking answers. His mind was fast and his body was as quick as a mountain cat's. He was still and all the hunted, the noble, agile, brave, hunted human being. Luku was not that, nor was he the hunter. He was slower than Matai but it was much more than that. He simply had no need for hunting, in either role. So he wasn't a leader nor a follower. He and Matai were close friends.

Arrano said, "New cave! I suppose it's five hundred centuries old like the rest but I understand the gristapo doesn't know about it yet. And on your way back you better watch yourselves. It's a different path than any you've taken, and there's one very wide jump on it, a small deep ravine but wide enough to make trouble. I'll give you directions. At least you won't meet either gristapo or the Civil Guard on it."

"Go on now. Go on speaking about Jon, but more quickly," said Matai.

"We talked about Gernika and those who perished there. His brother for one. Confusion and explosions. People who went into their cellars were the worst off. The fire bombs found a way in but there was no way out. I think Jon married the flames of Gernika. We also spoke of many of our old gudari friends. Jabier, Anton; these two were shot in Eibar right after the war. And we remembered how hungry we always were. We laughed too, remembering Atwater, our American, for whom we used to carry over the messages from Bilbao. The day the Americans landed in Sicily Jon was with Atwater between Gijón and Santander and they stopped at a garden to pick flowers. Atwater was filling the jeep with them until Arrano told him that in Spain flowers were only for funerals and he dumped the whole load on the road and in Llanes they found a man selling blood oranges and they celebrated by eating them. Atwater always talked a great deal about dignity and hate. He thought you had to hate. He was a good man but he didn't think our way.

Matai, you do understand don't you that Jon was trying to tell Franco something there in the same Gernika?"

"Well, it was his right but what made him think the old arrotz would hear? When has he ever listened to us? It was a waste."

"Don't say that, Matai. Jon fought Franco's war and then Hitler's and he was ready to fight Franco to the end but he was put aside. I don't know. Anyway, Matai, I tell you he's betrothed to those fire bombs. We each picked the wrong mistress."

"You never forget that French woman, do you? One would almost think . . ." From the valley came an irrintzi, the high-pitched yell and whistle and quaver, this time a warning signal; another irrintzi from a different place and another. All fell on the mountain and returned. Matai laughed, "Mascaró won't know which one to follow. Ospa, Arrano."

"All right, we'll go. Just let me tell Zakur where he's to take the sheep. What about your American? Do you want Zakur to take him along too?"

"No, we told him to wait there while we talked to you, but he's going with you."

"I don't need anybody with me."

"Do you have a gun?"

"How would I aim one?"

"All right. The American's a good strong fellow and he's studying Basque history so we're showing him some of it. You can help educate him. Right, Luku? He'll enjoy the cave paintings. He'll be somebody for you to talk to. You may have to wait in the cave awhile. We must go right back and find out what's happening. If it's dangerous somebody will come up to take you across the border."

"What's going on down there?"

"Automobile blockades, the usual, to pick up 'the leaders

11

of the terrorist movement.' So they're detaining fifty innocent people and you know the rest."

"I don't see you fleeing, either of you, why do you want to
take me across the border?"

"Eagle, you've done your part twenty times over. Why
should we let Mascaró work out his filthy hate on you? You
know he's waiting for a chance."

"Wasn't one blinding enough for him?"

"No, not enough. He'd like to cut off your balls."

"To replace what he lacks, the filthy andipuch."

They hailed the American and he arrived with Zakur, a
border collie who kept his belly near the ground when he
ran but who stood quite still while Arrano stroked his jaws
and talked to him softly.

The American said, "I expect that dog to speak at any
moment."

Matai said, "Not yet, Paul. Zakur has to hear before he can
answer. Eagle, tell him not to take the sheep too far away because we're sending Father Ander's little brother in case you
have to leave. Will he let the boy stay?"

"I'll explain it to him."

When Zakur got through listening he returned to the
sheep and made an invisible bar which they could not pass
because he patrolled it and then stood ahead of them and
gave them the sheep-dog eye until he had them in the order
he wanted. Then with sallies he moved them onto a path
that went off through the elder trees. His barks were short
and varied in pitch.

"Really, what do you need shepherds for?" asked Paul.

"The dogs need company. Sheep are boring. You wouldn't
believe how boring. With exceptions, of course. I've known
men who fell in love with ewes." Luku laughed.

Arrano went into his house and came out wearing a heavy
pullover. He didn't lock the door. He put the chair under

the roof overhang. Now he started, Matai then Luku behind him, all going full pace ahead, Arrano touching a stone or a tree with his makila. This was not tentative, not discovering but confirming objects within a blind landscape. Once in a while he stopped but hardly long enough for Paul, who was at the end and winded from the swift rush in which they moved.

Higher up they entered a mountain fog and the Basques kept up a joke about how lucky they were Arrano was blind; their own eyes would confound them. The cave entrance was near the bottom of Anboto crag, the mouth no more than a split in a gray cliff. There was a dolmen just beyond the entrance; free standing, its wide flat rocks were a protection against the sirrimirri into which the fog was turning. The four men came together under the dolmen roof.

Matai asked Arrano if he knew his way inside the cave.

"I can see it like a very precise map on the skin of my mind. And so can I see your path." And in Basque he gave the directions for their return.

Matai asked Paul whether he had a flashlight. "For looking at the paintings as well as for following the way. But keep close to Eagle."

Paul had a small flashlight. "I don't know how long it will last."

"Use it carefully."

"You mean we're going to stay in the cave with your friend?"

"We're going to leave you with him, Paul. Luku and I have to get back quickly but we'll send someone to tell the Eagle what to do, perhaps take him across the border. After that you can come back to Bilbao."

Paul looked around the foggy, rainy, craggy place, looked back at Matai and shrugged his shoulders. Matai laughed uproariously and joyously and Paul laughed with him. Matai said, "Don't worry, Paul. Arrano will give you one of his very precise skin maps." Matai and Luku disappeared into the rain.

Arrano touched Paul's arm and he spoke harshly. "Matai says your name in English but I have to say it our way with three syllables, Pa-u-le. We're in a hurry, Paule, but I should tell you that one enters the craw of old Anboto with reverence. Our fathers were protected by Anboto during the frozen ages. So Father Barandiaran told me. I showed him this cave."

"A privilege."

"What's a privilege?" Arrano seemed angry.

"To know Father Barandiaran."

"Of course, he is one of our greatest men, but are you informed about him?"

"Of course," said Paul in turn and the two seemed easier with one another.

"All right, Paule, it's a good thing for us to be friends because we have something of importance to do together."

"What?"

"If you don't want to . . ."

"I didn't say that."

"Without my consent you were given to me by Matai and Luku for company but I'll use you for more than that. Do you have a good ear?"

"I hear well enough."

"You must learn my footsteps the same as you learned the mass - I forget most of you Americans aren't Catholic."

Paul laughed but said nothing and Arrano laughed too, another version of Matai's happy earthiness. "We don't answer when we don't feel like it either. All right, Paule, the thing is this, just now put all your mind to learning how my footsteps sound. I'll be learning yours. By the time we push our way out of Anboto's rear we'll be speaking to each other through our feet."

"I thought we were waiting in the cave for Matai's messenger."

"I'll explain that to you as we go along. One thing at a time, Paule. Let's get inside now. I'll go first and you stoop when I tell you or the mountain gives you a pair of tortas worse even than Mascaró with his patented club. I nearly forgot, I have to leave a message for that blessed messenger. To save time give me hawthorn branches, not flowering, the dry ones. While you're looking get a strong staff for yourself. There's a hawthorn tree just above the dolmen."

Inside the dolmen, Arrano left his message, branches arranged so that they might have been blown there by the wind. Sometimes driftwood on a beach is placed transiently but immemorially by the waves, a statement in the ocean's language, storms fluted into white sand ruffles, versed and transversed minutely, too intricate for most men to read. That was the kind of pattern he made with a few branches but mostly twigs; his hands, sure of themselves, were not recording words but something the reader would know without words. Then he went into the cave, slipping between two folds of gray rock. Paul followed him.

There was an entrance hall, itself like a small conventional cave. It did not give space enough for two men so they were crowded, and Paul as well as Arrano was blind because the sideway entrance cut off almost all light. Paul waited until he had regained some vision. He saw that Arrano was part way down what might have been a hole but evidently had steps because Arrano's head lowered itself slowly.

"They're very uneven. I'll be at the bottom when you start down. I'll guide your feet. See?"

"No, I certainly don't."

Arrano's laughter filled the hole-path-steps. "I like to be

15

in here with a man with sight. For once I'm not jealous. My old useless sockets send out antennae like a grasshopper's but your eyes sink back into your stomach. Correct? You better put on your light."

At the bottom of the craggy stairway there was true darkness and also a state near to true silence. There were no noises but there were sounds which might have been the movement of rivers and rocks, echoes saved up for a millennium and just barely creaking in a reserve of strength and motion, or the sound of the tips of beech tree roots, a last, lacy, meandering, searching filament which moved a thumb length a year.

They stood side by side, Arrano's hand on Paul's arm. Arrano said, "Every time I come here I hear more of them."

"More of what?"

"More of them moving. I'll tell you something, Paule. You've probably heard professors argue about how the Basque language started? It started in a cave. Language of the rocks some have called it. Rocks move a little. Listen and you can hear them shifting their weight. Call it the language of silence."

They stood longer, listening, and then Arrano said there was a straight part ahead where they could walk and practice hearing each other's footsteps. "Use your lamp as little as possible."

After a while Arrano stopped and placed his hand on the head of a low entrance to what seemed to be a side cave. "Go and see the paintings. You may never be here again. Keep your light on and go through into the second grotto. I won't grudge you these moments of seeing Mari's cave."

The first paintings were of fringed bison and several small pretty horses. The wavering torchlight gave them motion. Paul would not have observed the entrance to the second cave if Arrano hadn't spoken of it. There were indented arches which dwindled for a half meter and became rock wall. The one that was an entrance looked not much different from the others because it was dark beyond, but he was feeling with hand and light and he saw the way to what his lamp caught as a herd of bison swarming the circular walls. Rock protuberances made the animals dimensional. The colors - yellow, a fluctuating mauve, brown, green - were strong in this secret haven, this hiding place of most febrile magic. The bison swam, they ran, some had tumbled and fallen but all together they were a crashing undulating herd.

He went among them. Oh recondite and beloved swarm of beasts, the heart of Anboto - but there must be a better word than heart, Paul thought. Then he saw there were no words here. He lay on the ground so the bison would not be molested by his importunate excitement. His light could thus discover one or another. The Great Bison was in the middle, surrounded, the centric point of motion. Paul got to his feet. He knew he was a pebble within the drum of some consummation he did not understand. He wanted to remove the rattling sound he made before the drum began to beat, the heart of the mountain began to beat. He hurried back through the two stone chambers.

Arrano said, "Yes?"

"You didn't see it before they made you blind?"

"No, but one or two have told me about it."

"It might be the greatest reason you could regret your blindness, Eagle."

"There was a raven in there once. Father Barandiaran told me about that."

"Tell me about it."

"Are you all right, Paule?" Arrano heard Paul's indrawn breath, sobs, whatever they were.

"Yes, I'm all right. About Barandiaran?"

"He'd just seen the cave, as you have. He'd seen other

caves so perhaps he wasn't as excited as you, but he was happy. He's eighty years old. You know he has his comparative religion laboratory, himself and his students traveling around. Seeing the caves is a religious experience for him."

"And the raven? You mean it was a sign of death?"

"Not at all. Don't confuse us with Spaniards. They're death people but we're not. He saw a raven in there, that's all."

"How could that be?"

"I asked him and he said, 'Since the cave is an opening to heaven it must be a heavenly raven.' Paule, the raven is one of the forms that Mari often takes and Anboto is Mari's mountain. They say she spends years at a time in here. For Basques she is the head deity of all."

"And do you believe in her? I thought you were a Catholic."

"Ah, Paule, that's a child's question or a student's." The blind man stood as always very straight. Paul put the light on him because he wanted to see as well as hear the words. "Paule, you know how mountains are when they're far away. They look like clouds, and clouds look like mountains, gray and white, but it's their size and their perfect form I'm thinking of. You fly to them. That's where you rest. You don't have to ask if you believe in the mountains, you fly to them and rest."

"It's that way with Mari?"

"It's that way with the caves. The Basque heaven is under the earth. From the caves there are doors into heaven. That's how the gods travel. Oh, they fly over the earth too. Mari flies in the form of that raven and sometimes as a winged horse. And sometimes Mari travels on a rainbow."

"You must miss those sights."

"They're still in here." He touched his forehead. "Come on come on, we have to hurry after all the talking."

From that time on they went very fast. Once on a steep wide ramp they met stalactites. "Hold onto them," said Arrano, "the floor is slippery." After three platforms of those formations, they came to the meeting of passageways. Arrano told Paul to flash on the light to get his bearings. Eagle was feeling the archways and the walls of one and then the other. They entered a passage on the right. The ceiling was lower than before.

"We're going out the narrow way, Paule. At the end we'll have to crawl like moles but it saves fifteen kilometers."

In bleak fear Paul asked, "Where are we going?"

"We're going to Bilbao. Isn't that where you wanted to go?" and the Eagle laughed, this time without restraint so that the sound entered each dark corridor and warmed the sleety entrails of the living mountain. "Don't be afraid, Paule. These are the roads of rivers cutting their way through solid rock. There's no danger from falling stones. The rivers took those with them when they left." Then he spoke very seriously, "Paule, I'll always tell you exactly what we're doing. That was how Jon and I treated each other. It was I who brought in the frivolity of that woman . . ."

"What does this flight of ours have to do with a woman?"

"Nothing. But it is not flight. Right now we can't use up the air talking, and you'll have to get along without your light. Keep your hand on the end of my makila. Don't lose it." He was on all fours dragging the makila behind him. Paul lit his flashlight once. There was a low stone passageway ahead, about like a mole run all right. But they were a jointed snake, inching along in the dark.

An exceedingly long time had passed when Arrano said, "Now we can walk." They stood up and stretched. "Not to waste time when we get out, Paule, here is what we're going to do. I have to go to Bilbao. There'll come a time when I can tell you why. All you have to do now is follow the route I'll give you. After we're out of the forests you're to lead. I will have told you where to go. You're ahead. You'll hear my footsteps behind you. And I'll be following yours. That's why we were learning the sounds the other makes; we will speak with our feet. You mustn't turn around at any time. You must ignore me. If anyone stops me, don't go back. Even if it's the Civil Guard and even if I shout."

"I couldn't possibly go off and leave you."

"Oh yes, you must promise that. Don't be a halfwit. You would have to get away as quickly as you could. No matter how you feel about it, I don't want you picked up. Otherwise I'll do it alone, and in Bilbao I'm not sure I could find my way. I know the streets but many other things have changed." He was pleading but he didn't keep it up long. "Listen. When we get to town I'll stop twice, each for a little while. The moment my footsteps cease but there are no other sounds, you are to wait. Stand within a doorway as if you live in that house, and wait. I'll come back. We'll be in Siete Calles most of the time. The streets there are full of cross alleys and dead ends."

"I live in a pension in Siete Calles."

"Good, then you'll find your way easily. But we're approaching Siete Calles from across the estuary. We come out of the hills into a part of town I don't think you know. It's bare. Mines, mostly. It's called Miravilla. Up there we're on Camino de los Mimbres. We go down to a little plaza called La Cantera. At the lower end of the plaza we turn left for half a block and then right, onto Laguna. I'm going to make one stop there. It's a street of whorehouses. If you want to, you can wait inside there. Laguna goes another block and we turn left onto San Francisco which takes us to Conde Mirasol. That street goes directly to the bridge of

Ortiz de Zarate. That's the one we want to cross on. The other side we're on Ribera until we reach the church of San Andrés of the Loaves and Fishes. We stay on Ribera and then to the Siete Calles. But in the end we go back to the church. You probably know San Andrés, next to the public market?"

"Yes, I know it. And what happens there?"

"The second time I'll probably go into it. If I do, nothing else will happen. You leave me there and as soon as you can find Matai or Luku, or Father Ander, tell them where I am and that they can forget about me. That's simple, isn't it?"

"Well, give me the order of those street names again so I can learn them. It's the plaza to Laguna to San Francisco. Then what?"

"Better I say them just before we get onto them, in time for you to learn but not forget. Does that suit you?"

It was raining heavily when they came out of the cave tunnels and for a while the trees made additional tunnels. They were dropping altitude rapidly, toward the city. Arrano taught Paul the street and barrio names.

They skirted small villages huddled in the mud, but as they approached one village of three houses and a church with its frontón, cows lowing from the houses, Arrano said they would stop there. He made for the farthest caserío. On the ground floor among the cows, a woman gave each of them a glass of heavy red wine. A man posted himself at the door with his makila, another went outside. The men did no more than greet Arrano and did not speak to Paul or to each other. The woman then brought them a country soup with potatoes in it, as life-giving as the wine. They stayed a very short time.

Outside, the afternoon was raining from a low thick sky, darker than before. The rain held when they reached Bilbao. The water obliterated any mark of them as soon as they passed. They went in the order Arrano had set, and by now they had learned each other's footsteps. On the wet paths and then the sidewalks the sound was different and Paul had to discover the differences and learn them; always the makila censured, admonished, was the teacher's ferule sharply striking a tree or the street curb. Paul threw away his stick because, unlike the Eagle's makila, it was nothing but voiceless wood.

The dark was solid around them. All went as the Eagle said it would. He made his two stops, the first short one in the street of Laguna at what might have been a warehouse but was, as Paul knew, a whorehouse.

The second and much longer stop was in Siete Calles. The house into which Arrano went had an inner patio at the end of the entryway, a concierge cage or small shop there, and then a double flight of stairs to the viviendas above. Paul did not try to see more than that and went a few doorways farther. He thought he became someone anonymous trying to keep dry in the heavy rain; nevertheless, one bland-visaged man with an exaggerated difference in the two sides of his face, startling and unforgettable, spoke to him in poor English. "The rain won't estop for long hours, mister. No use the waiting here." Paul did not disclose his own face, kept his collar up and his cap down. The cap instead of beret must have told the man he would understand English. Paul only grunted and the man laughed, not Basque laughter. The man then went through the door Arrano had left half open behind him. Paul did not know what he would do if Arrano did not return after a stop.

Arrano returned, running, light on his feet, feeling ahead with his makila, its sound almost continuous. Arrano passed Paul in his doorway. Then he slowed down and Paul passed him. By that time they were near the church of San Andrés of the Loaves and Fishes. Paul stayed on the side of the street opposite the public market and crossed directly into the doorway of the church, as he had been told to do. Arrano continued under the overhang of the church entrance and went through the church doors. Paul had to assume that because it was too dark to see, but there were footsteps no longer nor the tap of makila hitting the sidewalk.

Paul walked another block. By that time it was certain Eagle was gone. There was not a human being or a car or a dog in sight. Only the young man, Paul, who crossed the street again, then trudged along heavily toward the Ekilili restaurant, where he usually ate and often met Matai or one or more of the others. With those light footsteps behind him, in rain and dark and weariness, the American had taken on some of the fleetness of the man he had accompanied. Now he looked like nothing but a wet clod tourist, or clod student or whatever clod he was in the dense lonely city of Bilbao.

2

There are bells on the door of the Ekilili. Paul stood just within, searching faces. The tables were full, more men than women and all the men in berets. The proprietor, a very dark Basque, therefore nicknamed Jonbelz, habitually hunched his shoulders as if he were protecting his vitals; it made him look like a turtle. Jonbelz, in his turtle way, also protected patrons of the Ekilili. For instance, he would not have admitted Paul if he hadn't known about Matai's sponsorship of him - Jonbelz listened to his patrons' conversations when he felt like it. That he approved of Paul meant he personally had decided Paul was no danger to the Basques in the room, who for their part didn't question that double approval. Hardly anyone gave Paul a glance.

Jonbelz seated Paul in a corner and took his coat to have them dry it behind the kitchen stove. The sweater underneath the coat was also wet and Paul shrugged his shoulders uneasily. He asked Jonbelz to give him whatever

24

was ready to eat. He was still in that state of dazed sedulous attention into which he had put himself to remember the street names. He had remembered them and Arrano was in the church of San Andrés. Now he must find someone to whom he could give this information. He looked around the room again. He was waking up.

Father Ander was sitting with Matai's wife at a table Paul had scanned before. Paul was not well acquainted with either of them, but knew that Ander was a parish priest in Eibar, a town dominated by Star Pistol and its armament subsidiaries. The young woman's name was Isa, that much Paul knew, also that she had a brother and that she was very close to him. They too came from Eibar, where their parents had been shot in the forties along with many others; Eibar, first town in Spain to declare the republic in 1931, had remained continuously rebellious to the Crusade and there were massive recriminations from time to time to keep it subdued. These things had been told Paul, mostly here at the Ekilili.

Isa looked older than Matai and was extremely slender; her hands were long and thin. She was too serious to be pretty. She had two small vertical wrinkles just above the bridge of her nose. They did not always show. Paul thought she seemed detached from the crowd, which was made up of spirited people keeping their animation in some check but still talking intensely all around her. Besides the heavy-shouldered priest, there were a young man and woman at the table with Isa. They were looking at the priest.

The other girl laughed, a deprecating laugh although joyous, but there was silence afterwards. Someone called out, "Ay, Angeles, with Jon Arizeder in the trough of pain do you still find something to be merry about?" A few people looked at Paul and then at Jonbelz. There was no overt gesture from the restaurant owner but evidently he had satisfied them that it was all right to talk in front of Paul because neither was there a hitch in the conversation.

"Forgive me," Angeles answered. "I can't help being happy. Would he want us to mourn? He did what he chose to do."

"She's right, don't fault her," someone said. And there was a movement throughout the room as if all were withdrawing slightly, deciding they should not push themselves either for or against Angeles, but Isa reached for Angeles' hand, on the table, and held the ridge of her knuckles for a moment.

Paul rose clumsily, a log that had soaked up too much water. He sneezed twice and found his handkerchief in a pants pocket. At Father Ander's table Paul stood next to the priest.

"Sir, do you remember me? Matai presented me to you once."

"Of course. We wouldn't have let you stay among us if we hadn't known who you were. Sit down. You're from which university? I'll think of it in a minute." Ander was in his late thirties, therefore older than the young people with whom he sat. His voice was rather high.

When Paul said Matai's name, Isa looked up. She nodded, friendly but still very reserved. The wrinkles in her forehead tightened. She didn't speak.

"Father Ander, can you come to my table? Or perhaps we could go in the kitchen?"

"What is it? Have you a message to give me?" For all his bulk and strength, Father Ander was a delicate man.

"Yes, yes exactly. A message from the Eagle." Paul was so trembling cold in his wet shoes and so exhausted, he held onto the back of Father Ander's chair for support.

Angeles said, "Oh, please sit down. Jabier, give him a glass of wine."

Father Ander pushed Paul into an extra chair he pulled over. "You can tell me here. Please. These are friends."

With the wine warming him, Paul told the priest what the Eagle had directed him to say. The effect on Isa was immediate. In an anguished voice, but still quiet, she said, "Matai went back up the mountain. He was going to take him across himself. He said Arrano was in danger. He will have been coming and going, walking for two nights and a day. Why did Arrano come down?" She asked Paul accusingly.

"I've never met anybody as single-minded as Arrano. He didn't tell me why we came to Bilbao. He gave orders and in such a way that I obeyed them."

Angeles laughed again but almost in a whisper, afterwards looking around the room cautiously to see whom she might have offended. "I know him. I've been up there. We spent a week near there at Easter time. Have you been up there, Isa?" She spoke to the plainer girl with tenderness and respect.

"Yes, Angeles, I've been up there and spent happy times. It's just that I wish Matai hadn't gone for nothing."

Father Ander said to Isa very gently, "He'll be back soon, I'll take you to the house," and then to Paul, "You ought to go back to your own table. The police are coming in and out of here frequently tonight. Jonbelz can keep out the chivatos but not the police and you'd do better not to be seen with us."

"You might as well go back to being a tourist, Paul." This advice came from Angeles' young man, who up to now had been present through Angeles' radiance rather than through any quality of his own, although he was handsome.

Ander spoke again, "We need to hear just how you came into town, the route, can you remember? We'll talk later. I really think you shouldn't stay with us any longer."

Paul got to his table none too soon. It was not the police

who arrived but someone with news which overwhelmed every person in the room: Inspector Mascaró was dead.

First there was a universal indrawn breath, then speculation and questions. The newsbearer told all he knew, over and over. Mascaró had been shot just outside the door of his vivienda on Artecalle not three blocks from the Ekilili. It was reported that the wife and daughter had not heard the shot but heard the body fall against the door, and they went out. The wife kept screaming she had seen a man with a pistol, who had even come over from the staircase to the apartment door to make sure the inspector was dead, but the two women's descriptions of this man were contradictory. The hall was dark. The wife also said they saw a figure run down the stairs. She was ministering to the dead man and did not try to follow the assassin. None of the neighbors saw the man go in or out and as there were twin flights of stairs meeting at a landing, whoever killed him had evidently been waiting on the side Mascaró did not take. But Mascaró was dead, that was sure. The police were already all over the Siete Calles because of Arizeder but the wife and daughter had been so excited they had run around like wild sheep for some time before they called them. Yes, they must have had a telephone, because it was certain none of the neighbors called the police. Mascaró was dead, that was the one certain thing.

Drinks were brought around, each man buying for another and going from table to table. Someone sent a straight double whisky to Paul. A number of people left, among them Father Ander and Isa. Angeles was still at the table, sitting very straight. She was trembling. Her young man put his hand on her shoulder and she moved her head back and forth so that the soft black hair touched his hand. But then she held her head up straight and sat very still.

A man who had gone to the doorway to look out for the police raised his hand and the people were back at their own tables before the bell tinkled. The man who came in was a comisario in the gristapo uniform, rather untidily gotten up except that his shoes gleamed with polish. He looked at the bell and hit it hard, which increased the bell's clamor. People went on eating and drinking; if they glanced at him at all, it was casually. One or two stared at his shiny shoes.

He didn't shout; his voice was warm and rich, rather theatrical, "There are police officers at the back door so everyone stay where he is."

"Who is trying to leave?" It had to be one man saying the words but it was impossible to disentangle the voice from the crowd and it was possible to hear it as the voice of everyone present.

"I wish to know who was the last to come in here."

Jonbelz answered that question, "All have been here a long time having their dinner, keeping away from the rain, Comisario. It's still coming down hard, I see." After his bout with the tinkling door, the policeman had left it open and all could view the slant of heavy rain against jeeps double-lined outside.

"When did you come in?" The comisario was at the newsbearer's table, which was laden with plates of food half eaten or empty as well as a number of wine glasses which he had honestly consumed.

"I am just finishing my meal, as you can see. An hour, I guess. Jonbelz serves good solid food." The newsbearer belched but nothing worked for him; his jacket was glistening wet. The policeman slapped him across the face and this time shouted, "Come on in. Here's the first cabrón liar to take."

The four who entered manhandled the fellow in a practiced way. Two more came in, wearing Italian-cut civilian clothes and dark glasses. They hustled men to their feet and went over everyone for guns, slapping many, once kneeing a man and when he fell, kicking him. It was done routinely.

The comisario's beautiful voice said, "And you?" He was standing at Angeles' table. "Señorita, account for yourself. We were told you were seen in Artecalle half an hour ago."

Paul half rose to his feet. A few people looked at him, surprised, and he sat down. Angeles and her man were shaking their heads calmly. They looked up at the policeman with courteous puzzlement. She said gently, "You're mistaken, Comisario. Be good enough to feel my coat - perfectly dry." She let him touch the coat arm near her wrist.

"My compliments. You're clearly the most intelligent person in this benighted gathering. So you ought to come with me and help me find out what happened tonight."

"Happened tonight?" She was less relaxed.

The comisario's face had gone bright red but his voice was still mellifluous, "Yes, happened tonight. You'll soon know through your obscene underground so I may as well be the first to tell you. Police Inspector Melchor Mascaró was shot entering his house. The assassin tried to shoot the señora and also our comrade's daughter. They fled before him. I see by your sheep's faces that all of you know this already. You knew perfectly well what happened." He was aggravated, then furious. He shouted, "Inspector Mascaró was shot by one of you cabrones de mierda. He's dead." Now it appeared that this peculiar man was going to burst into tears.

The anonymous voice came in casually, "The word is that the French Jews have brought their executioners to Bilbao.

The inspector betrayed many of them to the Nazis. Isn't that true?"

"Those louse-ridden maricón Jews! We've already driven them out of Bilbao. Oh no, it's one of you. We'll find out. Or maybe we'll just send you all to a desert island to gnaw bones. What a relief that would be. Come on, señorita."

"Why do you take her?" It was one concerted sound from every person in the room but they spoke softly.

Then the anonymous voice, "Are you another woman savager, another Mascaró? And Mascaró is dead." The words were spoken reasonably but it was a threat.

The comisario looked around for his men. Somehow, and deftly, his men had been surrounded. There were six of them, four in uniform and the two wearing Italian suits, and each was within a tight clump of Basques, so close on all sides that to draw a pistol would have been difficult. There were jeeploads of police outside and the comisario could certainly shout to them. But after all, somebody had gotten Mascaró.

The comisario tried a sickening geniality, "You people are touchy. Why? Maybe it was the cabrón Jews. I'm just taking the young lady in for questioning. You know, we have to get these things straightened out."

"Questioning?" The word was an echo of exactly how he had said it, prissily, yet it was painful to hear, because that echoed prissiness showed they were helpless; although they could frighten him, he had the power and the machine guns.

The comisario must have heard the angry helplessness. He spoke briskly, letting his handsome voice march like a parade horse. "She won't be molested in any way. I see that her coat is entirely dry. Perhaps your great concern for her makes her valuable to us, who knows? But I promise you she will not be harmed."

Angeles stood up, the gesture saying, well, this charade has to end, let's end it. Jabier's face was despairing but controlled as he walked beside her toward the door.

"Do you have to take your amigote with you, señorita? If you need him . . . but I have better men under my . . ."

She interrupted, not quietly, "Please address me correctly. I'm a married woman."

"Take the señora to my jeep and guard her." The comisario opened the café door wider for her departure. He looked around the room and at random picked out five men to be taken in. Then he gave an exaggerated sign of seeing the American.

"Isn't your pullover wet, señor?"

He stood across the table from Paul, who looked up at him, was able not to drop his eyes. "It's almost dry. I got into a downpour while I was walking home from the Teatro Arriaga."

"Are you a music lover? Are all Americans music lovers?" The words sounded mild enough, with ordinary scorn-for-those-ridiculous-Americans in them but nothing virulent.

"When I got to the theater I found I didn't have the price for a ticket, so I walked here where I could get a good meal for what was in my pockets." By chance Paul had been thinking of attending that concert of a Russian pianist until Matai asked him to go the Gernika jai-alai and then mountain climbing, so he knew what the program was to have been.

"I didn't know Americans were ever without the price of a ticket for anything they want to go to. Except your hippies, and you know what happens to them in Spain." The comisario's voice went into a choked whisper. His oddity lay in the way he made no distinction in the objects of his rage; small or important matters met equal violence.

Everyone in the room was watching Paul. This was not

unfriendly; it was curiosity to see how an American acted under circumstances they themselves met daily. Abruptly the policeman said, "Your passport, please."

He handed back the passport. But as he left Paul's table he was saying, so all could hear, and with Spanish obscenity Basques seldom use, "Cowards, all cowards. Why don't they stand up and fight, so a decent man can fight back at them. Slime."

When he was gone, several of the men at tables spat on the floor and then stepped on the spittle. Others were sitting with their eyes closed, moving their bodies back and forth as if they suffered an intolerable muscle tension and were trying to throw it off.

"You were all right, Paul." Now it was Jabier standing by Paul's table. "I'll walk home with you. You have a room somewhere around here, haven't you?"

"What about your wife?"

"I can't talk about her. I'm sorry, Paul, I can't."

On the street and when they had accommodated their step, Jabier said, "Angeles will be all right until we liberate her. Meantime she's as brave as . . . as the Eagle. You said you knew him. She and he get along well." Jabier stumbled a little. They were in a street with cobblestones.

They had again matched their gait when he spoke.

"I didn't mean to be abrupt with you . . . about Angeles. When this is over you and she will get to be good friends. She likes Americans and America."

"And does she speak English?"

"Not much. She went to Nevada to visit her brother. Just for a little while."

"When was that?"

"Before we were married. I'll never let her go again. I might lose her to one of those agreeable Americans she talked about."

"You would never lose her . . ." Paul remembered Angeles moving her soft hair against her husband's hand. He almost felt it against his own hand.

Then Paul saw Jabier's lower jaw quivering, preparing itself. The irrintzi came—the same utterance he had heard that morning in the mountains, used there as a warning, inimitable certainly and notable in that place because it sprang out of air, rootless, giving no signal in its structure of who had delivered it nor where the man stood, a human sound become not inhuman but as if it were part of surroundings which did not deny man, simply made him invisible. That was how the irrintzi had seemed to Paul at Anboto; it had belonged in a vast scene: the mountains, the valley, trees, sheep, all in great detail, but no men in the cry although they might have been bodily present.

Now at close range the irrintzi was tied to the man who made it. Jabier's jawbone moved slightly but very rapidly to produce the quaver. Partly it was horses neighing. Paul knew the Basque word irrintzi was used for neigh and also for the high-pitched scream of a mountain leopard. And there in the middle of Bilbao, this crowded city, with old events and new in the air, the battle of Roncesvalles took form for Paul, and this had much to do with Angeles and Jabier.

It was not the actual warriors and their arms but the sense of it, maybe its meaning which, with the two years of study he had given Chanson de Roland, had so far escaped him. He saw now that the meaning was freedom. Basques on their small mounts were running under the oaks, man voice and horse voice matched, and joined by wild cats prowling in the underbrush. The lovers rode in that crowd of Basques but Paul himself was outside it and he was lonely; he wished he had been born a Basque.

Jabier's irrintzi was long and eloquent. The handsome

34

bridegroom of Angeles raised that intense feral quiver to the steeple top of the church which showed above houses. On that steeple Arizeder had once placed the Basque flag so firmly that the Civil Guard shot it down with arrows because they found no other way to reach it.

The bridegroom left his cry up there waving like another flag. "Run," he said. "We really better run before the Civil Guard gets here."

•

Back in his room, Paul felt nothing but exhaustion and loneliness. He didn't try to take a bath. The problem of hot water at this hour would have roused the house. He got off his damp clothes, arranged them on the back and seat of his typing chair, and got into bed. As he began to feel less cold his mind insisted on doing a review of the day. His left leg from heel to thigh was throbbing; that pain, which at the moment seemed to him would keep him limping for weeks, was the nagging voice that asked him what on earth he thought he was doing. He had come to Bilbao because of his study of the Chanson de Roland, on which he was doing a doctoral dissertation. Spanish was not even his special language, let alone this unknown tongue, Basque. He was supposed to be at the University of Poitiers respectably doing that thesis. Why was he racing through the dark streets of Bilbao with the Spanish police at his heels?

Indeed, although Paul was reasonably fluent in Spanish, the preparation in his subject had been done in French since the great chanson de geste about Roland was in the ancient form of that language and, equally, a great part of the analysis of the poem was in contemporary French. He had even read Menéndez Pidal's voluminous Spanish treatment in French translation. This was all natural because of his fellowship in French Medieval Culture at the University of Poitiers.

The extension of that fellowship and the Ph.D. to which he was aimed had so far kept him from being drafted for the Vietnam war, but he had never worried about that possibility. He had now been living in Europe four years, the last two concentrated on the study of Chanson de Roland and the battle of Roncesvalles.

For those two years he had kept himself within academic boundaries: which interpretation, Bédier's or Menéndez Pidal's, was most tenable and, of course, who might be the twelfth-century Turold whose name is in the last line of the epic - Ci falte la geste que Turoldus declinet.

He had come to Bilbao and registered at the university because from the distance of Poitiers it had sounded like a better seat of learning for his subject than the Opus Dei University in Pamplona, even if that was nearer to Roncesvalles. The reason he came from France at all was that, although still cut off by the moats of scholarship and theory, he had seen that the study of a battle which took place on the land of Pyrenean Spain (not Spain at that time, 778, but a country clearly not French, under sometime Moslem occupation, but always defended by people whom Julius Caesar called Vascones) required him to go to that country, now Spain; so he came to the provinces of what he had thought of as the Basque part of Spain. He knew at least that the name of one province was Vizcaya and the leading city Bilbao and another province was Navarra, which contained Pamplona and Roncesvalles. And he knew there was a Basque language. When he got there he found that none of it was Spain; it was the Basque country. And the language had nothing to do with Spanish.

Experienced in European housing, he had looked for the part of town where students and laborers could afford to live, had been delighted with Siete Calles, found a room, put in his books, typewriter and writing materials and asked directions to a good inexpensive restaurant. That was how he found the Ekilili.

His fluent although accented Spanish enabled him to talk to his neighbors either at the long central Ekilili table or the small tables. He met Matai and some of Matai's friends. For many days the subject of their conversation was almost strictly the Basque language, which attracted Paul because of its absolute difference from any language he had ever heard and for its almost total use of natural objects and not abstractions for word source.

The Basques he met were not accustomed to an American who wanted to speak Basque. There were some they had heard about or knew who taught Basque in American universities. There were even two United States universities with Basque studies departments and where the students were not Basque but mostly Americans, so they had heard; Paul discovered quickly that Basques knew about each other all over the world. However, the young men and the two or three Basque girls Paul met at the Ekilili still took it for granted that neither Basque language nor habits nor history interested anyone but themselves; those American universities were far off but here eating in the Ekilili was an American who had already bought a book about the Basque variations of Spanish in the city of Bilbao and was saving up his money for a Basque-Spanish dictionary. So it was he became their friend without their knowing much about him or, for that matter, he knowing about them.

By habit, Paul read whatever daily papers were at hand. Ekilili had some in Basque which Paul unsuccessfully tried to read. Mostly he got the local *La Gaceta del Norte*, and *ABC* which came from Madrid.

One morning Matai sat across from him and his deep

37

soft voice was a little aggressive. It was enough to make Paul look up. "If you have to read that garbage at least read *Madrid*. They'll close it down soon enough. Read it while you can."

"What kind of a paper is it?"

"You mean Falangist or what? *ABC* is supposed to be monarchist of course."

"And *Madrid*?"

"It's hard to say. They're intelligent young Spaniards, trying to get out a reasonable paper under unreasonable circumstances. We judge them by the fact that they sometimes report Basque events with accuracy. They even reported the protests against torture that Spanish Jesuits from the Pontifical University in Rome sent out."

"What about torture? I probably skipped the article if I came to it."

"It wouldn't have been reported in *ABC* anyway, but why would you have skipped it?" Matai was looking at Paul closely.

"Because I hate violence. I get enough of it in my scholarly reading. Have you ever read Chanson de Roland?"

"No, I haven't. I'm a typesetter, you know, and I get fed up with words. But what about Roland?"

Paul recited in French,

> "*Olivier now gallops through the fray*
> *His lance has snapped, he only has a stump*
> *And goes to strike a pagan, Malsaron*
> *He breaks his gilt, fleuron-emblazoned shield*
> *Bursting both his eyeballs from his head -*
> *His brain comes tumbling downward to his feet*
> *Then piles the corpse on seven hundred more . . .*"

He interrupted himself, but he had indeed said it well, with accents and pauses that the laisse demands.

The effect on Matai was to make him applaud but also laugh. "You're an actor, Paul, I didn't know that. But no wonder they don't teach the chanson in Spanish schools. That pagan fellow would have been a Basque, you know."

"That's what I came here to find out. There's a big lapse in French records. Charlemagne's defeat was concealed for a couple of hundred years - so I've discovered."

"And you've been wallowing around in pagan brains and eyeballs for how long did you say?"

"Better than the real ones."

"Vietnam?"

"I don't read what's happening there."

"Not even in *Le Monde* when you're in France?"

"Well, no."

Matai looked at Paul, or relooked at him as if he hadn't seen him before. Then he said, "We have a good *Le Monde* reporter around here. He comes to the Ekilili once in a while, I guess every time he's up here from Madrid."

"I'd like to meet him."

"He comes in here because this is a center of news about ETA." Matai said this slowly and with a pause before the last word.

Paul couldn't help hearing the emphasis. He said softly, "What is ETA, Matai?"

"I'm not sure it concerns you, Paul. Maybe you ought not to come to the Ekilili. See the two overcoats who just came in, sitting down at the last table? They're informers. I don't know why Jonbelz let them in. This is an ETA café. We know nearly all the chivatos so maybe Jon let them in to give them the illusion they're finding out something. He knows we wouldn't say anything while they're here. Put your *ABC* in front of your face and finish your rolls and coffee. I think they've been too busy looking around to

39

have seen you yet. I'm going anyway and I'll saunter over and tell them a few lies to distract them while you get out."

That was what Matai did, went over and had a joke and a laugh with the informers, who were attentive to him.

Paul was not at all inclined to leave the Ekilili; that obstinacy made him a good scholar because he seldom stopped until he had followed whatever subject to its end. So now he wanted to finish his breakfast and finish his conversation with Matai, who had not told him what ETA was. But the authority in Matai's voice, which had shown up in the tone of his first question and gone through the whole conversation, was also persuasive. In the last words his voice was hardly audible but he was giving Paul an order. And Paul obeyed, not out of fear but out of friendship, which Paul felt strongly toward this round short smiling young man.

Later Matai had told him something about ETA and about other Basques: ETA - Euzkadi ta Askatasuna, and it means the Basque country and its liberty - was a nationalist Basque organization. Basques had frequently opposed the Spanish government. For that matter they were against anybody who did not recognize their thousands of years of rights. They had always been for themselves and their old fueros which precluded the obligation to serve in Spanish armed forces and included a recognition of their inheritance laws and legal equality of their women. There was a Basque republic for a little while during the last year of the Spanish Civil War and many organizations had grown from that. ETA was one of several such youth groups but appeared to have the greatest popular following because although it had to work underground it performed acts of rebellion. ETA blew up statues of heroes of the Crusade; it had more than once robbed banks and there were indications that these forays were sometimes covertly and adroitly fostered by the Basque bank owners themselves; it had taken over radio stations for special broadcasts; there had been several jailbreaks. They hung Basque flags in unlikely places and they wrote words in Basque on walls. For these acts all known ETA members - by inference this included a great many young Basques - were pursued by the Spanish police.

But for Paul the facts although important, as were all facts to his well groomed mind, were overweighed by the affection that had grown in a few weeks between Matai and him and also between Luku and him. In a lesser way this included Father Ander.

It might have been that Paul was lonely and therefore open to friendship. He had not made friends in Poitiers. There, students and many of the professors were so wound up in French politics that an American was easily left out of the conversations. And this American did not seem interested in any politics, even those of his own country. Besides, the fast-talking French were too dissimilar to Paul. He felt at home in the Ekilili because of its particular pace. Who can say how this related to Paul's wheatfield background; he was from the American plains and those jagged mountains approaching and receding as the train entered the Basque country were disturbing. But the people were not. He felt at home; through them he felt this was a place he should have known long ago and that he might transfer his work from Poitiers to some university here (in truth the University of Bilbao was primitive for his tastes - the city police chief or chief policeman of that time had made a speech at the opening convocation, a flashy little man named Bonavit, who had managed to get into all the newspaper pictures with a visiting French physicist of some renown). But Paul had not failed to observe the student contempt for a physicist who was willing to be photographed with the ill-spoken policeman.

Paul questioned Matai and the others very little. It still seemed immaterial to Paul. For one of the few times in twenty-eight years he was not lonely. There were friends with whom to go to jai-alai and sometimes to climb the lower, easier mountains. Paul was no mountaineer and when the three-day excursions into the upper Pyrenees were planned, he was not included. It was only because of Arizeder's leap that he had gone with Luku and Matai to Anboto.

Even the peregrination with Arrano had not made him into a Basque patriot, although it had deepened his friendships. But the ecliptic effect on him of Angeles, an involvement and not merely a pleasant encounter, and this short walk through Siete Calles with her husband had bound him to them—and to Matai, to Ander, to Luku—in a way which was a step beyond friendship; or was it the distillation of friendship?

Father Ander and Isa had the good fortune not to meet Comisario Silva. They didn't hurry. Their pace and their moment of departure from the Ekilili brought them past the corner of a second alleyway before the jeeps roared along Belasticalle to the doorway of the Ekilili.

In those days the wife of Matai was a strong girl although she was thin. She moved quickly. The priest beside her was the tall, very heavy kind of Basque, a build of man found in wood-chopping contests, tireless but also synchronized in movement, not exactly light-footed, not at all the type seen playing in the great jai-alai contests, like the one the night before, when Arizeder jumped in flames.

The police had forced the players to go on; everyone said they had never seen such harsh powerful strokes against the wall, nor such violent speed of ball and man, reds and greens both letting out their anger, or their grief for Arizeder. That was what Matai's wife and the priest were talking about, softly, walking softly too and fast, now and then saying part of a sentence which the other might not answer, instead jumping the answer and the next one's remark, unspoken, and answering that second remark.

She said, "Father . . . know about the House of Everyone?"

"Not yet. Will he be there?"

Ander knew she meant the police. Isa knew he meant Matai. "God willing," she said.

Father Ander knew she was thinking of a home she and Matai might have together some time but he would not talk about it until she did. They believed that a thought was as strong as an act, so communication without words was stronger than an act and so each must guard the other's privacy. Since the event of yesterday, and more than that the news they had just heard of Mascaró's death, there would have to be flights and hiding, all of which would mean her climbing the mountains; she wanted the support of the priest so she could do these things and not be held back from following her husband whenever it was at all possible. She knew plenty of Basque women who climbed mountains and mowed hay and took care of a big house when they were pregnant - the pregnancy was what she had not been able to tell Ander.

She also knew that her husband, Matai, who was not from the country as she was, would have other ideas about a pregnant woman's activities. His mother was a dainty lady, part Basque in blood but not much else, proud that her husband now dead had been one of the mutilados of the Civil War, his mutilation a leg and an eye gone. Her husband's history and that of her other son, a Falangist since student days and still always on call to the Supreme Leader, had borne away the mother's basqueness; she wore spindly shoes and quite short skirts, and she wasted no warmth on Matai. He had warmth toward everybody, even his mother.

44

And he had been enough affected by her to believe a woman should be protected.

Father Ander said softly, "My daughter," although he was only ten years older than Isa. He spoke so because he felt she was in great danger, that someone was certainly following them now. Because of her courage it was her danger rather than his. He did not consider himself to be a brave man. His size deceived people, he thought. Like all active Basques he knew precisely the tortures that others had received, knew of course that Mascaró had been one of the most depraved of the torturers but that there were many others. He did not imagine for an instant that he would be brave if he were taken but he knew she would be, and this made her all the more vulnerable.

The priest said, "You're tired, Isa. Can you rest at home for a while? Do you really have to go to that pupils' concert tonight? Where is it to be?"

"At the parish house near the school."

"That means all the way across town." He paused. "Now that Mascaró is gone, won't it be easier for Matai?"

"Someone else will come in Mascaró's place. Maybe even Bonavit. And Matai will never let up, you know that, Father. They hate him for his good humor as much as anything. He keeps that no matter what happens and it makes them furious." There was a pause in which the rain, their footsteps and those of someone behind them took over. She listened but then went on in a lighter voice, "When he's in the mountains people tell him those Pernando stories. He brings them to me, to make me laugh. I suppose I don't laugh enough, Father, do you think so?"

"Don't blame yourself, Isa, don't do that. You're the one who's strong as stone and gentle as a nightingale, Isa."

"That's what he said to you, isn't it? Do you think he meant it."

45

"Why should you question that? Of course he meant it."

"I'm tired, Father. I wouldn't tell anyone but you. Let it just be that I'm talking to the wind." She put a closed hand in the air, opened it, and moved it as if it stopped a breeze, although the rain was heavier now than before. "I'm not strong enough nor good enough for him. I want more than those broken scraps of time we have together. They're so few. I need more time with him."

"Tonight he'll be back?"

"I don't know. Perhaps he'll sleep there in the cave. He needs sleep. He never gets enough. If he comes back he'll hear at once of the new events and it'll put him moving . . . And a lawyer for Arizeder . . ."

"No, we'll plan some way for Arizeder's release. But Isa, dear friend, I don't think I have ever seen you as despondent as this. You were courageous and wily when we arranged to rent the House of Everyone. What is it?"

"You're right, Father, there is something. When my brother and I moved out of our apartment into the House of Everyone, I brought a box of photographs I hadn't looked at in years, Father. They were from before my parents lived in Eibar even, so you see it was a long time. There was one of a house, a true caserío, my grandfather's it must have been because we never had a house like that. I studied it, Father. I thought to myself that's where I belong, the mother of a house like that with balconies of drying corn and peppers and the cows to tend. I could see myself with the white handkerchief on my head on the third-story porch."

"In time, Isa, in time. These hard days can't last forever."

Abruptly she said, "I'm pregnant, Father. It's four months now."

"God the Father's blessing." The priest's high voice was kind and apprehensive.

"Blessings of God the Father and the Holy Ghost," she

said, laughing. "Matai told me that story. You must have heard? Pernando was invited to dinner and that greedy son of his had no invitation, so when Pernando got there he said, 'The Blessing of God the Father and the Holy Ghost,' and the man of the house said, 'Why have you left out the Son?' And you know it . . . 'Oh, I didn't leave him - he's waiting at the door.' You should have heard Matai laughing." She didn't laugh but said abruptly, "Now we'll have a child and where will he be born?"

"In the House of Everyone and there will be rejoicing."

"That's right, that was why we got it, Father, wasn't it, so we could comfort each other and give a place of rest and refuge for our husbands, Kristiana and Angeles and I. Yes, of course. Give refuge to a baby . . ."

"So you see? But you shouldn't run all the way across town in the rain. I wish I had my car. I should never get caught without it. Does Matai know this yet?"

She laughed happily. "I can hardly wait to tell him. You know for weeks I have only seen him for a few minutes at a time. Today he was there ten minutes and I haven't the courage to tell him without a little preparation. I don't know how it will seem to him."

"Of course he'll be happy. Who wouldn't?"

"Have you ever met his mother?"

"No, I don't know his family at all."

"She's a proud lady. Not proud of Matai, though, but of his brother who is a very fine Falangist and was head of Falange at the University in Madrid. Oh yes, she points out Bernardo's merits to Matai whenever she can. Not that we see her much. But it's really not easy for an abandoned son to be a proud father, you know."

"I'm very stupid, Isa, I don't understand you. I'm blest with a gentle brave mother and I have no chance to know what kind of father I would be."

"Father, Father, I'm restless in this net of dangerous comings and goings. I may not look like one but I feel like a wild dove, caught. I have only my brother and Matai in this world, and now another coming. These three are mine. I want them safe but there is no safety."

"There will be. We are making that day of safety and quiet. Then I'll baptize your child with all the ceremony you wanted for your wedding. God will give us that reward."

"Maybe when I have my seventh child, Father, maybe then. You are to forget what I have said. I'll go to the pupils' concert and come home and wait for Matai. And when he comes we will rejoice together over the new one, whom I already know and love and to whom I'll present him. What could be more joyous than that, Father?"

They had walked slowly in the rain which had closed around them. Not many people were on the streets. When there were footsteps from behind Father Ander slowed down to let the person overtake and pass them. Shortly they were within the doorway to the building where the House of Everyone was established in a large vivienda. Father Ander and Isa had together found it and together rented it under false names. The priest's parish was Eibar, which had been Isa's childhood home, but when he was in Bilbao he stayed here at the House of Everyone, a stopping place for those working underground in the liberation of their country. Luku was often there. He had left his job in a bank to live as a liberado, moving from one house of this sort to another. Of the three girls Isa had named, she and Angeles lived there, each married to a member of ETA. Kristiana was still at her parents' but her husband lived underground so they were often seen at the House of Everyone. Isa and Angeles undertook the housework, although they had jobs. Isa worked in a clandestine printing shop after school hours.

"Are you coming up, Father?"

"I was thinking I might get a bus to Eibar and bring back the car. That would be three hours though. I would like to drive you to that confounded recital. What are they going to play anyway?"

"They're good pupils, Father. Some zoztzikos of course and the Chamberiana of Emiliano Arriaga."

"Well, naturally."

"Not only on instruments, Father. One of them, Pachico Gamboa, really sings like a zantzolari. His voice escapes him and carries for a kilometer."

"Do you sing a duet with him?"

"Yes, as a matter of fact, I do."

"Then I'll come back. You wait for me. I'll bring you home."

•

Father Ander heard the last part of the concert including Isa's song with Pachico. It was pretty and rousing - the boy at that splendid age of fourteen with his sudden new voice and Isa, eyes shining, weariness gone. They sang a classical Basque folk song, *Ai María Gavron Gavrona,* which lifted everyone's heart with courage for the return to wet streets and patrolling pairs of civil guards.

Isa said her goodbyes and got into Ander's car. He had heard the news of Angeles taken from the Ekilili. He had to tell Isa, but as he closed the car door and prepared the words he decided to let her have her small warm triumph all the way across the city. And when they reached the Siete Calles they were both thinking about Matai, whether he might actually be there. Ander could not break in on that anticipation. Then they saw the door and, wonder of wonders, Matai appeared to have arrived at that moment.

Matai opened the car door for the priest and shook hands

with him. "Kaisio, Ander! Is she hiding in there too? Thank you for bringing her."

She got out quickly and was beside him. They looked like children waiting to be let into their house. Neither spoke to the other, only to the priest, who, as it had been with Angeles and Jabier, was a reflector for them.

"Come up and have a coffee," Isa said.

"Or a glass of wine," urged Matai.

"Not this time. But, Isa, I must speak to Matai, only a moment."

"Shall I go up then?" Her voice was so clear that all small shadings could be heard in it, this time disappointment.

And Matai immediately answered that. "I'll be up right away, Isa. Why don't you come in, Father?"

"No." Ander was firm. "It'll not be but a minute. Good night, Isa. Your song was very lovely. I'm glad I came back."

"What?" Matai was quiet but cautious. He even looked up and down the street.

"In the Ekilili after Isa and I left . . ."

"Jabier met me on the road and told me . . . I was afraid something might have happened to Isa when I saw she wasn't here. I had just come out the door to go back to the Ekilili."

"You forgot about the concert?"

"If I ever knew. She and I hardly see each other."

"She doesn't know about this yet, about Angeles. Can you stay with her all night, Matai? Maybe we're asking too much of her."

"It's I who ask too much. You are her real support, Father, and I don't forget it. Well . . ."

"I know. I must go. Do you have some plan about Angeles?"

"Not yet." Then he shook his head, not in denial but to

50

shake off something - the responsibilities, the pain he knew Jabier was suffering? "Good night, Father. Your little brother will be all right up there. He felt important sleeping in Arrano's house."

When Matai was inside the hall he rested against the door jamb briefly. She met him at the top of the stairs.

"I thought you would be too tired to come back. Arrano shouldn't have come down. Should he?"

Still they hadn't embraced. They had to get used to each other. They stood in the half-lit hall in front of the door to their own room, again like alien children. By chance they were alone in the house. Nevertheless it seemed they could not embrace in any spot that was ordinarily public. He opened the door and she, entering, turned toward him, her eyes shining as they had when she sang. "Ay, Matai."

Within their room he took off her clumsy coat. He put his hands on her breasts.

"They're so little, Matai. I would like to have them bigger." It was a chance to tell him - but she didn't use it - that her breasts were growing bigger for a purpose which neither of them had really expected. They had not planned to have this child. Probably, and without deliberation, it was she who had permitted it. Now it brought its radiance into her whole slight body, which moved in delight for the child and for Matai and for the new dear kinship between those two. She remembered a wild-bee honeycomb of her childhood, up in an oak tree near the caserío of the picture - a fresh delicious recollection. She and her brother climbed toward it but fled pursued by the bees . . . Maybe she was even a kilo heavier and Matai would see that her breasts were growing, ever so little but enough for a man to notice. When he noticed, then she would tell him.

She said, "You must be hungry. Let me cook something for you."

"O Isa, pochola, pichona, my little hijachu, what makes you think I could eat until we have made love?" He asked the question as if it were a joke, a kind of song joke; both sang the love they carried, soft song, strong love. Once, while they were still standing and he was unbuttoning her blouse and she was clasping the hand that did it, he laughed again and it was part of the song - that wild benign laugh of Matai. The door came open. He reached a foot backward and closed it.

The sounds of their joy were like spring storms in the valley below Anboto. And no one came into the House of Everyone. It was their house.

She was able to tell him about the baby and the way it seemed to him was that another celebration must be made for the baby, who should share their extravagant pleasure. They spoke to him lying docilely within her; they told him they were making a feast of love for his sake.

It was dawn when she emerged to get food. She prepared it quickly and took it back into their room.

After the food and in the now quiet joy he told her what he had heard about Angeles and that he and Angeles' husband were going to Pamplona, where the police had taken her. Certainly Comisario Silva could not be trusted. They would have to try to release her as quickly as possible. It would take him and the others awhile to plan the Pamplona jailbreak. He would have to go into hiding while the plans and necessary preparations were made. Now that he had a family, whether son or daughter did not matter, he would not take unnecessary chances. He would be back safely after he and Jabier released Angeles and got her into France.

"Won't you come here again until that is done?"

"I'll certainly come when it's done, and I may come sometime during the planning. I can get word to Father Ander more easily than to you. He'll tell you if I can come. My star, my rosy heart, little mother, maybe I'll make a home for you up in the mountains and send Ander's brother to bring you to me. We would never leave it."

"We would certainly never leave it, Matai."

When Matai had returned to the cave and found the branch and twig message, he knew he had been a fool not to have observed that Eagle carried not even a sparse two or three days' food supply. He told himself he might have thought the Eagle kept food in the cave for a time like this but then he laughed at his own duplicity. In truth, he had simply not thought to notice and for a man living mostly in the underground this was a serious mistake.

Since Eagle had gone on whatever flight he had decided to take, Matai had a space of time he could call his own. He helped the small brother of Father Ander look for some strayed sheep and then he went down into the valley, stood resting, leaning on his makila, breathing the fresh green wind. There was none of that in Bilbao or its surrounding towns, where air was as clogged with factory refuse as were the rivers. Then he met a great rainbow which seemed to touch his feet, and then went off in orderly magnificence to

54

meet a far mountain. He started to hurry home. At a main crossroads he met Jabier in his parked car.

These young men, mountains their patrimony and salvation, shared the lack of any need to talk about what they saw up there. Others, even Paul, might have remarked on the complete rainbow which had them enmeshed. Jabier told Matai with no preamble what he had heard about Mascaró's death.

"Who do you suppose killed him? Does anybody know?"

"None of us knows. Maybe they sent someone over from France. What do you think?"

"Without telling us? We would have had to help with the escape."

"There's no word of an escape. We asked the Bermeo fishermen."

"Could it have been someone other than us? Many people hated him. Some woman he had defiled?"

"Not many of them would have known how to shoot. The bullet went into his mouth, so we heard."

"That sounds like one of our better marksmen or more likely one of their own. Could that be, Jabier? We've all heard he couldn't leave even policemen's women alone. Might it have been that?"

Then Jabier told him about Angeles. He said it as briefly as he could. He said exactly what had happened in the Ekilili. He knew she had been taken to Pamplona. In telling the story he did not mention Paul because to Jabier he was extraneous, but now he said, "That American friend of yours, Matai, what about him? Do you really trust him?"

"Yes, I do. He's taking the same risk we are. I was wondering how he got down from the cave?"

"He told Ander he came down with Eagle. What do you make of that?"

"Luku and I left him with Eagle."

55

"He wouldn't have lied and in fact taken Eagle to the police?"

"He might be afraid. Who isn't? But he's not a chivato. What did he say about Eagle?"

"That he was in the church of San Andrés and sent word we were not to be concerned about him. I walked the American home to his room to see if there was any more he wanted to tell."

"It's all right, Jabier, Paul's not a liar either. I'm sure Eagle's in San Andrés. That new young father from Lejona, what's his name, will take care of the Eagle. He's not in much danger now, anyway. We all know it was something personal Mascaró had against him and he certainly would have used Arizeder to get back at Eagle, but I don't think Bonavit and the others will be interested. It's too long ago. He'd even be safe up on the mountain. Forget about him. And we also have to forget about Jon Arizeder. That's tomorrow's problem. Now we must think about Angeles."

Jabier gave a cry, or perhaps it was some name he had for Angeles; after that the words rushed out, "Ay, Matai, what am I going to do about her?"

"They know . . ."

"Don't tell me that. Isa and she know, yes, that if something happens to us they're bound to be in trouble but, Matai, no matter what they've heard about prison and about an andipuch like Comisario Silva, they don't really know the things that can happen to them. What shall I do?" Jabier was crying, not wiping the tears from his cheeks.

Suddenly he stood still on the path, reached into his pocket and took out a knife and a piece of cheese. He cut some and, still crying, gave it to Matai, then cut a slice and stuffed it into his own mouth. While he chewed and swallowed, he had to stop sobbing.

Matai laughed and, chewing, said, "Brother, you must have learned that long ago. Who taught you?"

"That uncle of mine. You remember I told you about him? He was the old line like Arrano and Arizeder. Who can say what those men learned in prison and out."

"And taught their nephews? My father and his brothers were followers of the Gran Mutilado. They taught me nothing but hate."

"Not a bad lesson if it gives you the balls to break nine prisoners out of Basauri."

"So you think we ought to do the same in Pamplona?"

"I don't know. I have to do something and at least I know the cells and the passageways there. But I don't have your audacity, Matai."

"Let me think about it, Jabier. You know how I am, to make any kind of plan I have to think slowly and then act fast. Meantime, you find out everything you can about Pamplona, which policemen besides Bonavit are there, and about the sewer. Find out everything. I think you should go over as quickly as you can. Lucky you have a car. Go over and find out and leave word with Ander where I can reach you."

At that spot they parted company, agreeing not to be seen publicly together from then on. Matai walked so fast it was more of a run, posting himself toward Isa.

Six days later on a Sunday they made the try.

The plan had two parts. Only Matai and Jabier would enter the prison but there were others prepared to help the released prisoners, waiting in cars outside the wall to get them to the mountains. That part of the plan was centered around the many small villages above Pamplona; the group could be split up with some taking refuge in one house and others miles away in another. Then, in five small groups they were to go at different times into the mountains toward

Roncesvalles and cross the border in several places. Two of the groups were to join the romerías, which in black hoods and robes of penitents came each Sunday joyously rather than penitently to the shrine of the silver Virgin of Roncesvalles. The plan was good, and intelligent preparations had been made.

As to the operation inside, they were to use their knowledge of dictator prisons. Franco always needed new ones and the construction of these was usually contracted out to his friends' friends. Under this arrangement the new prisons were often not well built. Matai was counting on this. Both he and Jabier had occupied cells in the so-called new Pamplona jail, which was an addition to the very old fortress prison built against the city wall. They knew firsthand that locks were sometimes attached to doors made of rotten wood and that the quality of iron in cell bars was not what was found in the Pamplona dungeon built in other times. Matai knew that the switch opening the cell doors in the first basement, where new prisoners were housed, could be tampered with. They were bringing extra guns so, once the cell doors were open, they would have armed allies. They were hoping to liberate not only Angeles but nine or ten more, including the girl named Kristiana and her husband, Josu Mendez Guenberrena, who had been picked up the day after Angeles was taken.

Jabier would go in by the regular gate to visit Angeles, who had not yet been charged; they heard that Bonavit was moving carefully in her case. Through a barroom tally of non-Basques who had recently been in the Pamplona jail and had worked in the kitchen - a privilege never given political prisoners - they heard that the outside door nearest the kitchen opened easily from within. The plan was for Jabier to open that door for Matai. Before they went further they were to dislodge the trap-door to an iron ladder which went to the sub-basement.

There were two ways to get out: the door that opened from within was the simplest and most desirable way, but there was also an imperfect main sewer not large enough to make into a standup passageway but indirectly useful all the same. It had a badly planned right angle which held up the refuse and no one had been able to decongest this pipe. In the meantime, which went on and on, the sewage was diverted into a hole through the old wall against which the new jail was built and then into a ditch outside that wall. This hole was in the sub-basement below the kitchen and the makeshift trap-door and ladder led to it.

The trap-door was covered with pots and general refuse. It had never been considered an escape way, probably because a man would have to push his face and body through two meters of filth being carried out, and from what they had heard, there was no assurance that a big man could squeeze through. To be caught there by the guards would be an unsavory death. Also, escape through the sewer hole meant time. This was the weakest part of a plan which they hoped they would never have to fall back on. Nevertheless, they were to open the trap-door, and Matai had demanded that he be the one to make a delaying action in the corridor above while Jabier supervised the departure of prisoners - whether through the door, the hole, or both.

It was not unreasonable to expect the prisoners in the kitchen to lend help in exchange for being taken along on the break. The help could consist of guarding, warning, and even admitting Matai if Jabier didn't get there.

Jabier had luck. The man on the front gate was sick, perhaps hung over. He was supposed to take Jabier to the inspector's office above, but while they were in the corridor just before the stairs, the guard urgently had to go to the latrine.

Matai and Jabier had purposely made the visit at an hour when the squad was changed. Also it was Bonavit's day off and his substitute was known to be an old inspector almost ready for his pension. The three factors worked. The squad coming on was late; the old inspector was torpid - he may have been asleep in his office because he did not appear until much later; the one guard Jabier met had diarrhea. Instead of going up to the office, Jabier ran downstairs to the back entrance and let Matai in. Matai had the guns.

The kitchen prisoners made no outcry. Most of them were frightened by the guns but some of them were friendly; they all clustered behind the big dirty stove. The two Basques did what they were supposed to and then left them there. Jabier, white-faced but untrembling, and Matai, as always with his smile, came swiftly along the kitchen level, which also contained the cells of new prisoners and the switch which had only to be jiggled to operate. Jabier had not been sure exactly where the switch was; he had missed it on the way down. Matai did know where to find the switch. Now the purpose was to reach it quickly, open the cells and give guns to those who could use them.

So far even the sick guard had not reappeared. There was no alarm, although the imperfect cell switch might set one off; they were not sure. Jabier, a tall man, stretched his legs like a giant to cover the length of the hall. The switch was all the way back near the stairway.

"Behind the green door, behind the green door," whispered Matai. He couldn't run as fast as Jabier but his whisper carried.

There was noise from the cells, no shouts but a soft beating on the bars, the rhythm of the Basque hymn, *Gudari*.

Then they heard one long cry from Angeles, "Ospa, brothers."

The switch worked and gave no alarm. It opened the cell doors creakingly. The hall filled with people; Angeles, and with her Kristiana, Kristiana's husband, and about fifteen others. There were more people in the hall than could be easily managed. Neither Matai nor Jabier had been able to find out exactly the number of Basque prisoners in Pamplona. A van had been seen coming in the night before and some of those in the hall were new to the place, and confused.

In that moment of confusion, policemen appeared on the stairs at the end of the passage and near the switch; they stayed back around the stair corner, their machine gun muzzles poking ahead of them.

Matai, Jabier, and the freed prisoners had five pistols among them. There were about the same number of mitralletas visible. The prisoners were still not well spaced. The corridor was narrow and they were jammed around Matai.

"Get back," he shouted in Basque. "Get behind me so I can shoot."

They tried to do that, the three with guns staying near him, the others dodging around them.

"Kitchen door," still in Basque, "go to the kitchen door. We're covering." And he fired straight at the guards, who then moved up onto the stairway out of range.

It seemed to Matai they were going to make it. The preparations in the streets around the prison and in the countryside were good enough to carry it off even if they had to fight their way out. Where was Jabier? Matai called him, shooting to keep the police back. Then he saw feet in alpargatas sticking out into the hall. Jabier had worked the switch but he had fallen there, holding the green door partly open.

"Go out," Matai shouted to those behind him. "Josu, you're in charge, take them out. I have to get Jabier."

Jabier was dead. A policeman had plucked up his courage and stepped out enough to reach around the stairs and kill him. Matai came toward Jabier and he and the policeman were for a moment face to face. Matai dropped his empty gun and without losing the guard's eye picked up Jabier's. The guard ducked as Matai shot point blank into the stairway before he turned and ran back toward the kitchen end of the passageway.

It was impossible and although he had done other impossible things, he didn't do this. As soon as Matai turned to run, five men emerged from the stairway and one raised his hand to hold back the others. He could have shot Matai in the head or back but, carefully, he aimed for his legs. The mitralleta shattered Matai's left leg above and below the knee and he fell. His pistol skittered away from him but he half got up. The guard who had shot threw himself onto Matai, who was on his right knee by then, trying to reach the gun. Two other guards came into the hall with hand and leg irons and trussed up Matai. He was still lying on his stomach. Other guards ran over Matai and the men on top of him. They reached the kitchen. The door that opened so easily had stuck. Some prisoners were on the iron staircase trying to reach the sewer hole. Only one man escaped through it, a common prisoner.

Angeles, being returned to her cell, saw Matai bleeding but not unconscious. He shook his head as best he could. The ones standing over him with guns did not allow more than that. Then she saw the feet in alpargatas. They were almost opposite her cell. She tried to go to him. They held her back but such was her wild anger that they let her go. She knelt by Jabier. She kissed him. The old inspector, Bonavit's stand-in, permitted it. When she stood up after-

wards she put her hand on his sleeve. Matai could see it
happen. He knew Angeles' father was very close to her. In
her grief did she imagine this man was a kindly father? The
old inspector saw Matai watching and drew back his arm
and told the guards to take her. Matai dropped his forehead onto the bloody floor.

•

Matai was soon identified but the police in Pamplona,
even Bonavit, did not know Captain Zendejas' plans for
him, so although they treated him with proper barbarity it
was not what he would receive later. Chiefly there was
general delight that the Basque terrorist who was known to
have instigated the escape at Basauri a few months before
had run out of luck in this Pamplona try. Inspector Bonavit
led the rejoicing because he was the one who had suffered
the shame of a demotion and had only returned from Sevilla
to the Basque country within weeks. His particular saints
and protectors had done well by him with Matai, giving him
back his dignity. This inspector was a small, round, usually
cheerful man and from the moment he arrived at the prison
- called in haste - he was more cheerful than ever in his life.

He helped his men kick and beat Matai; then he called
the doctor to have Matai's leg taken care of. It was a bad
splintering wound which was not going to heal fast.

Matai came out of anesthesia on a cell floor, filled with
bitter anger at himself. He had destroyed an arrangement
which had seemed promising and which besides had had
several lucky complements. What had he done wrong? Was
it what Jabier had called his audacity?

Matai by both heritage and temperament was not a man
to dwell on guilt. It was not a question of forgiving himself.
He thought through everything that had happened and

decided that although the intention to liberate Angeles was right, it had not been the time to do it. They had acted too fast and had not known enough.

Carefully discounting the pain of his leg, he decided that the reason he had done it out of time was because he saw Jabier's great need for Angeles and he himself had added to that his own need and love for Isa. Was it wrong for them to have allowed that love?

Isa was safe and he thought her brother and Father Ander would keep her so. Angeles was a widow. He could find out which guard shot Jabier by listening to them around his cell. That comforted him. It could be a project to execute. Then he thought he must be having fever to imagine that some future retribution on the guard would alter Angeles' sorrow or his anger at himself.

He was taken to Cádiz and that trip was like an execution by iron maiden: the crushing pressure of the crowded van space and the swelling not only of his leg but his whole body. Nearly dead when he got to the dungeons of Santa María in Cádiz, he was put into solitary. No rotten doors and unfit switches there but tropical heat, cold stones, and all prisoners kept naked because of the recent escape of a famous robber.

In the following weeks his anger kept him alive although he was immobilized. His leg did not heal though a doctor attended it. Naturally heavy, he became bloated and unnatural. He thought it was the prison food, worse in Cádiz than anywhere, all starch. No longer able to stand by himself, he who could run up mountains had to crawl. His leg could not take the added weight.

Then one day he simply stopped eating. It was the day Captain Zendejas finally sent for him. Matai had not been exposed to Zendejas before. He knew about the famous Basque-catcher, but in solitary, Matai had no way to know what else besides the attempted prison break - serious enough - might be held against him. He had not been formally charged with anything, had been left like a big white slug which nobody had bothered to step on.

They gave Matai a crutch. He hobbled into the interview cell. The captain wore the air of a man who has solved a hard problem and, exhausted from his effort, is nevertheless as happy as it is possible for one of his temperament to be. He was a sallow man who often belched. He took small pills which brought on belches in clusters. Sun or shade, he wore dark glasses. He did not look up when Matai came in.

Finally he said, "Can you stand? I hear your leg is not healing."

"No."

Zendejas looked up at last. It was a calculating scrutiny; at least his dark glasses did not waver for quite a while. His voice was a thin military excretion, "Let him sit."

But Matai did not sit down. It was at just this point that the change in him began to take place.

The captain said, "You're a Basque, aren't you? How was it your father fought in the Crusade under General Millan Astray?"

"My father was a Carlist."

"And your mother?"

Matai didn't answer. He had found strength enough not to hear the words uttered by the tepid voice. It had no vitality of its own, but some extraneous and grainy substance, certainly not life, was sluiced into it. Matai knew the captain was both vain and ostentatiously religious. Had these two qualities crystallized into a sediment, the salt of cruelty?

Zendejas said, "I'm not astonished at your shame. We have already received a communication from your mother

65

deploring your associations and saying she is left despairing but not surprised by your latest indulgence."

Matai kept his silence. All he could think of was his mother's penchant for flowered hats. A flowery woman, all over; he had taken Isa to meet her in Burgos where she lived: Isa plain, like him short, but very slight, dressed in her teacherish skirt and blouse; his mother, beflowered, vases of them in the apartment, her face splotched as some exotic petals are, her hands beringed. She was young-looking, a match for her other son who had arrived while Matai and Isa visited, a splendid stylish young man, as slim as his mother; they made a lovely pair. Isa had been too shy to say she wanted to leave and they had overstayed their welcome, the handsome son finally the only one who made conversation. It was about horse racing in England. He had recently visited there, reward for his ardent student days. He had been sent to study the operation of computers but had spent most of the time at the race tracks, or so it sounded.

Finally they managed to leave that room with its two graceful people and the scent of begonias and English tea; at that moment it seemed to Matai that he and Isa were gauche and their future drab, but he thought this only until Isa began to talk about the race track in the same kind of English Bernardo had used. They laughed and looked for a restaurant and had merienda and went to their hotel to make tumultuous love. Part of the time he had pretended he was Bernardo and made love according to Falangist rules which they invented as they went along and which put them to laughing until they were exhausted from it.

Those things went through his mind. He did not need to sit down. He smiled. His face felt natural to him again. Even the combination of his señora mother and Captain Zendejas could not subdue him. He hardly listened to the captain giving him a religious homily. Then that characterless voice changed. The homily was over. Zendejas was saying viciously, "She will be infinitely grieved when she knows that you have confessed this despicable crime. Of course we will have to tell her, because I am going to give the news of your confession to the press in a few days."

"Captain, I'm at a loss to know what you're talking about. You'll have to admit I haven't been participating in much criminal activity since I received this wound."

"You know as well as I do that the crime to which I am referring took place before you were wounded."

"And what was it?"

"We have the complete proof, Matai José María Artazo Loigorri, that it was you who killed Melchor Mascaró." Zendejas arranged a pile of pills on his desk and then put them one by one into his mouth and chewed them.

Matai would have sat down then, in astonishment, but the young guard who at the captain's orders had earlier brought a chair for him now yanked the chair away; perhaps he too was surprised.

"Captain, how can you have proof where it doesn't exist? If I shot the inspector why would I put myself in danger of arrest by attempting a jailbreak?"

"That's exactly the point. You Basques are full of tricks." He was still chewing pills. Then the captain launched into a session of intensive belching. This was by no means the first time he had belched but before he had always placed his hand in front of his mouth during the bouts. Now, far from apologizing, he used his idiosyncracy like a rooster's crow. The effect was ridiculous, but Matai knew that the captain was then and there delivering a death sentence in this odd redundant manner; there were uncounted belches.

Matai noted that his strength was returning. He put the foot of his wounded leg on the floor to see how it took weight. He found he could use this painful act to offset the

67

unreality of the windy captain. He understood that what he was confronting was so absurd even in the Basque country with its tale bearers and surrealist arrests (thirty men, six jeeps, ten machine guns to bring in one unarmed priest) that he must keep it in its true dimension of fantasy: Zendejas, picking up his little pills with the yellowed long nails of his thumb and first finger, like a clicking beak, attention behind dark glasses given wholly to every white pill, and then the abandon and triumph of his gassy noises, was a monster figure in a child's fairy tale. But, Matai thought, they can nevertheless fairy-tale you right up to the paredón, and he could see Zendejas, still the absurd but scary wizard lifting two yellow fingernails to signal the execution squad. How does a man keep the upper hand when he deals with a chimera? Then Matai thought, not quite a chimera; the body of a goat is right and the tail of a dragon, but no lion's head. He was smiling to himself while he thought what kind of head would be appropriate.

The chimera said, "You understand, I am now arresting you for murder. You will sign your confession, I assure you, and until you do you may expect very little kindness. You will no longer receive the benevolent treatment you have up to now been receiving elsewhere and in Santa María." The captain belched out the last words, especially "benevolent."

Matai was staring at him and he said reflectively, "A rat's head is better than a rooster's. A big thin rat out of the sewers of Bilbao."

"Are you insane? What recristo are you talking about? Oh, get him out of here. Put him in the bottom tier." And to himself, "Maybe he'll sign quickly but what disgusting people for a Christian to have to deal with!"

5

Captain Zendejas' plan was to announce simultaneously Matai's supposed confession and the arrest of many other young Basques. He had a list. Matai led that list, which included the name of every Basque who had been mentioned in confessions made under torture as well as anyone presumed to be an ETA leader. Better to bring in too many than too few. Zendejas knew that some of the ones he wanted were disappearing and he was greatly chagrined by that.

It was not a plan that had been hatched overnight. Zendejas was an orderly man and he kept his master list hidden in the second right-hand drawer of the desk which for this investigation he had assigned himself in Basauri police headquarters. It was beneath a pile of newspaper clips of the columns he wrote under a pseudonym. The list had been there, growing, for six months, waiting for the event which would implement it.

Zendejas was not a stupid man as long as he did not attempt to understand what he was doing. For instance, his intuition told him that no one would disturb what appeared to be a disorderly collection of his published writing - the Viajero columns. His pride could not possibly have allowed him to say that the reason it was a safe hiding place was precisely because no one would be interested in reading his columns; nevertheless he instinctively hid his all-important list under those clippings.

Zendejas was both intuitive and cruel. It was his decision to deny the church marriages of ETA prisoners. If he were to be asked why, he would be confused and find it hard to give a reason. He knew there were others in higher places than his who knew the reasons and calculated the effect - who in short could find their way through the maze of religion and violence. He assumed this was their job. He and they were all Catholics but in different ways. He knew many higher-ups of his own service who didn't pretend to go to church - that was left to their wives. Zendejas went to church and came out refreshed. Religious practices were the only real remedy for his many physical ills. His stomach didn't ache when he was at mass. He sometimes thought he should have been a priest. For him it was a matter of offended religious beliefs that Basque rebels were allowed the comforts of the Church, religious marriages included.

Had he been able to stay in that world where everything was orderly in a God-given and incontrovertible way, he might have been a happy man. He was not that and the reasons were obvious. When he moved into a world of logic asked and given, where a man had to have intelligence, he was at a discouraging loss. He was not very bright. All the lists in the world (and his columns were often nothing but accusatory lists) could not make Zendejas intelligent. So, paradoxical or not, if he had not had that other experience of being sure of himself in church, where at times he was even happy, he would have been far more satisfied with his outside world. As it was, he simply had to make that outside world work: in the present case he was driven to capture every man and woman on his master list.

As to Mascaró, Zendejas had been exceedingly afraid of that inspector, who had had a far longer history of service to the Crusade than Zendejas. He was aware of some relief when Mascaró was dead, but at this point an elaborate system of forgetting set in. To be sure, Mascaró was an impious man who deserved death, but the carefully forgotten reason for rejoicing was that this death was going to make it possible for Zendejas' personal crusade to be activated.

With Matai standing in front of him on his infected leg, Captain Zendejas was, as it first appeared, not especially aware of him. It was obviously God's will that Matai had got himself shot in a disorderly prison break. A beauty of this God's will way of seeing things was that events so often fell into line decorously. For instance as soon as it was decided that Matai was the murderer, the list itself gained glory, because many of the people on it were Matai's friends and associates and this made them into murderers too, and the plan regarding them, which had been developed some time ago, could be put into effect.

Zendejas had decided that Isa should be one of the first to be arrested, and also Father Ander because he was a friend of Isa and Matai, especially since, with Matai in the Cádiz prison, Ander was probably protecting Isa. (At that point Zendejas had a few pious nasty thoughts.) But until the date set for the arrests, Isa and her brother and Father Ander were to be left alone except for the harassment of fear.

The address of the House of Everyone, along with those of other similar houses, became known to the police and all were listed in the Bilbao controlled press as hangouts of assassins and terrorists. A policeman was usually in front or at the back entrance.

The chivatos were given a new duty, to get misinformation to ETA members. Occasionally it was true information; Matai's suffering during the time in solitary in the Cádiz prison and the continued infection in his leg wound were reported with accuracy. But Father Ander heard he and Isa and her brother were to be picked up within the next two weeks; in fact the intention was to arrest them in two days, and Luku, whose mother lived in Father Ander's parish in Eibar, got word to him to expect the arrest much sooner than two weeks. Immediately Father Ander took his car and went to get Isa.

The logical man for Ander to go to was the bishop of Old Mogrovia, the church official who had Bilbao under his direction. At least he and Isa could take refuge there; this bishop, unlike the neighbor one of Donostia, who had blocked the arrest of three priests in his jurisdiction, could not be counted on to help them very much, but he had put out a letter over his signature deploring not only the violence of ETA but also that of several police organizations.

The simple fact was that whether Isa and Father Ander trusted the bishop or not they didn't know where else to go. The priest did not think it proper for him to take flight far from his parish; Isa, for her part, was not well enough to attempt an escape into the mountains, as her brother had suggested. She had never been a great mountain climber. Although she was strong she did not really come up to the standard of primitive health that country Basque women maintained. Her pregnancy and the worry over Matai had not prevented her from keeping up her music teaching and her underground printing work but the strain of fear was

apparent, especially in her greater than usual quiet. Zendejas had planned that well.

The House of Everyone was nearly empty because Luku
and others had to keep changing houses, one to a night.
Father Ander found Isa there with only the company of a
mechanic who was a university student as well. The priest
told her to bring a small valise and come with him. As the
student had an intense distaste for the empty flat, they took
him along.

Isa's brother had left that morning; he had wanted her to
go with him into the mountains, but now finally he had gone
on with three of his friends. This had her approval because
she had long since decided that her infirmities must not keep
her brother from escaping.

The highway to Old Mogrovia is very beautiful and the
priest's Seat made it quickly. Isa said, overlooking the great
seascapes on their right hand, "Why don't we go a little
more slowly?" She didn't sound tense, but rather like someone who is enjoying a rare outing.

"You're right," and Ander dropped to sixty kilometers.

"You don't suppose we could stop for a few minutes and
go onto that little beach ahead? It's called La Concha and
there truly are many seashells."

The student said, "Oh no, friends, no. We've been lucky
so far but let's not tempt our luck."

"Of course, forgive me, I really had forgotten. Once Matai
and I brought a meal and spent an hour there."

The bishopric overlooked the ocean; it was a handsome
place and had belonged to a millionaire mine owner who
had used it occasionally in the old impressive manner of
millionaires before the war. Now most of them lived in Madrid and traveled to Paris and London. This particular
gentleman had given his summer palace to the Church.

Etxebe, the student, was taken elsewhere, but the priest

73

and Isa were asked to go into a room with a window opening onto a garden of bulb plants. The former owner must have had a taste for English gardens. This one had hedges with tulips and daffodils following them all around. But now they were on only one of three sides. A gardener was removing the bulbs although it was not the time of year for that. In fact it was not the time of year for tulips, so they must have been force-bloomed. The gardener was concentrating on his work and did not look into the window. Once or twice Ander shook his head in dismay; the gardener was actually digging up the blooming plants. He picked the flowers first and laid them in the shade and then cut off the growing leaves and took out the bulbs.

"Aren't they going to replant them?" The process was inconceivable and disturbing to Ander, who was a gardener himself and although he had no English bulbs knew what ought to be done with them. Ander went to the window, impelled to tell the gardener he ought at least to leave on all the foliage. But he turned away. "He's doing it all wrong," he said crossly to himself. "Now they won't bloom next year."

"He'll surely replant them right away," said Isa.

Soon the gardener left, carrying the blooms he had picked. Except for these unnatural events in the garden, everything around Ander and Isa was normal and unfrightening. Even the boredom of a long wait was natural when you went unannounced to see a bishop. They themselves were ordinary looking, a country priest and a young woman who appeared overworked not so much from want but as if she did more than her strength allowed. She might be a factory worker brought by her parish priest to ask the bishop if he would help her trace a relative in America.

After the gardener departed they both sat with their

heads bowed. Once Ander said, "I wonder where Etxebe is. I think he had some cigarettes."

Finally two hours had passed. It was not the bishop they saw, but that was also natural. The bishop's secretary who admitted them to his office after the two-hour wait was a monsignor, a seminary instructor of Father Ander's; he was trying to be cordial but he was obviously frightened. His voice shook and he kept looking out the window beside his desk. He offered them chairs on the opposite side of his desk and glanced away from them.

When they were thus arranged he said, "Father Ander, you married this young lady - I knew her parents - to Matai José María Artazo Loigorri, is that correct, Father Ander?"

"Yes." Ander spoke harshly. "Yes, they're married."

"Did they also have a civil ceremony?"

Isa answered softly and thus balanced the anger of Ander's voice, and she smiled. The smile may have reflected in the corner of the secretary-monsignor's averted eyes. "No, Monsignor, how could we? We would have been arrested. Monsignor, were you in the home of my grandfather? When I was very small we lived there. It comes to me now that I remember you. You were kind and merry with all the children of the house." She held out her hands as if to include him in her life.

The man turned all the way around to her. "My dear and gentle little friend, what am I going to do? I will do whatever I can. If you and Matai had only been married civilly as well, I am sure I could have arranged to have you together . . . one cell . . ."

"One cell? What are you talking about, Father Simon?" Ander could not contain his exasperation. "We have come here for asylum. Isa is pregnant. Surely the bishop is not going to deliver over to the police a pregnant woman as well as a priest of his bishopric . . ."

75

The monsignor bowed slightly to Isa and pulled the curtains across that window out of which he had previously been staring.

"Do you mean, Simon, that you kept us waiting two hours so that the police would have time to find out we were here and come for us?"

"Oh no, Ander, no. I was trying to find a place to send you where you'd be safe."

"And we are not safe here under the protection of the bishop of Bilbao and Santander?"

"Where is the bishop? May I speak with him?" Isa whispered.

"His Excellency had to go . . ."

"Where?" demanded Ander.

"He has gone to Burgos to protest an order of the commandant of the district."

"To protest our arrest? When we are not yet arrested?"

"To protest the commandant's order to turn any of you in to him should you come here for asylum."

"Meantime you are turning us in until such an order is withdrawn?" All the force of Ander's large, muscled body went into the words.

"No, no, no, it was done by another priest, without my knowledge. He pretended to call the bishop, in Burgos, but really he called General Pedro Maldonado, the commandant, who then sent special orders."

"A pollution, a pollution of God's house," cried Ander, his voice high. "Harboring chivatos and traitors. Simon, you're a Basque. I know your family's caserío. Do you think God will forgive you for this?"

The monsignor wiped his eyes gracefully with a white handkerchief and then like a little boy wiped his nose with the base of his thumb. "Ander, listen to me. Maybe I can help you a little. Captain Zendejas is the one to be placated.

It's he who is gathering all the materials, making the arrests now. He is a good Catholic, not a Basque of course, but from near Compostela. I hear he has made the pilgrimage every Holy Year that has come around through his lifetime. I cannot believe he will afflict either priests or women. They say he also has a special devotion to the Virgin of Aranzazu."

"No, she's my Virgin, not his. Captain Zendejas is a friend of the Guerrilleros de Cristo Rey." Isa spoke firmly and loudly, the opposite of her usual voice.

The monsignor looked around and ended up with his eyes fastened on the window curtains. "Ah, please please, don't say things like that, Isa, please, remember my friendship for your parents."

She lowered her voice in volume but not in feeling. "My parents died together against a wall in Eibar. I don't know whether you were there to confess them or what your friendship to them meant. What does it mean?" Her voice faltered and dropped. Now it was a whisper. "Will you arrange that Matai and I are together, Father? Will you? I would rather go down to Cádiz to Matai's prison than be anywhere else alone."

Isa bowed her head and was silent. The monsignor had no place to rest his eyes. Finally he did look at her, and with pity. The glance jumped away at the same time his hands lifted themselves from the desk as if they were going to take action of their own, but he let them drop and in their handsome way they became desperately sad hands. That graceful and futile action was interrupted by Ander, whose hands were a wood chopper's, enormous, calloused, undeformed but shaped for work. With one fist he struck the desk and made the monsignor's hands tremble.

"Never mind about me, Simon. The apostolic delegate will take care of me if you and the bishop are too cowardly. But in the name of Jesu find a place to hide this girl."

77

"They know she's here. I'm sure they'll search every room to find her."

"Zendejas, that good Catholic, will search every room to find her?"

"The bishop is not here. What authority have I? And it is not Captain Zendejas out there waiting. They have sent Comisario Silva."

Ander put both hands on the desk to support himself because his body shook. Isa reached one of his hands and laid both hers over it. "Say the Our Father, say it with me softly."

Over the murmur of the two Basque voices came the sputter and grind of jeeps. After the Our Father, Isa went and pulled open the window curtains. The parking patio of the palace was crowded with jeeps. Whether from restlessness, the pleasure of a successful hunt, or because it was time to eat, the mechanical and human noises were building up.

"We shouldn't wait here," said Isa.

"Yes, by Jesu, let them take us here in the office of this chivato without conscience. Let him see what he's done."

No one of the three spoke. The room was full of cumulative silence, then noise and silence side by side; there were shouts in the patio burbling down into sobs, then one unbearable scream, then shouts and laughter. With laughter came more revving of motors.

"That was Etxebe. What are they doing to him?" the big priest asked the monsignor in a whisper, giving him the responsibility, who could not accept it but crept as far as possible back into his desk chair.

Yet when the knocking came on the heavy handsome door of his office the monsignor stood up, pale, slim, erect, in his well-cut soutane and his biretta. Unwavering, he went to the door and disengaged the lock. Ander pushed Isa behind him and put the desk between them and the entering men, who did not seem to be the monsignor's allies or even his kind of people. They shoved one another through the wide opening, two carrying machine guns. None showed any respect nor removed his headgear in the presence of this Church dignitary, and the first words spoken, in the slurred Spanish of Sevilla, were, "Are you protecting these Virgin-fucking terrorists, Monsignor?"

Before the monsignor could protest, another voice shouted lispingly, "Look at the Eibar prietht. Ith it really a prietht? With hith whore tucked in behind him? A whoremongering prietht that'th what they're protecting."

This was an elegant and well-proportioned room, distorted only a little by clerical touches - three varnished chairs in a row against one wall, a safe, an unflattering picture of Pope Paul VI. The rug, the desk, its chair, the large high window were all noble and possibly snobbish, in all events handsome. And so was the monsignor. The policemen were still clustered near the entrance, he apparently holding them back although they were not looking at him but beyond to Ander and Isa. Now the monsignor raised his arms and stood like a cross in their way. They did not touch him but went around both sides of him. The man with the lisp said, not loudly, "Be careful, Monthignor, you don't want to get in the way . . ."

But then the noise began. The monsignor, stranded on an immense formalized rose, an island in the elegant rug's pattern, dropped his cruciform arms but kept his feet among the curving petals. With his head bowed he was appealing, as some factory-produced figure of a pleasant saint might be. Now he crossed his hands on his chest as well as bowing his head. He became invisible and his room crashed around him. The old sergeant from Sevilla when he lifted his voice did not shout, he bawled, a sound unlike cattle, resembling the non-animal and dehumanized roar of some black, slime-drenched tenement alley. Its ingredients were cruelty received and cruelty given, death and pitiful birth. It was mostly fearsome and that was its executor's intention.

Father Ander paled before the ferocious incoherent bellow. When the Sevillian struck his face the red mark showed precisely, a palm against the white skin. Ander reeled and reached backward to keep from falling on Isa. Ander's size made him a component of the sudden violence; there had to be some kind of strong recipient. But Isa was as much out of place as was the saint-monsignor. She too stood very quietly. She wore an unstylish print dress, rather loose to cover her pregnancy but very fresh and clean. Her face too had a fresh look, not as strained and tired as before. Although her hands were shaking, she opened her purse and took out a rosary.

If that hadn't happened they might have left her alone or at least taken her away decently and quietly. The Sevillian was busy with Father Ander, getting him into handcuffs and leg chains. The younger men were still not sure how to treat Isa, but the rosary which she was now saying, her eyes open, her lips moving, became too much of a link to their sad overburdened mothers and to the glistening little shrined Virgins of their country towns. Isa could not be disregarded. There was a pause. The room shifted, perhaps trying to regain its decency. In truth, that shifting was the sound of Comisario Silva banging a hall door, then coming noisily up the stairs.

As he entered he said in the beautiful voice no one ever forgot, "Put handcuffs on this infamous woman. Take her rosary away."

The young men competed with each other to obey Silva's orders, hustling Isa as though she were resisting them, tightening the handcuffs, striking her in the face and then throwing her purse to Silva, the invented bustle performed with shouts and laughter, each man proving he was the most assiduous.

They took Ander and Isa, bound, to the jeeps. The monsignor was still praying. Silva threw the rosary to him. He didn't catch it, although after they left he leaned over and picked it up from the handsome carpet. Then he abandoned his refuge flower and laid Isa's rosary on the desk.

Following are parts of a statement Father Ander made for his lawyer.

"I was in the company of a young woman and a young man. I was arrested on October 5 at the bishopric of Mogroviejo. The evening of that day we arrived at headquarters of the Social Brigade of Bilbao in Gorodoniz Street.

"Inside the entrance of the police station, officers were gathered who forced us to go between their double file. Many asked me if I were the priest and when I said yes slapped me across the face.

"They made me get onto a sort of board and began to give me blows with their rubber bludgeons mainly on the stomach. They also gave fisticuffs on my ears, all with gross vulgarities on the subject of women.

"They grabbed me by the hair from above to make me stand on tiptoe, and in the same way threw me onto the floor. The young woman and man arrested with me received the same treatment. The girl was not beaten as hard but she was addressed with enormous vulgarity.

"When the police got tired, they took us to a lower level of the station. We were followed by young policemen in plain clothes who insulted us. They took us in a file and put us in a cage. The young men outside clutching the bars of the cage looked like wild animals. An older policeman called to their attention that this was an open cell where they could be heard. Since our arrests in the bishop's palace, we had been manacled.

"Another group of young plainclothesmen took us out of the basement and put us in different cells. They began to beat me. I could not help screaming and I heard terrible cries from the cell where they had taken the young woman.

"For me there were many bludgeon blows on the sides and belly and on the testicles. One was hitting me on the back with his wooden club and another on the buttocks with his baton. When I bent to try to avoid a blow they would kick me in the chest and in the ribs. I tried to get to the door, but all that happened were more blows from the truncheons and more kicks.

"I remember once during this time they said they were going to do the 'roue.' They made a circle and passed me from one to the other, each beating me in whatever manner he fancied. I was unable to complete the circle and fell to the ground. One of them lost patience and threw me against the wall. The circle lasted a long time.

"They held me to the wall with a baton against my throat so I could not twist or bend, which were the only ways I could get relief from the irons on my wrists fastened behind. One of them would reach around and hit the irons with his stick. After this they fastened the handcuffs with my hands under my legs and made me go about squatting until I fell down. They beat my buttocks to make me get up. They took off my shoes and put a weight on the toes.

"When they had enough of that, they made me hop around squatting while one went round on an old bicycle they keep down there and each time he passed me he would beat me if I was faltering. After that it was the exercise, up and down until the legs couldn't do it. They made me count the times . . . And after that the operating table . . . and after that I was tied to a chair with my hands chained behind my back and kept there for many hours. These men had a fund of filthy words beyond any I have heard. Once I was on that chair so long that I had to urinate in my pants. The humiliation of that and of the bicycle were the worst; you feel like an insect that has been stepped on and is flapping around half dead.

"I was kept six days in the police station. I was taken every night for maltreatment. One night I was allowed to go to sleep on a sofa and told I would not be disturbed. I was wakened in five minutes for interrogation. My body was bruised all over. My toes and wrists were crushed, my face was swollen and I did not have the courage to ask for a doctor. Once I asserted myself to demand that my bishop be notified and that under the law I could not be arrested without my bishop's permission. Their answer was that my bishop had already washed his hands of me and so had my mother, and then they gave me another beating. I was moved from the station to a prison and kept there in secret for twenty days more."

One part of Ander's experience is not recorded in the statement. He told it but his disgust would not permit him to write it down.

He finally came to the last of the six days in the station house of the Social Brigade. Although the special duty of this branch of police is tracking down subversives and terrorists, and although Comisario Silva belonged to a different police group, Captain Zendejas had great faith in Silva, having used him in earlier Basque court-martials and importantly in this one.

The torture and interrogation of Father Ander by the Social Brigade's special squad had not produced anything like the results Zendejas wanted, which was nothing less than a full statement of how the dispatch of Mascaró had been planned on such and such dates in the monastery of the Fathers of the Epiphany and with so and so present. When, no matter what they did to him, nothing really forthcame from Father Ander except, in lucid moments, a repeated statement of his religious beliefs added to the screams and supplications which his high voice frequently emitted, Silva was called in to take a hand.

In that pseudo-logical way in which a movie house owner will, if he has one horror picture to show, show two, so Zendejas, admiring his own adroitness, decided that the very man to seduce a real although deluded priest was a spoiled priest. Silva had been dismissed from a seminary near Cádiz.

Comisario Lucas Silva was born in the Canary Islands but was not a true Canarian, who are guanches and have a creditable history, the known part going back before the time of Columbus, who used to check his boats in the Canaries for the long pull to the Indies. Columbus had a lady love on the island of Gómara. Her Spanish name proved she was not a guanche but daughter or wife of an official. Another story tells about Columbus' pursuit of a guanche maiden, tall and swift. His men were betting, some on him, some on the maiden who was compared to a doe. She was caught. So were most guanches, the last living in caves, leaving behind them traces of their dark skin color in the Spanish population. For that reason, any pure Spaniard knew this race was inferior and huntable. Silva grew up with that idea, all the more so because his skin was rather dark. Also the guanche caves and the Basque caves may have been associated in his mind.

Silva's family was poor. He was a bright boy. A priest on the island of Lanzarote, living in exile there among the camels and cochineal bugs, saw the boy was teachable. The priest was old but at some time had been energetic enough to make a nuisance of himself - one of the religious or political nuisances exiled to the Canaries. He wanted to help an intelligent boy. The priest managed to get Silva into a seminary near Cádiz. It was the most effort he had made in twenty years - writing old friends, getting a few pesetas out of a family farm to give Silva a dowry. He died afterwards.

None too soon to avoid the disappointments which would have been his. Silva, even with a lovely singing voice, did not do well. He couldn't abide the mixture of students in that seminary. Also, he considered the priests socialist and subversive so neither could Silva abide them; he was there during the few years of the republic. Perhaps he needed and even longed for paternalistic repression, in some part of his mind knowing his own shortcomings, including treachery, and wanting them controlled by someone other than himself.

When the rise of Franco began in the Canaries, Silva had reached his third year at the seminary. One more and he would have been an ordained priest. He never talked about what happened to bring his dismissal. In view of his eventual career with Franco, it may have been something the Crusade found meritorious: the priests may have caught a letter of his in which he offered to go back to the Canaries and help the general and if so, there were probably other letters not intercepted. That seminary was destroyed and the prior killed with elite savagery when Cádiz was over-

86

whelmed by the Crusade. One thing that Silva talked about was the beating he gave a fellow seminarian, a trial run which Silva could not forget. He left the boy blind. Some said he was Silva's denouncer to the priests, others that he was merely a homosexual.

Basques knew these things about Silva because they made a point of learning all the facts they could about Spanish policemen stationed in their country, especially those encountered in torture cells. Silva was well documented; so were Bonavit and Mascaró, but names were not always known, for instance the corporal from Valmaseda and one called The Mustache who was famous for tickling prisoners into dreadful hysteria, and a man who would appear in tandem with Mascaró and then disappear. Also there was the old Sevillian whose nickname was Powder Puff. The torture squads were sent wherever they were needed in Spain.

·

So, Silva joined the Franco army and to his great glory took part in the Sevilla massacre in the working class district. After this there was a blank in Silva's life. The Basque investigation turned up nothing certain. Perhaps he ran onto a decent commanding officer who did not countenance his flamboyant brutalities, but some said he spent the time in one of those ill-manned insane asylums of the war and first postwar times and that he was recruited from it for police duties too revolting for regular men, if there were any such after Spain's fratricidal war. He never gained much rank. In his own peculiar way he was outside Franco's Spain; certainly he was not part of the new rich who grew so fat.

He was scrawny and to those who knew him professionally this seemed to extend inward. He always appeared to be ashamed of himself. He had a scar on one cheek. One might guess, unfairly, that his was not a battle scar. But it was that, given him with a hoe by a woman he was trying to rape in Sevilla. He forgave her the wound, was proud of it and touched it fondly, but he never forgave her escape or at least he went back to those streets of Sevilla every time he could, looking for her.

So Silva was a pitiful man, scarred, resentful that for all his talents he had never made much impression. The approval he was receiving from Captain Zendejas was a balm but it had come very late. Etxebe, the student taken with Father Ander and given to the comisario to handle, said Silva arrived early one morning at the Social Brigade prison and began to beat him, meanwhile berating the policemen who were there because the prisoner hadn't already confessed. Etxebe said that when Silva stopped hitting him the insults began and lasted at least half an hour. The insults of Silva were worse than his blows, Etxebe said, because with that face of failure and the malice pushed down into the roots of his being, when he started his vituperation nothing stopped him. He wasn't afraid of saying anything that came to his mind. He lacked respect for whatever he had been able to find out was the most sacred to the prisoner.

After the rabid insults Etxebe was hung by his feet in the elevator cage, his hands manacled between his knees. He signed the statement that had been prepared for him.

The next morning early, Silva had Father Ander brought to an interrogation room. It was a more respectable habitation than the bicycle cell in the basement or the one with the operating table in it. It was as if, this not being Silva's home but that of a relative or friend, he had been given the best they had in which to receive his visitor.

It was well known that these men made their real homes

in the police stations. Abhorred by the populace, away from their own towns, often disliked by their wives (as was said to be the case of Melchor Mascaró), not unlikely since their vocation of torture must finally erode whatever goodwill they had, the station houses were their refuge. It was told of one of them in Bilbao who used that ordinary opening gambit of an arrest, "Come on down to the station with me, not an important matter," with such cordiality that he was convincing and some went with him thinking he meant what he said. In a way perhaps he did. Since home is a habit, then the urine-smelling entrance, the light that never went on in the third section beyond the scuffed swinging doors, the bicycle even, might have taken on a dismal familiarity and so become the place to which a man belonged. That policeman might as readily have said, "Come on home with me and have a cognac."

Raddled Silva spoke pleasantly that morning. "We must have something to say to each other, Father. We come from the same education."

Ander smiled as best he could with his puffy mouth. "Yes? I've heard you were in a seminary."

"They kicked me out because I couldn't sing that puñetera new music of theirs."

"Oh. What music do you like?"

"Sit down, sit down. Have a cigarette."

Ander motioned to his swelled lips, shrugged, and shook his head.

"They shouldn't have treated you so. I'm sorry." Silva laid a baton on the floor by his chair.

Ander watched Silva with pity. Ander was a man who would stop his parishioners from beating their oxen and the man before him was less than any ox he had ever seen because as everyone knows cattle have dignity, and Silva looked downgraded, degenerated below any member of the animal kingdom. This one is bound for hell, thought the priest, and he felt very sorry for him and tried to smile at him.

Silva was speaking. "What do you mamones do for your sexual needs?"

"Nothing. Chop wood."

"Have you ever had a woman?"

"No."

"So you like men?" Silva made a sad gesture of male to male lust but it distorted his face and his hand into something so wearily obscene that Ander did not restrain himself from reaching toward him with his own gesture of comfort and revulsion. He said, "My friend, you must know some priest you can go to. You need . . ."

Still Silva did not strike down the hand that had reached to him. Still he sat in his chair across from Ander. His aspect was of a deprived object, even his clothes seemed disarranged and soiled. Of the two of them, although Ander was purple from beatings, it was Silva who looked as if he had been tortured - lines clove his face, his head hung down.

"There is no one who would want to help me." Self-pity came up like fat on a dish of entrails cooked for a dog. And then his manner changed; he had reached a depth from which he had to rebound into anger. "But not from you, you maricón, you don't know how to sleep with women as a man should. Nor with men either and you despise me because I do." He began to pant like a ridiculous actor. "Because the priests made me into a half-man you mock me . . ."

"No man or woman would sleep with you except under force," said Father Ander coldly. Even his tolerance had worn out.

"What's that? What are you saying now?" It was not the

priest's cold deprecating words that Silva heard but what came after. Ander was speaking Latin.

"Acunctis nos, quaesumus Domine, continua pietate custodi: ut quae insola spe gratiae caelestis innititur, tua semper protectione muniatur. Per Dominum . . ." He blessed himself as best he could with his manacled hands.

Silva blessed himself too and cried out, "Alleluja, alleluja."

Ander rose. "They haven't let me say mass since I was arrested. Will you say it with me now?" His hands lay on the battered table between them. "Shall we make an altar of it?"

"Let me lock the door first. The cabrones de mierda who use this police station wouldn't understand. I know all the answers for the high mass. I know them, Father. Can you sing the high mass? I can sing it all, the whole mass. It's the day of San Lucas the Evangelist. Today is his day and he's my saint. Did you know that? Did you know my name was Lucas?" Silva was very excited.

He turned a lock in the door. As he came back the beautiful if stagey voice (he overpronounced the Latin while Ander gave it a Basque sound) came out with a most glorious Prefatory, "Per omnia saecula saeculorum . . ."

And "Dominus vobiscum," answered Ander's poor voice.

"That's right. You sing the answers. I know the whole mass. They never let me sing it but of course I know it. Surely with this voice they should have let me sing it. Will you let me now, Father?"

"It's a profanation . . . you're not a priest."

"Leche de la amada! A profanation? You let terrorists and malcontents use your church for their purposes. I'm an officer in the service of a great religious crusade. Let me sing the mass, hijo de puta."

91

Ander stared pityingly at him. "Sing it then, sing it. I'll give the answers."

Silva was appeased and friendly. "That way we won't have to take off your handcuffs. You see? Now, you kneel here." He moved the table under a crucifix which was part of the room's equipment.

Silva began to sing the high mass. He seemed to be unaware of Father Ander kneeling where he had been told, giving the salutations and answers required of a server. Silva was floating on his fine voice. This did not change his looks much but he was not quite the same malicious man he had been, and he maintained his flight up to and through the Acclamations and himself took the Amen, amen, amen, in a musical elaboration which almost turned the hateful room into a chapel. Then as if this had been an affirmation of some nobility in him, Silva raised his arms and sang the Lord's Prayer triumphantly. All this in Latin, and it brought him to the rite of peace.

"The peace of the Lord be with you always," he sang, now in the vernacular.

Ander answered, "And also with you."

The actual breaking of bread and taking of wine was upon Silva. He had never performed this part, and of course they had no goblet or other paraphernalia. Or what undid Silva may have been the ritual that was supposed to happen just before the communion and after the server's peace response: an embrace given by the celebrant to the server, and in most churches carried from him to one of the people attending the mass and person to person among them all. Silva turned around as if he were going to perform this part. The resonance of the words he had last sung warmed the room. Ander's inadequate rendition of "And also with you" had not deleted that.

Ander rose from his knees, as was correct. His face was

lighted with some form of joy - it was not terror - even this strange mass had comforted him. He seemed to expect Silva to give the embrace of peace although he could not open his arms to receive it. There was a mighty silence which could have contained the transfiguration of some minor but terribly lacerated demon into an angel (still lacerated but in heavenly ways). Silva's arms were raised at his sides like wings.

The priest's face showed the changes taking place in Silva. Ander looked forlorn and then shamed. Then fearful. He turned away from Silva's face and ran toward the door. If he had been able to hold back his fear, Silva might have expended in some other way the paroxysm to which he had built and which should have culminated in the raising of the host, instead thwarted by that unlucky rite of peace and now released by his victim's terror.

Even in this situation, Ander was thinking, "Anyway, he's been going to mass." That was because of the lapse from Latin into Spanish because it was only in recent years the salutation of peace was given in more than words. But the recognition of Silva as a mass-goer did not lessen Ander's terror, although he had got back to his usual pragmatism; he was a strong man who knew other men's minds but who at this moment had no way to defend himself from one who had chosen to defile him. He pounded with his manacles on the locked door. He could hear someone on the other side trying to force the door.

No one entered and what happened was not the cold or laughing routine of torture; it was ravishment, a beating as furious and prolonged as the orgasm of some man who has been unable or unwilling, or in spite of himself long deprived of such an occasion.

Police batons used in this district are either twenty-five centimeters long or fifty. The shorter one had been tested out and modified, measured and proven by Melchor Mascaró and it was named after him, a mascaró. It could put out a man's eyes and eternally damage his eardrums. It could prod all parts of his body. It was this kind of baton Silva had laid down but snatched up to use.

The door was finally pried open from outside. Captain Zendejas stood there, not as inflamed as Silva but very angry. He was in uniform, tidy, dark-spectacled.

He said, "Comisario, I understood you wanted me here to witness the confession. I hear you've been singing mass instead. You don't learn, Comisario. What recristo is this, will you tell me?"

Silva gasped. He didn't try to speak.

The captain lifted Ander's bloody face off the floor with his shoe. "If he weren't one of those Basque animals, he'd be dead and then where would our case be? As it is he has to go to the hospital." He pointed with his baton, a long one, to the men behind him, "Take him there. The cabrón reporter from *Le Monde* is sniffing around. You keep this father well protected in the hospital. Hear me?"

The sense of the room which had been some sort of chapel and then an unequivocal abattoir was now of the deepest imaginable despair. Ander was unconscious. Silva had not only returned to his particular and fearful anguish, he had entered some new labyrinth of it.

He said, "I'll go home. I'm tired."

"A chuloputa like you has no home." Zendejas laughed sourly, and so in their different ways, mostly in embarrassment, did all the men with him. The two who were to take Ander laughed breathily between their efforts to get hold of the heavy body.

"Give the comisario a bottle of wine and let him go to sleep in the squad room, Inspector." Captain Zendejas sounded tired himself.

The inspector said, "Captain, why do they keep him? Thank God, he isn't in our service."

"I am terribly humiliated that his indecent profanations of our Church took place in your station, Inspector. He does a good job every once in a while. I really thought he was going to get the confession. He got that young fellow's."

"I know."

They went away. One man, designated by the inspector, stayed to clean up the room.

7

The only thing that was simple for Arrano during that day of his and Paul's expedition was his entry into the church of San Andrés. For some reason he got into his mind this was going to be the risky part of the trip, that having left Paul behind, he was going to meet some terror just inside the big door. It was true the door brought him into an unlit vestibule, or so it used to be. Then when that specter of danger did not take shape and he was not attacked, he shifted ground and told himself that he must be careful about depending on the way things formerly were. If the vestibule were lighted now it could be a trap. He would be seen and that might easily be more dangerous than meeting someone in the dark, but it could only happen if he were followed and he had no sense of pursuit, or flight, in spite of the events inside the house where Melchor Mascaró had lived. When he finally recognized that this kind of thinking was his reaction to being alone in a populated place for the first time in years he got back his natural healthy caution. He stood perfectly still in the vestibule, not breathing in order to hear anyone else breathing. He believed he was alone and he followed the wall, touching a bulletin board, then a door which led to the gallery and then the wider door into the church. Unless they had been moved, which seemed unlikely, the confessionals were on the left side of the altar (he had heard that some renovation had been done in San Andrés). He had entered right of the altar so he must cross its steps. He went onto his knees, and got to the other side. The confessionals were in place and he laughed inwardly thinking of a game of hide-and-seek, he and the confessionals. The old Gothic altar had been changed for something the description of which gave him no picture, except that there was an immense golden cross suspended in the lofty gloom above the altar. Again it was the gloom upon which he reflected.

If someone entered later than he, that person would not yet be able to see him, but if someone were kneeling in the church he would by now have gained partial sight. Unless that hypothetical man moved (in the small entryway he could have heard the breath but not here) there was no way for Arrano to tell whether or not anyone was there. So he attuned his actions to the assumption someone was there. He found the priest bell alongside the confession box, rang it, and it made the rounds of the arches and crevices of San Andrés. Immediately Arrano went to the second box and pushed open the half door and knelt. He felt around him. Apparently the boxes had changed, if not in situation; there was a curtain above the half door. He pulled it across. The sides appeared to be solid except for the confessional grill. He waited for what seemed a long time.

The priest had not yet arrived when Arrano clearly heard someone enter the church, but he was well into his box and at that moment the priest came into the confessional and opened the grill on his side.

Arrano spoke at once, "Father, if the man who just entered goes into the first confessional, please hear him and let him go. I'll be waiting for you. I am an old Basque." The word "old" was a signal that he needed help.

The priest said, "Not as old as God," which was the answer to the signal. The priest shut the grill.

Drawing a total silence around him and filling the box with it, Arrano listened to the other man stumbling on the altar steps. (So San Andrés is indeed very dark, Arrano thought, checking this for possible need.) Once the man muttered in Spanish. Then, still stumbling, he rang the priest bell hard and very nearly fell into the first confessional. The priest waited a moment before he opened that other side of the grill. Arrano could hear nothing. Although he was used to open spaces, his life had brought him more than once into closed niches: in rocks waiting to cross a border, in a crowded gathering of trees, in the loft of a house - all connected with waiting. He had long since made up a ceremony for this waiting and it came back to him now. His heart of course beat heavily, and without word or sound and in the heart's rhythm, he sang it a song; a Spanish hopscotch rhyme he had learned on the streets of Bilbao forty-five years before: "Fanfarrista, fanfarrón/Muy amigo de baladrón."

After that he laughed at his heart and said, "Sleep now, sleep until I need you." Then he was ready and his heart didn't get in the way. He could hear the murmur of the priest. Once the man in the other box cried out and, even muffled, it was the sound of anguish. Not long after that the man left the box. Arrano heard clearly that he went to the back of the church and knelt.

The priest opened the grill. "I'm going to take you with

me but he's at the back. We'll wait until he goes. I'll tell you when that happens."

"I can hear him."

"He won't be long. He's in a great hurry."

The man at the back of the church rose and it sounded as if he ran out. There was a door there into a side street.

"Do you wish to confess or have you come for another reason?"

"Yes, Father, I want to confess, but when we're out of these boxes. Oiba, they make me uneasy!"

The priest laughed softly and lightly. "In the garden?" he asked.

"Anywhere there's a tree around."

"Who are you?"

"Arrano, the blind man."

"Blind Eagle." The priest correcting him sounded young and respectful. "I think there's no one in the church now but I'll go out to be sure and if it's all right I'll lead you to where we go. Otherwise I'll kneel on the steps of the altar until I can come for you so just wait."

It was safe. They went through a door beside the first confessional and the passageway led to the priests' quarters. For just such an emergency as this a room was kept prepared. It was in the basement of the old monastery which housed the priests' residence, a school, and the teaching nuns' residence.

The young priest insisted on giving Arrano food before he heard his confession. Then he took him to the refuge. Once there, Eagle felt out dimensions of the place, climbed on a chair to reach the ceiling. He said, "You're kind to give me this protection, Father, but I can't use it. I would start pounding on the door and shouting. I'd have the police on your necks in no time, not to mention scaring your little nuns to death."

"Our little nuns are mostly old ladies and they've lived through a war or two. But what shall we do?"

"The simplest is the best. A room like this at the end of all those clever passageways would be the first thing the zipizopos would find. Can't you get me out of Bilbao tonight? Some fisherman . . ."

"I'll talk to my fellow priests about it. Meantime can you at least stay here while I do that? Look, you must need sleep. Asleep you won't be pounding on the door. Lie down, Eagle, I beg of you, and let us priests think up some simple solution."

That was certainly the least Arrano could do for his hosts. He was a man who slept quickly. He had made the confession, in the grimy little garden back of the monastery under a grimy chestnut tree which was trying hard to come into bloom. Now he lay down and slept.

When the young priest came back and saw him he let him alone. He sat down and waited.

But Arrano awoke almost at once. "Thank you, Father, that sleep was what I needed. Now I'm ready to follow any plan you propose." Arrano sat up on the bed and pushed back the hair that had fallen into his eyes.

"First, Eagle, there's important word that has come to us through the back gate. Mascaró is dead."

The silence between them was unruffled. Arrano said softly, "So that is the word that has come. Do they know who killed him?"

"No, but the police will be watching every fishing boat up and down the coast and they'll be blocking the roads more diligently than ever. Two such events. Arizeder and now this. The city will be under guard at every single corner."

"Oiba! It seems I got into San Andrés just in time. So you want me to stay hidden, is that it?"

"No, we can't dictate your actions to you. I only wanted

to say that we can't get you out. Anyone making an effort to flee Bilbao in these days would himself be in danger and we would be taking a great risk if we tried to arrange it."

"I don't want to put you in danger."

"One of the priests, God bless his soul, has another idea. He says that by now, from your solitary way of life, you've taken on the appearance of a monk. I should tell you, that priest was in the back of the church during our little game of salistrampas and he saw you."

"Ujuju! How could he have been there and I didn't hear him? I can hear a louse whisper."

"You can take that up with him when you meet him."

"What's his idea? Go on, my young friend, and tell me." Arrano stretched his arms to touch the wall on either side and he brought them down with an exclamation of pain, "Ala, just so you don't want me to stay in this cricket trap!"

"He says you look like an ascetic monk and it so happens we have the brown habit for one of our celebrations. That's not important but we have one. A little short for you but the sister superior is having it lengthened."

"So?" Arrano was still wary.

"So you will be Brother Telesforo, named after that great pope and martyr. You have come from - where would you like to come from?"

"Valley of the Gypsies," Arrano answered promptly. "I have always wanted to live there among that wonderful accursed folk. So, long ago I took myself to an ermita there."

"Better if you had lived in a mountain cave. The Civil Guard might know the ermitas but never the caves. They'd have a case of titiritear at the thought of a gypsy cave. How much do you know about the gypsies?"

"I never had a gypsy girl for a sweetheart, if that's what you mean, although I've heard others talk about that too. But I knew many gypsies who came to the market in Gernika.

I've walked that valley of theirs in war and peace. Would that be enough?"

"It sounds enough to me. This was before . . . your blindness. Forgive me, Eagle, but if you should be asked about different villages, the roads . . ."

"Everything was before my blindness and I remember everything. Today is the first day since then that I've been alive. You know that. Ospa, let's get the sackcloth and ashes and see if they become me."

"There was one more stipulation. My brothers invite Brother Telesforo to have supper with them but they want the brother to know he has a great reputation as a storyteller."

"Well, Father, I may have lost the way of telling stories. Your brothers, God bless their souls, may be disappointed in this rural hermit who has lived too many years in a squalid cave among the squalid gypsies. And listen, young brother, I'm not forced to sleep down in this hole? Under that poor gasping chestnut would be more appropriate for Telesforo."

Sporadically these priests lived well. They depended on the charity of the inhabitants of Siete Calles who, themselves sometimes pressed for food, knew what a discomfort hunger was. This was one of the good times. And except for a sparse small infrequent bottle Arrano had had little wine and the priests brought out their best.

They were right: Arrano looked the perfect hermit. Even his feet were tough and bruised enough, since not always owning alpargatas he had walked barefoot on Anboto's rocks. With the wine they settled down together, a small company: the pastor, his assistant, the young priest, the porter Bachi who was in confidence and kept an ear out for the bell, and two seminarians. There was equality in the group.

First they talked about Arizeder. Nothing else could be said until that subject was fully explored. They understood why he had done it, that was not at issue, but they needed to tell one another each scrap of information they had heard - how he was handled when the police put him into the ambulance; what the Basque doctor who was called from the galleries had said exactly word for word; who were the doctors that would treat him at Holy Saint Anne Hospital. They agreed that the fact Basques from every part of the country had now heard about the fiery dive and men waited at the hospital entrance day and night, would probably guarantee decent medical treatment for him.

After the situation of Arizeder had been examined carefully the name of Mascaró came up. The first words were said by a seminarian from Vitoria, "Is it certain he is dead?" as though Mascaró himself might walk into the monastery.

The pastor didn't answer although the question had been addressed to him.

Arrano spoke, "Is he so frightening, that Mascaró?"

"His offenses against women are the worst I have ever heard." This time it was the young priest.

"And against men?"

"Through their women. Of course he tortured men, and at the same time he made tapes of their cries and forced their wives to listen when they came to beg help for their husbands. Much more than that. Now that he's dead I want to put his sins out of my mind. I've heard the stories of too many women he has afflicted with his cruelty."

"He had a wife himself, I've heard, and a daughter. How is it those two women could have tolerated him and shared his home?" This was Arrano.

No one answered at once. Then timidly the seminarian from Vitoria said, "I've heard his wife couldn't leave him. She had nowhere to go." After a pause. "She's not Basque and she's not Spanish and there was some reason she couldn't go home. To France, I think."

Bachi spoke. "It's been on my mind, Fathers. She and the daughter come here quite often. Maybe none of you see them because they come in and kneel at the back. I thought the girl was ill, she really looks ill and walks stooped, and once I went back and said to them it was a little warmer in the front of the church. The wife glared at me, a very frightening woman . . . handsome but really ugly, if you understand me."

"She had a great deal to bear, with such a husband . . ."

Bachi was scornful of these soft sentiments. "If the inspector had not been such a devil I would have said he had a burden to bear with a wife like that. But it was the girl who took my attention. When I spoke to them I thought she really wanted to move up front. She even said, 'I want to go to confession, maman.' The 'maman' was in French; I don't know why I remember except I couldn't imagine calling that woman any kind of mama . . ."

"Yes, and so what happened?"

"Mama shoved her back into her seat. She said something about when we go to confession it's to the monsignor . . . What monsignor? I never saw them around when any monsignor came here to say mass. Did they ever come to communion, Father?"

"Bachi, we have no right to discuss their situation. Since they didn't come to us we're obliged to respect their silence." The pastor was stern.

The young priest, evidently experienced in a situation like this, picked up the words quickly. "They're suffering enough. Let's leave them alone. And Brother Telesforo has not even begun to keep his promise. A story, Brother. What story will we have tonight?"

"It ought to be about Arizeder," said Bachi.

"Arizeder or you, Arrano, or both of you." The seminarian from Vitoria was growing surer of himself.

"The flag?" Because although that story of the flag hung on the church steeple seventy-seven and a half meters high was well known it always brought pleasure to Basques.

"Yes, the flag."

"Maybe you don't know what results it brought. You must have been children, all of you. Nineteen forty-six. Or not yet born."

"I was no child. I was never a child. Who's childish during a war?" Bachi said. "Anyway I remember it. We lived near that plaza. My mother always sent me out for the milk for the younger ones. God knows what time the milkman had to get up but his cans and the bones of his horse were clattering away out there before sunrise, and I was the one who had to meet him at our corner. He couldn't believe what we saw and I couldn't either. That flag was up there looking as large as all Europe. How did they get it up the last five meters, Eagle?"

"Basque luck, or desperation. But it was well planned. Jon is very good at planning. He left the doors to the bell tower cluttered with boxes marked *Danger Dynamite*, so the firemen were delayed. Anyway they couldn't reach it. There was the Basque flag flying - and it was a very big one, Bachi - on the tenth anniversary of Franco's takeover. If they hadn't left the church fifteen minutes earlier than they had planned they would have got away. Jon had some young fellow with him who insisted his mother didn't know where he'd been all night and she'd be worried, so they pushed up the time all along. Fifteen minutes later would have been safe. Worse luck for them. That boy's mother didn't see him for two years."

"You were saying that afterwards . . . ?"

"That was the best part, Father. The big flag up there

came down in burnt tatters from their arrows - well, you know that, but did you know how Basque flags multiplied themselves a thousand times over in the next months?"

"I was in a boarding school in Bidasoa and those brothers were not the ones to let us out because of Basque rejoicings . . ."

Arrano's voice warmed. "Suddenly thousands of Basque flags, small ones made of paper, were fastened to trees or telephone posts or walls, all over, even in tiny villages. The police couldn't keep up with them. And in Archanda on the exact site of that last battle before Bilbao fell, someone, well not one man, several, and I could name them, painted the word Euzkadi in letters two meters high - it could be seen from many parts of Bilbao. They wore masks and did the job by flashlight and until it was over held prisoner anyone who came by. The best of the paintings, I think, was one on a building directly in front of the police station of María Muñoz." He sighed. "That was a time to live. They wrote *Muera Franco* and *Muera la Falange* for the gristapo to read."

"But they caught those who did it?"

"Some, yes. Or others in their stead. I think most of them got away that particular time. I was taking a rest. I couldn't afford to get caught because of the other work I was doing . . .

The last words slid downhill as if Eagle thought he had talked enough. Every man was silent for a while. Then the seminarian said, his voice breaking because it took all the courage he had to say it, "Why don't we have festive celebrations like that now? Everything now seems sad and hard."

It was the Eagle who spoke up to reassure him, comfort him. "We'll have them again. We'll have the flags up again. And we'll have the fires atop the twenty-seven peaks.

There are other things we have to do now, my friend. It's still just as true, more, more I think, that the good Vizcayan - and you from Alava too - never give up, not in a cockfight not in a street fight. But he laughs at the same time. Let me just tell you this and I'll stop. I was in Donostia. Maybe that's why I like to go out in the harbor there. It reminds me of that day. It was long after I was blind. It wasn't more than ten years ago. Franco was taking his vacation that time too. It was another launch, not as fancy as the *Azor* but everybody knew it of course. Anyway how could they help seeing his red and yellow flag? So there he was having his daily tour on the blue Cantabrian waters he so often mentions, when one by one every small boat in the harbor put out its Basque flag. Three thousand flags, either paper or painted on wood and floating on the water. Oiba, what a sight! And there I was blind as a mole. They didn't have the police or the boats to arrest three thousand people. There were no flags in the boats they caught up with. Jon started something with his flag on the cathedral."

The six men were still silent.

"I haven't told you any great tale, have I? There are enough of them. Txomin. He got out and was in the United States making a good living as a guitarist but he came back. And he was arrested. And Peru. Next time I must tell you about Peru. And Mikel and his Japanese students. There're a thousand stories but maybe not a thousand nights. Can't we get any new word about Arizeder, Bachi? What's the matter with your information service?"

And they did keep track of Arizeder's condition. Whatever news there was, whether about him or others, any underground word or even street gossip, came to Bachi and usually soon not late. Within a week a diary written by Jon Arizeder got to them through the back gate.

This paper came clandestinely from France. It turned out

that Arizeder had been writing a book for a long time and had mailed the manuscript to a friend in St. Jean de Luz a few days before the jai-alai game. He had never mentioned any of this to Arrano, whom that fact piqued a little. But Arrano understood his friend's reasons from the excerpts which had been copied from the manuscript and brought for him and others who knew Jon. Evidently, further along, the manuscript told of the fire bombs at Gernika and of the prison life that Arizeder and Arrano and many gudaris had lived after Franco's victory, until they died or in some cases were exchanged and sent to France - men like those Arrano had talked about when he was supposed to be telling his story - Peru, Txomin, Mikel. These later sections were mentioned but what was copied seemingly whole was an introduction both to the rest of the book and to the event at the frontón. This had been written during recent weeks. Arrano had shared with Arizeder some of the days mentioned, including the one at the harbor, told without Arrano's name because Arizeder had been punctilious about omitting names of those of his friends who were alive.

For Arrano, of course, all of the diary came through his ears; the Vitoria seminarian read it aloud in one sitting:

AUGUST 20

I am now in Urkiola, a beautiful corner of my Vizcaya. Yesterday I climbed toward Anboto, the marvelous valley at the foot of that mountain where I have walked so often during these times of forced retirement, when because of complications and problems related to my having fought in the Resistance, I was counseled to avoid being implicated with groups which are now being followed by Franco's police. I have loved this valley very much and I can never forgo returning to the old cross situated toward the top and that records the death of an old-time mountaineer . . .

I also hunted for mushrooms, my favorite recreation and sedative for a troubled mind. I remembered an old trifling event, when at the border in Etxalar mushroom hunting served me as a justification to the Germans of my presence there. What I wouldn't give to return to those days! I would still be able to do it because I feel strong and my spirit has never betrayed me, but all that is nothing now but a far-off recollection. I'm going in another direction and the road sign says to the end of everything.

AUGUST 22

Today I went over to the Sanctuary of the Fathers of the Epiphany. A pile of stones and a tiny Virgin. In my time I had a great devotion to her and I used to pray there for my country and for my cause. Why couldn't I pray as I used to when I heard the priests' choir intone the psalms? I was there and I was absent. I desire to keep my faith, believe in something, but it escapes me.

AUGUST 24

Today is Sunday and with my family I went to a deep valley called Iturri-gorri. We found mushrooms in a beech wood. I love the forest but sometimes it frightens me. Man is changed into a dwarf. All the greens that nature has created are there. Even the stones are green. And in the woods there is a contrast of silence and noise which is startling: sometimes the murmur of the foliage is soft but it becomes violent when the wind chooses to sweep the earth . . . Many times I have felt like an intruder entering where I have not been invited and I have been afraid and looked for the way out to the sun, which with more right than I have to enter is still prohibited. When the leaves fall and all the vegetation sleeps then comes the white cover, snowflakes falling from high branches. My fear is greater in that heavy white snow. Today man is destroying the woods as if he wanted to destroy this fear but I would like to die in the forest.

AUGUST 25

I slept well. Lately I have not been tranquil but the last excursion tired me physically and rested my mind. I don't sleep as deeply as I used to a few years ago. I am preoccupied with something which has to be done soon or more exactly something I am considering doing. The truth is I am afraid not to do it. I believe it is my duty to risk everything and die for the cause. To protest one more time. But what does it matter whether it's now or a little later? Every man has to leave this world. Some depart having done nothing. I want to go leaving something behind. I want something after death. I want to live in the memory of my people. Death means being nowhere but I want to remain in the hearts of those who think as I do. To give them courage, faith, and hope in Euzkadi.

AUGUST 28

I have the impression that some of my friends are avoiding my company. They consider me compromised. My friendship is a risk because they think I'm impassioned and partisan in matters which inevitably involve risk. Knowing my temperament they think that sooner or later they'll see me arrested. I don't reproach anyone. That's the way the world is and man has become weak and clutching when it relates to survival and profit. Anyway for me it is the feeling of intimacy that is important and there I have the certainty of knowing I have many friends, and yet nobody knows my real plans.

SEPTEMBER 4

Am I tired of life? No, none of that simply because I am considering departing it. I submit that I am going to die in order to protest against injustice and hypocrisy, and against persecution.

But above all because I remember Gernika, symbol of the liberty cherished by Basques. I want to relight that fire which destroyed our liberty and do it in the presence of those who are responsible.

I have no intention of killing Franco. He's a man in his dotage whose followers keep him on his feet by force and in order to maintain a myth. He's only a decorative figure. He has been touted as a man of providence but all men of providence die in bed of a head cold. He's presented daily as active and capable of holding tight on the reins of government. The insistence on photographing him surrounded by piles of books and documents is interesting. I doubt if he is able to read the morning paper. The ordinary man has an age of retirement. A dictator doesn't have this because the wolves who live off him want their posts insured. Private enterprise would never choose as director an old man with the abilities of Franco.

So Franco will die by himself one of these days. Why give him a push? What I want to do is simply protest before him. Several times I have had him at three meters from me. I could easily have made an attack on him. I admit I passed some bad moments and that violent ideas went through my head. But I let him walk away, reviewing the troops that were honoring him.

A few days ago I was taken for a suspicious character. It was at the Donostia harbor. Someone had loaned me a boat. The pier was cordoned by police. The accesses were closed to prevent the crowd of people who congregate when the Chief of State goes by to get on his yacht. One of the port employees knew me and asked the police to let me go in to get aboard my boat. I was carrying a package with exceedingly innocent contents. When I came to the end of the pier, I noticed I was being followed by a sergeant of Franco's guard and a policeman in civil clothes. They reached me and asked very correctly for my documentation, but they didn't insist on that because what they were really interested in was the package. "Do me the favor of opening it," said the sergeant. Apparently they took me for a terrorist and thought the package might contain a bomb. How embarrassed I was: in it there was a mushroom torta and a fried trout I had brought along for lunch . . .

This raises an interesting question. If during our war I had had Franco in my hands what would have been my duty? I know the answer for myself. But for the world? Then it would have merited a decoration and the man who shot him would have been a hero. Now he would be an assassin, a terrorist. What has changed? Then it was war, of course. But at what point did the war end? When peace was imposed by one of the sides? Did the problems that brought on the conflict disappear then? Why may I not insist on my right to consider myself still at war against a law which is not legal, and against a system which does not respect the most fundamental human rights?

SEPTEMBER 6

In my time of war and action I had moments of depression but at that time I was one cog more in an enormous wheel which forced us to action at an appointed hour. I remember the long waits before coming out of the trenches. There was great possibility of death but we who went into the danger were many and in that macabre lottery there was always some possibility of escaping death.

But now I see no escape. My mission must end in death and nothing is served if I don't die. But with dawn and this radiant weather my spirits rise and the pessimism disappears. Death doesn't seem so horrifying . . .

SEPTEMBER 7

I've never been a heavy drinker and very rarely drunk. Alcohol is a method of evasion and worries drown in liquor. I am worried but I don't feel like getting drunk. I don't know the drugs that are so much talked about but if the only way to arrive at my goal were to take one of them I would do so. But I prefer not to depend on anything artificial. I think from now on I will not drink more than I usually do. I don't want to fall into dejection.

SEPTEMBER 9

Today is Sunday. It was overcast but didn't look like rain. I went in my car to the crest of Artikutska where there is a leafy wood, and in the moss a great variety of mushrooms. A misty rain had already begun when I passed the crest which leads to the woods and I was not wearing proper clothes. But I went in little by little, not thinking of a return. Then came the kind of rain with which my country is prodigal - dense, penetrating. A heavy fog wrapped everything and obscured the outlines of a few sheep that were no longer browsing but stood quietly waiting out the downpour. I also stood quietly under the branches of a large beech tree. It was a protection of short duration because when the leaves were soaked, water fell in torrents. I like to get wet and I let my clothes soak up the rain. I wasn't cold and I thought I would stay there a while to enjoy the things of this earth. I drank the raindrops that fell off my nose.

Before, I used to come to the mountains with friends. Now I prefer solitude, walking at my own pace alone.

SEPTEMBER 12

Violent action has two contradictory sides. What is a terrorist? Is it the man who believes in violent action in order to instill the terror which will force his will or his program? If this is so then Franco and all those who support him are terrorists.

But that is not the way it is in this hypocritical world. Suppose a man has made armed resistance in the name of a high patriotic ideal. And in this war (because we are in war) suppose that man kills a civil guard. He is immediately called a cowardly assassin and a terrorist. But let's imagine that he's leading a group and in a bold coup he defeats and destroys a thousand civil guards. The next day the world press will be talking about an army of liberation and about a general, the same terrorist who in the beginning killed one civil guard.

What will I be called? I don't aspire to anything more in the reports of the Franco press than the title of terrorist because I do not aim to kill a thousand Francos, nor even one. I want only to see the terror reflected in his eyes . . .

SEPTEMBER 13

I had a son whose death marked my life forever.

My son had an ephemeral life. He reminds me of the tree of Gernika, sick from the lack of pure air necessary to freedom.

My son didn't want to die. Nevertheless we buried him on the day of his sixteenth birthday. I didn't look at him in his coffin. I had already embraced his warm body just after life escaped it.

I have put him up as security that his life and mine have value.

In his innocence he said, "I don't want to die." In my wisdom I say, "I want to die." He was youth which could have accomplished much. I have left my youth behind and I also want to leave some accomplishment behind when I go . . .

SEPTEMBER 14

If I don't die it could mean a failure. I don't want to stop halfway and find my bones in a dirty prison cell.

I have often considered how to state my personal faith before Franco. As I have said, I am not looking for his death.

For me to accomplish my protest two circumstances have to meet. One, I have to be willing and prepared and, two, I have to be in an opportune place and moment. I don't have firearms. I don't choose to have them because I don't want to cause innocent victims. Two hand bombs would be enough to terminate the dictator, if one wanted to do that. One shot would also be enough.

But that's not my idea. My intention is an old one of mine. I want Franco to suffer the fire which he lighted in Gernika, that fire which he swore was lighted by us, the gudaris. He said this in order to discredit us before the world. This calumny came from his mouth. It is a filthy lie and he has never chosen to admit it or confess it. I want to carry this fire to him because it is his.

SEPTEMBER 17

I have always admired those Buddhist bonzos who, to protest injustice in their country, burned themselves publicly. Or that young Czech Communist rebelling against the Soviet occupation of his country.

Am I not able to do the same? Do we Basques not have reasons to protest before the world? Why do the democracies ignore us? Why is the Vatican silent about the dozens of imprisoned Basque priests? . . .

·

Nothing that his friend said surprised Arrano but it did leave him reflective. The manuscript had come by the hands of a fisherman from Bermeo. Fishermen like other friends brought food to the priests' house and the manuscript lay there in a catch of merlusa. When the cook gave it to the pastor, he saw what it was and at once gave it to Arrano and told the seminarian to read it to him. Then he and then the priest assistants read it. With the interruptions of their work this took two days. Arrano, having heard it first, had the two days to reflect. At the second dusk he sat under the chestnut, his head covered by the brown cowl. The young priest came to sit with him.

"Your friend is a hero."

"He wouldn't want to be called that."

"I suppose not."

"You could say there are no Basque heroes."

"How could you say that?" The young priest sounded angry.

"That European use of the word hero is an offense, don't you think?"

"Ah, I see, Sperrle bombing Gernika with his condors was a German hero? Is that what you mean?"

"It was a Basque who led other Basques at Roncesvalles. And defeated Charlemagne. But I think you don't know his name."

"It's Roland's name we know."

"Poor Roland." Arrano let out a long laugh. "Can you see

116

him there? He won't blow his horn, and no, and no he won't blow it in time to save himself and the flower of French knighthood. So with his brains coming out of his ears he finally blows it. Too late. Charlemagne hears it on the other side of the pass but he can't get back in time to save his favorite or any of them. All dead because of the false pride of a golden knight, lying with what face he has left looking toward the Basque country the better to tell his lord he would have gone back to fight if he could." Again he laughed. "Thanks be to God we don't play that game of heroism . . . superhuman deeds, shame if he's not the best."

"Could it be, Arrano, that those who are not heroes are not cowards either?"

"I'm no philosopher, Father. I've known Basque cowards. Not many. But among the gudaris if a man was a coward, he told us about it. It's the one who doesn't admit it who's the dangerous coward . . . and maybe, too, the hero."

"You sound like Unamuno, Eagle."

"Yes? I've heard Basques say he is no Basque even though he was born in Bilbao, but I never forget how he answered the death cry of that creaking old Gran Mutilado - and there's a hero for you - with his own kind of cry."

"And Unamuno died very soon after that. That could be a Basque joke!"

The porter had joined them. "I knew him. I knew that creaky old Gran Mutilado. He looked like the sewed-up horses Spaniards goad into the bullring to be regored. If you ask me, he was mad with fear. Long live death! What kind of man would say that?"

The young priest remarked, "Have you a message for us, Bachi?" because the porter often got so interested in the conversation he forgot what he had come for.

"Oh, to be sure, there's an American at the back gate asking for someone named Arrano. I told him we had no one here by that name."

"Young?"

"So-so. He looks scared."

"Your guide?" from the young priest.

"He might be. I'm afraid it's no good news if he's come here. I never even suggested he do that. Do you want to see him first, Father? Just to be sure who he is."

"Bachi, put him in the priests' parlor."

"He said to tell Arrano he had just come from Pamplona."

8

They didn't stay long in the stiff parlor but went into the refectory for whatever the cook could find to give Paul, who had a look of fright and excitement. Finally, with some soup in his stomach, he could talk. He told them everything he knew about the events in Pamplona. It was what he had heard in a Basque bar. The one common prisoner who had escaped, an old man not Basque, was not reapprehended until he had confusedly told many people what he had seen. Apparently he talked continuously up to the moment the police found him, beat him, and took him back to jail. At least he had been bought plenty of drinks while he was free.

He had been working in the kitchen. At first he hid behind the stove. He was sure the man who came through the kitchen door at the beginning was later wounded, a short very heavy man. He himself was small and thin. Just before he escaped he scampered from his hiding place, and briefly ran into the corridor. He saw prisoners being hustled into cells. The shooting drove him back but he heard a woman crying wildly, and he saw several men on the floor with guards around them. Even though it washed him in shit, he got out by the sewer ditch which he could have used much earlier; it worried him that he delayed so long while police were looking for him. It seemed as though he thought he might have returned to his home in Casceres if only he hadn't gone into the corridor.

"Did you know about this ahead of time, Paule?"

Paul shook his head.

"Maybe some of it's not true," the young priest murmured. "That old man was in no state to see things clearly."

"We have to believe Jabier was captured. And whoever was helping him was wounded. It sounds like Matai."

"If Jabier escaped we might not have heard yet."

"Paule, how did you happen to be in Pamplona?"

"I heard she had been taken to Pamplona. I caught the bus over." It seemed to be hard for Paul to explain and this made him careful and slow. "Well, on the way home from the Ekilili Monday night last week her husband said they, I mean Basques, would release her."

"But you said you didn't know about it."

"No, I didn't know anything definite. They don't tell me things like that. A man living at my pension told me she had been taken to Pamplona. So I went over. Maybe I could have helped them."

Meantime Bachi had re-entered. He was unusually quiet and sat down at the end of the table, hands folded in his lap, looking at the floor.

Arrano spoke to Paul, "If you had helped them you'd be dead tonight. Don't think Inspector Bonavit wouldn't have liked to shoot an American if he had such an obvious duty to shoot - you trying to liberate Basque prisoners. My God, Paule, you heroic Americans are the worst dumbheads."

"I didn't know I was heroic. As a matter of fact, I'm a coward."

Bachi spoke very mournfully - they often laughed at him when he used this voice - "Jabier is dead."

"How do you know?"

"The broom seller just came by. He says Inspector Bonavit announced it."

"It could be a lie."

"No, Jabier's family has gone over to get his body."

The young priest knelt and said a prayer. Arrano sat up straight. Bachi knelt. Paul laid his head on the table.

As soon as the prayer was over, Arrano said, "It could just as well have been you, Paule, if you'd been helping them."

"So what?"

"You mean better you than Angeles' husband, is that what you mean?"

"I suppose so."

"But it wouldn't have worked that way, Paule. It would have been you and Jabier both. Don't you understand, Paule, you can't get mixed up in these things."

"I helped you, didn't I?"

"Yes, you did, but I don't take the risks Matai does or that most of the young ones do."

"There was a time when you did. The French woman - all that."

"What French woman?" asked the young priest sharply.

"Oh, I talked too much up there on the mountain. I hadn't seen anyone for days and I got to talking when Matai and Luku and this fellow came to tell me about Jon Arizeder."

"I want to know what I can do now to help Angeles," Paul interrupted sullenly.

"Why do you want to help her?"

"I'm sure it sounds absurd to you, both of you. I love her."

For a moment it looked as if Arrano were going to laugh at these words but he did not. Instead he took Paul by the shoulders and spoke seriously and quietly. "But you just told us, Paule, that you were her husband's friend."

"I was. I was anxious to help him. But he's dead. She has no one to protect her now."

"And you want to protect her?" The words were said sadly and with much irony but most of all they brought up level after level of the realities which Paul's brash words had leaped over; that now the police would, if they chose, charge Angeles with knowing about the prison attempt; that Captain Zendejas, if before he had felt restraint in his treatment of her, was no longer constrained, that in her sorrow and distress even the sage Angeles might make mistakes. Perhaps Paul heard the echo of some of those matters as they went through the minds of Arrano and the priest; he said in the same dispirited voice, "Couldn't I at least pay for a lawyer for her?"

"Not many lawyers will dare to defend her."

"There must be some."

The Basque reputation of Americans did not include the doggedness that Paul showed. He shook his head as if he were a dog with a bone.

"Maybe we have to take you seriously, Paule. The trouble is, the police'll get you out of here if they have any notion what you're thinking. Or put you in jail. How do you stand with your own embassy?"

"I haven't the slightest idea. When I went through Madrid and registered they made a point of warning me about drugs, and I don't use them so I didn't pay much attention to what they said or how they acted."

"Mr. Nixon has announced he will visit the Spanish

Chief of State; maybe you can talk to him." Eagle did not try to conceal his anger.

"Don't confuse him and yourself, Arrano. Because he's an American doesn't make Paule into Nixon." This was the young priest.

"Paule, I didn't mean to insult you, but let me tell you, Arizeder was a courier for the Allies in the war with Germany, working out of the U.S.A. Bilbao consulate. Have you heard any present defense of him in the papers of your country? You see the Paris *Herald Tribune* and I'll make a wager that the connection of my friend hasn't been put into print there." He was still angry.

"Eagle, you're making a confusion again. Look, this Paul is willing to help a young Basque widow - whether or not he loves her is his own heart's story but I respect his feelings. So to whom shall we send him to offer this help?"

"Send him, Father? If we send him to anyone he'll be in jail or at the border in six hours." Arrano was beside himself.

The young priest was embarrassed. "I haven't had much experience in these matters, Eagle. I was responding to your anger. Paul should be permitted to help, should he not?"

Paul stood at a window which opened onto the drab garden. Perhaps he did not hear them. Turning around suddenly he said, "Is that man allowed in the Pamplona jail?" And he turned back to the window.

The other two exchanged glances; they knew Paul meant Comisario Silva and their mutual pity for the American closed the argument between them.

Arrano answered, "I don't think Silva's jurisdiction includes Pamplona. Take heart, Paule, Angeles is one of the strongest girls I have ever met. I know her. She and Jabier were up in my valley for a week last Easter. She's a woman with a deep sense of joy."

"Joy," Paul said.

The young priest went to a cupboard and got a bottle of wine and glasses. They sat together drinking very slowly.

Finally Arrano said softly, "Paule, you told me your reason for being in Bilbao was to find sources about Roncesvalles. And that you hadn't been able to get up to Roncesvalles yet. So go there in those mountains. Talk with the abbot at the monastery. To begin with limit your talking to scholastic matters, although I know he has ideas on more up-to-date events. But he loves to mull over the details you students relish. If you wish, tell him you know me . . ."

Paul looked through the red wine, his eyes magnified by it. "Well . . ."

"Don't make any objection yet," said Arrano. "Whatever happens in Pamplona, if it's known it'll be known up there. Roncesvalles is only arriba-abajo from Pamplona. But most of all it's a way for you to stay here in case you can help. Your papers say you are studying this subject, do they?"

Paul nodded. "I have letters from my professors in Poitiers."

"All right, do what I said. If you get too uneasy you can come back here, but it's safer for you if you're there. And really your safety may help her the most. Do you understand?"

"And about the lawyer?"

"Yes, the lawyer."

"I'll find some money. I don't have the money here. But I'll get it."

"It will have to be sent from the United States?"

"Yes, wouldn't it come through?"

"Oh yes, yes. There are bankers who would receive it and . . . aren't there, Father?"

"Of course. I have a cousin in the Banco de Vizcaya. He can arrange it."

"Then I would leave it in your hands, Arrano, to reach the right people. How do you get a lawyer here? At home I'd ask a friend who was the best lawyer for this case and telephone him. It could be fixed up in a day."

"It'll be done here as fast as possible, Paule. You see, Father can't act directly. Nor really can I. But the way will be found."

"Yes, Arrano, I believe you."

•

He took a bus that very afternoon. The rain, his friend, covered his departure from the priests' residence. He went out through the church by the same route Arrano had entered, that door from the priests' quarters to a confessional, in which he rested or made his mind blank so he could go through the routine of catching the bus - the terminal for Pamplona was across town but there was no remedy for that. He decided to walk rather than get involved with other buses, or taxis. He had walked from there when he came a few hours before and in the rain he felt hidden. No police accosted him either time.

However, in Pamplona some hours later, the station was overflowing with police. Some boarded the bus at the stop before Pamplona and before anyone was allowed to debark. They looked at everyone's papers, including Paul's while he put on a certain scholarly air which he hoped was the most suitable mask. As a matter of fact, he knew they saw through him and his mask. Then with the bus pulling into Pamplona, the police leaped off efficiently, to join their numerous fellows. Paul surmised their intention was to find out who was aboard and be ready to arrest those they wanted after the crowd had cleared and the unfortunate

125

ones were in empty streets on their way home. He was sure they would do it all very well.

This time he took a taxi to his pension even though he had often heard that every other one of them was driven by a secret service agent and the rest by chivatos and he did not feel prepared to cope with either type. He was exceedingly tired by that time; he had imagined that during the trip he would sort out his mind and to some degree he'd done that, but by wearing himself to tatters and in the end simply leaving an unmitigated dedication to a girl with whom he had scarcely talked.

The taxi man was saying, "They came out fast, didn't they?"

"I'm sorry, I didn't hear what you said before."

"The priests, twenty of them, and the assistant bishop. They all read the letter at mass this morning."

"I wasn't in Pamplona. What was the letter?"

"It's all in the paper. Don't you read the paper?"

"Usually I do." Paul knew it was dangerous to respond like this.

"Man, it was strong language. You know, condemning Bonavit, chief of the Social Brigade; the monsignor had been to the prison and talked with some of the men who had been beaten."

Paul wanted to ask, "And Matai?" but only brought out a grunt of understanding.

"The strikers at Dow Chemical, you know. Twenty men and two women were taken in two days ago. They had all been badly beaten and some worse than that. The monsignor said one was blind. Do you think they'll let them out now?"

Obviously the man knew nothing about Matai and Angeles or was so involved in this other affair that he was not interested. After a silence he said shyly, "You know my son is in there. He's eighteen. We were so glad when he got that job at Dow Chemical. You're an American, aren't you?"

"Yes, I am. And I wish you good fortune, you and your son." He shook hands with him.

"Good night, good night." From the taxi man's voice it sounded as if Paul had done him some great favor.

Paul gladly took the comfort the man had given him, even if it didn't belong to him, took it with him into exhausted sleep.

The Pamplona paper the next morning was filled with only one subject: the same terrorist who had planned that scandalous jailbreak in Basauri some months ago, releasing terrorists and murderers to prey on the land, tried to break the Pamplona jail (this story had not appeared in the local papers up to now); was it any wonder that with dangerous unprincipled men like this man, Matai José María Artazo Loigorri, the police were sometimes over-assiduous in their arrest and even occasionally in their treatment of culprits? In this case, the adventurer Artazo Loigorri and his colleague Jabier Ojenbarrena, when cornered, had attempted to jump out a second-story window. The police had had to shoot and Jabier Ojenbarrena was dead, but the principal malefactor had not been wounded. He had hurt his leg in the attempt to escape through the barred window; the police surgeon said it was a mere sprain. However, the prisoner that very morning had been taken to Cádiz, a move dictated by the necessity of avoiding any possibility of his being released by his accomplices.

There was a small paragraph on an inner page, announcing that eight of the twenty-two terrorists arrested at the gate of Dow Chemical had been released. The others had attacked members of the forces of Public Order and, in the interest of law and order, would have to be examined at more length.

There was always much gossip if one could find a safe source, but Paul did not like the look of the angry woman who ran the pension so he made no inquiries of her. He asked for the laundry he had left with her two days before. She looked at him with contempt and said it was not ready.

"I'm leaving today."

"Where are you going? You Americans are always running back and forth. Don't you have anything to do?"

"I'm leaving at noon today and I'll need the laundry."

The only bus for Roncesvalles left at one; he didn't really care whether or not he caught it but he meant if he could to keep his promise to Arrano. While he was waiting for the landlady to iron his things, he walked toward the prison, following his map. But within two blocks of it he saw there was jostling and shouting. While he was trying to see more, a closed police van approached at slow speed. The barred window was tiny. She could be in there, he thought, they could be taking her to Cádiz too.

He made his face look as calm as he knew how; he stood facing the van. If she saw him she would know he was a friend. She would remember him from the Ekilili. She had given him a glass of wine. The van was still moving slowly when it came abreast. A man with a mitralleta sat beside the driver. Apparently in jest, because he laughed as he did it, he pointed the machine gun at Paul. Without meaning to, Paul ducked, and the man slapped his knee and laughed outrageously. Then the van speeded up and put on its siren. The driver, in the mood of his companion, took the next corner at high speed.

•

Much in Paul's life had come to him by chance but not his college education; that had been planned from the day of his birth. His family was one of those typical to a pervasive degree far beyond the number of such families in America: a strong-minded and virtuous mother, a less strong and less virtuous father, and often, although not in Paul's family, a passionate love between these two, all the more lasting because it was like the banked fire in the living room stove which the father tended. (Both love and stove had to be pushed back a generation in Paul's family; there were indications that the passion was an every other generation affair.) But there was something else banked up in the father, and had been in many of his progenitors: love of adventure. So it was that missionaries and ambassadors came from these families. Paul's inclination for travel was a paler form of that drive and his parents agreed with it and fostered it because it combined both parents' frustrated ambitions.

The mother had the kind of mind that should have gone into getting a doctorate and being a professor. She would have loved both parts of a life like that - the study and the university infighting. For her, a subject of study ought to be as theoretical as possible; erudition was doubly that if it related to an obscure subject. But she throttled her intellectuality, if that's what it was. It was literally unthinkable for her to move ahead of her husband, who ran a hardware store and made good money at it. Meanwhile, his real longing was for dangerous travel.

Each of them had a heavy investment in Paul but so far he had met his mother's secret needs more than his father's. A Ph.D. on the Chanson of Roland was a solidly recondite and suitable subject. But in recent months Paul had caught himself thinking, "My father would like to be here." This had nothing to do with his father's politics or even his kindness or cruelty toward people. Paul had no idea whether his father was kind or cruel. But it was to his father he wrote about getting money out of his own savings account (which in this family was also begun at birth with a five-dollar gold piece from the grandfather, who in physical fact did bank his own living room fires). It was also to his father Paul wrote about going to the state capital and looking for a good lawyer. It was enough for his father that Paul said this was for a girl he had met and who was in trouble.

No "What kind of trouble?" from his father's lips. If he thought it, he would say to himself, "About time Paul had a little excitement." From his mother, yes, there would have been distrust of the word "trouble," but she didn't know about it yet. She would never know from her husband. He disliked her too much to tell her anything important. Not that they ever openly brawled.

The non-brawling muted Paul. He knew about silence. He had even thought about the kind of silence with which he was familiar while he and the Eagle listened inside Anboto. The kind he had known at home and which many times had driven him out of the house was not the aggrieved-wife silence of American folklore. Both man and woman contributed to this silence; between these two there was ground which had once bloomed with flowers (Paul's mother was a famous and astute gardener but these were wildflowers). Field columbine, primroses, small wild roses wide-eyed. They had all been seared away. It was a battle-ground but, and even though there had never been any battle which Paul witnessed, when the reports from Vietnam talked about flame throwers, that silent ground was what Paul thought of.

The summer after he finished his junior year in college, doing brilliantly, all perfect marks (that was how he got the first fellowship to France, that and another year of excellence), as a prize his father gave him a trip around America, a bus trip entitled *See Your Own Country First.*

Paul and a friend were going to take it together but the friend got a serious ear infection and Paul had to go without him. It was a lonely trip, a preparation for later and more acute loneliness in France.

This particular *See Your Own Country* tour was special; it was built around notable local fairs and typical events. As they got west there were plenty of rodeos, a tennis affair in Del Monte, and then a Basque festival up in Nevada. This was held in a fine stand of trees.

There were log chopping races, which Paul never did see in the real Basque country; there was a tremendous and well-prepared dinner. Not everybody in the tour bus got invited to dinner. Paul was alone, tall, thin, and one of the buxom girls who had prepared the fine meal decided he was the ideal recipient of such food - and she thought he was a student in the same college she went to and that time invested with him might be returned to her in some form. They found it hard to talk and she despaired of any increment from her kindness. Then, from somewhere much deeper in the woods than where the tables were set, came singing and a flute. It was not a real txistu, the girl told him and explained about that, but there weren't any txistularis in their part of Nevada. She explained all the Basque words carefully. She said there would be dancing though. He said he would like to dance, if it was folk dancing. She said it was Basque folk dancing and very very difficult. He fell silent again.

From that place of laughter and the dancing which was too difficult for him came one irrintzi.

"What in the world is that?"

She told him the name and all about it.

"Really made by a man?" he interrupted her.

"No," and she was cross now, tired of his hearty appetite

and his shyness. "It's a woman doing it. I told you the oldest in the family was taught it, didn't I?"

Anyone more sophisticated than Paul would have known from the girl's voice that this irrintzi-giver was someone very much the center of the happy sounds from among the trees, and that she was probably very pretty. There was laughter and clapping after the irrintzi. A man's voice shouted, "Do it again, chirripita."

She didn't do it again. The music began. Paul didn't go over there. He and his chubby hostess seemed equally alien to the merriment. He said goodbye stiffly, and found his way to the bus.

But it was a fact that the irrintzi stayed, nearly forgotten, in the back of his mind.

Another bus from Pamplona brought him to the town of Roncesvalles and he decided to walk from there. An avenue of plane trees went up toward the pass and to the church of the silver Virgin of Roncesvalles and the monastery. That plane tree road was exceedingly inviting. Unpaved, it called friendly small plants and walkers to share its side paths.

He knew Roncesvalles meant valley of hawthorns and he looked for them. Although the hawthorn is too proud and spiny to share human roads, it was visible in many places along the way. It set off and clustered around the large pilgrims' cross marking the cutover to the abrupt Roman road aimed at the pass. That was where the army of Charlemagne had marched, Charlemagne and half his men already through and on the French side when the battle began.

For the present Paul swung around and left behind him the church and the old college with its documents to read and scholars to meet, including the abbot whom Arrano had recommended and who had written a book about Roncesvalles. Paul wanted to follow up any material that presented itself - that was his nature - but now on his way to the physical scene of the battle upon which he had made such exhaustive observation, all his work seemed to him dry and remote.

He was confronted, honestly and painfully, and suddenly, with what appeared to be reality. At least he was suddenly transposed to a real-life viewing of the site of Roland's death. Around him were hills from which Basques must have ridden down onto the French rear guard, giving their irrintzis, blowing their horns. He had only that once in his life heard an irrintzi before he came to Bilbao. He had known that the Song's listing of enemy Persians and Saracens and Blacks was decorative fantasy of the author, Turold or whatever he was, and that it was Basques who attacked Charlemagne's rear guard. Still, never until a few days before had the living fact untangled itself from the notes and subnotes of scholarly inquiry.

Angeles, by causing a fusion of what he called love for her with anger at the foul treatment of his friend, Matai, had precipitated reality. He could mark the exact moment that event took place, knowing then, and now in Roncesvalles, that when the police van lurched past him and he ducked from the machine gun of the guard, his action, including the fear in it, had committed him to the side of Angeles and Matai and Father Ander; even Isa counted in it.

But he had no idea what he could do about it, apart from paying for a lawyer.

•

He was looking through a valley and at first it seemed very still, although it wore harsh wind marks, the trees swept into wind shapes, splayed trunks bent and heavy. Sometimes it appeared that a tree might have been kept at bay so long that in defense it had sent up three squatty stems instead of one tall one.

Within the quiet he began to hear a minute vagrant sound of blowing in the trees, but different for each kind of tree, a murmur and a faint whistle, and then a soft roar in those with full branches. Yet there was no special bending or movement.

The rocks were also marked by wind. There were broken ones, their matching portions lying together to show how they had fitted. There were no sharp thrusts. Every part was smooth. Storms must have carried sand particles to polish the rocks, as the ocean does. Paul lay on the ground, facing downward but with his chin holding up his head so he could see. He perceived the sense of wind as if it were the ocean. Did it have waves of its own kind? Because only centuries' repetition could have done what he saw in this valley.

On the left ahead of him there was a black mountain with very green grass growing wherever it could and a stream of rocks cascading down, motionless now, yet motion had been established forever in the fall of stone.

His eyes fell to the ground directly ahead of him. He saw a tiny oak tree perfect in form, then a larger dead but erect tree skeletal white and as beautiful as the mimic tiny tree. Behind them were fallen trunks and again the sense of water because they were lying together in a channel, branches, multiple horns rearing out of immense fallen trunks all white. On the ground under the one erect but dead and one small living tree and approaching the splendid jumble of fallen ones he saw wild roses and columbine; the columbine was gaunter than tame ones, petals farther apart and small, the horns widely separated.

There was a fuzzed white plant and a shrub with strawberry leaves. There were strong blue seed pods and on the same plant above the pods pale blue flowers. Some plants grew flat against the ground, not risking a raised head. These had stars on them, constellations parallel to those living in the night sky. And there was dun-colored lace growing on the ground with pink flowers star-shaped too, the parent plant almost invisible.

Still looking along the ground he saw small papery wild iris, heavenly blue, and what in his own land he called Indian paintbrush and red columbine and a very small daisy with yellow petals and a black center. Not an inch of this ground was bare. Ahead in rocky places there were pennyroyal and lupine and from all around came the smell of sage and sheep dung.

With the constellations of small flowers there were constellations of twigs, their patterns intricate but clear. Neither wood nor rock seemed to grow or fall by chance. There was no such thing as a random heap. Fallen bark found its way into this ground pattern of stars and planets and streaks of light. He saw the heavens lying on the earth with all units of it drawn from hiding and displayed. Heaven as carpet and pavilion, both were acceptable.

Then he stood up in order to look on all sides of him: vast castle rocks ahead and, nearer, a stand of aspens. These were a colony; they had drawn together. Even so, the wind must have doubled many when they were young because trunks were set at a horizontal and made a seat, and then the rested tree had, he supposed, become strong enough to grow straight once more. To a certain height the bark was as rough as an elephant's hide, then it became as white as aspens usually are. Underneath them there were currant branches bearing translucent red berries and one tall bare stalk with a primrose flower, brightest pink. Back of the castle rocks stood a great calm mountain.

The pass was narrowing. No more docile mountains now; every rock was in motion. On one side there was a crag with orange protrusions, on the other side one that looked like a vast animal dusted with snow, recumbent but not stationary. The trees, even afoot, were stricken, an immense fallen one directly ahead. Gone were all its small branches and twigs but that tree still had a score of enormous branches attached in concentric circles. It too seemed mobile, asserting its age, review of time changed into proud motion.

Now it was a place of stones, some gray, some white with red-brown markings, and in one place a long wide white strip going straight down the fall of them. There was a precipice above. He looked up to the rim. There were caves, the entrances like the one Arrano had taken him through. The Basques attacking Roland must have come out of caves instead of riding the ridge as he had first surmised.

There was a round formal open place below, a series of square rocks in an amphitheater. That could be the place where Roland stopped to meet those lithe small horses, each one double-ridden, coming out of the caves. Echoes of horns and cries ahead of them would be the first knowledge the French had of attack, and after the sounds the sure-footed, tiny, mountain-cured horses and the riders strong as their mounts.

In the silence of these mountains (a bird said bee-bee-bee and then took an indrawn breath unrecordable and that was all) Paul rehearsed the noise of Roncesvalles. Knights, weighted down with plunder and armor, had their cry which repeated their banners, heavy, gilded, splendid banners, and they shouting the heavy, holy, confident "Montjoy," bastardized word but a word, not prime unworded sound. Had they formed themselves in a protective circle, horse heads out, the gleaming banners above, the fine romantic shout rising higher than the banners? And out of the caves down the river of rocks and dead trees, stars under their feet, the Basques came with their irrintzis which picked up sound where the knightly cries left off, pitch up too, high, very high above their own wind-tattered banners.

Paul felt tired, as if it had been his battle and he had ridden it a thousand times. But this time he had seen it differently from ever before. And he wanted it over with. The brutal priest-warrior Turpin had always annoyed him but now the whole knightly crowd seemed boorish, whatever they did, done for show. That was why he was tired: it was with them and their bad manners he had always ridden, the affectation of courtliness overlying treachery - that the fine game they played, Ganelon to Roland, Roland to Ganelon, everybody afraid he might be thought less brave than he wished to be considered. Paul had carried their showiness two years; he had assumed, in what he now thought was simplism, that the side of the knights was his, that those who attacked them in this mountain pass were his enemies too. But now he had ridden with the enemy, carrying the anger they carried for the destruction of their city, Pamplona, and the deaths of their children and he found they were his friends.

So what was he going to do? Walk back through the pass to the college and talk with that abbot of Arrano's?

Not yet, because something was happening in the amphitheater. First he saw color. It was scarlet as explicit as a bird's wing and more so than men's clothing. But it was exactly that: there were seven men in red sashes, red berets, white clothes. Then flute sound came to him. Drums followed the flutes. He sat quietly to listen. The musicians had started together, but now six were silent and only one flute voice came up the mountain. Paul looked around. Spotted among the rocks there were other men than he. He stood up and across the valley someone not only stood but started swiftly down and toward him. As the man ran he raised his arm. The music stopped.

Paul waited for him. The other didn't speak until he was within low voice distance. "Why are you here?"

"Only by chance, friend. I am going down to the monastery to talk with the abbot."

"He knows you're up here?"

"No."

"You're not a Spaniard."

"No, but what's it to you, really?"

"I'm sorry but I must see your papers." The man did not seem to have any other weapons but he held his makila like a club.

That won Paul. Arrano and his makila and the sound on the sidewalk: this must be a friend. He got out his passport.

"Oh, I've heard of you. You're Matai's friend." The man changed, but offered no slavish courtesy or explanations. His voice dropped in pitch still more. "Do you want to go down nearer and hear them? One of the best of all of them is down there."

"Why are they here? Of course I want to hear them. What an opportunity."

"Go and hear them. I'll take you down. Afterwards I have to go up there again."

"Is there a celebration of txistulares here in Roncesvalles?"

The man raised his arm and a flute began again. All he said was, "Listen."

It was dusk going into dark. The sound was deeply suited to the hour that has its special name in Basque, illun, the moment when the day dies. This was not the plaintive cry

139

of some gentle wild man in his field. It was simple in the manner of artistry. And here was the place and time for it. Once it had belonged in a village festival but where were the festivals? Of the seven men in the amphitheater three were old. Each played his dream and desire.

In a pause Paul asked again, this time of a boy who with others was there out of respect for the masters to whom they were listening, "Why are they playing here in the mountains?"

The boy said, "Oiba! Because they go to prison if they play in the towns."

One of the players spoke, "Today we're playing in honor of friends already in prison. Father Ander is a txistulari. He has composed for it."

Another said, "Franco has forbidden the txistu, you know, unless the Civil Guard is present and who wants to play for them? . . ."

•

Paul's stay at the monastery was more satisfactory than he had imagined it could be. The abbot was eager to read what Paul had written on Roncesvalles and urged him to go back to Bilbao and get his papers. They gave him a cell-workroom. Any other time in his life this arrangement would have been paradise for him. He got his papers and on that trip to Bilbao he saw Arrano, who sent back a letter to the abbot:
"Dear friend,

Your kindness to the American student is appreciated by him. No doubt he has told you that. It is also appreciated by me. I will tell you why and present a way in which you can help him even more. Aside from his good intellect, this young man although he hardly knows it has great restraint and courage. I'm sure he hasn't told you that he considers himself pledged to one of the Basque prisoners being accumulated by the captain of our common dislike. He knows almost nothing about her although he is raising money for her lawyer. I think he needs to hear all he can about her the better to understand his situation. He is, I think, living puchurrusquillas. No doubt his mind is trained enough to keep up a studious appearance but in fact, my friend, he daydreams much of the time. You and I know that facts, no matter how bitter, are the only salvation. I ask you to help him. I will get word to the family of the girl, and one of her brothers, or anyone else of the family who wants to go, will take one of the romerías to your church, and there the relative and Paule can talk. You may not know that I myself have become a brown hermit. Probably that is why this churchly plan has occurred to me. The relative will make himself known to you. And send the American down to Bilbao every so often because I am struggling with myself becoming resurrected. Sometime I'll tell you the symptoms. Paule helps me. From your old friend of the aviary."

It was Angeles' youngest brother, about twenty, who came. His family had cousins in a village sixteen kilometers from Roncesvalles, so it was easy for him to join the romería there: strong young men were always needed to carry the big crosses. It was pleasant to see a jovial young head and hear a sweet singing voice emerge from the hangman-black gear, robe tied with a hangman rope. The abbot had word when to expect the Duarte boy and told Paul the romería that day was especially fine and that it was worth his while to attend the eleven o'clock mass. So Paul had the experience of seeing just such an emergence, like a bright amaryllis from a dung pile. The abbot introduced Paul, and when the other young men went off for their picnic in honor of the romería queen, the abbot said to these two, Paul and Duarte, "The kitchen brothers will give you your own picnic. Go for a walk together into the pass."

The boy, Victor, was young and brash enough to quickly break the constraint between them. "The Eagle told me you think you love my sister Angeles."

Paul paled to hear the astounding truth said so bluntly. "Yes."

"Everybody's in love with Angeles. Jabier was a great boy but I don't know how it was Angeles chose him from all the others."

"She loved him, no doubt."

"I do doubt it. She was in love with his beliefs. Are you by any chance in love with her beliefs?"

"Well no, I respect them. But it is she I love." He wanted to talk about her hair and her voice but restrained himself.

"We all respect them. The family is proud of her, but . . ."

"You mean the rest of the family doesn't feel the same commitment as she does?" He looked for another word and then for clarity added in French, "Consécration."

Victor answered, "Jabier brought on her consécration, as you put it. That's not a word a Basque uses. Frenchmen yes, Spaniards I suppose, but I don't know anything about them. Apparently Americans. You look rather saintly yourself, Paul."

"You couldn't be more wrong. Listen, you pronounced that French word with a beautiful accent. Does Angeles speak it that way too?"

"Our parents believe strongly in travel and education. Angeles and I both went to school in France."

"You have other brothers? Is she the only girl?"

"Two brothers between her and me. One went to America."

"Where in America?"

"He was in Nevada first and then he went to Idaho. That's where he is now, but I think he'll come back because of Angeles."

"Have you visited her, Victor?"

"I'm the only one they let visit her. You know they arrested my mother and father and they charged them with aiding Angeles and Jabier. They didn't hold them long but they won't let them visit her."

"But you can go see her. Please tell me about her."

They had arrived at the circle of boulders where the txistularis had played. Paul stood but Victor sat on a rock. His face was young and happy under the beret. Paul felt old in contrast to the boy. How comforting Victor's visits must be to Angeles. "What do you and she talk about?" He thought how intrusive that sounded but decided not to apologize.

"We talk about good times. The sidewalk in front of our house and Jabier's house was a playground. We had it chalk-marked for various games . . . she was older and used to monitor the games."

"Bostari. Chucarrisa," said Paul softly.

Victor was startled. "Do you know Basque?"

"Oh no, the Eagle's teaching me a few words. I think he must have had a good childhood. He often talks about the children's games he played. Chucarrisa must be what we call leapfrog" - he said the word in English - "In a row and the last one jumps over the back of the one in front and so on. Is that how you do it?"

"Yes. You say the words with a fine pronunciation. I'll tell Angeles about it. She'll laugh at that word 'leapfrog.' What a nice word." He said it again in English.

"Does she know English?"

"No, not much. You know she visited my brother who was in Nevada."

"Yes, Jabier said something about that."

"But only for a very short time. I think it was only a week she was there. My brother moved to Idaho just then. She helped him move and set up house for him. But the whole visit was less than a month."

"What year was that?"

"Really I can't remember. Let's see. Let's see it was while I was still in school in Paris. My parents were going to send me to America too but the teachers wouldn't let me go. I never had good school ratings the way she did, so . . ."

"Was it summer?"

"Yes, summer. Why?"

"No, it can't be, but ask her, Victor, if she was at a Basque festival in Elko, Nevada. It would have been summer five years ago. Ask her. And ask her if she gave an irrintzi that day."

"I am going over to Pamplona this afternoon and see if Bonavit will let me in to visit her tomorrow. I could come back this way and tell you. Shall I?"

"I suppose you have to be careful. Would it be better if I met you somewhere else?"

"In Pamplona no. No, it's better here."

"How did you happen to come here today?"

"Didn't the abbot tell you? The Eagle and he arranged it. That Eagle is a real friend of yours. The way he says your name, Pa-u-le! Of course I wouldn't have come except that he spoke for you. He's a good friend of Angeles too. Have you been at his little place near Anboto?"

"Oh yes." But Paul was thinking about the picnic at Elko. No, it wouldn't have been Angeles. But he also knew that whether it was she or not, the irrintzi joined them like a quivering shining band of light. That was going too far. It bound him to her, that was all he could really say.

Victor came back in two days. Yes, she had been at a

144

picnic in Elko but she didn't remember giving an irrintzi. Perhaps she had. Because she was the oldest in the family, she knew how to give it. She had no recollection of seeing Paul, but of course there were two hundred people there. Anyway she sent her thanks to him for his help about the lawyer. Victor knew about the lawyer from the Eagle, not Paul. He and Paul did not talk about the lawyer at all. She had asked a great deal about the pass of Roncesvalles. Victor delivered a message from her to Paul that the amphitheater of stones was where they would meet after the trial, when she was free. There she would thank him and give a wonderful irrintzi for him, to express her gratitude and also her joy at being out of prison.

"How do they treat her there?"

"No prison is a thing to rejoice over, Paul. But Isa is the one who is truly suffering."

"Where is she?"

"In Bilbao. They say she would have died after the first ten days. She lost her baby. They are leaving her alone now but her situation is very bad. We all weep for Isa."

"And Angeles?" He spoke in a low tense voice. "I saw Silva, you know."

"From what we hear Silva has been taken off the cases. He went too far. Something about a mass and Father Ander."

"Angeles?" Paul demanded.

"No, Paul, she's all right. She's strong, my sister's very strong."

"Please when you see her, tell her . . ."

"I'll tell her she has a friend: Paul, her friend."

•

Victor was allowed to see her only once more. Then she was moved to a women's prison, still in the Basque country but in the province of Alava. It was run by nuns. She was

145

no longer allowed visitors. She was kept there until the trial started.

Paul saw Victor several times when he went down to Bilbao. Since Victor's mother came to San Andrés for mass (Victor himself was no mass-goer) it was easy to get word to him. Yet he and Paul never again reached close contact. This bothered Paul. Arrano told him it was because Victor was becoming more and more troubled about Angeles' chances. At first he had been able to think she would be released as soon as any trial action was taken. Now months were going by and her lawyer, an intelligent, abrupt young man from Madrid, spoke very seriously about her situation. He had found out that Zendejas was claiming she had been an ETA courier. The lawyer, Galíndez y Navarro, had a chance to see Angeles and afterwards was so restrained about her situation at the nuns' prison that her family was afraid she was not in good condition at all. Arrano said that Victor's lack of voice was because he was worried and had no way to express it. This didn't make Paul less worried.

◄10►

Resurrection meant for the Eagle the dislodgment from a safe place: the island behind his eyes. Sometimes he called it the Isle of Reil and he didn't know where he had found the name.

With blindness he withdrew from life; that was natural. After the event of blinding he walked up the mountain as far as he could, through sunlight, graying shadows, and then the dark, where he stopped and died.

He began physically to live again little by little. He relearned the mechanics of that, mostly by building his house, and he let no one help him. In other times he would have followed the Basque custom of asking neighbors to come together to build a neighbor's house. He had no neighbors. He chose not to have.

With the solitary building his body came back to being alive and that was different from the way it had been before. He increased and exaggerated Basque preoccupation with concrete objects. Hammer, nails, adze, shovel became more real to him than they had ever been and life was merely a series of physical acts involving these objects. He wouldn't let himself think beyond what he was doing while he nailed together the parts of a fence. That fence, house, sheep-pen were the place he made to replace the one he had lost; naturally he did not want to see people who lived in the lost world nor even know their motives for being alive. For that time being he discarded motive.

Jon Arizeder was the first to enter the new place of cabin, a few sheep, the oaks and beeches, and Arizeder did not intrude beyond the limits his friend set for him, but little by little, and it took years, he was allowed to move freely in the part of Eagle's life where objects possessed the unique intensity of merely being. They didn't talk about it but Jon could tell by the way Eagle handled a shovel that the act of blind shoveling was something a seeing man could not comprehend. Then, again little by little, abaaba in Basque, Jon was able to take his friend fairly often into his own life like that trip in the boat the day Franco was in San Sebastián.

And they talked. Usually it was about the old splendid combat from which they were excluded now, and it was seldom about any personal part of their lives. For the Eagle, that had been transposed into the Isle of Reil.

When he was forced to meet Paul, the short but compressed journey (compressed in every way: speed, teaching Paul how to hear, the purpose of the journey, the excitement of seeing the paintings through Paul's eyes, which might seem the slightest event but was not) became Arrano's tentative re-entry into a living world, not the same one as before because it still had components of his blindness, and these sharpened his old perceptions. But a habit he had had of entering another man's mind began to come back to him, to see as the other saw, hear what he heard. He had to use this faculty in the cave or he could not accomplish what he wanted to; so Paul, who was in every way a stranger, became suddenly well known. And Paul's view of events startled and interested him. They had not talked about this, but Arrano every once in a while found himself thinking abstractly, not a Basque habit but the way the young American scholar often thought. The Eagle laughed at himself but he kept on testing events through Paul.

This was, most importantly, the situation of the Basques in prison for Mascaró's death. He felt he had a part of the responsibility but he was not suffering for it. Torture was worse now than ever before because the Franco impulse for torture waned and waxed with the tide of Basque opposition. These young people - some of whom had become the Eagle's friends because he lived on a mountain they often climbed - knew the horrible facts about torture yet continued to do those things they believed in and which were bound to bring pursuit and arrest; Arrano found himself questioning what they did, not doubting but testing, as if he had to find the roots of their bravery and also the roots of cowardice and betrayal (not theirs). He looked at his own life but he saw no answers there. It was Paul's voice, in himself, saying, "Can it be that the courage and dignity of the Basques like a poultice draws out the cruelty of a beast Mascaró? Is that bravery or the counterbalance of evil?" Then his own voice answered strongly, "No and no, it is courage and its color is scarlet."

These were some of the things Arrano had been considering when Paul arrived at San Andrés from Pamplona. Paul's reversal of his estimate of Roncesvalles enlarged the questions and answers. Paul used to think easily and conventionally, so he told Arrano, who took him to mean

European and American sentimental conventions, the romantic hero, the pure and valorous knight, Roland, Galahad, Blondel. Paul told him that it now seemed to him the imbecile blond knight was precursor of Lieutenant Calley, hero of My Lai.

"If so, is the battle of Roncesvalles the prelude to Vietnam? And Roland winning this time?" Eagle asked.

Paul shook his head. "I don't know. Maybe." He told Arrano that the change in his thinking came about not so much in the pass as when the police van rushed along the Pamplona street. He had assumed of course that Angeles was in the van and although he now knew she had not been and that it was Matai on the floor bracing his wounded leg while the playful driver went around the corner, his encounter with the van was a landmark for him.

During these talks in the San Andrés refectory and under the tree, Paul became Arrano's friend, or Arrano his, because Paul was still not quite sure enough to be the active friend of anyone. His precise, scholarly ways were very amusing to the young Basque priests but Arrano admired him for them. His courage had to be scholarly; he was no Roland. His falling in love, as it is said in his language, was a long due event for apparently he had led a celibate life. So to fall in love with someone unapproachable was logical. This did not mean he was insincere. He had arranged the money for Angeles' defense.

The next time Paul came to San Andrés, Arrano had girded himself to talk about his blindness.

"How many blind men do you know, Paule?" he began abruptly. (They were in the garden and by some spurt of magic the tree had a dozen blossom candelabras on it.)

"None but you."

"I hear there are not as many of them as there used to

be selling lottery tickets or chiclets on the street corner. Is that right?"

Paul said in his country they used to sell shoe laces. "There are less because many infants are saved blindness at birth, you know with disinfectant drops. And they're taken care of better when they have measles . . ."

"Even in a backward country like Spain there are some of those preventatives." But the right things weren't being said. Paul's "none but you" had been what the Eagle needed but it was not enough; he wanted his blindness sealed and proclaimed an ordinary condition.

So he went on, "Basques don't like children who are blemished and we don't often have them. In my village there was a bachelor, a good man, who found a badly deformed baby on his doorstep. This is not to say he was the father. He took the child and brought her up. Some years later a woman, with a pretty daughter younger than the deformed one, came and said she wanted to be his housekeeper. The two girls became great friends. The bachelor loved them both. It was a happy household. Yet if it had been his own child he might have given away the deformed one."

"It's a beautiful story, Eagle. Is that how you would have done it too?"

"I suppose so. What I was trying to say was that although I wasn't born deformed, if blinding had scarred me, many of my friends would have had to turn away from me. You can't tell by looking at my eyes that I'm blind, can you? Yet that disgust which they might have dealt me was one reason I lived on the mountain. Do you understand that, Paule?"

"Yes, I understand it. I'm glad you told me, Eagle."

"It's never been said to anyone else."

"Thank you."

151

He couldn't tell Paul or anyone, and never did, that in his long head behind the blind blue eyes there was the Isle of Reil. It wasn't going to be easy to abandon it, he could see that. Everything he had ever beheld was there, and having had eagle sight, there were plenty of pictures to store. The first, the outermost layer was the scene around him when the blinding started and sometimes he was sorry it was not nobler, although there was a great oak tree in it. The house of the border guard was under that fine tree. When the German told him what was going to happen he looked around with all his might. He tried to see every leaf on tree and on the ground. He did not want to see the French woman. He heard her voice and that was enough.

He saw Mascaró's back. Mascaró had a stoop although he was a handsome man. The braid on the collar of his green uniform was yellow - Eagle could see it along the back of his neck. Once the policeman put up his hand to brush away dandruff or a hair; probably it was the terminal fixity of Eagle's eyes he felt clinging to him.

Eagle saw the stubble on the German's face, the door of the guards' hut, nothing splendid except the tree. But the colors were strong and brave; they came out in colorless places like the dusty ground and they came back to him any time he asked for them. If for some the blind world is dun and gray it was not so for the Eagle.

The German medical technician told him how long it would take for the alcohol injected into the optic nerve to take effect - he was a decent pimply young man who wanted to be a doctor and he had put the alcohol in a depo solution so the span of blinding would last long enough for the captured Basque to get back to his mountains. But the colors dimmed fast in the world Arrano was leaving. Saffron and red streaks down the sides of Monte

Jaizkibel soon came to drab. But in the island of Arrano's head there was a wild glow of color.

There were gray scenes inside there but only if they had been like that in life - the prison of Santoña was one. Yet not every scene in Santoña was dull. The sadness of the scene created the gray. From the room where he and Jon Arizeder slept - during most days they were in a patio - there were going to be some taken out at early dawn and shot. As it was not known ahead of time who they would be, the prisoners tried to find a place away from the door. That part of the room was crowded. Arizeder and he decided to force their luck and sleep near the door. The bad part was that the condemned men had to stumble over them on the way out. Gray dawn, gray sorrow. Sometimes they were brave enough to give the condemned man a word, even tell him a dirty prison joke, seldom a prayer and only if the man himself were praying.

When Arrano's vision went, the other senses changed their quality. As he expected, they grew stronger but they also lent themselves to the deprived eyes in a different way.

Before, when he was sighting a border-crossing from the top of a rock, he would cover his eyes with his hand so that afterwards his sight would be clearer, and it was. The help that hearing and touch gave his dead eyes was a little like that; they abetted the inner vision and he saw things he had not known about before.

.

Paul had to go. He had to hurry back to Roncesvalles because a scholar in Basque history was visiting the abbot and Paul wanted to hear what he said. So Arrano was alone under the tree. He began to talk softly to himself and with hesitation. No one was with him.

153

". . . When we were young . . . we could look at the hide of an ox and judge his strength and from that his use to us . . . Why do I say we? . . . we ran our hands over the ox's hide and we heard how the hair sounded. It was in order to judge the animal's value and how much we should pay for him. But now those other benign senses do more for us . . . They give us the whole living ox (why do I keep saying we and us and who are those who were with me then and are here now?) . . . In the Isle of Reil he becomes pure ox. Those with sight have no way to know the joy of this and there's no way for us to tell them . . . Sound becomes sight; the animal is there, complete and himself, moved from the stable yard to behind the eyes. I see him there but I do not know whether this seeing is by ears or hands or eyes. Is he the real ox?" This question was amusing and Arrano laughed, but it was not derisive or demeaning. It was a true laugh.

". . . I have not been asked but I say that this applies to people as well as cattle . . . Someone I knew well - Arizeder - is closer and clearer. If my eyesight were suddenly returned and there were the changes that years and disappointment must have made in him, I might choose to return to the Arizeder on my island . . . not a rosy stuffed dummy of a man but maybe a truer Jon. Since I am saying this aloud for the first time it comes out with hesitation. I know it is right for myself . . ." And he was silent.

What he knew was that he had come to the French woman and he couldn't talk aloud about her. He couldn't even say her name. He had laughed at Paul and his falling in love but that was because Arrano's only reference to love was this woman, red-haired as all temptresses should be. Had that hair in life become the ugly gray that red hair becomes? That was the absurdity of it: she was flaming away, hair and all, all of her hair, in the island mind. She

154

was well preserved, like the corpse of Lenin, as fresh as at the moment of her disappearance. But she had the advantage over Lenin of being able to move, running along the path shaking her fist at a German strafer. No doubt her fist was a sign to them; they flew low enough. He knew that, nevertheless he could only see the grace of gesture, tightening of her buttocks under a tight red skirt, her mocking feet in alpargatas. It was enough to make him put his hands over his ears.

On her back in the corner of the rock shelter he had built, not for safety but for their privacy so others couldn't hear her crazy moans and meows, she would wave her legs and feet in supposed ecstasy. Her legs on the path expressed the same ecstasy. Right then in the garden of the church of San Andrés her feet laughed. That was one island image he had to destroy. Or, on the other hand it might be what would keep him in the Isle of Reil. Up to now it had been wholly durable although he knew it was as false as the French woman herself.

He was not quite through. His blind eyes could feel the island images. Not only the laughing sound of her abominable swift feet but he felt them, a male hand to a female foot, the instep, the heel . . .

If she was intruding so flagrantly it was because he had found out she was wife, now widow, of Melchor Mascaró. (The young priest told him and said it was known, but never mentioned, by a few other Basques.) No wonder her husband hated the Eagle, and Arrano used that name for himself: it put him face to face with Mascaró. He understood now that Mascaró had kept him at bay up on his mountain. But was it she who had kept Mascaró at bay? When that inspector wanted to kill someone he had no trouble finding a way to do it in line of duty. Why did the young priest - or was it Bachi - say she couldn't go back to France? He remembered well that once (and he had thought she was joking) she told him she had killed a general. He thought she meant a German and congratulated her. Her red hair was tied with a bright green ribbon and she had orange polish on her nails. It was of great remark among their friends that she carried her nail polish into the Pyrenees. She used to change the color. Another signal?

There she was, green ribbon and green dress, barefoot, laughing, telling him she had shot a general. She was cleaning her rifle. They were sitting on a broken wall. As punishment for that killing, and now he supposed it had happened and conspicuously enough so they might still remember it, she had lived with Mascaró for twenty-four years, more punishment than she would ever have received in France.

She was married to one who also had a mountain cabin. To this he took wives of prisoners, those whom the pastor had mentioned so delicately. Arriaga, the doctor called from the stands to look at the civil guard and Arizeder, came to see Arrano every now and then and once it was to try to forget a prisoner's wife brought to him after a night in Mascaró's hut. Dr. Arriaga had to tell Arrano about it to get it out of his mind: shredded from waist to knees as if an animal had clawed and chewed her. And her face around the mouth. Arriaga had heard there were others who had not dared to go to a doctor for fear it would mean more torture for their husbands.

The chewer and shredder was the Eagle's French woman's husband. Eagle's island vision refused to go further into the matter.

.

There had been no reason for him to leave the priests' residence. He could keep himself better informed there than on his mountain, not only about Jon but everyone. There were no rumors he was being looked for. His life had taken an odd turn - that was how he sometimes thought of his resurrection - surely a more vivid passage except for his sorrow over the suffering of his friends: Arizeder, Matai, Luku, who was the last to be arrested and had been shot not resisting arrest and had nearly died. Even his mother hadn't known about it until much later, but he was the same Luku, according to his lawyer, Rufino Thevet, gentle but with the voice of a valiant giant; nobody could destroy that energy, the lawyer said. Isa and Matai troubled Arrano most. Zendejas' ferocity toward those two was limitless. For instance, word had come that while Matai was in the van and pounded on the front panel because the pain of his leg had reached a peak, they filled the van with Mace; that information came through a man who worked in a petrol station and saw it happen there. He said the driver was in high spirits. As to Isa, the reports were too painful to repeat.

They all had defense lawyers, a collection of people as brave as the ones they were defending. They took the risk of threats, assault, deportation, car burnings, fines; this had happened in previous court-martials but now it was worse; the Guerrillas of Christ the King had taken a hand. Some of the lawyers were from Madrid, one of them an older famous attorney and a leader in Pax Romana; a few were from Barcelona, including one of the best, and the others from Bilbao and San Sebastián. There was a Basque woman lawyer defending Isa.

There were sixteen lawyers, and sixteen prisoners including three women, Isa, Angeles and Kristiana. The report was that Kristiana was very nearly mad from torture. Also there was a second priest besides Ander. Of the remaining eleven Arrano knew well only Matai and Luku and Isa's brother, Gorka. Angeles' husband would have been among them, of course, and Arrano had known him. But in a way all Basques knew all the prisoners, calling them by name and family and caserío.

Arrano had some business with Matai's lawyer, Suertegaray, a bilbaíno whose younger brother Jabi had been shot recently by the Civil Guard. Since Suertegaray was crippled with polio and it was difficult for him to get around, Arrano made his first sally from San Andrés dressed in his monk's habit. The lawyer's office was in an old building on the Gran Vía and the rickety elevator frightened the Eagle more than the Civil Guard he could recognize by their footsteps. The elevator gave him that feeling of being trapped and he had to recite the couplet about fanfarrista, fanfarrón. He walked down when he had finished talking to Suertegaray. Arrano under all circumstances was to attend the court-martial which had been announced for early December.

Meanwhile Zendejas was getting his case together with great care. Arrano imagined that behind the eyes, well protected with exceptionally dark glasses, there was a brown area, like a rather peculiar film screen. On that brackish background facts were registered so hazily that truth could hardly be distinguished from a lie. The one permanent and dramatic feature of that screen would be the scarecrow crags of Zendejas' terrible fears. Of course they were the same dull clichés by which he lived but behind his eyes they looked grand or at least frightening.

One of the feature pictures which Zendejas prepared was a case for the death penalty. Bachi was brought the gossip that Matai was to receive a death sentence from the court-martial and that many current judgments were for the purpose of accustoming the populace to this. There had been one death sentence, for Carrasco from the town of Vera, but pressure from all sides reduced it to life in prison. The next time it might stick. Meanwhile eight years of prison to the priest Erroka Ibaieder because underground pamphlets were found in his car, six years to the Capuchine father, Mikel Lezama, for having distributed a manifesto of ETA, ten years and four months to another Capuchine for a similar offense. Sixteen, fourteen, twelve and a day and so on for boys who were found with underground publications. And a young fellow arrested without being given any reason and attempting to escape in his car had his legs shot off with a machine gun, instead of the police firing at the tires.

There were absurdities too, mirthless authority with iron mirth in its wake. Near Vitoria a poor fellow was shot by the Civil Guard while the man was ringing the church bells. The Civil Guard thought he was signaling terrorist friends. When it turned out the village bell ringer was an old fighter in Franco's Crusade and still an ardent crusader, in short an informer, a policeman was arrested.

Every Basque arrest meant torture, automatically. In preparation for the Burgos trial about two hundred had been arrested. Some of these had to be released and of these some told what had happened to them.

There were protests. The Jesuit twin brother of a general, Franco's chief of staff, made two public statements from the Pontifical Gregorian University of Rome. In a round table on the tortures in Uruguay he said they should first discuss those in Spain and gave examples. So did the abbot of Montserrat, lamenting the silence of the Church on this subject; he said Church indignation should apply to these cruelties as much as to Soviet tanks in Praga. Meantime the Soviets were getting twenty-three fishing bases in the Canaries. If there was humor in that the Basques would find it.

159

It was a delirium, injustice so flamboyant it destroyed reality, Zendejas' monsters unleashed. In his way Zendejas was a minor prophet, and Arrano thought he was not the only one of that species to confuse himself with his villains. The captain had no heroes.

Zendejas is a name rhyming with the Spanish pendejas, a form of which, pendejo, is used in Mexico to express mean contempt and from there incorporated by bilbaínos returned from Mexico into their own kind of Spanish. The captain was commonly called El Pendejo; Arrano did not choose to use the nickname-epithet.

Arrano had met other men in Zendejas' pattern - it was not unique - and from Arrano's observation these men had in common a head lacking in original thought, its vacuum filled with clichés. But for these clichés they are willing to kill, occasionally even themselves but always plenty of others. These men were apt to have a certain kind of face, the outward demonstration of their digestive systems. Since their stomachs were invariably out of order the poor face (with mouth as center - the eyes were concealed by dark glasses) became the banner of internal misfortune. Sometimes the face was twisted, sometimes caught in the rigidity of constipation, but always distressed. Zendejas' countenance had been described to Arrano as distressed.

For Zendejas the stomach face was not a detriment to his career. On the contrary. It gave a ludicrous but menacing preview of his intentions. Whether it indicated cramps, flatulence, stone-hard accumulation of immovable waste, the face was a graphic chart of oncoming moods. Zendejas used very few hand gestures.

Arrano gave Zendejas so much thought because he was the one to determine how the arrested Basques were treated. Others would handle the prisoners but the captain laid down the rules. Zendejas had to have his master plan substantiated; proof came from torture. He already had experience preparing court-martials including that of the Carrasco who had received a death penalty. Zendejas was proud of having "cut into the heart" of ETA and often announced he had destroyed the leadership. This time he was boasting he would cut out its heart altogether.

.

After Isa had been in the Gorodoniz station house for twenty-seven days they wanted to move her but they were afraid she would die during a trip of any length; the nuns' prison in Alava was the indicated place for her. Not only the distance but the fact there was no doctor there prevented her transfer.

Isa would have preferred to die. Singularly, it was the military doctor attending her at Gorodoniz police station who saved her life. It was true that those above him wanted to bring her to trial and had instructed the doctor to keep her alive, but his motives were not the same as theirs. It would take a long time to understand why this slender, gentle, middle-aged man from Galicia was a career medical officer in the Social Brigade.

Every time he entered Isa's cell, even when she was nearly unconscious, a spider thread of understanding spun itself between them. Since there was usually a guard present, the doctor said very little except to ask medical questions. He always protected her privacy as best he could; he told the guard to get out if he had to examine Isa. It was not at his order she was given medicine which along with the beatings brought on the premature birth and death of her baby. He first saw Isa when he attended her at that time.

The comfort he gave her was through his hands. He

161

never touched her except with respect. After the inhuman and lecherous mauling she had received for days from the squad headed by the Sevillian sergeant, those curing hands, even when they gave her pain, healed her. She understood she must never tell anyone about his kindness.

Sometimes after he had visited her (while he was in the cell she would force her mind into as clear a present awareness as she could) she was able to remember the joys of her life. She thought of Matai continually but she tried not to see him in the form he had - the heavy, well-proportioned body she knew, the face with its smile; during one of the deliriums she went through she became convinced that if she thought of Matai like that, it would harm him, that if she brought him to such a clear image, someone else - maybe one of the dreadful men she had come to know - would also see him clearly and then they would do to him some of the things they were doing to her. So her mind, defending her and him, gave him other forms. One was a great oak.

She pulled her wretched blanket over her head. She was standing under the oak. Then she sat leaning against the trunk. She reached her arms above her head and touched the bark. There were many birds in the oak tree. An owl sat high in a leafy redoubt but sometimes she heard him. Swallows didn't stay long; they dipped by and she was refreshed by their curving flight. A cuckoo speaking softly and the turtledoves moaning because all doves are afraid of the nets at the mountaintop. Little birds without names flitted from side to side of the cell. And there was a raven, black-bronze and beautiful. She saw the raven clearly before the whole beloved scene departed.

There was another as comforting. It was a road leading to a caserío. The house must have been the one belonging to her grandfather but she saw it from farther away than in the photograph she had. There was a stream near her and a bridge. The road was on the bridge. The water of the stream quenched her thirst. She was fevered and the water was cold and clean. The grass was clean. The road made a loop to the left. There was a high hedge on each side. The house gardens and a house tree took her to rest, let her be drawn between the rows of beets and in the tree shade. The great forest trees began above the house in a valley that went to the white mountains. In the forest she could sleep. She looked down onto the road which was below her now. There had been no people in this scene (nor birds, although she knew the birds were in the tree of the caserío) but now she saw two people standing close together on the bridge, looking into the clear water. Ay, Matai.

•

Zendejas' mind could be known down to its most minor pathways because under the name of Viajero he wrote columns for controlled publications (but those which carried an even more drastic line than the official one, so, in truth, requiring little control). The Viajero columns were battering-rams of old ideas - the international plots against Spain and the vile use of the Black Legend; the Jews were there too; Zendejas simply used the words zoological and bacteriological instead of Jewish.

He did frenetic columns when Constitutional Article 18 was abrogated. This abrogation meant giving the police free rein - no time limit to holding prisoners for questioning and the right to arrest without reason given. In general the controlled press, often in identical words, delivered reassurances about this: the respectable silent majority should not be alarmed, none of their necessary rights were touched. Only miscreants and terrorists should be alarmed. But Viajero-Zendejas frankly said that civil rights ought to be abrogated. What bothered him were the persons who, however mildly, protested the constructive destruction of those rights.

Arrano had learned from Jon the general trend of the Viajero but one day when Paul was there, Arrano asked to have a Viajero column read to him. Paul went out and got the current *¿Que Dice?* a paper supporting the Guerrilleros del Cristo Rey, who in the last week had destroyed two bookstores in Madrid by breaking the windows and throwing red paint around, and in Barcelona had torn up and cut up a Picasso exhibit, although in Barcelona they had met with opposition. In *¿Que Dice?* these attacks were reported by inference; there was a column, not Zendejas', lauding "recent patriotic actions" of the Guerrilleros but not saying what the actions had been.

"Go on, go on, read what the Viajero has to say."

The young priest who was to read glanced over it. "It's a little more mixed up than usual. I suppose he's been so busy he didn't have time to cut it down and make it neater. He seems to have thrown in everything."

"Read it and stop talking, Father," said Arrano.

"'. . . In these days when hell is raining impiety . . . when the fire that is spit from its flaming entrails lights hate and passion and attempts to reduce to ashes the flaming love we feel for the Crusade . . . We say down with the ecumenists and impudent berriganists!!'"

"Is he talking about the Berrigans in my country?" Paul interrupted.

"It must be . . . it says berriganists."

"Go on, Father. If we have to hear this rubbish at least let's hear it read fast." Arrano spoke angrily.

"'NO, NO. It is not enough that we are for God and Spain, against revolution, against its accomplices and its hidden hordes . . . No! A nation of free men, sincere and decorous cannot merely blame Communists. We must also blame persons of the elite, of high intelligence with contacts with the highest levels of international circles, who have contributed to the absolute confusion.'"

"Ala, confusion is the word," said Arrano.

"'From religious communities and public platforms, from universities and judgment halls, hammering at young minds, pouring into their heads destructive philosophies, values, judicial procedures, zoological professors waving the flag of evolution have been dropping day by day the insidious calumny, the defamation of organizations, corporations, of moral concepts in order to reach pure nihilism step by step, vandalism and the negation of all established order.'"

"This is really the worst pendejo I've ever heard," said Bachi.

"'Priests dressed in secular clothes, women who look like priests in their long black coats and other women inappropriately dressed like men. To these last it is useless to tell them this is an abomination in the eyes of God, as they can read in Deuteronomy, because their frivolity makes them blind, as Isaiah says, so they can neither see nor understand. A woman in pants is costumed as a man but she cannot deny her sex. She's like the monkey dressed in silk who is still a monkey.'"

"He hates women, doesn't he? Do all Spaniards hate them?" asked Paul.

"All crusaders, yes," said Arrano.

"'The volcano which has vomited and is vomiting scandals, calumnies, and campaigns against the Spanish state with the purpose of weakening it, disparaging it, returning to the old tricks of confrontations, homicides, and the climate of civil war leading to the establishment of Russian and Chinese Communism in our country.' Wait a minute, that doesn't seem to be a sentence," said the young priest.

"Oh well . . . 'One of these aspects is the overt posture and underground activities of the Spanish ecclesiatical hierarchy. Another aspect which must not be forgotten is that the idealogical and governmental system flowing from our Fundamental Laws creates a whole, perfectly adapted to direct the present and the future of the Spanish people with maximum guarantees of real liberties, of secure authority, effective peace, and internal progress. But our Fundamental Laws have the profound wisdom and precision of clockworks, exact and precise. Any part that is oxidized or deteriorated disturbs the proper functioning of the mechanism. We say this because we have insisted without interruption on the necessity of a categorically serious application of the Law, up to its ultimate consequences, and we say now that if this inexorable application were applied there would be no necessity for repressive measures because that would make impossible the formation of those brews and miasmas which afterwards infect the gangrened sectors of society which have backed ETA.'"

"He took a long time to get there. What a windy fool," said Bachi. "Finish, Father. They need a paper twist to start dinner cooking."

"Here's the main point, I think. Here's where the captain speaks from his heart." The priest had been reading ahead. "'. . . sensational lies from those who attack the highest magistrates of the regime; while they make calumny against the loyal functionaries of worthy institutions, they present themselves as being barbarously treated. This unchaining of a bacteriological offensive should be a disgrace to each one and all Spaniards. The impressive point is the sinister danger of an opposition, infectious but with the symptoms not yet recognized, incisive, fluid, but in our opinion EASILY ATTACKED AND EXTIRPATED. This humble column is one of very few which, when the law of Press and Publication was approved and promulgated, opposed the liberties of expression that law guaranteed. VIVA the censorship of the press. And of the movies, theater, books, radio, television. The suspension of these and other liberties has become a necessity. Is this because we are Nazis or Fascists? NO NO. It is because we are lovers of the TRUTH. Liberty under God's reign in His Justice in our country ONE GREAT AND FREE, not yoked zoologically to the carts and carretas of those tyrannical libertines, those violent despoilers of Spain by decatholicizing it, disarming it, and enslaving it.' "

"Not more?"

"Only a paragraph. 'The moment has come for the regime to offer once more the testimony of its deep, profound, indestructible strength. During the three decades the war has never ceased because the red armies, beaten and disarmed, have been relieved by others who have continued the battle. In this 34th triumphal year we have never ceased being combatants for God and for Spain, exactly as it was on July 18, 1936. This is because, possessing and enjoying VICTORY, we have never forgotten that the victor must conquer constantly with more victories, and that it is worse not to know how to defeat the enemy than to be defeated oneself . . . Those countries like Spain which are founded on VICTORY, in order to keep it, must constantly demonstrate that they desire and know how to conquer the conquered.' "

Each man walked from the room in silence. As the young priest left he dropped the paper at his feet. Bachi picked it up, tore it into strips, and put a match to the pieces. Arrano's face was as gray as the ashes. Paul put his arm through Arrano's as they went out.

Three weeks before the opening of the summary court-martial Paul moved over from Roncesvalles to stay in Bilbao. Arrano had dealings with the lawyers and needed someone to help him get to their offices. He had tried to go alone and didn't like it, the young priest wrote Paul.

The day after he got there he took the Eagle to see Suertegaray. He was waiting in the antesala when the lawyer on his crutches brought Arrano out. "I have a message for you from Luku's lawyer, Rufino Thevet. Luku's sisters ask you to go over to Eibar to see them - next Sunday would suit them."

"Of course I'll go over, but what do they want to see me about?"

"I understand it's a message from Angeles Duarte."

Paul's hands tightened on the magazine he had been reading. Then he laid it on the table carefully. "She's still in the Alava prison?"

"Yes. You see her lawyer had to go back to Madrid and he left the message with Rufino. In any case, you'll get it straightened out with Luku's family. Here's Rufino's card introducing you."

"Do I have to wait until Sunday?"

"I guess not. I think they just wanted to cook you a nice dinner."

"I'll go this afternoon. Is that all right with you, Eagle, I mean you don't need me this afternoon?"

The bus ride all along a river would have been beautiful except for the scum on the water, a white foam seen close up to contain every kind of debris, rags, dead fish, boxes, food. This was the most heavily industrialized part of the Bilbao area. After a while Paul stopped looking out the window. Eibar itself was as desolate as an abandoned city. There were no trees: even the dead trunks in the plaza had been removed.

The apartment house was like dozens of others, built for the Star Pistol employees (Luku's father was one) and sold, not rented. They were not old buildings but the general erosion seemed to have reached them too.

Luku's mother let him in. She accepted him with no more identification than his own word (he merely said his name) although he held out the card from Rufino Thevet.

Energetic and talkative, she wanted to show him the apartment and, above all, Luku's pelota trophies. Luku had used a den as his bedroom; now it was den again, the trophies on a shelf there. The two sisters shared one bedroom; the other was the mother and father's. She went through each room and explained it. She didn't allow a chink of silence for Paul after he had introduced himself and it gradually came to him that she thought he didn't speak any language she could understand.

Finally he topped her voice, not easily, and shouted in

Spanish, "Will the two señoritas, your daughters, be home soon?"

She was as surprised as if he had grown a foot taller standing there in front of her. Then she burst into laughter. "You must have thought I was very rude, Paul - that is how you say your name, isn't it? My son spoke of you several times. Do you know that his father and I saw him in the Siete Calles? We were just going into a restaurant there and he came out from an alleyway, as if he had known we were going to be there. It was after all the others were arrested, but Luku is very clever. He kept himself hidden just walking around Siete Calles. His father said to him, 'Son, are you content with what you are doing?' And Luku embraced us both and said yes, he was doing what he had chosen to do. He had already been a liberado for a year, more than a year, but before that he had a good job in the Banco de Vizcaya. A week after that they caught him." Her word torrent was stemmed for a moment.

"Did the wound heal all right? Have you been able to see him?"

"Oh yes, yes. We have seen him since but not in the hospital, you understand. They wouldn't let us go there. My daughters and I are going over to Burgos to the court-martial. The lawyer tells us the prisoners have nearly all been brought to Burgos already. The prison there isn't as bad as Santa María. In Cádiz, you know. That's the worst. But Burgos is cold as the North Pole."

"Were he and Matai in Cádiz together?"

"No, they move them around like chessmen. One here. One there. They treat Matai the worst."

He couldn't wait any longer. "Please tell me what you can about Angeles, señora."

"The girls will be here soon and they will tell you everything. We have known Angeles for many years because she and my daughters went to the same nuns' school in Deva."

"Do you know if she is well?"

For once the woman stopped talking or preparing to talk and looked at Paul carefully and shrewdly, that Basque use of the eyes called begiak, which means the truth within. The one so surveyed must return the same look. Her eyes lifted his and they met and held until there was no way for him to show anything but his exact thoughts and emotions.

"They say you feel great affection for Angeles. I see it's true."

"Yes, señora, it's true."

"The girls will tell you the message they have for you from her. They know her well not only because of school but also because their brother cared very much for Angeles."

"I didn't know that," and it seemed to him a lack in him not to have known.

"She didn't accept Luku's affection, love; anyway they were too young. But Luku had really already made up his mind that with the life he led a woman would suffer too much."

"Like Isa . . ." Paul said.

"It's better they don't marry. I was sorry to see Angeles marry Jabier because he was so deep in his work. They were bound to suffer, both of them."

The front door opened. It was as if a flock of cheery birds or possibly merry bleating lambs had come flying, gamboling in. The two daughters, like their mother, kept talking every minute but their voices ran the scale, lifted, hovered. They shook hands with him and then the one with auburn hair - he had no idea who was older or younger because they were both so pretty - put her hands on his arms. It was still formal, but affectionate.

"He's nice looking," she said to her sister as if they had discussed him beforehand.

"Sit down in the dining room, you three, and I'll bring in a cup of coffee."

Humbly, but quickly because he did not want them to start talking about other things, he begged them, "Please tell me anything you know about Angeles."

"Yes, yes. Well, to begin with, her lawyer who is from Madrid, a fine lawyer named Galíndez, knows Luku's lawyer. They are old friends."

"Is there a message for me from her?"

"Wait, just wait a minute." It was the auburn-haired one. The other one had been talking. "Go on, sister, tell him."

"I just wanted you to understand how the message came. Angeles told this señor Galíndez to tell Luku's lawyer to tell us . . ."

"That Angeles feels she has known you all those five years since the picnic in Nevada, and that for that reason, since you are old friends, she wants you to know that, that . . ."

"She feels that the friendship you and she have is the most important friendship she has, and it has given her very great comfort during those awful months with the nuns . . ."

"Was there more?" Because both girls seemed to be waiting to say something else.

"Well, señor Galíndez said she said that if you wanted to give either me or my sister a kiss, she would permit us to accept it for her."

"I will give you each a kiss." He was crying.

The mother had just come in with four coffee cups. "You may give me a kiss for her too, Paul."

He asked them to tell him how, by what miracle, it

was that Angeles could come to feel she knew him and could trust him.

"By now we all know you're trustworthy. That was no problem. As to the other we have a word for it, it's called long love. You see, we don't often marry early and we may have to love the man we want to marry for many years before the marriage is permitted. But we think about him a great deal, all the time. Sometimes he has even gone to Venezuela or America. We know he will come back for us. And the long love is what keeps us happy."

"Do you think it has really made her happier?"

"Oh yes. The second time he saw her señor Galíndez says she was joking and singing . . . She always used to be like that, but it surprised him to find her so in prison and we think it can only be that the long love began for her."

Paul stayed with them until late that evening, until the last bus he could get back to Bilbao. They went for a walk and they showed him Father Ander's church and parish house. Paul became the member of a family and he was glad to be that. When he got back he didn't tell the Eagle everything about it. It was a family secret.

•

He went with Eagle to Burgos for the court-martial, arriving the day before it opened. They left Brother Telesforo and his hood behind with the priests, and the Eagle emerged in a beret. They looked up a hotel in the old part of town, one Eagle had used when he was a courier. They soon found out the same family was no longer running this hotel in Franco's chosen nest. The present owner was a pure zipizopo, stupid, overbearing, and too talkative for toleration. Of the original family - and the Eagle had had real friends among them - a few had died of natural causes, many had grown so loyal to the Crusade they had burst with pride (as might well happen to the zipizopo) or they had had the chance to go on to something better than running an unprofitable hotel. Some dead or alive were not mentioned because they were godless traitors. Was it possible these had been his friends? asked the owner. But since the Basque gentleman was blind he would not turn him away. Arrano was preparing to leave in anger but when they passed the door of the little restaurant and smelled the savory food, Arrano decided the owner couldn't be a total beast or he wouldn't be able to keep or be married to so good a cook. So they stayed.

This was a very cold December. Although cathedral lovers are addicted to its cathedral, Burgos under any conditions is not really a beneficent city. It is one of those stone places of guilt and persecution, which was probably why Franco picked it as his headquarters during the war, like the onion finding its way into a porrusalada, thought Arrano, enjoying the onion-Franco with its dozens of slipping skins and a tiny heart

The hotel room was frigid but they could warm themselves with brandy in the restaurant. Not to be sentimental but to state a fact to himself, Arrano at those times remembered the prisoners who had been brought from all over Spain to Burgos and could not warm themselves in any way whatsoever. It was said that the three women were in the coldest of the jails, an old fortress formerly a convent.

From the hotel they went directly to the military headquarters, which was away from the center of town, a large red-brick building with a square odd tower. Paul said it looked like the top of an old-fashioned elevator shaft, not an attractive idea since the Franco police (if not the military, strictly speaking) had their unpleasant uses for elevator shafts.

There was a good-sized crowd, mostly Basques, looking at the building, and soldiers to keep them in their place. Luku's mother was there and so were her daughters. The three came to Arrano and Paul as soon as they saw them and their cordiality was as great to Paul as to the blind man. Arrano called the girls his chirripitas and gave the mother a hug. She told all about her brother in Idaho in the United States. There are many Basques there and it seems her brother had prospered and had found a way of telling the officials of that state, some of whom were American Basques, what was happening in the Basque county and she had hopes for some kind of intervention on their part. Arrano listened to her of course but didn't tell her he thought that process was bound to be slow. It would have to go through the Madrid embassy, and the current ambassador was Franco's friend, not the Basques'.

They walked around the outside of the building together. Luku's mother was known by everyone, Arrano by fewer people but enough to make him feel part of the crowd. For all his prison travels, he had never been inside this particular military headquarters. They heard from some who had that only a hundred persons (and this meant prisoners' families, friends, really any Basques) could get into the courtroom after allowing space for the president and other members of the court-martial with its soldier entourage and then the uniformed police, the secret police and the chivatos. Also there were pressmen, many from Spain but also from France, England, United States, Germany, and farther off. The presence of these foreigners was very distasteful to loyal crusaders who, from the gossip the Basques heard, thought the Spanish press would not have had to attend at all if these shameless intruders hadn't

175

pushed their way in. The French were the worst, *Le Monde*, *Figaro*, and that direst of enemies, the liberal Catholic *Le Croix*. There they were, demanding seats; several of them with cameras were circulating among the people that day before the trial.

However reluctantly, room also had to be made inside for the prisoners' lawyers and for the prisoners themselves, who were to sit in front of the judges but in a hollow place not quite deep enough to be called a well. Their heads would be visible. There was a small bench near the judges for witnesses, and also some benches for visiting lawyers.

At least five hundred Basques had come to Burgos, so there would be plenty of waiting. Arrano was thinking that some people might remember the cold while they waited outside before each session as vividly as they would re-member what happened inside; already it was like being in a war - deadening cold and incipient exhaustion. Never-theless, the crowd increased and there were not only Basques.

A short fat man dressed in black, even a black hom-burg, and escorted by seven taller men who were evidently police in plainclothes (although the correct small gentle-man hardly seemed a policeman) came across the square, walked cater-cornered from their black cars. The people drew away from the group, although the little gentleman was most amiable and called out salutations here and there. He saw Arrano and switched direction so as to meet him. Arrano and Paul were still with Luku's mother, but she veered away, taking her daughters and saying to Arrano, "It's that black beetle, Bonavit. What does he want of you?"

"Well, my blind friend! How many years since I've seen you?" The inspector held out a hand. (Paul noticed that in spite of the sedate and expensive clothes and hat, the man had dirty matter in the corners of his eyes.)

"Since I was in your jail in Barcelona, Inspector." Probably Arrano knew the hand was there but he didn't take it.

"You don't hold hard feelings, do you? Each man has his job. I hear you have a nice place up on the mountain."

"A nice place for a Basque but too primitive for you luxury-loving policemen."

Bonavit laughed cheerfully and clapped Arrano on the upper arm.

Eagle drew back and then checked himself. "Inspector, I hear about you too from time to time. I hear you had some kind of battle with the Sevilla pickpocket children. Is that right?"

A couple of Bonavit's tall attendants scowled, but Bonavit said, "Yes, yes, yes. Worse than my own children and I have a houseful of naughty brats. What a job to give a grown man. Well, I'm back in my own territory now. If I can help you in any way, Eagle (he too said the word in English and Arrano's face showed his displeasure), let me know." It occurred to Paul that the inspector had had to keep up this conversation until he got a sign of resentment.

Bonavit left, waving a backhanded goodbye.

•

In some other place and time Bonavit might have loved children. It has been said that people who resemble them are apt to like them and Bonavit was small and round. But the pickpocket boys declared war on him so how was he supposed to like them?

When he was demoted from the head of the Social Brigade in Bilbao and sent to Sevilla, the pickpockets were dumped into his lap. Nobody wanted the job of rounding them up. They had been no problem while the old man who for many years was régisseur of pocket picking was left alone to rule in his own way. The trouble came from the editor of *El Garabato,* a scandal sheet which, indeed, was now covering the Burgos trial. This paper had a scummy little office in a bedraggled part of Madrid but Muñoz Ramírez, its editor, always hired bright reporters, not hacks, and very good cameramen. *El Garabato* made a specialty of graphically covering ax murders and the like; its sales were large. It stayed out of politics.

Naturally there was a subsidiary business of blackmail. What was not published was as profitable as the gory material that was. The editor had an accurate file of the affairs and peculiarities of fairly important people. He never went above a certain level of politician or businessman or policeman but the pickings in that selected area were rich enough. It was said he kept the same careful information on those above the dividing line he had chosen, but he didn't use this information. He kept his records in a shorthand of his own invention.

That was not quite all. The editor had been a red during the Civil War, had got out of Spain and worked for the *London Times.* He came back in twelve years, protected by information he had acquired before he left but amplified and verified with proofs remaining in London; this information was about someone high up in Franco's government, some said Franco himself. There were two men in London and none in Madrid who could, if necessary, give the name. The editor used this as blackmail only to the point of being allowed to publish what he pleased in *El Garabato* and it was, obviously, a scandal and sex sheet. He never attacked the dictator's friends. It was said that

Muñoz was not romantic enough to think one man could overthrow a corrupt government but pleased himself by showing the untouched picture of crime under that regime. He told a novelist who had an introduction to him from a London friend that the way to write a story of Franco Spain was to take the full file of *El Garabato* and make a continuous and not artificially connected record of the violent crimes of thieves and pimps and murderers and that he would then have the shadow history of the Crusade. So in a way Muñoz had kept his integrity.

The old man who managed the pickpockets had his police connection. Muñoz knew the connection but he didn't think much about it until his own pockets were picked one day in Sevilla. He caught the boy, who had a runny nose, mean eyes, and the hands of a violinist. Muñoz made the boy show him how he got the money out of an inner upper pocket of his coat.

"How much do you get out of it?"

It was fifty pesetas to the boy for a haul of five thousand.

"Goddamn!" Muñoz had kept a few phrases from his London days. And that was the start of an exposé; the old man refused to pay up. Perhaps Muñoz would have used the story anyway; the one percent of the fifty thousand offended him. It was not often that the injustices he saw were as uncluttered as that.

The old man retired to Santa Cruz de Tenerife in the Canary Islands.

The boys began to carry on business for themselves and the alarm of respectable persons was unbounded: a wave of juvenile crime had inexplicably crested in the city! The police were arresting enough children but evidently not the right ones. There was a magnificent scandal, fully reported and beautifully photographed by *El Garabato* when the son of a member of the cortes was arrested.

At this point Bonavit arrived and was given the mess to clean up. With the old man gone the pickpockets had no one special to hate. Bonavit provided them with his person. He also offered a relative of his as a substitute for the old man in Tenerife. The pickpockets retaliated by going in a quiet relentless group to Bonavit's house and literally picking the clothes off him. They then cleaned out all his food and drink. Ten masked boys did this job. As there were three hundred pickpockets working in Sevilla it was impossible to identify the ten.

Bonavit was above *El Garabato* magic line. Muñoz had one of the richest files he had ever gathered on the inspector; according to his rules he could not use it. So the pickpocket boys who were carrying on a successful war with the police suddenly lost their ally, although *El Garabato* knew that Bonavit had all the pickpockets he could find rounded up and beaten with mascaró clubs. Fifty boys at a time were herded into the basement. Three died. The young policemen who were ordered to do the beating began to protest. It was too much. The arrests were finally stopped by their own weight. When Bonavit was not in the police station he took on his affable, open manner, so nobody would believe the stories that went the rounds.

Some of the boys had to accept Bonavit's relative; some petitioned the old man to take them on in Tenerife. One group began to work the Madrid-Paris train. They were the hardiest. Up to their arrest at the border they were still on their own. Now they were in prison in Burgos, where they were not being badly treated.

•

Next morning Paul and Arrano settled the matter of getting into the first session by arriving before dawn. Then they went from the first session back to the line in order to get into the second. As to a midday meal they found a good enough system. Since even before blindness the Eagle had developed waiting and standing as two of his great talents, he could make himself into a Basque rock when Paul would have got nervous. So Paul went for food. By the second session, the people in the line became friends and permitted without protest this deviation from the quickly established rules. Eagle was the only blind one there and that had its effect, but soon their method was extended to the sighted, who would leave one person and it was permitted that another go for food and drink. It was the police who bothered everyone, joining hands and shoving them back roughly. This gave photographers a chance for action pictures, something of which the police were not unaware.

Finally they were in the courtroom, in one of the last rows, Paul told Arrano, but how could one grudge the nearer seats to mothers and sisters, and grandmothers and occasionally grandfathers of the prisoners? Some families had not seen their children for more than a year but knew through the underground they had been tortured brutally. Isa had lost her baby; everyone knew that; Isa had no parents to attend, and her only brother was among the prisoners alongside her husband.

Eagle was surprised by the voice of the president. He was a cavalry colonel and famous polo player of whom the Basques knew a good deal. The colonel had presided at other Basque court-martials and in all (up to now closed sessions) heavy sentences had been returned, and Eagle expected more brute authority in the voice. Instead the colonel spoke in a cultured way, although he clipped his words; Arrano had noted that many modish horsemen did that, especially polo players, to match the stylish clacking of hooves. The voice was of someone who knows there is an elite that can cross boundaries. He would talk French, which no doubt he knew, in that same not quite supercilious hoofbeat rhythm.

Paul whispered to Arrano, "Small eyes."

For the first session, before Arrano had a chance to hear Paul's more complete observations, he had to depend on a courtroom scene within his own mind. He knew the pictures he saw were ludicrous; and they were also impertinent, not to the army officers but to the prisoners over whom this court had such complete power. Zendejas was demanding six death sentences and seven hundred and fifty years of incarceration for sixteen Basques. It was evident from the lugubrious reading of the interminable apuntamiento, which contained a savage but boring disregard of truth, that the end result was foreordained no matter what ridiculous aspect it had in Arrano's mind: he couldn't help seeing these powerful judges as barnyard animals.

The dapper horse was of course the leader, but there was a cow, a donkey, a pig (from the snorts to which one of them was committed to as his form of expression). The ram was the mumbling reader of that fantastic accusation. There was no ox. An ox is a Basque. The Eagle played this intermediate game until he had some facts to build on and he could have conducted the whole trial with these barnyard participants, but the matter was too serious for that. Beasts seldom bring in death penalties for their own kind. Two stallions may fight. So may rams, although this one was only an old, pelt-clotted, desexed male sheep, more old lady than ram.

After Paul described the actual men to him, Arrano had no trouble moving them over from animal to human being. He had diagnosed them fairly well. The one for whom he hadn't found any form was Captain Zendejas, the central figure, the hero of this enactment. Jackal? Coyote? Not wolf. Paul said he was thin with a distended belly and Arrano couldn't envisage any animal with that appearance unless it was starving to death. Receding hair which he stroked tenderly and with a handsome pair of hands, although his fingernails were very long, Paul said. Arrano couldn't fit in those hands either. But it is true that the devil not only has his particular sense of justice but occasionally has striking and unaccountable beauties. They had told him that Comisario Silva had a handsome voice.

That first session was not all one toneless reading of amazing and sometimes absurd statements, as when Lieutenant-Colonel Ram intoned the news that ETA being essentially a Communist organization naturally kept in touch with other Communists, in one proven and damning instance having contacted the Communist Chinese ambassador in The Hague. The Chinese ambassador in The Hague represents Formosa.

Paul and Arrano would have laughed if they could have and not risked being thrown out - others did laugh. The president of the court must not have heard the statement previously because he too looked amused. "A withered smile under his mustache," Paul whispered.

Perhaps because of the president's suppressed amusement at the blunder, those who laughed out loud - mostly pressmen - were not ejected; the lieutenant-colonel who was reading shuffled his papers. It was not his mistake but Zendejas', and in Arrano's island he could see a bristling jackal not knowing from whence the attack comes but raging and cowardly, half and half.

There was another small laugh brought on by the older and in a conventional sense most respectable defense lawyer of them all - Calvo Peralta from Madrid. Arrano remembered his voice. Several years before he had gone with Arizeder to hear this lawyer give an interesting lecture in Bilbao. Arrano recognized the Madrid accent and the deep, sweet, unbreathy voice that spoke to the president of the court without exaggerated courtesy but no sarcasm, "The crucifix is placed on the wrong side of the president's chair. We take this as an offense to the Church. According to statute number 586 it should be on his right . . . I speak in the interest of the dignity of the court. The crucifix is also hanging crooked."

There was a bustle, background orders to someone to rehang the cross. And there was hushed laughter, very distressing to the officers present because this carelessness brought all of them a kind of shame they could understand.

They had been there two hours when the first break came. During the breaks the people in the public seats were brought to a patio, the same one used sometimes for periods between sessions when they were suddenly punished for being there at all. A minor break lasted about a quarter of an hour and no one was permitted to sit down or speak, although they could walk around a little. Miraculously there were toilets available. The discomfort of the lack of that service was in Arrano's experience the most anguished humiliation forced on a petitioner, a status which in Spain automatically included the families or friends of any prisoner whatsoever. There was absolutely no talk allowed; there were soldiers with mitralletas all around to enforce that rule.

During this first intermission the soldiers discovered Eagle was blind, and in their back-country way they made use of the knowledge to push him against doorways or walls or in any other way make him stumble. So Paul held on to him and they walked very close. Arrano's prison tricks came back to him and Paul was apt at picking them up:

when a soldier jostled them and there was a noise of faltering and regaining footsteps they would exaggerate it and Paul would use it as cover to tell Arrano something, their heads together.

In that first break the Eagle found out a little about the judges: the thin bumbling reader with bone-rimmed glasses which enlarged his eyes, and with spots on his uniform and old but well-polished shoes. Zendejas' appearance he already knew; after all he had brandished himself around while becoming the expert on Basque affairs, so Arizeder had seen him more than once and had told the Eagle about him. Also there was a judge who was a lawyer, the only one on the Board.

As to the president's appearance, Arrano had made a pretty good guess. "How tall?" he asked Paul.

"Five feet six," which Arrano had to translate into meters.

Paul found the rest of the officers colorless; one seemed sleepy.

Paul described the prisoners coming in, chained two and two, Matai and Isa far apart.

"Angeles and Isa chained together?"

Paul said yes, and, "Her hair is beautiful. It's grown long. She's wearing a dark red sweater and dark slacks. I think she looked up and saw you."

"And you?"

"Perhaps."

"Of course she's looking for you, Paule."

Arrano didn't tell Paul then, because there was no time or way, that he heard Angeles' voice when she came into the court saying to someone, "You know I'm nervous. I can't imagine why."

Arrano told him about that later and it made Paul cry; he said, yes, she had stopped for a second and spoken to a woman lawyer, an observer, who, they had learned, was

Belgian and was from the International Federation for the Rights of Man. This conversation took place the first evening in the hotel restaurant. They had decided not to search elsewhere but to eat there every night because the food was good although the people were not friendly. They used low voices there. Arrano was trying to teach Paul the way they did it at Santoña, and other places, almost under the breath. It would be a help in the courtroom if Paul could do it, but there was a trick to projecting the faint voice. He almost learned it. The only trouble was his natural voice took over when he was excited. But in the restaurant he got it pretty well.

The first night neither of them said much because both were absorbed in Angeles. For Arrano it was to try to understand what her voice and these few words meant. It could mean that she, and at least some of the others, had hope in the court-martial. Arrano could not find a way to tell Paul about this but he knew that if the prisoners had hope then all Basques ought to have it. Another thing was that her mother and father were attending the trial, bravely, because some people hid away after an arrest and imprisonment; so Angeles may have been trying to raise their spirits with her jaunty carriage and her joke.

And then there was what solitude and cold and dirt can do to anyone. Perhaps her gaiety had been a try at comforting herself, since who else was there to do that? To be honest, Arrano had heard desperation in the gay voice. And also, to be honest, although he did not doubt Paul's commitment to her, how could she, not knowing him, make any comforting commitment to him? How did she keep up her courage? Her family, even the young brother, had not been allowed to visit her for the last seven months. She was more alone than Isa, who until she died would be circled by her love for Matai and his love, even after his death. Angeles' marriage had been an extension of the happy family she had come from. She had known Jabier from child days in Bilbao, playing on the sidewalk in front of their next-door houses. Ay, Angeles, ay, my happy child, I hear your voice there on the sidewalk and if ever desperation had come into it someone would have hastened to assuage it. This is what Arrano was thinking.

And now she and the other two girls were shut up in an ancient dreary provincial prison without enough blankets to keep them warm and their families denied the privilege of bringing them more; they would have only icy water with which to make themselves presentable for the court. The latrine they would be allowed short use of would smell of age-old excrement. Her hands were chapped, Paul saw that. But her hair was brushed and shining. Of course Paul saw that first of all. She must have fought to keep some rusty prison-guard nun from cutting it. They had cut Isa's hair, Paul said, making her look like a sad, small, hungry boy.

Arrano was half in love with Angeles himself. She was the kind of Basque girl he had always secretly loved. He had not had the time to marry one but he had been attracted to all the Angeleses. They sang and they danced; they were the beloved heart of their families, usually with half a dozen brothers who kept guard on that female gaiety which was heart of the family's heart. So now she had come from a year of mistreatment, although the word was that Angeles had been less tortured than Isa, by far; perhaps she had been able to summon the older brother even in those twisted men of the torture squads.

Paul interrupted Arrano's thoughts. "Would she ever be able to hear me, Arrano?"

"Learn to speak Basque." And they laughed for that best of all reasons.

187

They had heard in the Ram's dreary voice the sentences that had been asked. Twenty years for Angeles.

•

The summary of the charges took the untidy old lieutenant-colonel a day and a half to read. It is true he was often interrupted. The defense lawyers again and again said they couldn't hear. The senior lawyer from Madrid complained the summary of charges was not that but an accusation.

Arrano thought it was the unending schoolish composition of a bully boy, about fourteen, who had recently learned that writing too can be a bludgeon. His habit took over: to attempt to enter the mind of this man or that. So it was with Zendejas and his document. Arrano kept seeing him writing it, or more likely dictating it to some small red-faced soldier who had been barely taught the high science of shorthand and didn't do it very well, so giving Zendejas a chance to blow up often enough to draw off the worst pressure of his hate for the Basques he was so exuberantly trapping. Or maybe he himself typed the first draft. After all he did write the Viajero column and he probably wouldn't have used a military stenographer for that. So there he was over a splendid germanic electric machine as heavy as a tank, its power and size making the man more minor than ever. He was typing with two fingers and there were some phrases that sounded as though they had been done with one finger. But the face above the machine, with or without dark glasses, was always aglow. This excitement had brought on the bungle about Communist ambassadors and a good many other curious errors as well. The one involving the Czech revolver amused Arrano the most.

Zendejas assigned Matai this Czechoslovakian revolver 7.65 Astia №956192. Matai loved good firearms and seldom had them. He tried to achieve the Pamplona jailbreak with an old Star pistol. All Basques knew that, these details the folklore which helped maintain their spirits in their largely underground life. The next more trenchant point was that when Matai was tried by the civil court for the Pamplona jailbreak attempt no Czechoslovak revolver was mentioned or produced. Yet here was Zendejas saying that this Czech revolver was the same one found on Matai after he was wounded in Pamplona and that it was also the one that killed Mascaró. And the Czech revolver was right there in court.

It was easy to imagine the bully fourteen-year-old's chain of thought: Czechs are some kind of Communists; ETAs ought to be Communists judging from their pugnacious lack of respect for the Crusade. It turns out there is a Czech revolver in the store of guns (not necessarily taken from ETAs but arrived at in some way). So Matai - who has been picked out as murderer because he is such an affront to the police with his laughter and jailbreaks - is assigned the Czech revolver with which to kill Mascaró, and the gun expert is told to make the proper statement about the kind of revolver that did that. The problem came from the position of Pamplona authorities, including Bonavit. When they did not revise their statements to admit the Czech revolver a little rift might have grown between them and Zendejas. Or maybe there already was a rift between Zendejas and Bonavit. These jealousies were well known.

12

Arrano had to see the trial whole, in perspective. How was he to get that?

Was it two faces confronting each other? One must be of Franco and his Crusade, that word which has its special effluvium in the controlled press and is otherwise used mechanically or cynically, but everywhere sums up the assumptions behind Franco's power. This face is as stony as the rictus of death. The other face is that of the Basques with their old innocence which is not stupidity. Their assumptions are also there and at least these are more alive than the ancient general's. Their face is mobile. They adjust what they do to what the other face shows.

In this dialogue the old one is worldly, rigid, so sure of himself that he never questions his supreme rights, although he still needs support from the Black Legend. The other keeps testing this motionless opponent, whose aspect may change a little when he is shown to be ridiculous or slow-witted. It never changes when he is shown to be cruel - it is his assumption that cruelty and torture are his prerogatives. Nor when he is shown to act illegally. That is his right. Under all circumstances, including ridicule by the foreign press, he will attempt to keep his air of dominance, even correct dominance. But the acid-washed bones of the Old Mutilado show through.

Life against death. In how many places is that tune being played? The Eagle is a Basque, so for him this particular performance is the most touching of all.

The sportive or dung-clotted barnyard animals departed in procession from Arrano's island mind. Their bleats and snorts were not exactly pitiful; every creature knows when it is going home, whether to stable yard or to the merry red corridors of hell.

In their place entered the careful stiff courtroom, the picture of a youngish Franco set perfectly straight on the wall. The crucifix was still crooked, although now on the right side of the president of the court. There were straight lines of chairs, the ornate uncomfortable ones of the judges or the plain uncomfortable ones of the defense attorneys and observers, the benches of the audience, everything lined up in parallels. But from the beginning to end there was one untidy spot - a pile of guns and other evidence thrown near the judges' dais, guns and books and pamphlets which were said to have been seized when the prisoners were arrested. Ho Chi Minh and Hegel could be made out alongside Gorki's *The Mother*, and *Mila 18*, and *How to Learn Basque Rapidly*. More than once someone passing the judges' table stumbled over the guns and books, but no matter, each day they appeared and each time more jumbled.

The trial began at 9:35 A.M., Thursday, December 3. The judges were in place, upright in all ways. While they sat in the empty courtroom before that first session did they feel any vague qualms in spite of the power they so formidably contained? There had been closed court-martials but this was the first open one. Basques had a devil-given cupidity and energy, although if the judges thought it out clearly, what risk was there? Everything was bound to go smoothly. Arrano, doubting that, was in the mind of the Ram.

The president, it is certain, had no qualms. For him it was like taking a difficult horse over water jumps; he knew he could rely on his own skill. But the Ram had no special skills. Of course he could read. He was by nature a follower. His self-discipline was sporadic. For instance he had left off his sabre.

That had happened before, but in a secret court-martial in which he had participated. That time nobody made a fuss. He had remembered it himself before any mention was made of it, let alone reproof. He should have known it would be different this time. It was that difference that bothered him. In his untidy way he had been something of a star in that secret court-martial. He had his old-boyish way of sounding rough. But all that was amateurish in comparison with the rectitudinous surroundings in which he now found himself. His throat was beginning to feel sore; there in the anteroom where they had congregated he had been repeatedly clearing it of the surru, until finally the president asked him to find a spittoon and be done with it.

So they sat themselves down in their ineffable respectability, and the president, Colonel Emilio de la Vega y Morales, ordered the public to be admitted along with the reporters, who could be heard ill-manneredly arguing with the soldiers assigned to guard doors and check documents. In the antesala, members of the court-martial were told by the president they must treat the press civilly. That was a difficult burden and one that should really not have been asked of a loyal crusader. Captain Zendejas - his Viajero alias was well known and also that all his journalistic experience acquainted him with the savagery and lies of the foreign press - added his admonition to the president's. And the president had not liked Zendejas doing that.

So the press was not the only problem. Lieutenant-Colonel Ram understood in his slow obstinate mind that if there were to be tensions among members of this court-martial it would be Zendejas who would create them. Unfortunately the captain was a vulgar man and a shade absurd. He had better not make scandals with this president who had his own ideas how to handle beasts, bitches and Basques. In his mind the Ram laughed at the alliteration - not original with him. There was great repose in the thought of the president's vigorous command of authority. De la Vega was a gentleman. The Ram sighed and shuffled his enormous pile of documents. He knew he ought to try to do it quietly but it was not easy. They had been typed up on a kind of paper with which the Ram was not familiar, slippery and hard to keep in order.

The reporters were pretty well settled in their seats, pulling out notebooks and writing boards, but approaching seats opposite the defense attorneys (and what sly fellows these were, mostly Jews, the Ram had heard) came three arrogant persons who, it appeared to him, had no business being there at all - clearly foreigners - and they seated themselves near and almost on a level with the court.

His neighbor at the table, an artillery captain, whispered to him, "Legal observers. Can you imagine?"

"Why is such an affront permitted?"

"I hear they are from outlandish places. The large woman is from Belgium or Holland, one of those Communist countries. The other I don't know but she certainly looks like a Jewess. The man is from Algeria."

"Algeria? A black?"

But Eagle was tired of the muddy Ram mind and left off trying to stay in it.

•

Now came the prisoners, two and two. After Angeles, chained with Isa, it was Josu Mendez Guenberrena whose appearance struck Paul the most; at the intermission Paul described him and Arrano told him that Josu resembled himself, Paul. Young and old at the same time, and also he was a student and looked it. Josu was married to Kristiana and sometimes during the trial they were chained together, but not this first day.

Josu threw a glance around as if he were seeing everyone from some place far off, a look of absolute calm, almost absent-minded. As he and his companion sat down, Josu was trying to loosen his jacket. It was hot in the room and cold from where they had come. His gestures were meticulous. He did not fumble, although he had the shackles and his neighbor's arm to contend with. He got the jacket as far back as he could, sat still and looked around once more, this time at the judges. He could not have seen them well from where he sat, but he brought up his head as far as he could. This disconcerted the Ram, who was nearest to the prisoners. The president did not return the gaze but was aware of it because he composed a gaze of his own, absolutely contemptuous. Anyone can express contempt by looking down and then up sideways, but the president could express contempt while looking straight ahead, and, as Paul had observed, his eyes were uncommonly small - thus it was all the more of a feat.

194

As soon as the court was declared open, the defense lawyers began their legal attempts to get the handcuffs off their clients. One of them tried three times to be heard and was disregarded. It was Arga Lorenzana, the Basque young woman lawyer, who got her "con la venia" recognized. Maybe the president wanted to see how a Basque woman conducted herself in court: she was first eager, then angry. She said, "Con la venia, Mr. President, may we be informed why the prisoners are handcuffed?"

The colonel looked surprised. From the sound of the voice, Arrano conjured up the idea he had a plastic bag lying between his legs along with his sabre; in it he kept the expressions he allowed himself, all of them suitable to a nimble horseman. This one was of conventional surprise - eyebrows must have been raised, head cocked. "Public order - security . . . what else, señorita letrado?" Then he spoke to the officer of the guard who was half visible standing in the pit. "Lieutenant, on your honor, would you take the responsibility for removing the handcuffs?"

The man sounded confused, although he answered quickly in an ingenuous voice, "No, Colonel, I wouldn't take that responsibility. No."

"Refused," said de la Vega loudly.

Arga spoke furiously. "Never since the Inquisition has such an indignity been heard of."

So the Basque woman lawyer was turning out as might have been expected. De la Vega pounded on the table. Arga had not even asked for the venia.

Matai's lawyer, Suertegaray, handsome, tall, romantic but with legs shattered by polio, so held up by crutches, then attempted to discuss military law, articles 770 and 772 which he said give only the president the responsibility for order in the courtroom; therefore consultation with the officer of the guard was illegal and a subterfuge.

De la Vega was perhaps deferent to the crutches. He spoke mildly. "That's possible, señor letrado, but in the situation I find myself, and having consulted the law, I am making the decision. The accused will remain manacled. I beg of you not to insist further."

Rufino Lares Thevet did insist. "Mr. President, one of the accused has constrictions in his arm. Can't the manacles at least be changed to the other hand?"

"No. A muscle constriction is not really painful if he holds his arm still."

Thereupon word was given to the Ram to begin reading the apuntamiento, or judicial report. What was this document which was read in monotonous voice for three sessions plus several hours? By definition a judicial report is a neutral résumé of the thousands of pages of dossiers and other information. This fundamental document is meant to inform the judges of the accusations against the prisoners but is not itself accusatory. Objectivity is its intrinsic quality.

Arrano laughed when, later, he gave that resplendent definition (which he had gotten from Suertegaray) in answer to Paul's question.

In fact the defense attorneys frequently interrupted the reading, indignant at the lack of impartiality.

"This isn't a judicial report but an accusation," said Lares Thevet, and the president told him to be quiet and said to Flores, "Go on reading."

The other judges looked around, only barely interested. The exception was Zendejas, who listened with fleshly pleasure. He leaned forward, following every lip movement of Flores. Of course the report was his; he was the investigative member of the court-martial. All that was lacking for Zendejas was applause for his efforts.

From time to time the president stroked the plaque of carved horses standing on the carved table in front of him and his carved chair. His sabre was between his legs, according to the Military Code of Justice, ✗1174.

Calvo Peralta, the older Madrid lawyer, interrupted the reading. "Con la venia, Mr. President, we observe that the recorder is not wearing his sword, contrary to the strict order of the Military Justice Code, article ✗1174. This deserves an admonition."

"It could nullify the procedure of this case," said Arga.

The Basques understood that the tactic was not flippant; on the contrary its object was very serious - to remark on the grotesque ceremonial, its lack of meaning obvious to all participants. The president smiled vaguely as if at some agreeable recollection but he spoke vigorously, "I order you to put on your sabre, Lieutenant-Colonel Flores."

The judges looked high above the heads of the public, Flores-Ram made scribbles on paper. A very rare event was taking place - the humiliation of a court-martial Board and so of the whole army caste. At last the sword arrived. Flores took it nervously and it fell from his hands. There was a repressed laugh among the public.

"Silence or I'll empty the court." De la Vega lost his horsey manner.

The recalcitrant sabre was at last subdued and placed between the legs of the Ram. Peace restored, the session was immediately suspended for fifteen minutes.

The court reopened with more protests from the lawyers: the guards had prevented them from talking with their clients.

"I will register your complaint," said de la Vega, who had altogether regained his composure and spoke in an unhurried voice.

Lieutenant-Colonel Flores, properly sabred, put on his glasses and proceeded with the reading. It was hot in the room. The prisoners could not take off their sweaters or coats. A defense lawyer tried again to have them unchained.

"That question has already been settled, señor letrado."

The lawyer insisted. The president ordered the guards to release the manacles one by one just long enough for each prisoner to take off his coat if he wished. There were clicks as each pair of handcuffs was released and then relocked. The silence behind these little sounds was made up of the indrawn breaths of each prisoner's family.

The session was suspended at one o'clock and fifteen minutes, to resume at nine o'clock the next morning.

That afternoon reports began to come in of the kidnapping of the German consul from his house in San Sebastián. The Burgos papers, the Bilbao papers, and, as they arrived, most Madrid papers, the government-directed majority, announced uniformly and with not a falter that the kidnapping was another violent act of ETA, that the consul might already be dead, although ETA was using him as a hostage against the conviction of prisoners in the Burgos trial.

The Eagle had a bad sleep that night. He felt as though Jon's fire was consuming him. When the Eagle dreamed, which was not often, his dreams were too horrible to repeat; they came to him that night. By morning he was in real waking distress; perhaps the imaginary flames were a fever but he could not take the chance of finding out if that were true. Nothing was going to keep him from the trial. He decided it was best not to discuss the consul's kidnapping, not even with Paul who had gathered all the papers he could lay hands on. Eagle urged him to wait for *Le Monde*, which of course might be prohibited if its report was too disagreeable.

At the morning sessions they managed to get seats very near the front. The room seemed small and hot and crowded.

Carafes of water and glasses appeared on the judges' table and on the desks of the defense attorneys. The journalists were surly; they had been skin-searched outside the chamber. An old Italian reporter was saying furiously that the last time he had been treated this way was by the gestapo in 1943 in Venice.

As soon as the session was open, Luzarra asked to be recognized.

"No," said de la Vega dryly.

Other lawyers protested. Even now with de la Vega's intentions becoming clear, astonishment was apparent in their anger.

De la Vega was not abashed; he said to one, "I prohibit you from speaking," and to another, "You do not have the floor." Tension increased. The courtroom was not only suffocating but filled with taut lines of furious communication between the colonel and the lawyers. Empty ritual had gone out the window.

Calvo Peralta intervened. He held onto his self-possession. "Are we to conclude, Mr. President, that we cannot be assured of defending our clients freely?"

Luzarra said, "The kidnapping of the German consul Conrad is preventing this court from presiding with the serenity and equanimity required of it. We should adjourn this trial."

The president told them both to be quiet and threatened all the lawyers with penalties if they continued their disobedience.

"Disobedience?" exclaimed Arga. "This is not an elementary school, Mr. President."

All along there had been a muted struggle going on in the prisoners' well. At this point Matai and Angeles both got to their feet, pulling their companions with them and pointing to the ears of all four of them.

"Their ears have plugs in them," said Arga in rage.

The lieutenant in charge of the well was half-apologizing. "Mr. President, we put them in on the way from prison so they can't talk to each other. Some of the guards forgot to take them out."

"Well, take them out. What's all the fuss about?"

The lieutenant obeyed him.

"We haven't heard anything that's been going on in the court," said Angeles. "They try us and they don't let us hear." A guard pushed her down.

Matai was not as easy to handle. He stood for several moments, shaking his head as if to clear his ears.

Luzarra and Suertegaray in turn tried to get the venia. The president silenced them.

Luzarra again asked permission to speak in order to protest that he had not been given permission to speak. The president gave him permission to speak in order only to register his protest that he was not allowed to speak. There was no laughter but there was a pause, an unsighed sigh.

After that the president signaled to the Ram to again continue reading. The apuntamiento had arrived at the interesting point of accusations against eleven persons not present, some having fled and others being priests who had not been arrested because the bishop of Bilbao had used the prerogative given him by the Concordat to prevent the arrests. These eleven were said to be members of ETA and it was becoming clear that not only the prisoners in court but the whole organization of ETA was under attack. There was hardly any further pretense that Mascaró's murder was the subject of the case. The brittle dryness of de la Vega's voice increased when he spoke during these accusations against the absent eleven: he or persons above him seemed not only to have decided this matter was to proceed rapidly, but that the roots and meaning of the case should be made clear.

When de la Vega announced the noon recess Eagle could easily hear that the president had stayed behind the other judges and that he was pacing back and forth. Eagle wanted to listen so he held onto Paul pretending he was dizzy. One of the observer lawyers approached the president. From her walk it was the heavy-set Belgian woman whose direct gaze and absolute attention to the case impressed Paul.

De la Vega spoke to her amiably in French. Now he was a parlor gentleman. "Do you have much trouble following the proceedings, madame? It's all very long and boring, isn't it?"

Her voice was deep and the Eagle thought it sounded tired. "Not at all, Mr. President. I was interested in everything. But, with your permission, I am indignant that the prisoners are kept chained and that the lawyers have no immunity at all from you, Mr. President."

He laughed very politely. "You must be commended for your frankness, madame."

"As another lawyer, I admire the lawyers for their courage. It isn't easy to make a defense when at every turn you remind them you have all the power."

"Oh, madame, I didn't say that to them, at least not in those terms. As far as the handcuffs go, don't you understand that? I am sure you're a sophisticated woman. Things can't be so very different in Belgium than they are here. You must know orders come from above."

He pointed upward and laughed a short neigh and shrugged his shoulders. He had thrown his first cigarette away and he took another, offering her one, which she did not accept. He said, "As far as asking the officer in charge his opinion, that was one of our precious formalities. I wouldn't expect you to be so ingenuous. Actually the lieutenant was opposed to the prisoners being kept in handcuffs."

The lady said quietly, "Even in the colonels' Athens the accused are not chained during trials."

As she left he bowed and said with that straight-glanced condescension he had perfected, "Adieu, madame. Let's talk again."

During this conversation, the prisoners had been held in their well. The lady had brought herself and so de la Vega as near to the edge of their hole as possible. Paul didn't need to tell Arrano they had been listening; Arrano could hear their attention. And it took no special faculties to know they were aware of the hopelessness of any conversation with this mechanical horseguard. Yet the lady's courage must have given them courage, the deep good bell of her voice against the tinny words of the other with its casual insults to their rights.

As Paul and Arrano went out, the Eagle was saying, "Greek colonels, Spanish colonels, betibat."

"What does that mean, Eagle?"

"The same. One and the same. Ujuju!"

In the corridor outside the chamber they were met by the usual throng of chivatos and guards. One of them came at Paul and Arrano. He jostled the Eagle so hard he nearly fell.

They finally got everybody out of the corridors by pushing with their batons. Cattle to the slaughterhouse, Arrano thought, Jósus, it's all a man can do to remain cattle during a march like that - he needs more self-control than for any attack on the enemy.

Paul said, "Let's catch up to the observer lawyer. She's ahead with Luzarra."

"Our place in line?"

"I'll manage that somehow. Come on!"

A crowd had gathered around Luzarra and the Belgian lawyer. Luku's mother's unconquered voice was telling the woman observer how hard it was to get into the trial. Another woman was thanking the lawyer for attending the trial. "You must help them, they're very young."

Arrano saluted Luku's mother with a fond "Kaisio!" and then said, "Paule, we might as well go to whatever café Luzarra takes the lady."

It was cold. The warm air inside the café was a respite. Arrano had come to associate the cold with the gristapo. Some of them in civilian clothes came into the warm café and chilled it. They sat at a table near the lady and talked arrogantly to one another. Well, this was their town and their time.

Arrano had a terrible headache. It was as though the dead eye nerves were growing and little good it would do them. Paul understood Arrano's pain - the prisoners standing chained listening to the vapid horse-trainer. Paul put a brandy into his friend's hand.

A woman came to Luzarra's table. Arrano motioned Paul to tell him about her. Paul said her face was furrowed as if she were old, but her voice turned out to be very young.

Luzarra said to her, "Sit down with us."

"No. I have only a word to say to the lady."

"What is it?"

"About Mascaró. Do you know what he was?"

"I have heard something about him," said the deep voice of the woman attorney.

"But maybe you don't know what happened when he died. That night in all of Euzkadi we sat, as you are, in cafés. But we were laughing and singing. There wasn't one bottle of champagne or any liquor left on the shelves of bars or stores. Do you understand what that means?" She turned suddenly and went out as if she would weep if she said anything more.

They sighed at Luzarra's table. They sighed at Arrano's table. "I know her, Paule. She's a wonderful woman. She matches the lady lawyer!" One of the gristapo called an ugly name after her. They didn't have the heart to introduce themselves to the lady as they had thought to do. Instead they hurried back to the line.

Naturally they didn't get their good seats again, but were in the very last row. In some ways it was better to be as far as possible from what happened that afternoon.

When the session began it was apparent de la Vega was anxious to move it even faster than it had been going in the morning. He tried to hurry Lieutenant-Colonel Ram, whose throat had gotten very bad and who was asking to have a blond male puppet-doll assistant read in his stead. Almost everyone had learned the Ram's monotone and was able to follow it. It was hard to understand the doll. But what was being read was extraordinarily important. Each side had the right to ask to hear certain evidence which had been left out of the apuntamiento.

First the defense requested the verbal but recorded testimony of the wife and daughter of Mascaró. What came out was that these two women, after allegedly identifying Matai in Santa María prison in Cádiz, had never signed the statement. They simply didn't sign it. There was nothing the prosecutor could do about that. Pressure must have been put on the women and it was astounding to Arrano that they had not signed. Nor did they choose to testify at the court-martial; their letter to the court said they would not present themselves because of fear. They did not say of whom they were afraid.

The next testimony had again to do with the gun that killed Mascaró. The bullets taken from the body of Mascaró were said to be from a Czech Vizor pistol, model 50, caliber 7.65. The pistol was there in the pile. It was held up to view, but the bullets from it were not presented as evidence. Then the blond baby substitute for Lieutenant-Colonel

Ram read from a paper handed him by the Ram. The paper said, as if quoting a witness, that Matai shot Mascaró with this pistol. He shot from the top of the stairs and hit Mascaró who was just about to enter the door of his apartment, but it was not said who was being quoted. After that there were words identified as coming from a gun expert. According to this authority, the pistol had belonged to Matai when he and Jabier Ojenbarrena attempted to free Angeles Duarte from Pamplona prison.

The link, however, was again omitted: that when Matai was tried for the Pamplona attempt no Vizor pistol was mentioned or connected to him in any way. It was Matai's lawyer, Suertegaray, who insisted on the reading of these additional documents, and he put emphasis on the dates. When did the Vizor pistol appear on the scene? There was no mention of it in any document until well after Matai's trial and conviction for the Pamplona attempt. Where was the Vizor at this time? As always, Suertegaray (now it seemed that the president had a special aversion to the crutches and he became more and more abrupt with their owner) pushed this point as far as he possibly could.

Then, through her lawyer, Arga, Isa asked to have her wedding certificate read. All along there had been statements about amorous relations between Matai and Isa and between the other two girls and their husbands. The reading of the religious wedding certificate did nothing to curtail these references. The Ram snickered and shuffled his sabre; others brushed back their hair. The gestures and sounds were of men enjoying a very poor dirty joke.

It came out that Arga was trying to make it possible for Isa and Matai to share a cell for the remaining time but the court was never as violently negative as in this exchange. "They were not married by the civil authorities, they are not married," said de la Vega, his half smile visible.

"They believe in the validity of the religious ceremony, Mr. President."

"That is very touching. They will remain separate and indulge in no more illicit behavior."

For little Isa this may have been the very bottom. If she could have been close to Matai for the days that remained, she might have been able to tolerate the rest. Most Basques knew some of what she had suffered because a book about the tortures was published in France and it circulated underground in the Basque country. There was also word-of-mouth reporting from bribable guards. The book itself had forty statements, many sworn to lawyers, others smuggled out. What was omitted from the capsulated stories was as important as what was said.

This was Isa's statement made to Arga Lorenzana: "Here is part of what I was forced to submit to: With my hands and feet tied, I was given blows with their fists in the stomach and other parts of my body, and then kicked while they said, 'Let's see if she'll die right off.' Held by the hair I was whirled around. One group of men, who had taken off my dress, passed me around while they spoke to me in foul words.

"They showed me what they called the operating table. My hands were tied behind me. My feet were tied. They stuffed my mouth with paper. They struck me on my breasts and above all on my thighs, until they were exhausted.

"They also used a thin plastic wand and a hose.

"Having put me on the operating table, and everyone knows the position, they beat me again and poured water into my mouth, sometimes drop by drop and sometimes all at one time.

"After some of these operations they would take me out of the cell. If I wasn't able to walk they kicked me and beat me with the wand from behind. It seems to me that more than once I lost consciousness . . . Once when I woke up I was inside a car. My body was asleep, without feeling . . .

"They forced me to take medicines. Sometimes when I could not walk I was carried in the arms of these beasts.

"The interrogation that accompanied the mistreatment continued night and day. The last night I was left in peace. I was not beaten on the last day.

"I was always treated like a prostitute. You know the language these men use. They talked to me a great deal about my husband. They were trying to drive me insane, telling me he was in their hands and that one of these days they would cut off his head . . ."

Isa herself did not come up from the well to give court testimony. Arga told the colonel that Isa was unable to do this. And now it was time for these face-to-face encounters. All of them but Isa had their twenty minutes or so. Matai had eight and a half minutes.

When this part of the proceedings was announced, stirring and the sound of a pair of handcuffs being unclipped came from the prisoners' well. Just then the sleepy judge said he wanted a certain procès-verbal read; it sounded as though he had been told to make this demand but had forgotten or been asleep until now. During the reading of the document, which was a repetition of the charges against Matai, Suertegaray asked where the statement was taken. By whom? In prison or in front of an examining judge?

"Withdraw those questions," said de la Vega imperiously.

"With your permission, Mr. President, on the contrary I request that my questions be answered."

"May I remind you, señor letrado, that this tribunal has every right to bring action against you and disbar you. Who do you imagine you are?" De la Vega was getting more and more sarcastic and noisy. He had nearly lost his rigid self-control and a fifteen-minute debate took place between him and the defense lawyers with the president doing most of the talking. At the end Luzarra thanked the president for his illumination of the law, and Luzarra's sarcasm was the more biting because it was quiet.

Calvo Peralta, always calm, demanded the suspension of the process. "We are obliged to refer to the officers of our bar associations. According to Article 23 of the by-laws of our guild we must do this."

"No, I order you not to leave your seat."

"Defense is impossible under these circumstances."

"I withdraw from you the right to speak." De la Vega was truly beside himself.

In this atmosphere the questioning of the prisoners began.

Valentín Lizaldi Aranzazu was the first called to testify. Paul told Eagle that Lizaldi appeared very calm and that he wore a sweater over a frayed shirt; because of the mood created by de la Vega's noisy anger, Paul risked speaking outright although softly.

Lizaldi was quiet, leisurely, not distressed. They knew he was a chemistry student, twenty-one, the youngest of the accused. The prosecutor asked him, "Do you remember distributing illegal propaganda?"

"I did it because . . ."

"Answer yes or no. Have you distributed copies of *Zutik?*"

"That depends, I . . ."

"Yes or no?" from de la Vega.

"I am a militant of ETA. I am explaining to you why I have fought all my life against fascist oppression."

The president was pallid and menacing. "I order you to be quiet."

"I was tortured." He covered the president's voice. "As were all my comrades here."

Then very quickly Sahagún Velarde asked for the venia

and without waiting questioned Lizaldi. De la Vega couldn't follow quickly enough. Was he tired from the recent combat? He leaned back and listened - extraordinary conduct.

Sahagún asked Lizaldi why he had fought all his life.

"I chose to fight for the working class and I shall continue until absolute victory. To battle merely for reforms is not enough under fascism . . ."

The bellicose statements contrasted with his gentle manner. No gestures. No apparent emotion. From the start of the interrogation he sat serene and motionless.

"Your opinions are not pertinent," said the president crossly.

But Sahagún kept on. He asked quickly, "You were arrested on the eleventh of October by the police of Bilbao?"

"Yes, I was arrested with three friends in a house on Artecalle. We had been mountain climbing and had come back to our rooms to get a change of clothes. The police were already in the house. They were in the room next to the one we entered." The voice was gentle and calm. "They began by wounding Simon Sarraga in the stomach. One of the policemen was seized by a kind of hysterical fit; he kept bellowing that he had to allay his tension, those were his own words, by killing at least one of us.

"He went for me. I was already manacled. The other policemen had to hold him back and the chief was explaining to him that we still had to be made to talk. The hysteric kept pointing his revolver at my head and inquiring into the details of my obligations in ETA."

"How long were you held in the central offices of the Social Brigade?"

"Nine days."

"Were you the object of threats or bad treatment during this time?" Sahagún threw the words away.

"No, I was not subject to bad treatment. I was subject to systematic torture. They beat me savagely all over the body. I vomited blood and urinated blood. They gave me the torture of the circle. Thirty policemen punched me back and forth like a ball, this one to that one, to see who could hit the hardest. The men who tortured me are the agents of law and order, of that which is called authority . . ."

"And the operating table? Were you subjected to that treatment?"

The president interrupted. "Señor letrado, no, that's enough. Leave the subject alone."

This was the first time in Franco's years that details of torture - and all Basques knew the often playful names and nasty forms - had been mentioned in any Spanish court. The Spanish press was stupefied. No wonder de la Vega was numbed into silence.

Lizaldi was permitted to finish his testimony. This had to do with the condition of his friends, that when he met them in the police corridors or saw one in the hospital they had been beaten beyond recognition, that only by their voices could he identify them.

Again, the president seemed to be begging for understanding in his difficult position. No doubt other lawyers in other cases had been more cooperative than these lawyers, although in a way Sahagún answered the colonel's plea for he did not ask any more questions about specific tortures. "One more question, Mr. President. Valentín Lizaldi Aranzazu, can you swear before this court that the depositions you made were given in conditions of all necessary liberty?"

"How could I swear that? The judge had only to look at me at the time I signed. My face was swollen purple.

I was covered with bruises. I had signed a complaint against the police."

"Which does not appear in your dossier."

"No, because they kept me twenty-three days in solitary before a doctor saw me, and then he said I was healthy enough so if I was careful I would still be able to stand before the execution wall."

"You are not to testify on the opinion of others but only on facts," said de la Vega, somewhat placatingly. But then as if he couldn't allow himself this good humor, he added sententiously, "Anyway, we are not here to judge the police. If you have something to say on that matter take it to another court."

Sahagún had picked up the colonel's uneasiness. "Just one more question. Under the torture which you suffered, had you been asked if you killed Mascaró, would you have answered that you were the murderer?"

"Without any doubt. I would also have sworn that I had assassinated this entire court-martial."

That was the end of his testimony; he went back quietly to his friends in the well. His manner had not varied during any part of the questioning.

It was getting late but they were going to squeeze in one more prisoner. This was Father Ander.

The Eagle knew him, knew him well. His high voice reached Arrano through all the layers of his blind eyes. Ander said he was thirty-seven. He sounded as if he were seventy-seven. What had they done to him? The answer was easy. Eagle had heard the record of his torture, well-planned and systematic like that of all the others, perhaps made more deliberately humiliating because he was a priest. Ander's statement spoke of the terrible shame he had felt during the bicycle and also when he could not help urinating in his clothes. The other prisoners were in their twenties and he was thirty-seven. Is there a point in there somewhere when dignity must no longer be sacrificed? Arrano tried to remember from his own life if that were true.

Ander was in the middle of saying he had formerly belonged to JOC, an organization of young Christians, when his voice broke and he cried out, "This morning the Civil Guard shot Eli Peralta. In Eibar, my parish, in a protest against this very trial. I should be there to comfort his parents."

The sleepy judge coughed, then half-laughed. It was hard to know what that man thought he was doing but Ander took it as an insult to the memory of Eli Peralta. He turned to the court (up to now he had been looking down into the prisoners' well and it might have been that he was comforting them because they had just heard about Peralta's death) and spoke to that judge in a voice of great severity, "You laugh at the murder of another young Basque, a good boy, decent and moral. You laugh."

Arrano was afraid the priest was not going to keep his self-control, but his attorney helped him quickly. "Father Ander, will you tell the court what you consider to be the duties of a priest who lives in a Basque industrial parish?"

Ander's voice came out sweet and strong. (They haven't destroyed him, Arrano told himself, and it was all he could do not to make the sign of the cross.) Father Ander said, "In the face of injustice and oppression the priest's temporal involvement is necessary. Neutrality would betray our Lord, who was always on the side of the afflicted." He looked up. Paul told Arrano that his face was radiant. "I would not know how to exercise my priesthood without revolutionary action. So it is in accord with my faith and my religious vocation that I belong to ETA."

Arrano thought: Well, he's had a chance to say it and that's what the trial is about.

"Do you believe in violence?" asked the lawyer.

"I'm a peaceful man but if necessary I will use a revolver to protect Basques against true violence, that of the political police who machine-gun my people without warning."

"That's enough," said the president. "These considerations don't interest us at all."

So the lawyer switched the questions back to the tortures and as Ander tried to answer, attempting to recall the nightmare he had been through, speaking of the taunts about women, about homosexuals, which, apparently, had been chorused throughout his interrogation, Ander suddenly stopped talking. He pointed, with the first finger of his left hand, at a man seated just ahead of the Eagle and Paul.

"That's the man . . ." shouted Ander. The priest was unable to say anything else.

The man was repectable enough looking, so far as could be seen from the back, but his hair was badly combed, longish - combed over tangles, was the way Paul put it. A murmur went through the room. The man crossed and uncrossed both his arms and knees until everyone around him was looking at him. The man murmured, "Lying puto." The woman next to Arrano whispered, "Silva, God burn his soul." Arrano thought it was a prayer and hoped God would hear it. The president was pounding the table for silence.

Ander had been Arrano's friend. Now he was ten times that. The priest's terror of that uncombed torturer made the Eagle love Ander many times more than ever before. Ander became his son, his brother, his mother, his confessor.

All these years he had saved a place in his island for someone he could love completely. He never had had anyone to put there but he had kept the place clean swept, the ground white, green trees to shade it, and comfortable chairs for the beloved. There they are in their well, he thought, and Ander will lead them into the green shade. Each one will have a view of whichever is his favorite peak - Txindoki or Itzkorri or any other.

The depression which came over Arrano that night had not left by next morning. Each day was colder than the one before. Cold in itself was not the malefactor. He had known more than one bright freezing dawn - the frost glistening like diamonds, but vocal: the sound of feet on it as sharp and precise as the words of a well-spoken versolari, except that by analogy you would need two sets of feet. Or like laughter. That would all be in the mountains. Cold in a prison is the ill-smelling breath of Satan. The whole city of Burgos was a prison and the cold it offered each dawn was unbearable. The six with their demanded deaths might be the lucky ones.

That was how low in spirits he had fallen. Then he and Paul walked along the dark streets to get into line, and perhaps because in the dark he could be more independent than in daytime; he was able to tell himself that this trial which weighed him down so deep was a trial of all Basques, and that he had better find more courage in himself because cowardice if felt in one part of the body (the feet, say, or the eyes) can easily spread to more notable parts like the liver or heart. What one Basque feels is often felt by all, and the danger of infection was multiplied with so many of them crowded together waiting on this trial, dependent on its outcome. Weakness in one would all the more easily reach the others. What was needed was laughter.

He tried to laugh, and Paul took his arm, alarmed by the snort.

"What are you thinking about, Eagle?"

"About the abduction of the German consul," and he was, although he had only begun to do so.

"And you think that's funny? It seems to me to be a mistake, a bad one."

For a moment Eagle was angry at him with his sure pat American judgment. What did he know about abducting consuls?

Paul went on, "Tell me what's funny."

"At least two things, Paule. It may not be an abduction at all, or rather, yes, an abduction but arranged by the police."

"To cut into the newspaper space the French press is giving the trial? A red herring?" Paul said the last words in English. He liked to match Basque expressions by citing American ones.

"It could be, Paule. You have no idea how clever the Franco police are with their red herrings, except that the pamphlets they write in Basque are a lexicon of words no Basque uses. If it's that, most probably they hired someone to do it and it'll come out. In any case, the consul is married to a Basque woman so they couldn't have picked a more unlikely victim if they're trying to say that members of ETA considered him an enemy."

"And if somebody connected with ETA did really abduct him? What then?"

"Then it's a joke and it may be a dangerous joke but I can see why they did it."

"Why?"

"For the same reason Calvo made the point about the crucifix. Without doubt they have the consul in some house ten meters from a police station and are going earnestly into that same station to give complicated reports about someone who saw the consul one hundred and two kilometers from there. And a Basque can be convincing, Paule."

"So I have found out," and Paul did manage to laugh a little.

"You don't think it's funny that the police of two countries search for a man who may have been kidnapped on the orders of their superiors, or who may not have been kidnapped at all but has gone away with friends and who, as the police well know, is anywhere except where other friends report him to be?"

"I don't think it's funny if Franco gets what he wants out of it, to create the impression that ETA is terrorist."

"Well, you'll see, the consul will turn up in a few days in that house next to the comisaria. If it was a mistake to have done it, at least we may as well enjoy the laugh while it lasts, and there will be more laughs in it yet."

They had reached the little stand where they always got a fine strong cup of coffee before they started the first wait. There was more news being talked about and it was not especially funny. The council of ministers had met in Madrid the night before and once more declared a state of emergency. This was said to be because of the German consul. With all guarantees abrogated the police could pick up anyone they wanted for any reason. Those they wanted were probably not consul abductors, if any, but leaders of the innumerable protest strikes. Forty-six thousand people on strike in Bilbao, the men at the coffee stand were saying; Pamplona was slowing down more every day.

And from a voice in the darkness beyond the stand, "They better send the butcherboy Bonavit back home to Pamplona."

"He's afraid to go." That second voice was Basque.

The stand owner shouted, "Get away, all of you. This stand caters to the Civil Guard."

"Certainly I'll be off." "Indeed I'm off. I never share my bread with that species." Two voices spoke together.

Paul and the Eagle swallowed their coffee and went too. "We'll have to find a new coffee stand," said Paul angrily.

At the queue there were mostly women and they were mostly silent. It is said that women can bear the cold better than men but Luku's indomitable mother looked frozen and had her head and mouth wrapped up. She and her daughters were the first in the line; it occurred to Paul they might have been there all night.

The session started late. When de la Vega entered he gave an ironic salute to the defense lawyers. Other members of the court made ostentatious noises with their sabres when they sat down. They appeared more than ever sure of themselves, as if the lot of them had come from a briefing and were relieved by the decisions announced there.

Certainly conditions throughout Spain that day could give them no reason for self-congratulation. The line had been talking about more protest strikes in factories and universities, in Madrid, Sevilla, in Franco's home province of Galicia. To be sure, they also spoke of new interrogations without limit and of helicopters over country towns. In one of these, for the benefit of the helicopters, the republic had been proclaimed in the town plaza; with that news laughter went up and down the line.

Each day had had its drastic happening to start it off: the kidnapping; the shooting of protestors including Eli Peralta; the state of emergency. The foreign press was learning Spanish secrets, an invasion of national privacy.

Another thing was certain. If haste had been heretofore advised to the court-martial, the briefing they had come from must have ordered more haste. The words heard from the court most frequently that day were: a matter of no interest, don't answer that question, no connection with the facts, no one asked you that. One interdicted subject was of course torture, but besides that any explanation whatsoever of prisoners' motives for whatever they had done.

Adoni Cardenas, not a member of ETA, never before arrested, had driven a former ETA leader and his sick wife to the French border; for this he was charged with banditry and terrorism. When asked why he had driven them he attempted to answer and was instantly silenced. Thereupon Sahagún in exasperation interrupted the colonel, "How can you judge a man when you won't hear him?"

It was not easy for Arrano to keep track of the exact order of the testimony, but afterwards, especially during the night, he would rehear the Basque pitch and tone - most have musical voices and the speakers were young, the judges all much older. Those young voices drowned out the drill sergeant's rebuff "that's of no interest." The passages of what the prisoners said filtered through his mind. Isa's brother, Gorka, or Spanish Jorge as the court insisted on calling him, was asked about ETA backing by the Basque clergy. Gorka himself had been a seminarian. Trying to answer, he was instantly interrupted by de la Vega, but managed to ask quietly, "If the priests and the people are not backing us how could I and many others live a clandestine life for years on end?" Those voices alone could tell Arrano what he wanted to know, but the words were a splendid complement.

As to voices, the legal officer - the only lawyer on the court-martial Board, rarely noticed because he was given so little to say that no one was familiar with his voice - startled the whole courtroom on the fourth day while the people were waiting to go out for a break.

The Italian newsman approached the legal officer. "Major," they heard him say, and the Italian's voice was strong, "why are the prisoners still chained?"

The answer began with throat clearing. Paralleling Zendejas and his stomach this man's throat was the part of anatomy in which he lived - so it sounded to Arrano. It was a loud old voice wallowing around in a phlegmy vast cavity - one of nature's amusing eccentricities. There were actually echoes: a comic actor would have made a world reputation with such a voice. It said, genially even with all its trappings, "Look at them. Isn't it obvious we have to keep them chained? They're dangerous. They're mad dogs. Señor, you must have been in the United States. These Basques are exactly like the blacks they have so many of in the United States. They're ugly and dangerous. You can surely see that." The words made an echo tour of the room, passing young Franco and the crucifix.

For the effect they should have called up next some prisoner who resembled a mad dog or who was at least unpleasant-looking, but unfortunately there are not many ugly Basques. Angeles Duarte was the one called and she was the handsomest woman in the room. Her hair was shining black, long. She wore a dark red sweater set and black slacks. She covered her fear with jaunty femininity. Arrano could feel Paul's excitement.

Captain Zendejas started the questioning with the old insinuations of illicit cohabitation. It was clear that for him it was the only approach to such a lovely woman, or maybe any woman at all.

She answered him in a quiet contemptuous voice, "Captain Zendejas, you know perfectly well that I was a Basque wife and that I am now a Basque widow."

"Already married and widowed?" Perhaps he, like the Ram, was trying to prove he was a man of the world; a concupiscent lout was what came through.

"My marriage had nothing at all to do with what you mean by marriage, Captain. I will not answer questions concerning it." No member of the Board could completely conceal his pleasure at Zendejas' annoyance.

Then Galíndez y Navarro, Angeles' lawyer, put her a question about her education. Most of it had been in a nuns' school in Deva where the speaking of Basque was punished with whippings and long periods of standing in the position of the cross.

De la Vega brought out his smile. He murmured, "Those punishments are not only for the Basques. We all know about the nuns . . ."

Galíndez asked Angeles if she were a member of ETA (the accusation claimed she was an ETA courier). "No, I never joined ETA, but my sympathies were with my husband's work."

"What was his work?"

"He was fighting against the fascist oppression from Madrid. I believe in that fight."

The sleepy judge, the same captain of artillery who had awakened once to ask for a procès-verbal but who had never really made his personality clear, spoke up as if on cue, "She's attacking the Spanish state. I am an officer of this country. I cannot sit here and listen to insults delivered in the presence of strangers." An odd statement, Arrano thought. Would he have sat there and listened if strangers had not been present? The artillery captain went on, "I demand that this court go into a closed session." That was another cue. Several judges joined the captain. It was decided by the colonel-president that from now on the prisoner must wait to answer each question until the president decided whether or not the question could be answered.

They went back to Angeles' reasons for helping her husband. She was after all explaining a Basque marriage, and she did not sound as if she liked having her privacy breached. "It is different from . . . some marriages. We choose to put that love to work for the battle we are both fighting, the battle of the Basque people . . ."

"I tell you to be quiet," said the president as if he were talking to a very irritating child.

Suertegaray pulled himself up on his crutches and still half standing he said, "In this court you are asking for the death of six men and for seven hundred and fifty years of prison and you treat a woman who has already lost her husband with supercilious . . ." He interrupted himself. Now he had got himself erect. "No one can deny this is a political trial and yet you refuse the prisoners the right to speak of their battle or of their beliefs." He turned to look at the president; up to then he had been regarding Angeles. "What is it you want from this prisoner? The police broke her ribs when they arrested her. And now you want her to chatter about her embroidery?"

Angeles was allowed to go on with her testimony. It concerned the mistreatment of her parents and herself after her arrest; to her also the police described what they would do to her husband when he was caught. He was to be hung in the elevator cage; his head was to be opened with stilettos. "It's inhuman . . . an inhuman system," Angeles cried out.

De la Vega snapped at her, "Your opinions are of no interest."

But he couldn't stop her. He may even have had some respect for her. She said, "Our jailers here are nuns again . . . they are fanatics, despots . . . Sometimes I wonder if they are really women."

This time it was Captain Zendejas. "That consideration is entirely immaterial. It has nothing to do with the matter of the trial."

At that moment Calvo spoke up. "Mr. President, I wish to call to your attention a fact which has not been observed before, or perhaps has only occurred today. There are two extra revolvers and one extra mitralleta in the pile of evidence. None of these weapons are identified as having anything to do with this case."

The foreign press took note of the matter, but the court did not reply. Instead it called a recess and cleared the room. When the recess was over the extra weapons had been removed.

It was finally Matai's turn and the barrage of interruptions took most of the time allowed him. If the intention was to make him ineffective it did not succeed. True, no evidence was admitted. Not Ander's alibi. Nothing about the gun. But at the very end Suertegaray asked him, "Matai José María Artazo Loigorri, did you kill Inspector Melchor Mascaró?" And the answer "No, I did not. I swear it" was given in a shining, living young voice. Arrano knew it was the truth but so it seemed to him must everybody there. Of course with some that was not the issue.

And so it came to Luku.

Arrano could tell his footsteps just as he could when he walked on his mountain. There was the sweet strong voice and the tenderness. Arrano was thinking as they swore Luku in that one loss, not the least, this accursed farce was bringing to all Basques was that no young woman was ever going to derive the joy of that tenderness. Zendejas was asking the death penalty for Luku and sixty years to back up any possible default of death. The tenderness he expressed there and then, was for the rest of them in the well. His was the final testimony so he was the voice of all, summing up the trial, speaking a little more for Matai perhaps because Matai was his close friend and because the court had so shabbily kept Matai from speaking for himself.

Without anyone asking him Luku said, "I am a member of ETA. I attest to that. I am responsible for the labor front."

Empty knocking for order: the prisoner is to wait until he is asked before he answers.

Then from the prosecutor, "Have you been delegated the responsibility of the left bank of the ría of Bilbao?"

"That question is not correctly put," answered Luku.

The colonel gave him a spontaneous second look, not one taken from the plastic bag. "Limit yourself to answering the question."

"How can I? I've sworn to tell the truth. I am ordered to answer yes or no. Neither yes nor no would be the truth. If you will allow me to explain . . ."

"Put the question another way," said de la Vega curtly to the prosecutor.

"Did you attend the gathering which took place in July in the monastery of the Fathers of the Epiphany?"

"That isn't one question, it's three." Luku was no longer gentle nor tender, but neither was he argumentative.

De la Vega was determined not to lose his temper; the joke had gone too far but the foreign press was following with attention. Military dignity was the only tactic he had. It must be enforced on the court-martial.

This was not easy for the prosecutor but he tried. "Accused Larandagoiti, is it true that on the sixth of May you attended a meeting in the House of Everyone in Artecalle, at which a decision was made to deposit twelve bombs in various parts of the Basque country?"

"This time you have asked four questions." Luku went on, and was uninterrupted. "On the sixth of May there was a meeting in the House of Everyone. It is not true that it was decided at that meeting to place the twelve bombs. It is true that ETA had possession of twelve bombs. It is not true that those attending the meeting had the right to decide what to do with the bombs. So you see, Mr. President, there are four questions. Which shall I answer?"

Mechanically de la Vega was saying, "Of no interest. Of no interest."

Rufino Lares, Luku's attorney, asked him, "What is ETA?"

"Of no interest. Don't answer the question."

"I submit, Mr. President, that the accusation against this prisoner states that ETA is a separatist, terrorist organization. What are your political views, Luku Larandagoiti?"

"We are not separatist. We are not terrorist. We are fighting for the same objectives as are the people of Andalusia or, for that matter, the people of Vietnam."

"This court is in no way concerned with the people of Vietnam." De la Vega was at the very end of his patience.

And the court began to fill with voices. De la Vega kept saying, louder each time, "Be quiet," "You have no right to speak," and others of his overworked silencers. Luku's voice, detailing the activities of ETA, was louder than de la Vega's.

But the president finally came on top of the duet, shouting, "I order you to stop talking. You no longer have the right to speak."

Luku shouted back, "I am a prisoner of war and I demand my rights under the Geneva convention."

With that Luku took several steps toward the court-martial, his fists lifted. His guard had him covered; another held a gun on the defense lawyers. Luku approaching the platform of the judges shouted, "Gora Euzkadi Askatuta."

Zendejas and the sleepy judge drew their sabres. Bravely they kept the table between them and Luku; nevertheless they defended the picture of young Franco. Perhaps they also defended the always askew crucifix.

It was not over. The prisoners in their well, with one impulse pushed off their guards, rose, and began to sing the Basque hymn, *Gudari*. Luku led but all of them sang. Their parents could hear each voice. The families on the benches joined the singing. They could not have been quieted short of someone shooting every one of them. Luku was bound, muffled, rushed out of the room.

All persons in the court were then ordered to leave, except the defense lawyers. In their reluctance, mothers kept their eyes turned on their children in the well, stumbling because they could not see their way out. The prisoners stayed on their feet the better to receive the warm gaze of love. When the room was empty of family and press, and the prisoners too were departing, each one of them in one way or another and each speaking to his lawyer, usually by name, said, "I forbid you to continue my defense. You are a person of great courage and have my confidence, but not one of us recognizes the authority of this court. Therefore we do not choose to be defended in this court."

This was said while the soldiers prodded and yanked the prisoners out of the room but the words were fully audible to their lawyers and to the army officers on the Board.

It was the last public session. Colonel de la Vega proclaimed triumphantly, "I pronounce this court-martial to be in closed session."

◄ 13 ►

Immediately after the courtroom was cleared of people, press, and prisoners, the lawyers asked permission to depart. At first all their voices piled up in anger and other emotion; then they stopped and gave Calvo the floor, on their own account not out of deference to the colonel - that was evident. Calvo said they wished to leave the courtroom at once since they were no longer representing their clients.

Colonel de la Vega was riding high. Up to now he had usually responded to Calvo's good manners with his own version of that commodity. The issue was plain. Without a lawyer to defend him, a prisoner on capital charge may not be convicted. The judge could appoint puppet defenders but that took time and it was apparent de la Vega was determined to get this unwholesome affair over with now. He smiled faintly. "Señor letrado, I most earnestly beg you to remember we are still in session and beg you to accommodate your remarks to that fact. This is a summary court-martial in spite of what some of you would like to think."

"You can call in other lawyers," said Luis Luzarra stiffly and bluntly.

But the president was playing a hard game and enjoying it. Now his little smile came out from behind his mustache and showed itself completely, but his eyes had never been harder. "Not one of you may leave until the court permits it."

Without a venia Arga spoke loudly, and this created an odd effect: she spoke as if the colonel were deaf whereas that which she was expressing was her deafness to his power. "I am here against my will and under constraint. Your orders oblige us to go against our consciences and our professional duties."

"Señorita letrado, your petition to leave is refused." He spaced the words well apart and paused longest before the last one. During the words there was an increasing sense that at the end he would burst into laughter. Had he laughed it could not have been more insulting than what he did.

Suertegaray requested the venia and explained the bond between lawyer and client which could not survive being broken by either. "We have no authority to remain here, Mr. President," he said gently.

There was no acknowledgment of his words.

Calvo had remained on his feet from the time of his first petition. He seemed dazed, certainly angry and dismayed. He faced de la Vega, slowly turned his body and head to do it. "Mr. President, I have worn this lawyer's robe for forty years. During this hearing you have worn your uniforms as officers of the army. I ask you to consider that for us, as lawyers, there is also the honor of our robes. We cannot be forced to continue the defense of prisoners who have disallowed it."

There was no answer from the president.

227

Suertegaray standing on his crutches, said, "If we are kept here by force we are nothing but a collection of bodies. We are no longer lawyers."

At last de la Vega spoke, harshly, that hard, strong part of his character permanently taking over, so it sounded, "Refused, refused, refused. I order you to sit down." He signaled the Ram to begin reading.

This was in effect a rereading, since the apuntamiento had said all this about the punishments asked by the prosecutor. There was slight variation in a few sentences, the black joke of taking sixty days off a forty-year sentence. The total came out the same - six deaths and seven hundred and fifty-two years of imprisonment and millions of pesetas of fines.

With one exception, no one in the room paid much heed to the reading of those demands. The other defense lawyers had removed themselves from the scene and left only the bodies Suertegaray mentioned but Calvo gave attention to every word and every gesture and to the expression on the faces of the judges. They could be sure this man would remember them and their characters as long as he lived.

At the end of the toneless, emotionless, brutal reading Calvo again addressed himself to the court. "On principle I do not wish to open my mouth in this court again but I am forced to make an observation, Mr. President and judges. Your carelessness in the conduct of this case is an offense to all of us who are lawyers. Thank you."

Then as if such restraint and dignity were intolerable in that place, Lieutenant-Colonel Ram said, "Mr. President, may I have your authorization to leave the room, just for a few minutes, to satisfy an imperious physiological need?" The boy, somehow left behind in fun and games, too big, too awkward, trying to catch up by being coyly vulgar, hoping he sounded like a gentleman? The adage is that a Spanish gentleman is so clean he washes his hands before but not after a visit to the latrine and when Ram returned from his urgent mission he held his hands awkwardly and conspicuously. He also wore a self-congratulatory simper. His sleepy captain neighbor gave him a complementary but minor simper.

De la Vega was extremely busy presiding at an imaginary session. "Señor letrado don Agustín Sahagún Velarde, you now have the floor in defense of your client," with flourish.

Sahagún Velarde said he no longer represented Valentín Lizaldi Aranzazu; therefore he had nothing to say. He was extremely serious.

This was repeated fifteen times with different names and each time de la Vega replied, "During its deliberations this summary court-martial will read the written statement of counsel."

There remained only one more rubric in the liturgical text. Then de la Vega's military conscience could take a vacation. According to Article 931 of the military legal code each prisoner must be asked, "Accused, have you anything to say for yourself?"

In order to save everyone's priceless time de la Vega ordered the guards, after bringing in each prisoner so he or she could be asked that question, immediately to conduct the prisoner to the van which would deliver him or her at the gate of the appropriate prison.

•

The prisoners, hauled from the court after Luku's outpouring and after their universal denial of representation by their lawyers, were in a state of provocation, perhaps awakening. The effect was by no means identical in each. Although the unanimity of their danger (and of their aims) made for certain common emotions, what had just happened in the court aroused other emotions they must hardly have dared to feel.

The hall outside the door to the court-martial chamber was narrow. Door and hall were familiar to the prisoners, leading to the latrines; and to reach them one passed holding cells. Luku was in one of the cells. He had been buffeted by the guards as they pushed and dragged him out. His face and hands were bleeding. He had attempted to return blow for blow and he had not done badly until they got him chained. They had had to whip him across the face with handcuffs. He did not appear to notice the several guns aimed at him; when the other prisoners passed his cell he was panting and still fiercely yanking his wrists apart. He pushed one of the mitralletas out of the way as if it were too much of an affront, obstructing his view of his friends.

"I'll go in with him," said Father Ander.

"Thank you, Father." The guard captain let Ander in with Luku.

Most of the men prisoners were put into cells. Kristiana and her husband, chained together, were left standing in the hall not far from the door. Kristiana was crying, and the two shackled hands rose from time to time to wipe away her tears.

Isa and Angeles were also standing outside the cells. In her chains Isa appeared withered, tiny and, beyond all, helpless. She was held on her feet by the support Angeles gave her. Isa's short badly cut hair gave her the look of someone recovering from an illness or entering a mortal one. Here also the two shackled hands moved together. They touched the buttons on Isa's blouse. Angeles shook her head. The guard captain passed them. Angeles, pulling Isa's hand with hers, took his sleeve.

"Señor guardia, she's going to faint. Can't we give her a drink of water?"

He unshackled the two girls. "Go and get the water. There's a tin in the first latrine."

Isa, standing alone, tried to arrange her hair. Angeles

spoke to Matai when she passed his cell. "Get him to let you out. You must." She returned and gave Isa a drink and then with what water was left in the tin washed her face and bathed her wrists.

"I'm all right. I have something to do. Help me, Angeles," she whispered.

Word came from the president that the prisoners were to be ready to come in one by one. There was bustle of extra guards crowding the passageway. They pushed the prisoners into a sort of line. Matai in the confusion which was supposed to be order or perhaps even with the help of the guard captain (who with the beating of Luku apparently came to the end of his day's allotment of violence) was standing almost next to Isa, only Father Ander between them. And Ander tried to shift positions with Matai but one of the new guards prevented it.

Beyond Matai stood the prisoner to whom he was now chained; it was Kristiana's husband, the quiet and exalted Josu, who seemed hardly to notice what was going on.

"Speak to her," murmured the priest. Then, "Speak to him, Isa." But on each side of him there was silence.

They turned to each other. Isa with the support of Angeles and the priest stood straight. Matai pulled Josu with him until he was facing Isa directly.

"Matai, speak. I'm afraid she's decided to do something that will hurt her too much." Angeles said this aloud, recklessly. All the prisoners knew that on the last day of Isa's torture the sergeant from Sevilla, who was in charge of that squad, attached an electric apparatus to Isa's breasts, suction cups charged with current on each nipple; her breasts were burnt beyond repair. She had been wearing a high-necked sweater but today she had on a gray buttoned-up blouse.

Matai did not answer Angeles. Isa stood up straight. She was as tall as Matai but very thin. Their eyes met. Every person around them, now even Josu, was containing them in the curved palm of his love, guarding this gaze and protecting the silence around it.

"The first prisoner to enter will be Valentín Lizaldi Aranzazu," the guard captain shouted.

An exact court record of these confrontations was made. A close-cropped army stenographer, whose wife on that very day was bearing twins, one of each sex, not as hoped a pair of identical sons, made the record. Certainly he was in no situation or frame of mind to observe the passion of these entrances and exits and the words said each time, but the passion was there. Door opening, stiff guard with submachine gun but not necessarily devoid of emotion; then the prisoner, hands chained behind his back.

How could anyone, including the lawyers, know what the prisoners felt - fear, anger, hope, courage, despair? Even the court's expectation of them may have had its effect - a simple enough expectation - that the prisoners conform, obey, go to death or forty years and one day of prison quietly and not be a nuisance to anybody because there are after all certain civilized rules of human conduct which can be expected of each man, even a Basque prisoner. Behind and beyond, above and below aphorisms, a human being walked through the door to do the best he could, one human being after another.

The question "Accused, have you anything to say for yourself before you are judged?" was not put into the record every time it was asked, but it was asked every time.

•

"Accused, do you have anything to say for yourself before you are judged?

232

"The accused Valentín Lizaldi Aranzazu: In a loud voice he said a number of words which appeared to be in the Basque language. The president ordered him to withdraw. While he was doing so he turned and cried out in the Castilian language, apparently to his lawyer, Ay, Agustín my friend.

"The accused Simeón Sarraga Nuarbe: He said a series of words, which appeared to be in the Basque language, among which the word criminals, spoken in the Castilian language, could be distinguished, and the president ordered him to withdraw.

"The accused Kristiana Ureuta: She said she withdrew the mandate which she had given to her defense attorney and that she considered this tribunal a farce. And the president ordered her to leave.

"The accused Carlos Urederra, a priest: He said some words which appeared to be in the Basque langauge and the president ordered him to withdraw.

"The accused Jorge Aranzamendi Beteta: He said very loudly a number of words which appeared to be in the Basque language and as he entered the room he shouted stentoriously, Gora Euzkadi Askatuta. The president ordered him to withdraw.

"The accused Andrés Aranbarri Celaya, a priest: As he entered the room he said he withdrew the defense by his attorney, and after having said a long series of words which appeared to be in the Basque language he left saying the same Gora Euzkadi Askatuta which he had said on entering.

"The accused Obineta Najara: He said, I have nothing to say because I do not recognize the authority of this court-martial and because it is the Basque people behind us and all people wherever they are who seek their freedom that this court is attempting to condemn. And the president ordered him to withdraw.

"The accused Jesús Mendez Guenberrena: He said, As long as I live I will fight fascism, and the president ordered him to withdraw.

"The accused Isa María Dolores Aranzamendi Beteta: She said, I withdraw the mandate I gave my attorney, Arga, to defend me. Quickly she cried out several words which appeared to be in the Basque language, and with her hands which appeared to be manacled as were the hands of all the other prisoners, but which in her case were free, she unbuttoned the clothing she wore on her upper body and she displayed her breasts. The president ordered her to withdraw. As she left she cried out Gora Euzkadi Askatuta.

"The accused Luku Larandagoiti: He said, We will see who is condemned as the assassin of our comrade killed in Eibar during the protest against this illegal proceeding. And the president ordered him to withdraw.

"The accused Sabino Lasarte: He said some words which appeared to be in Basque and the president ordered him to withdraw.

"The accused Matai José María Artazo Loigorri: In a low voice he said words which appeared to be in the Basque language. Then in a low voice he said he renounced any defense made on his behalf. The president ordered him to leave.

"The accused Sabino Bidea Etxebe: He said, as he entered the court, I withdraw the mandate I gave my defense lawyer. The president ordered him to withdraw.

"The accused Antonio Cardenas: He said that he rescinded his legal mandate to his lawyer. Then he exclaimed, Gora Jabi Suertegaray. After that he shouted Gora Eli Peralta murdered yesterday by the Civil Guard in Eibar. When the judges asked if he had anything to say for himself, he said, Yes, Mr. President, I have something to say. The drain in the floor of my cell is stopped up. I wish someone would repair it. Then he again shouted, Gora Jabi Suertegaray. Gora Eli Peralta killed yesterday by the Civil Guard. Gora Euzkadi Askatuta.

"The president ordered the recorder to take note of the insults to the Civil Guard and also observed that attention would be given to the prisoner's complaint in regard to the drain in his cell. This complaint was referred to the prison director. He ordered the accused to withdraw.

"The accused Simon Ojenbarrena: He said, Gentlemen of the Defense, this trial is a farce. They are trying to condemn the Basque people through ETA. Then he said several words which appeared to be in the Basque lanaguage; then he said, Gora Jabi Suertegaray and twice more Gora [not identifiable] and the president ordered him to withdraw.

"The president then said, The arguments are closed. This court-martial will now meet in closed session to deliberate and bring in a verdict.

"At fourteen hours and forty-three minutes on December ninth the court adjourned. The judges met in closed session to deliberate and return a verdict."

•

When Isa returned to the hallway, her blouse was still unbuttoned. She walked by Matai as if she did not see him. Angeles, weeping without stint, reached for her and did up the buttons.

"What recristo is this?" murmured the guard who chained the two women together. "Come on. He says you have to go to the van. Come on."

During this, Matai's turn came and he went into the courtroom.

•

Many people were still waiting in front of the military headquarters.

When they first came out of the building they were exalted. Some were too old to tolerate such an emotion. Several fainted. One of these was Father Ander's mother. She had a son with her, not the little boy who sheep-herded for the Eagle but another, in his teens. He tried to lay her on the floor under the seats until she recovered but the guards wouldn't permit it and she was carried out by the boy and Paul. They took her to a frozen grass border and laid her down. There were two ambulances drawn up near by. After quite a while an attendant got out of one and brought some smelling salts.

The boy asked him to give her a shot. "It's her heart."

"Then you should carry medicine with you. These ambulances are only for emergency."

"What kind of emergency?" Arrano asked him.

"Suppose someone were shot?"

"During a court-martial?"

"Who knows? We have orders only to accept emergencies and only at the order of the president."

Someone had meantime brought a bottle of brandy and they got along without the attendant. When the old lady revived she began to cry. Many around her could not bear to hear such a very old woman cry and they went away.

This was an eddy in the sweep which carried the crowd and spread to those who were already waiting outside. Some as they emerged had still been singing the hymn. This current of joy that came out with the people was perfectly intolerable to the guards, especially those who had not seen what happened inside, and the soldiers expressed their feelings with extra shoves and butt blows.

The people turned back on the guards as if they were going to re-enter the building. Then they stopped in their tracks and did not budge in either direction. The newsmen had come out first, which put them farthest from the entrance and so the least subject to police action, but some members of the foreign press protested at the shoving and rifle-butt treatment of the people, as if the time had come when it was no longer acceptable. These newsmen moved with the surge of the people and with them held their stance. The guards began to get anxious but still attempted to disperse the crowd. Six persons were arrested but that made no difference to anyone's conduct. An anonymous voice came from the center of the crowd, "We're going to wait here until we see the lawyers. We will not move or speak."

Even the Spanish pressmen appeared to be amazed, surely not by the police and their rough tactics, so it must have been by the events they had witnessed in the courtroom. The reporter from *El Garabato* was pale. His paper had been giving the most complete report of any Spanish paper. The old Italian, who happened to stand next to him, said, "How are you going to report this session, eh?" The other answered, "Maybe I'll tell the truth. How would that do?"

A lieutenant, with a mitralleta held by its neck like a bottle, appeared from around a corner of the building. He raised the gun to shooting position and scanned the crowd with it. No one budged except three reporters, who drifted away uneasily.

The lieutenant said, almost good-humoredly, "Those who want to wait here may do so if there is no disorder . . . Silence," he suddenly commanded. There already was silence. Only he and his men made any sound whatsoever -

237

their natural military clanking. Newsmen who left did so without noise.

It looked as if the crowd would stand there forever; the sounds of the guards subsided. This immobility drew everyone together, Basques, newsmen, and soldiers, not into congeniality but into waiting, most elemental of emotions.

"They're coming," said the voice from the center of the crowd.

The lawyers were carrying their robes over their arms. Arga was first. Emerging from the main door each walked alone as if each had undergone a deep, scathing, individual experience. Then as they came down the steps and saw the silent crowd they fell into small groups. Calvo Peralta drew up to Arga. She let him move ahead as if she were not yet ready to share in any public announcement whatsoever. There were tears on her face which she did not conceal.

He said, "We have done what we can . . . Your courageous children . . . Be proud of them . . . Keep your courage." When he was abreast of those newsmen who had waited he said, "Gentlemen, press conference at the hotel." After he had got out these words he took his handkerchief from his cuff to wipe his eyes.

·

Paul told Arrano he had a letter to give to Arga.

"But she's not Angeles' lawyer."

"I feel better giving it to a woman."

They caught up with her and Paul asked her if she could get the letter into the prison.

"Is it in Spanish?"

"Yes."

"Too bad you can't write Basque." Arga sounded rude. That was how her sorrow came out.

He knew she meant what she said but that she also meant yes she would get it in some way. It was only one thin sheet. His writing, left-handed, was small and clear. He didn't put Angeles' name in it anywhere.

"My beloved,

"You are helpless who should not be helpless. But even they can't take away your beautiful strength so you are not really helpless. I was standing beside you today and I was warmed, heartened, inflamed by your strength. It should have been the other way around. I should have been warming you. And that is what I will do the rest of our lives and whether we are together or separated.

"I will learn your language so we can say whatever needs to be said. Be perfectly sure that I will always have you in my mind and in my heart. There is nothing else I want to think about except you. What can I do for you? I am not your countryman but there must be something I can do. I will ask Arga and your own lawyer, of course, but without asking anyone I'll find out what I can do for you, my beloved. People have made up many words of love and names of love. Forgive me if they don't come to my mind. That's because you, not names to describe you, come to me. At all times. Forever.

"When you spoke about a Basque marriage I felt you could not think of marrying anyone but a Basque. Can I become a Basque? I'll talk your language. But anyway when we walk side by side on the street or in your mountains, it will only be you who will be seen. Alongside your beauty I shall be as invisible as I was when I stood beside you today in the court.

"You know how I walked near Roncesvalles. That was when I had first seen you and I have been there many times since. Those who see me think I am alone. I am not. Everything I see there is you, the trees, the rocks. Someone played the flute for you that first time. I listened. I am listening to you now. I have never loved anyone but you. Sometimes if your heart takes an extra beat, remember it is my heart beating in you. I hear yours all the time. p."

When Calvo's words broke the silence the people began to look around. They had been pushed out in such a rude pell-mell that families were separated, but besides that, like the lawyers now emerging from the military headquarters, each person in the crowd, no matter how close bound they looked, was isolated. Calvo released them. They returned to the human state of intimacy.

Paul had kept hold of the Eagle by gymnastics and force. Now he saw they were crowded next to two women and a man and he saw that the older of the women was determined to stay near Arrano, who looked around him, evidently aware of the attention she was giving him. He couldn't have helped feeling her bump against him.

The woman said very softly, apparently to herself because it was not the undervoice of a Basque, "The Eagle." She clicked her tongue against teeth, "What an Eagle. Still flying."

The girl with her, taller than she, took her uneasily by the shoulder, "Please, maman." The girl was exceedingly nervous, one might say she was dying of nerves. She said to Paul, "Please let us through. We have to get out."

At the same time, Arrano caught Paul's arm, "Paule. I need a brandy and so do you. Get us out." Paul had never heard a voice like this from Arrano: fear, confusion; there was almost despair.

The knots of people were in any case loosening. Paul got Arrano through; people were helping each other, and since everyone attending the trial, or attempting to, knew Arrano, they made way quickly.

"Not one of the near bars. Go away from this section. They'll try to catch up with us. Let's go fast. Who was it that was watching the woman all the time?"

"There was a man with them. I thought he was with them. Eagle, it was Silva! But he looks much more presentable than usual. I hardly knew him." Paul's arm and hand with which he was guiding Arrano trembled.

"The opera singer and he sat in front of us when Ander was testifying? Oh yes, oh yes. Stop for a minute and lean against a wall. Now double your fists and hit the wall until you hurt yourself . . . Now you won't be trembling . . . Anyway Comisario Silva's not on your trail."

"If he isn't I'll start following him. I want to meet him, Eagle."

"Stop talking like Hugo's *Hernani*, 'Oui de ta suite, o roi!' You don't want to meet him but you may have to if he's been put on the woman to keep track of her."

"Who the hell is the woman?"

"Señora viuda de Mascaró."

"She's extraordinary-looking. Terrible wild eyes. She looks insane, Eagle. Why was she cozzening up to you?"

"I think I hear them following. Listen. There are only two pairs of steps. That was her daughter back there with her?"

"You heard her call her maman."

"I can tell Silva's footsteps but I'm not sure which woman it is."

"I don't see any of them."

"They're around the corner. They'll turn this way in about a minute."

"Shall we go on or do you want to meet them here?"

"I don't want to meet them at all any more than you do. And for much the same reason."

"Please don't make your riddles, Eagle. Hurry up, we can get around the next corner before they see us. What's your reason, Eagle?"

"While you strangle the comisario I'll strangle señora Mascaró."

"I don't know what you're talking about."

"Because I've loathed her every day of twenty-four years, that's my reason. I didn't know she was alive until fifteen months ago, and in that time I've been trying every way I can to get her out of my thoughts. When I didn't know she was alive it didn't really matter if she was alive but for this last year I've been wanting to kill her. Now she's running after me to be killed. Probably that's all she ever wanted."

"She isn't worth killing."

"That's what the young priest in San Andrés kept telling me."

"She's the French woman."

"Of course, of course. Didn't you know that?" He brought Paul to a standstill. "Let me listen again. It's she, all right. The girl's awkward, but that one has fairy feet. All right, I have to let her talk to me."

"What do you want me to do, Eagle?"

"Pick out a café that looks poor and empty. Go into it.

243

Sit down. Get us three brandies each and set them in front of us. By the time we get to the second one they'll be there. I see you aren't trembling. I'm not either."

She was a terrible woman to behold. Paul's first impulse after he had a good look was to thank God that Eagle couldn't see her. No hate on earth could make you want to have a woman you had once loved look like this. She was terrible to look at but not in the way of ugly and beautiful. From some points of view she might have been considered a beauty. Once she had been that from any point of view. Lately the word had rarely been applied to her. She had not been the beautiful wife of Inspector Mascaró. She was spoken of as the inspector's wife and no one had to say which inspector.

He thought she was on some powerful, demanding drug although she was very calm, talking softly to Silva. They ordered café capuchino. She was facing Arrano, the policeman in profile to her and to Paul, who watched her because he couldn't help it. She turned her eyes away from the Eagle and gave Paul a nod, which he found disconcerting.

Paul didn't know women very well but he had enough natural instinct, stored up and seldom used, to see that this woman had been every kind of female at one time or another. He was pretty sure she had even been some man's beloved wife once for a little while. Perhaps she only had to be each thing a short time each, had been one of those babies who at seven months appears to be four years old, thirteen years at four years and so on, and doing everything easily. Precocious. So she had finally become precocious in murder and betrayal. Precocity isolated, unattached to a great talent, might be a sickness; a mortal one to judge by her.

She turned to Paul and nodded again, then smiled in self-congratulation, it seemed to Paul. She had told him he was

244

thinking along the right lines and then complimented herself on reading his mind. That was the first time her face had not frightened him, then, when she smiled. The smile surprised him. Next he surprised himself by thinking, I'm not the one who has to hate her, that's for the Eagle. And it was almost as though the hate was a privilege, not a burden.

There was no doubt about it: he was Arrano's surrogate in this situation. Having recognized that, Paul saw that the encounter was a great moral event, not because the woman was a grotesque or because she and Silva made a devil-hitched tandem, fascinating and so far unexplained (for Paul, Silva had weasened down considerably from the proportions with which he, Paul, and out of terror no doubt, had endowed him), but because this was the meeting after twenty-four years of two persons, one who had caused the other to be blinded and the other who, for some reason, had needed the blinding. They must have fitted together like hand in a fine suede glove. As the Eagle's stand-in, Paul thought they must still fit that way. So had he become surrogate to find the way to draw the hand out of the glove?

Arrano had gone into a state of not being present, except that once he muttered, "I may have to have twenty of these." He was finishing the third brandy and Paul went to the bar cash-stand to get them each three more.

As he passed the woman she was saying in a hoarse voice, "Of course, of course, Lucas, but the girl has to be somewhere by herself and you have to pay for her room. You understand."

"Yes." Silva kept his eyes on her; there was no doubt Silva was dwarfed by the French woman. He was fondling the scar on his forehead.

As Paul put the six small glasses on the table, Arrano

spoke in the voice of a wakened deep sleeper. "Let's get it over with."

To Paul the voice said, "Let's kill them both and get it over with." He sat down close to Arrano.

"She looks like the devil's wife. She's planning some kind of high jinks with that leper she's with. And she's very far gone on heroin, I think it is . . ."

"Paule, I know all about her. Nevertheless, I have to hear what she came to say. So you must help me."

"If I can, Eagle."

Silva got up and talked to the owner of the café. The man closed and locked the front door, then disappeared through another door behind the bar, closing that behind him. Silva brought a bottle of brandy and placed it on Arrano's table. Then he went back to his table, asked the French woman to rise, drew the table closer to Arrano's and reseated the woman with a flourish. Paul was constantly surprised at how respectable he looked and how well he wore his obviously new clothes.

During this time Arrano did not move. His hands were clasped in his lap. His blind blue eyes were staring at the woman; Paul thought again about the deliverance Arrano's blindness was to him.

She spoke, her voice soft and pleasingly hoarse, "Are you really blind, Eagle, or are you fooling me?"

He didn't answer.

"Maybe you can see that I've kept my hair dyed red for you."

Paul put his hand on Arrano's hand.

She licked her lips. Paul thought she wasn't getting done whatever she had come for or she needed whatever drug she took to bolster her. And just then Arrano grasped the table with his two hands, and laughed. Silva put a hand on his gun, but the woman showed only relief and then expectation. The laughter shook the man, the table, the glasses, the coffee cups on the other table.

"Are you perfectly mad?" asked the comisario rather primly. "Stop it and listen to señora Mascaró."

But Arrano could not stop. That laugh and the sobs it went into had to cover the stretch of twenty-four years. Paul had heard the Eagle laugh many times but this was half a life put into the sound that man alone can make. Finally Arrano laid his head in his arms on the table and was silent. Then he sat up and drank the two remaining brandies.

He said, "I was thinking how señora Mascaró has you policemen boxed in. I suppose you thought you had her boxed in." Next he spoke to the woman, and she leaned toward him. "You must be wanted in France even now for the murder of that General whatever-his-name; so, poor soul, you couldn't go home. You kept them running in circles with their tongues hanging out, while you identified Matai, and another ETA, and another, and went to that beautiful prison of Santa María where, to make it easy for you, they had the prison director and some cop recruit standing one on each side of Matai. Oh yes, that's the man, you said in your best bed voice."

Arrano's voice was tired but he pushed on as if there were a set amount he had to say before he could stop. However, he turned so the woman could not see his face and she reached toward him, to comfort not to capture. He spoke to Silva, "I know, you policemen harassed her but she's a hard one to harass. She said it was Matai but she simply wouldn't sign a statement. What were you to do? How sad if the widow of Mascaró should happen to get beaten to death by her husband's comrades! How did you get yourself assigned to her, Comisario?"

During all this Silva kept his hand on his gun. At the end

he said, "It's not correct for me to listen to his insults." His lips quivered.

"Are you going to cry about it, Lucas?"

"You promised me," he said.

"I promised you. I'll keep my promise."

"What did you promise him?" This was Paul out of pure curiosity, as sharp as pornographic curiosity.

"Well, Little Boy Blue" - the name was said in English - "I promised him something that's important to him. Being a close friend of my husband's, he knew quite as well as I did that my husband was normally impotent. Yet many times, oh, many times Mascaró told this old friend that he and I - I - . . ." She got stuck on the word.

Arrano interrupted before she could get started again, "Be silent."

She managed only, "I promised to show him how that was done."

"I'd better tell you, Little Boy Blue" - Silva's English pronunciation was not as spry as the woman's but it could muster and he was half singing in his lovely voice - "that having shared these confidences with you, before you leave the café I shall collect the passport I let you keep in the Ekilili and you will be out of Spain in twelve hours. O.K.?"

Arrano had not let go of the table edge, still held with both hands. He spoke quietly, hardly to be heard. "Why did you want to talk with me, Louise?"

The sound of the gentle pretty name said in a low voice, a name heard for the first time by Paul, was more painful to him than anything that had happened so far.

And she answered in a pure young voice as simple as a brook. "Because I saw you on the stairs of Mascaró's house."

"Then why didn't you tell them I was the murderer? Your friend here? All of them?"

"Because I love you, Eagle."

Paul wanted to shake Arrano, pull him to his feet and away, but he didn't have to.

The woman said in another voice altogether, as if she were the vicious mother of the girl who had spoken in the first voice, as if she were standing on a balcony and pouring scalding water on the girl and her strong true love, "How could I have thought you were the murderer when I was sure the bullet came from the other stairway where Lucas Silva was hiding?"

Silva stood up. "What rehostia are you up to, you lying, God-pissing bitch? You told me you wanted to talk to him about your daughter. And you never told me he was on the stairs. That would have been a different story."

"Even if they had known, Eagle wouldn't have done them as much good as the squared-off young man. Be quiet, Lucas."

"What about your daughter?" Arrano had let go the table as though he no longer needed it; he was at ease.

"Your daughter," she answered.

"I have never had any children."

"Because you never slept with anyone but me. This one is yours."

"And if she is?"

"I have to do something about her. I don't really like her. She even resembles you. She's no child of mine. Besides, you can't want her to be around me, can you?" It was said with no play-acting, nor pity for herself or her daughter. Then she went back to the scorn and jealousy that Paul noticed was her usual tone when she talked about the daughter. "Not that I haven't kept her chaste. She's half Basque so let her be chaste. I'll swear to that."

"Don't swear to anything. What would I do with her?"

"Take her up on your mountain and let her keep house for you, you fool," said Silva.

"Maybe your young friend could take her to the United States. Eh, little boy? She's a virgin. I've heard that's exceptional in your country. Couldn't you get her papers, Lucas?"

"How could I get them? That means dealing with the American consulate. Of course the colonel could get anything he wants there. But not me." Self-pity rose to the top, Silva's mark.

"I couldn't take her to the United States if she had all the papers in the world," said Paul.

"You could if you were married to her."

"Señora, thank you for your confidence. I couldn't do it. I'm already pledged to another girl. We're talking nonsense."

"Now we'll talk sense." Silva pushed a small package over the table toward Paul. "Open it and smell it, or aren't you familiar with these things?"

"Don't touch whatever it is, Paule," said Arrano fiercely.

"Certainly not, but what sort of crazy thing is this? The comisario is a comedy detective, isn't he? And why are they so eager to get rid of the girl?" Paul spoke English, which the Eagle could mostly understand.

He answered in Spanish. "Yes, he's a comic all right, and whenever you think life is a great suppurating wound remember him and laugh. As to the girl, I suppose she's too honest to have around, whatever they're up to. What else?"

The woman mimicked him, "What else! Eagle, you never get over thinking I'm some sort of witch. What else? Doesn't it occur to you I may be trying to help my daughter? If you'd ever thought of me as a simple decent woman we might still be together."

Arrano answered with flat anger, not laughing not crying, "And you wouldn't have had to sell me to the Germans to blind or give them the names of every Basque in the maquis battalion. Is that right?"

She answered coldly, also flatly. (Paul was thinking, now it's almost over.) She said, "You're too proud of your blindness, Eagle."

Eagle's head jolted back as if she had slapped him. Paul looked at one and then the other. If there were going to be a reconciliation it would come now. He spoke to the woman, "Señora, may I ask you what your plans are?"

"Well, Boy Blue, he couldn't expect me to be faithful to him forever, could he? The comisario and I have had an abiding friendship and now that I'm free we're going away. Maybe to Algeria. I've kept my French citizenship. Why shouldn't we go away?"

"Why not?" Paul's relief was evident in his voice. Nevertheless the woman still charmed him while she revolted, bored, angered him. He had played surrogate long enough.

Arrano spoke bitterly, "What's the matter, Paule? Don't you understand how fortunate you are to have participated in this scene of monstrous truth? I owe you more than I can ever pay." Then he asked the woman abruptly, "Now. Where is our daughter?"

"She's on the other side of that door," and pointed behind the bar. Looking at Arrano's face she laughed. "Of course I knew you were listening to our footsteps, so I had her stay a long way behind and Lucas put the owner outside to show her into the back room when she passed the café." This seemed to give her innocent pleasure. She was not laughing meanly. "We were a notable pair while we lasted, weren't we, little Eagle? And I must say you've developed your hearing to a fantastic point."

"At least I can hear the poor girl listening at the door. What's her name?"

"Matilde Arcángel, a sus ordenes," the woman answered mockingly.

"Poor Matilde. I wonder how she stayed alive. Matilde, come in."

But she didn't. There was a pause. Both Silva and the woman rose. Arrano motioned them down. "Go on, Paule, you bring her in."

She moved against the wall as he opened the door. Her eyes were cast down, her arms straight at her sides. It was apparent she wouldn't go into the other room unless she were forced, so he put his arm gently around her shoulders and talked to her in French, "Come with me, the Eagle and I will protect you." On the way he stopped at the bar and still not letting go of her took a bottle off the shelf. Then he sat her down at Arrano's table and poured sherry for her in one of the empty brandy glasses. He took out his handkerchief and wiped the table of spilled brandy. "You drink your sherry now, mademoiselle."

"Dear Bleeding Jesus," said the French woman, "you certainly make a nicely matched pair. She's scared as a fawn and you . . ."

"Be quiet, you fool." It was the first time Arrano had shouted at her. "Matilde, what do you say? You heard all that was talked about, did you?"

"No one at all wants me." She spoke without feeling and she wiped the palms of her hands on the sides of her skirt. She couldn't seem to raise her head.

Eagle said to the woman, "You will have to give me a sworn statement that she is my daughter and it must be registered wherever such a document is registered. In Bilbao, so the monsters there can't take her away from me."

"Anyway she's your duplicate, Eagle," Paul remarked.

"All of those papers, yes, yes, of course." The woman spoke testily.

"And tonight Matilde will stay at the hotel where the lawyers are staying. She'll be there with the woman lawyer. Tomorrow we'll go together and do the legal business."

The girl's head rose and she spoke sharply, "Aren't you going to ask me what I want to do?"

Arrano put his arm around Matilde's shoulders much as Paul had done. "Thank God they haven't gutted you of pride. I am asking you. Do you want to come and live at the feet of Anboto with me? To tend the sheep . . . ?"

"Not to tend the sheep. The dog can do that. I'll help him. But I will come because you're my father."

"Did you know I was your father?"

"Oh yes, my mother spoke of it often enough. It didn't make her husband like me any better."

"Why didn't he throw you out?"

"No, my mother wouldn't let him do that."

"Do you love your mother?"

"I suppose so, but I want to come to you."

"Why?"

"I've followed you as best I could. I saw you twice with that old friend of yours - the man who jumped in the pelota court. You're both handsome men. I'd like a handsome father. Your friend was brave and probably you are too."

"All Basques are brave." She laughed at that, and so did he. "You'll be lonely, Matilde, up there on the mountain."

"She's always been lonely . . ." Her mother sounded jealous. "I don't really know what you want of her. Are you going to sleep with her?"

"Oh, Louise." With his elbow on the table he made a back of the hand to her, not altogether the usual scorn of that gesture, rather a farewell to Louise. He said, "There's one other part to this arrangement and now I'm speaking to

253

both of you, the señora and her friend. Paule is to be allowed to see Angeles."

"You mean the prisoner, Angeles Duarte?" Silva was shocked.

"Is that the girl he's pledged to?" The woman spoke pensively. "What a thing!"

"It's impossible for him to see her," Silva said pontifically.

"I can make trouble for you, Comisario."

"What trouble?"

"The *Le Monde* reporter. Your hiding on the stairs."

"I'll shoot him, and you. Both of you."

"I know you're not that stupid, Comisario."

"She said she saw you on the stairs."

"Listen, I have known all along someone else was on the stairs. Now I know it was you, Comisario, but I think there's one more step. I'll talk to the lawyers as soon as I get to their hotel."

"You know it's too late to change anything now," said Silva, but he sounded worried.

The woman laughed, "That's right. And anyway the one to see would not be your lawyers but the great pendejo himself."

Silva was still distraught. "I suppose I could try to arrange to get him into the prison. With some money."

"Paule has some money."

"Of course you can do it, Lucas. You don't know your own power, and you don't need money. You've never been so well off." The woman spoke with sweet cruelty and the wonder was that Silva seemed to accept the words.

"You can do it, Comisario." Then Arrano said to Paul, "We'll stay at the Gran Hotel ourselves tonight. We want to know what's going on." He spoke to the woman. "So?"

"All right, Eagle, I'll go to the prison with your friend.

I haven't asked any favors. Surely they'll let me visit the three women accused."

"I'll leave it in your hands, señora Mascaró." The name amused him a little. "I'll be at the Gran Hotel. You bring Matilde there as soon as the visit to the women's prison has been properly made. Paule, you're to take care of Matilde. As a matter of fact, you can let Paule bring her back to the hotel. That'll save time for you and Silva. You be there in the morning though. And no picking up of passports."

Silva started to say something, cleared his throat.

Arrano interrupted him flatly, "Paule must have a paper signed by you, Comisario, so he won't be bothered in any way. Write it out now."

The French woman laughed. "I doubt if Comisario Silva can wait for all these complications, Eagle. Maybe we better call off the arrangements."

"You know how to keep men waiting, and it looks to me as though you'll do some waiting of your own. You don't get the little present without preliminaries, eh, Louise?" This time the name was said in plain mockery of his first pronunciation of it.

"You're a cruel . . . Basque." She was ready to burst into tears.

He gave his attention to the girl. She had drawn back into herself with that reflex she couldn't control - wiping her hands on her skirt and bowing her head. Her shoulders shook. Arrano said harshly, "The first thing is that a Basque woman very seldom cries. Forget your mother's example. Your head is up. Find where it belongs on your neck. Your shoulders are held back. You're a tall girl, almost as tall as I. So you'll take long easy steps. No mincing."

"I don't know how to mince," Matilde said angrily.

"All right, but you'll practice long steps while you're with your mother and Paule. The only time Paule will have to leave you is for the few minutes they let him in to see Angeles. They're asking twenty years of prison for her. He must see her, so you'll wait for him even if you're alone with guards like Silva. And then Paule will bring you to the hotel."

She was ready to go, and her self-assurance swept up her handsome corrupted mother and the Canarian. They went toward the doorway, all three in a hurry, whatever their different reasons.

Paul waited to speak to Arrano. He was breathless. "It's too fast, too fast. Will they let me see her? Do you really think so, Eagle?"

"Insist on it with Silva. He and the woman can do it. You must see her, Paule. If it takes every misca of courage you can dredge up. If you never do another brave act in your life, do this."

"I know." Then he said, "How can you get to the Gran Hotel alone?"

"You know I can follow the echo of our footsteps back to where they came from. Not to mention the footfalls of two damned souls who walked behind us. Forgive my jokes, Paule, dear friend. I have never been so tired in my life and weariness will lead me to a bed. Anyway, don't worry about an old plucked eagle. Put your mind on getting into the prison. When you hold her in your arms whisper that Arrano also loves her."

"In my arms?"

"Go on. With those two chums you have picked up you have to strike while the iron is hot. Isn't that what you say? Keep Matilde next to you. I'm sending her to help you."

15

"You three walk ahead," Silva told them when they were outside but still in front of the bar. To Paul, "How much money have you?"

"Fifteen hundred pesetas."

"That won't be enough."

"Eighteen. That's all I have except a few pesetas to leave in my pocket."

"I'll see what we can do with it. The nuns won't need much but that governor is as difficult as a rusty saw." Silva divided the money in two parts and put them away one bundle to a pocket. Paul supposed he was keeping half for himself and nine hundred pesetas didn't seem much of a force to use on Spanish prison doors. As they started to walk he was putting his hand into his pocket to add whatever was there when he felt Matilde's hand on his. "No, if you give everything you have they won't help you. Give him

257

more at the end. We can get some from the Eagle . . . from my father."

"Is it really enough?"

"He seems to think it's enough."

"I can't hold back anything to help me get in."

"I understand, Paule." She said his name without strain the way Arrano did.

They passed a pair of civil guards who looked with curiosity at Paul. Matilde dropped his arm as soon as she saw the guards.

"Do you need help, Comisario?" one of them asked.

"No, no. My gun's right here. I don't want to make a fuss. You know the puñatera newspaper men."

"Why? Are you taking him in?"

"Precisely, but let me do it my way."

Silva had a reputation which even the incident of the mass had not altogether demolished. Zendejas had kept that as quiet as he could. The version which got out was a squalid black joke on the cabrón priest while it showed Silva as a wild, unsteady, but frightening policeman. Also, in the twists of hate and fiction it made him out a profound Catholic. It was known Silva had requested the job of keeping Mascaró's widow under surveillance; naturally there was talk about her and him but it grew from curiosity - through her husband's boasting she had come to be considered a hot bitch, whereas, from whorehouse gossip, Silva at best was supposed to be a sexual oddity.

So the civil guards, whose lewdness lay on their tongues with their spittle, sized up this procession - the daughter walking with Paul honestly troubled them - as one of Silva's juicy vagaries, but they did not doubt what he said.

"I'm taking him to the provincial prison, if anyone asks," Silva called over his shoulder.

Since this exchange was police to police it was in their

258

argot, incomprehensible if untranslated. Paul understood pretty well; Arrano had taught him some of it while they waited in line at the hearings. Matilde had had her own special course in it.

"Did he say he was turning me in?"

"He said it but he's lying. You'll see. It's a good way to get into the prison."

He wanted to ask, "And to get out?" but he controlled himself. He had seen Silva stripped down to a forked stick and a rag by the French woman, so for the present he was not afraid of him, but the bland way the other two police-men spoke of him, Paul, as inanimate property, terrified him. He was freezing from head to foot. His heart and his lungs defied him, one pounding exacerbatingly, the other denying any breath at all.

The provincial prison was a very old building on quite another plaza than that of the military headquarters. It was directly in back of the majestic heavy cathedral. The prison had once been a monastery and the small windows and high arches he could see made it seem colder than any Burgos building Paul had encountered; freezing air came out of its doorway.

He thought he had to escape. His lungs were giving him a little respite, enough so he could run into the cathedral, which he supposed would be a haven. Instead, he picked up his feet to get over the high board along the base of the prison gateway. The man who had opened the door to Silva was carrying a whip. Paul looked at him once and became as blind as Arrano. Now his eyes were denying him their function and he thought this was just as well. The man with the whip disappeared and an officer came in his place.

Paul did not hear most of what Silva said but that voice was the only warm thing in the place. He did hear Silva say, "Yes, Captain," overcourteously. There was no visible exchange of money. There was no arrest of his person; he had his hand on his inside pocket ready to show his passport. He heard the French woman laugh in a polite superficial way. Now he was aware of Matilde talking to him.

"My mother is telling the governor that you were with her when she saw one of the women accused on the street. Together you saw the woman with the murderer in the early morning of the day of her husband's death. She wants to take you in to find out if it's the same woman. It might not be of importance now but she is nevertheless curious and is asking the governor if, out of his friendship with her dead husband, he will permit it."

At last Paul was able to hear what was said. He could also hear coughing and hawking. Evidently there was a prisoners' patio somewhere at hand. He discovered he was nodding his head to what the governor was saying. The three of them, the governor, the woman, and Silva, were talking with great animation and charm. They seemed each one to be an old friend of the other two.

The governor said, "I'll send for one of the nuns. Will you wait here, señora, señorita, señor. I'm sorry it's so cold in our old prison. There is a little sun entering this room. Please wait here." And then, "Comisario Silva, may I ask you to accompany the visitors? The corporal and the madre will show you the way. I have to stay near my telephone in case the court-martial should bring in its verdict."

The nun was the embodiment of Angeles' doubts about whether prison nuns were sexed. Dressed in a mud-colored habit which had the advantage of not showing the dirt, she was evidently ashamed of her dirty hands. They were large, chapped, the nails mistreated, and she avoided shaking the pretty hand held out by the French woman, instead got hers into each opposite wide sleeve, and bowed angrily.

260

"This way. Follow me. What do you want of the prisoners?"

Silva answered royally that it was a matter of identification.

"I should think everyone would know who these women are after the display they made of themselves in court this afternoon."

"How right you are, madre," murmured the French woman.

They had to go underground to reach the women's section. The dark passageway destroyed any normal feelings Paul had mustered, stopped his breathing again and made real and sensible the expectation of freezing to death.

They emerged in a small patio and Paul, relieved at getting out of the tunnel, could see that it had once been very beautiful with three excellently proportioned arches on each of the four sides. Paul could not help giving the patio his approval, but a dreadful smell of decay (cabbages - softer matter, he thought) overcame the lovely arches. The French woman went absolutely white. They stood there waiting for their nun guide to ask premission from her superior - as she left she muttered, "Lazy things, we can never get them to keep things clean." Like the hiding of her hands, the complaint from that hideous abandoned hulk was sad. Who could have used her for anything but what she was doing? She resembled a woman Paul had seen plowing like an ox near Santiago de Compostela. Paul had not forgotten the woman in her field of stones. He knew he would not forget this dismal nun.

Then he shoved everything out of his mind. He had not thought he would ever talk with Angeles; he had done everything he could to put off the realization he was there near her because he was afraid they would take the meeting away from him if they knew how much he needed it. In truth until this minute he had hidden from himself that seeing her was a life-and-death matter for him. She was behind one of the doors around the walls of the patio. He was not at all afraid now. He would have stayed there in that patio for all his life if it meant seeing her.

A different nun came back with the keys. The door she opened was straight ahead of where they stood. "The madre says you want to identify one of these prisoners. I'll bring them into the patio. It's too dark in there for you to tell one from the other. There's one I'm not sure can come out. Let's see."

The corporal with his mitralleta moved to cover the doorway. He was a dark sickly boy, obviously from the south somewhere. Silva flicked a glance at him and smiled. It took the women inside the door a long time to come out. First it was Kristiana, looking frightened and bundled up in a ragged quilt. She dropped it when she saw the four people in the patio. Then she leaned against the wall as if she were faint. And the second was Angeles.

Paul walked the three steps to where she stood and took her in his arms and kissed her.

"What do you mean . . . ?" The nun put her fist to her mouth but she did not separate them. Silva stood next to the corporal. "It's all right, brother," he said. "You're from Lanzarote, I can tell it. So am I. I'll explain it all to you in a minute."

"Maybe I should shoot them, no?" The boy had a speech defect together with a Canarian accent. Nobody there but Silva could have understood him.

"No, no, not yet."

Paul and Angeles clung together whispering.

"Speak up. You must speak Spanish here and loud enough so you can be heard," the nun said.

262

"I am asking her to marry me, madre, so no matter how long she goes to prison she'll know I am waiting for her."

At the same time Angeles was saying, "Go to the house of my mother and father or find them here in Burgos and tell them I have given you my word."

He spoke directly to the French woman, "It's been extraordinary your bringing me here. I cannot identify the other woman as the one we saw that day, señora, but this girl is one I met at the University of Bilbao and we fell in love. Then she disappeared. I haven't seen her since and I find her here."

"It must be God's will," said the French woman piously.

That he had attended all the court sessions and had not recognized Angeles was left unexplained and hopefully there was no one there able to pick that up: certainly not the tongue-twisted Canarian, and the nun probably had no way of knowing he had attended the sessions, although he couldn't be sure of that. Maybe his strange statement would hold water.

The French woman said, "I think all this should be explained to the governor. Don't we have to go now?" She was asking Silva.

Before he could answer Matilde spoke. "No, maman, listen. You remember we saw the monsignor from Pamplona. Remember? He said he was staying at the bishop's house. He stopped us in front of the hotel."

"Of course I remember, Matilde, what about it?"

"The one who used to be your confessor at the cathedral in Bilbao when I was little. Are you sure you remember? You like him."

"What are you saying, Matilde?"

"Go and get him. The bishop's palace is right here. Go and get the monsignor. He'll be willing to marry them."

"Why don't you go yourself and let Silva and me be off?"

"They wouldn't let me out and in again alone, maman, you know that. But you and Comisario Silva could do it."

"Better if only the comisario goes. I know he'll be back. You have too much faith in me, Matilde. Anyway, I shouldn't leave you here alone. What kind of a mother do you think I am?"

Matilde sighed.

"Are you willing to go, Lucas? All you have to do is tell him that the señora Luisa viuda de Mascaró asks him to come here at once." She spoke very fast.

"Another Eagle?"

"Oh, no, no. Anyway what difference would it make? You ought to be proud I have friends like the monsignor."

"I may have to tell the governor."

"If you have to, tell him. We can't make miracles even if Matilde invents them for us. Go on, now." And he went. "I'm getting fond of you at this last moment, Matilde."

"Let's get it done fast so we can stay good friends while it happens."

"While what happens?"

"While they get married, maman."

"What's a wedding, you stupid?"

"I don't know. I never attended one before." Matilde went to Kristiana, who had pulled the quilt over her shoulders again and moved into a pale ray of sun. Matilde leaned against the wall next to her.

Paul and Angeles were talking in low voices. The nun stood guard over them and evidently could hear enough to satisfy the rules she went by. They paid no attention to anyone. They did not seem to notice Silva's absence.

The nun spoke up once, "How can you make plans like

that? You don't even know what her sentence is. And, you, you don't know him."

"I've known him a long time, madre. Madre, I'm sorry if I spoke against you nuns in my testimony."

"Well, yes, it was a cruel thing to do. For my part I forgive you but the superior is angry. I wonder if you know what we suffer in our Christian labor?"

"I don't suppose I do. Madre, can't Isa come out? I want her to meet my friend."

"You'll have to help her out."

Paul decided he better pretend he did not know Isa, to give some sense to his explanation (no matter how friendly this nun, she would have her orders to report whatever she heard). So when Angeles brought out little Isa, he asked to be introduced.

"It's very sudden, Isa, maybe it's madness. We love each other," said Angeles.

"I see him and I see you. No, it's not madness for you. I'm glad. How did he get in? Will they let me see Matai?"

The nun, not unkindly, took her to the railing of the arches and sat her down. "It's not as cold out here, Isa."

●

There was silence in the patio, cogent and painful. It was evident the soldier's arm was aching; he shuffled but he did not put down the mitralleta - the nuns were reputed to be great snitches and not only on prisoners. Paul and Angeles were intently considering one another's hands, to which the nun had so far not objected. Matilde appeared to be dozing.

Her mother was staring at each girl in turn. It was women like these Mascaró took out to his shack - all younger than she. It was after he let the woman go - sometimes he had to push her out of the car and would tell his wife about it half joking ("I can't get rid of them, bijou, what do you think of that?") - that he and she had their most satisfactory encounters. For her this meant he was impotent - naturally after what had happened - but she was not. He and she took pleasure from that. More often than otherwise his clothes were bloody. She took them off him. She never knew the exact details of the preceding encounters.

•

The uncle who brought Louise up was a mechanic, which involved his being oil-stained and smelling badly. He was not a nice-looking man, had none of Louise's natural grace although he was brother to her mother, a beauty who died during the flu epidemic. The mother's lover disappeared. The child was placed in an orphanage and was cherished there because she was so pretty; she looked enchanting in the blue uniforms. The uncle took her out precisely because of her prettiness; he had that much feeling for beauty. His wife was passive about the little girl. They had no children of their own. It turned out he had to begrime her beauty if he could. By the time she was six he was calling her slut and whore instead of her name. She came to think badly of herself, yet she knew she had to escape before the uncle made good on sleeping with her: her objection was not moral but to his ugliness. It was also because she had heard her aunt screaming when her husband was in bed with her. Once the girl met her aunt in the latrine after one of these times and she was bleeding on the floor and mopping up the blood.

Louise was not brave. She never stood up to the uncle but put him off and did not defy him. When she was thirteen and began to menstruate, the sight of the blood had an unusual effect on her. It made her want to sleep with the uncle, and she did as soon as possible. He was a nasty man. And she accepted those things, even enjoyed them.

The wire she did not enjoy; taking the blood of the lamb, he called it. They were alone in the house when this happened and Louise found herself mopping up a great deal of blood, exactly like her aunt. As soon as she was able she ran away. Being pretty, she had plenty of admirers.

From then on and until she met the Eagle she was a sexual tease. She became constantly more beautiful, and she was intelligent as well, and crafty, but there was a warp in her intelligence. On the one hand she became active in the French underground and was an asset to them, then she went over to the Germans and was valuable to them. She did this turn cleverly, although she was not brave; indeed her alliance with the enemy may have been because she didn't like to do dangerous things without a protector, and the maquis had few men to spare for that role. When she spied on her old friends and brought them to capture and death, she was always under the protection of some Vichy or German official. All this was well done; the warp was that she could change, not frequently but totally, into a naïve, subnormal adolescent girl. Even when overcome by this stupid clumsy part of herself she was as classically beautiful as a figure on a coin; her stupidity in this bewitching body was itself seductive. But she made mistakes.

One of them was the French general, a Gaullist. He searched her out, hearing about her beauty and her good reputation as an underground fighter. She preserved that reputation and the general was not careful enough in his inquiries. She shot him not because he was a Gaullist but because he tried to sleep with her.

She had worked it out for herself that her lovers or those who thought they were her lovers were older men whom she pleased in more sophisticated ways than ordinary simple sex. Also, she liked impotent men; they suited her best. Her protector of whatever moment was usually that. She stayed away from young or virile men of any kind.

This general was an unplanned casualty. He was young and big and handsome. She had closed her legs to him; they were in his hotel room and he had not even gotten her clothes off. He had a dagger in his belt, which along with his trousers had fallen to his ankles. He said, half joking, never in his life having encountered this kind of woman and reaching for his dagger, "I'll get this between your legs if you don't let this in." He had a very fine-looking sexual member. She got his gun, which was also handy, shot him in the head, pulled up his trousers and went to tell her protector, on this occasion a German, that she had killed a French general. It was toward the end of the occupation when the Gaullists were coming into their own and since the dead general was popular, and close to de Gaulle, they hustled Louise off to the Pyrenees to infiltrate the maquis and gudaris who were fighting there.

It was a real love affair between her and the Eagle, if a perquisite is that lives of the participants are changed. The Eagle was an innocent. It was this that won her. He didn't know what she was up to with her teasing. Basque men don't usually marry when they're young; he was in his thirties and had been fighting since his teens and had never had a woman. She was also an innocent even if that had been caused by perversity. But her relations with Arrano were blissful, abandoned, a spell. They could have made love all day as well as all night and if they were not in the very heart of some patrol they would take every chance to

268

do that. Eagle was wild with it and what he remembered as her ecstasy was real.

But the worry was too much for her. She knew the war was nearly over and the Germans defeated. She conjectured that the Eagle would kill her when he found out she was a German spy. What she did was deliberate. She did not feel glad about it or sad either. If she had any feelings that day at the border it was relief that she no longer had to have feelings. Mascaró suited her. He was not old but she could tell by the way he touched her, on the one occasion she let him do that during an earlier crossing she made with the Eagle, that he was also without feeling. For him, her beauty - then at its peak - was something to defile. Defilement was his substitute for emotion. Perhaps she knew this.

She didn't know she was pregnant when she led the Eagle into the trap, and she didn't know until it was too late to abort without danger to herself. There were times when she got a great deal of joy from the little girl. Physically she protected the child from Mascaró, who was perfectly ready to beat her to death. It was the stupid adolescent part of Louise that took pleasure in her daughter. She was not a worse mother than many. She had hoped to marry off Matilde early because Louise intended to leave the Basque country and, if possible, go to America. She wanted to go alone, start over again, was how she put it.

But no one wanted to marry Matilde. Mascaró's reputation did not greatly affect Louise's life but it made Matilde undesirable, even to policemen; in spite of his power, as a father-in-law Mascaró was not a healthy prospect.

Mascaró's death changed everything. For one thing, her husband had supplied Louise with her requisite heroin. That was also where Silva came in, but it was not the only thing about Silva which attracted Louise. It was unknown to Louise herself exactly what she planned to do with Silva but there were enough possibilities along with the need for the drug to justify keeping him in tow.

•

Silva and the monsignor arrived. The priest was white-haired, ruddy, cheerful, carrying a large bag. Even the prison smell did not seem to alarm him.

"My very dear señora, the comisario has explained your noble impulse. It can't make much legal difference, excuse me but so it seems to me, since the court has not allowed the validity of the other religious marriages, but as I see it the grace of God is stronger than any man's rule so why shouldn't we help them to the grace of God? I've spoken to the governor. He is a religious man and he agrees with me. He says as long as there's no newspaper publicity - you know how the foreign press would treat the story - he won't object. He said he thought something romantic was afoot when you came in. I never met a more softhearted man."

Paul and Angeles approached him. She said in wonder, "You're going to marry us, Monsignor?"

"Yes, providing the young man's a Catholic."

Angeles looked at Paul longingly, lovingly. "Would you mind if he baptized you, Paul?"

"No, I don't mind."

"What about his religious instruction?" asked the nun, really worried.

"She's been instructing him ever since he entered, madre," from the French woman.

"Madre, don't be distressed. I'll ask him the important questions, then I'll baptize him, then I'll hear their confessions and then I'll marry them. Then they can take communion." This jolly monsignor was a man of action.

"Yes, Monsignor," the nun said dubiously.

"Can I really take communion, Monsignor? They haven't let us have communion since we came here. Isa and Kristiana will be my attendants so they can take communion too, can't they, Father?"

The monsignor looked up to heaven through the murky cobwebs that caparisoned the arches. "How many souls we are comforting today!" He had everything with him in his bag - he said he always carried it when he traveled - even a small portable altar. "We won't have to disturb the other madres," he said.

So the ceremony went ahead, confessions and all that and then the nun served for him. Paul was wearing his parents' wedding ring and used it. Paul was to become a naked new soul lying in the palm of Jesus, so the monsignor told him. Isa arranged Angeles' hair, having asked the nun permission to bring out a brush. The three girls and Paul took communion and for the first time Isa seemed relaxed. Poor Kristiana didn't speak but she knelt with them. The other two women also knelt although they did not take communion. Silva stood stiffly beside the soldier, whose mitralleta was allowed to rest butt on the ground. The two policemen bowed their heads when the little bell rang that told them transubstantiation had taken place.

When the priest had given the final blessing, the bride and groom rose to their feet holding hands and standing silent. Isa and Kristiana remained kneeling.

The soldier put his machine gun back to its active position. With all his aplomb, the monsignor was dazed by what he had done. He put away his holy paraphernalia and the nun helped him. A very cold wind swept through the festoon of cobwebs. Then, Matilde broke the spell, whatever it was. She approached Paul and Angeles and took off her sweater, a heavy warm one, and held it out to them. "It's a little wedding present." Paul took it from Matilde and

271

wrapped it around his wife, then held Angeles in his arms, unaware of anyone else.

"Now we really have to go," said the French woman restlessly.

"They aren't going to be alone for an instant? There must be an empty cell, madre, where we could let them stay for five minutes. I doubt if it would take them that long." Silva, laughing, flicked the peephole on the cell nearest to him.

The nun and the French woman made sounds to show they were scandalized.

"There was no such permission given by the governor. Only that they could be married. We mustn't presume on his kindness," said the monsignor in haste.

Angeles stood away from Paul. "Yes, Monsignor. We are indebted to you for your kindness. We do not presume on it. And this is not the place for my husband and me to be alone. I wouldn't take him into one of those cells. Our marriage will be celebrated in Roncesvalles." Her voice wouldn't carry her any further. She started to say goodbye to Paul but could not. Isa and Kristiana stood one on each side of her. It did not seem possible to Paul that Angeles could go back into that fetid cell.

He grasped Angeles' hands and he could only say, "Always, always" and her name.

"Lawyer . . . family," she answered.

The others didn't meet the prison governor on their way out. The man with the whip told them he was still waiting near the telephone for the verdict.

Immediately outside the prison door they separated into three groups and no one in any group appeared to have anything to do with members of the other groups, until over his shoulder the monsignor said, "Remember, nothing to the papers." Then, "Señor Paul Fowler, you'll have to come to get the marriage certificate. Bring him to the side door of the bishop's palace, Matilde. I'll be there in half an hour. Since I have gone this far I must finish it properly." He was talking to himself and he went away quickly.

Silva and the French woman had disappeared during that speech.

Paul said to Matilde, "The monsignor is afraid, isn't he?"

"Of course. Why shouldn't he be? Zendejas and the colonel won't like it. The monsignor is impulsive, everybody knows that. As soon as they hear they'll be after you too, Paule. I suppose you better go. You must have the certificate though."

"I have to stay near her."

"They won't let you. Will your embassy help you?"

"People keep asking me about my embassy. I have no idea what they will or won't do." He fell into reflection.

Matilde did not try to interrupt his silence. Finally Paul said, "Is there some way I could get warm clothes and blankets to her?" Only then he observed that Matilde was shaking with chills. "Let's get into a café. Excuse me for not seeing how very cold you are."

"All right. We'll drink one brandy. I have a coat at the hotel. I have to get my things anyway. We might do that while we're waiting for the monsignor. It's this way. Let's get my things first of all." She turned a corner half running and he followed.

At her hotel they found a suitcase standing just outside the concierge cage. "Your mother left it for you," said the concierge.

After she extracted a coat Paul took the case. "Can we go now and get the certificate, Matilde?"

In the waiting room beyond the side door of the bishopric the monsignor came to them at once with the paper in an envelope. Paul opened the envelope and looked at the document carefully.

"The father registrar was not very pleased. He may report the matter to the bishop who may very well report it to the court-martial. Matilde, I can stand between Angeles and the authorities to some extent and if it comes to that. But there is no way I can protect señor Fowler. You ought to leave Spain, sir, as soon as you can, and positively if there is any publicity at all."

But with the certificate in his hands, Paul was able to drop both his strange ill temper (fear, he knew that) and the unreality into which he had been pitched. The only thing that had seemed real to him since they had begun this venture was Angeles' presence. Deprived of that, he was lost; but now, by some absurd student reasoning, a piece of paper had restored his strength.

As they left the bishop's residence, he was even able to laugh at himself. He had the envelope in his hand and he kissed it. Now he could feel Matilde's relief.

"We had better get it xeroxed and I'll mail a copy home."

"If there is a place we can trust not to take a copy for the press."

"Silva would be the one who would know."

"Silva is busy," she said, not bitterly nor gaily.

And Paul was fully aware of her at last. "What a monstrous life . . ."

"Paule, I don't want you to say that. Anyway, when we get to the Gran Hotel I will have escaped it. Escaped," she repeated it reflectively, a monstrous life reflected in the mirror of a word and then discarded.

Finally they went into a bar and had their brandy. They lifted their glasses in a toast.

◄16►

Matilde and Paul found Arrano talking with Suertegaray, the blind man seeking out the crippled one as if they two had special faculties. The lawyer saw the young people in the doorway even before Arrano knew they were there. But Arrano spoke first.

"Do you have money enough for us to stay in this hotel, Paule? It's an expensive one."

Suertegaray broke in. "I already told you, Eagle, we'd be glad to arrange for both of you. Paul is Matai's friend so he can certainly share my room, and you have any number of offers."

"Has the young lady any offers?" said Arrano. "Shall I present my daughter, Matilde Arcángel, señor letrado Suertegaray."

The lawyer, grave and romantic, took her hand, then bowed a small lovely bow. "I wish we had had you with us earlier." He was examining her face and bearing. "Will you tell me, not necessarily this moment but while you are here, exactly what you saw that rainy afternoon?"

"I can tell you at once and in very few words, señor Suertegaray. I saw nothing, because with the first shot my mother pushed me into a closet and locked the door."

"When did she let you out?"

"When the gristapo arrived, while they were still on the stairs."

He showed Matilde to a chair. "You would have made a very poor witness then, even if we had been allowed witnesses. Did your mother by any chance tell the police you had been shut in the closet?"

"Of course not." Matilde laughed.

"A good Basque laugh. We welcome you back to your own country, Matilde."

She nodded to him and immediately turned to Arrano. "Paule has a great deal to tell you, Papa. None of you will believe what has happened. I think you ought to call Angeles' lawyer if he's here."

"What is it, Paule?" Arrano anxiously went to Paul, who had been silent, standing with Matilde and then behind her chair. The blind man touched Paul's face lightly and felt down his shoulders and arms.

"Did you give her my message and under the circumstances I suggested?"

Still Paul didn't speak. Matilde cried out, "Papa, Papa, he's married to her."

Angeles' lawyer, Galíndez y Navarro, and some of the others had just barely come into the room as she said this. All of them looked at Paul with amazement. Galíndez exclaimed, "Every saint in the calendar! What did you say?"

Paul spoke slowly; he was talking to Arrano. "I saw her come out of a dark hole. She had on her red sweater - she had pulled it up over her hair it was so cold, and over her hands. Her cheeks were red too. I took her in my arms, how could I help it, Eagle? There was nothing more to it. She loves me as much as I love her. A monsignor came into the prison by some chance - I don't know who arranged it . . ."

"Matilde, I should think," said Suertegaray.

". . . He came there and married us. She is precious and brave and lovely."

Galíndez was standing exactly beside Paul, crowding him. "Granted, but did the monsignor give you a marriage certificate?"

Paul handed it to him. "I want to get a copy immediately to mail to my lawyer in the United States, to my parents' lawyer."

"What for?" Galíndez was hard, and wary.

"If it's registered under American law, I thought it might make it easier to help her. She told me to discuss everything with you, although when she and I were talking it was not about the certificate because we still didn't know we were going to be married."

"We have a copy machine here with us."

Arrano said, "Matilde, will you tell us in simple order what happened? I think Paule can't do it. Something enormous has come over this Paule. If you are really married, Paule, let's sit down quietly with a bottle of the best cognac this house can serve and after we take a drink, my daughter will give us the information in proper order."

By this time nine of the sixteen lawyers were in the room. The twelve people found chairs or seats on the sofa. Paul held up his glass and said gravely, "To my wife."

They drank the toast.

Then Matilde spoke. "We met the Civil Guard on the way with Comisario Silva . . ."

"Dear God, is Silva in this too? And you're sitting here free?" This was Suertegaray.

"Go on," ordered Galíndez.

"Silva told them he was taking Paule in. I was terribly afraid. Paule, why don't you tell them the rest?"

"It was I who was afraid. I was never so afraid in my life. I wasn't able to think of Angeles then. I wanted to run away when we stood at the prison door and saw that man with a whip . . ."

"Old Bimbo wouldn't have hurt you. But what about the governor of the prison?"

"He's a friend of my mother's," Matilde spoke a bit shrilly.

"Your mother was escorting Paul? You and your mother and Silva?"

All of the lawyers laughed with such pleasure that Paul, who was the only one there who wouldn't naturally have understood why they laughed, could not be offended.

"So the governor didn't arrest you, Paul? All of it is simply beyond belief." Galíndez was still making a little fun of Paul. "Were you cold when you went through that filthy tunnel?"

"I would have died of fear if Matilde hadn't been there."

"I think it's about time you said so." Suertegaray spoke softly.

"We waited, and a nun unlocked the door of their cell. Angeles came out. I thought I would never see her again and there she was. It seemed as if we had known each other a long time. Well, we have. And she had the letter."

Arga wasn't there so no one but Arrano knew what letter he was talking about.

"Money," said Arrano, "did you give anybody any money?"

"I gave Silva the money and Silva must have distributed some, but if he did, it was done discreetly."

"Silva seemed to have a good deal of money of his own,"

said Matilde. Arrano and Suertegaray were interested in this. Arrano started to say something but stopped. Galíndez hadn't noticed the attention of the two others, so engrossed was he in the story. He said, "You'd think we were talking about the anteroom of some member of the cortes. Arga and I are the only two who have been in that prison, I guess. You can hardly imagine the filthy garbage dump of the place."

"It's a beautiful patio," said Paul severely.

They laughed uproariously this time. Paul and his scholarly tone was unlike any American they had ever met. They were laughing at their ridiculous and amazing brother, and now Galíndez clapped him affectionately on the back.

"As a matter of fact," said Suertegaray, "it is a national treasure, listed in guidebooks as the patio of Santa Monica, fifteenth century."

"I knew that. Not the name, but I knew it was beautiful."

"Some day you'll be telling your grandchildren you and Angeles were married in one of the small jewels of . . ."

Galíndez interrupted. "What I want to know is, how on earth did this monsignor get there? What monsignor is he? One of our friends?"

"No, one of my mother's friends." Matilde's timing was so perfect that once more they laughed and this laugh did really seem to break the tension.

Arrano said, "Ujuju! The monsignor and the comisario and the señora Mascaró. Anyone else? I feel my hateful filthy love seeping away from my heart. And as it departs my sweet and virtuous daughter approaches nearer and nearer." Arrano stood up and found his way to her. He stood behind her chair, touching her hair now and then. "What else happened, Matilde?"

"There was a young soldier with a mitralleta and the

nun of course. It was the first wedding I've gone to so I noticed everything."

Each man took a deep breath and let it out. Arrano asked Galíndez to pour another brandy. "This is to my daughter."

They drank that toast. Then Galíndez was all bustle. "You and I better talk, Paul. Lets go to my room. May we confer with some of you gentlemen if we need to? We must see how to use this marriage for the salvation of Angeles."

"He'll have to leave the country, you know that, Galíndez. Of course he can wait until they put him out, but if he wants to get that marriage certificate registered . . ."

"I understand you . . ."

There was a long pause after Paul and Galíndez left. Then Matilde told them about the governor's stipulation that word of the marriage should not reach the newspapers. Most of them thought the news wouldn't help them at this point; waiting for the verdict, as they were, it might seem a frivolous side event. "There may be a time, though," said Suertegaray.

"How would we do it?"

"Tell *Le Monde* and the *New York Times* we have a story and ask them to reach us at once if they hear Zendejas has something he's announcing. In other words they'd beat Zendejas to it . . ."

"Would it be better to tell them outright, rather than hint at the story?"

"The *Times* man is absolutely honorable."

"Then tell him about the marriage, under the circumstances you are saying."

"And he would tell *Le Monde* if we were breaking the story?"

"I think we can trust *Le Monde* too."

"As a matter of fact, so do I, but that reporter has been

pushed around so much by Zendejas he might love to beat him in a move."

"Let's let Calvo decide."

"Ala!"

"What about the governor at the prison?" Matilde asked timidly.

"Yes, we have an obligation to him. Maybe he wants the news out. He has a feud going with Zendejas. Can we find out what he really wants? It wouldn't do him any harm if it did come out. Zendejas will twist it so as to show the government's ineffable clemency. So maybe the governor would rather set it up for his own benefit."

"Better not ask him anything."

"Paule and Angeles were never left by themselves, I suppose, in a cell or anywhere?" This was Arrano.

"No."

"It's better this way, Matilde. To have a baby in prison . . . I've seen women in prison with babies."

"Paule could have taken the baby."

"You don't know the Franco prison system. The baby would have been used as a poor little frightened pawn. Brought up by nuns . . ."

"There won't be any baby so what are you going on about, Papa? Where's Arga? I want to find her and talk with her," as if Matilde had all she wanted of men.

"We're running shifts waiting at the military headquarters. Arga and Calvo are there now."

"Does anybody know when the judgment will come?" Matilde was still distraught.

There were headshakes. Several of the men picked up the papers they had been reading. It was evident Matilde shouldn't have used the word judgment, with its jolting finality. These men had worked together to keep a ball in the air, to keep the judges unsettled so that the decisions now being made in some comfortable room of the officers' quarters in that ugly brick building were put off as long as possible on the chance that world opinion, if not justice, would work for their clients. And each time the ball was thrown and astutely caught, a sense of reality had been asserted, as against the hand-of-Death verdict asked for: six capital judgments and hundreds of years of imprisonment and the enormous fines. Certainly a binding web had been woven for an appeal, for a reversal, but those things could not happen unless the old general died. The lawyers were in league with a decent future, not the decaying present. They were bright and pragmatic but they had allowed themselves hope - resilience demanded it. Judgment, said unaffectedly by a young woman outside the circle of the particular suffering they understood in their clients, was like a true word spoken by a child. Their hope shriveled away into a dark corner. Matilde understood most of this but she did not know how to mend her brashness.

Suertegaray said, "I heard through the *El Garabato* man that the Young Captains came in this morning early and are talking with the Board now." He was wooing back their hope, not for their sakes as much as for the girl's. He had seen her distress.

"Yes, I heard that too. Does that mean Díaz Alegría has a say?"

"It certainly seems to mean there won't be a decision tonight. They'll have to listen to the Young Captains."

"The telegraph office is bogged down. If they make the usual mistakes in delivery we may get some of the telegrams ourselves."

"I've never had a telegram from the pope," said Suertegaray, and they laughed as best they could.

But then they all stood up. They had heard the front door close.

282

"It's Arga." They were all saying it but no one moved from where he stood.

Arga came in weeping. "We're to be there to receive the sentences at ten tomorrow morning. But I talked to the Italian newsman. He's wormed it out of Lieutenant-Colonel Flores. There are nine death sentences. Nine."

•

Three men had two death sentences and three had one each. The lawyers went as ordered the next morning to hear the rest of it. Paul and Matilde and Arrano saw them off from the hotel.

Only Lieutenant-Colonel Ram was in the courtroom to receive them; he read a many-paged document full of paragraph five of article 286, articles 257, 258, paragraph one million, three hundred thousand, and six. The document was also full of terrorism, assassination, incarceration. The two lowest sentences were twelve years and a day, the day added to counteract any future amnesty toward prisoners with twelve-year sentences. Angeles' sentence was fifteen years; Isa's was raised from twenty-four asked to fifty years given. Against Matai there were seven counts. He received one death sentence for assassination of Mascaró, and the other for banditry and subversion and armed subversion. He already had been given thirty years for the Pamplona attempt.

Lieutenant-Colonel Ram's voice was hoarse. He read with dignity he had never before shown, perhaps because he was alone there, the sole person responsible for his caste, his country, the Crusade. Or maybe it was because he had to read the word death so many times; tangled up in legal phrases it stood out like a big red bloom on a tree of matted vines with sticky leaves.

At the end of the reading, the sixteen lawyers shook hands with Lieutenant-Colonel Ram. He had accomplished this minor duty with decency; perhaps he was the least vindictive man on the court-martial Board. Perhaps he had been against the ferocity of this judgment. Not likely that he would have stood up to de la Vega but he might have opposed the jackal snappings of Zendejas. In spite of anger, dismay, and the sad anticipation of having to inform their clients, the lawyers had sat listening with absolute attention, testing the legality of each word, each fatuous denial of truth. It was as if they themselves were to stand against the paredón.

They went back to the hotel as a stern solid unit. They might have been the judges. They had to confer before they went to the prisons to tell the accused, still not the convicted until General Pedro Maldonado, military commander of the Burgos district, signed the sentences; and until that signature was written there could be no clemency demands from lawyers.

Paul, as still as a statue, was waiting for them inside the hotel door. Galíndez y Navarro whispered to him, "Fifteen years, five less than was asked. A little better, and it may mean somebody's friendly. I'm going to see her. Send word with me if you want to." No one else spoke to Paul. The deaths they carried as a joint weight put them outside communication. After they had passed him he went onto the street and walked up and down alone, preparing the message for Angeles.

He wrote a note and the lawyer, fortunately, out of his experience memorized it on his way to the provincial prison. New restrictions had been promulgated by the nuns, by the governor of the jail, by someone higher up. Angeles could not receive any piece of paper whatsoever. Galíndez could only recite the letter to her.

Arga went with Galíndez to inform Isa and Kristiana. Captain Zendejas' rage to punish Isa for being Matai's wife was not equal to the rage for punishment of which de la Vega and the others were the instruments. Besides that, her husband and her brother were both under death sentence. Arga had to give her this news. Walking over there with Galíndez, the woman lawyer tried to comprehend before she went into the prison. To punish women is a tenet of the old savage church of Spain. Was this hatred of the vile female body something that had been siphoned into the church, donated by some pale, self-worshipping, self-abnegating, paulish regent or a noble of the purest caste? The Black Legend is true, Arga thought; she did not love Spain - she was thinking that those who love Spain have to explain to me sometime how it is that de la Vega and the man above him, and above him, could permit the crushing of a virtuous, gentle girl. What had she done to suffer so? She is brave and Matai is brave - that's what they've done. Those were Arga's thoughts while she walked along the cobbled street.

The captain-governor of that jail must really have had a soft heart, as the monsignor had said. He brought the two lawyers into his office. "I have been censured for what I did yesterday. So I have to be strict about every rule, no papers, no letters, absolutely no warm clothes. What can I do? My cook has prepared a strong blood broth. There it is in a thermos bottle. Take it to them. Bring back the bottle." He bowed them out, strained muscles around his mouth and his eyes closed.

The three women were in their cell, arms around each other, trying to warm one another. Angeles had put her new sweater onto Isa, who was in a chill, her teeth chattering. Since yesterday in the court when Isa had been able to take her part strongly, she had been constantly diminishing in size and force. She looked as inanimate as a white root in a cellar, except for the shaking. She was not crying.

"Arga, what am I going to do for her? Can't we possibly get some blankets? She's so cold nothing we have will warm her," Angeles cried out.

Isa spoke in a whisper, "Arga, you've come to tell us. Tell us."

"Let's bring her outside. We have some broth for you. Drink it first."

Galíndez found the tin cup which was about their only utensil. They filled it halfway for Isa first. "You must drink it all, every drop. Dear Isa." He wanted to put his arms around her but as he started to do so, the pitiful nun with big dirty hands made a move toward him. He said, "The governor sent the broth," because it really looked as if she might take that away.

Isa drank all they gave her. It seemed to revive her. The other two took their turns and the bottle was closed to keep the soup warm.

Then Arga drew back her shoulders. "It's no worse for Matai and Gorka than we expected, and even before the announcement there have been petitions of clemency coming in. There'll be more . . ."

Kristiana and Angeles cried out against the verdicts of Matai and Gorka. Isa was silent at first but then she began to moan as a very sick baby does. The moans turned into words. "Arga, we were together for a few minutes yesterday. When we were waiting to go back one by one the guards let us stand near each other . . ."

Kristiana interrupted suddenly in a loud voice, "The same guard who let Josu and me be chained together part of the time. He would have let them talk but they didn't talk."

"Only Father Ander was between us and he pushed himself out of the way as best he could . . . He blessed us . . . Matai was there beside me . . . death." It was said as low as an indrawn breath. "I had not . . . seen him . . . close that way since our baby was killed. I didn't know, Arga, if he would want to see me after what happened . . . the guards . . . you know all that. But his eyes told me it was the same for him as it was before, Arga."

How could Arga tell her about Matai's two death sentences - if one failed or was set aside the other would be waiting for him. And Arga could not open her mouth to tell the increase in Isa's own sentence. What difference could that make to her?

But Galíndez was of a different mind. He signaled to Arga to stand beside Isa. "Isa, we must give you all the truth."

"Tell me . . . all the truth. Matai and I . . . have always told . . . the truth to each other."

"They increased your sentence to fifty years."

She cried out, "What did I do? What was the charge?"

"It was garbage," said Arga very angrily. "I'll read it to you if you want to hear it, Isa. We'll appeal, we'll get it reduced."

"How could you get it reduced? Every time the matter was brought they would double the sentence. Isn't that right, señor Galíndez?"

Arga answered, "It's a monstrous injustice. I think all the world will protest it. The *Le Monde* reporter left for Paris at once. So did the man from *Figaro*. They say there'll be strikes all over France. Franco can't hold up his ugly revenge for the whole world to see and not expect to be condemned."

"Arga's right, of course. I have no words to express what I think," said Galíndez.

"And Gorka, my poor little brother . . ." Isa put her hands

over her eyes. Then, "You must tell Kristiana and Angeles what their sentences are."

"Angeles has fifteen years. Kristiana is exonerated . . . but you must go back to the mental institution, poor child. We can visit you there. Kristiana, dear friend, your case is not at all hopeless. Since you were exonerated, in time, soon, we can get a medical certificate that your mental balance . . ." This was still Galíndez.

"And Josu?"

"The thirty years they asked for."

Kristiana put her head back as far as it would go. It was unnatural and disturbing. She went rigid in that posture, her hands at her sides. The nun came toward her as if she were going to wrench her back into normality. Arga stepped between them. "Madre," she said with authority and the nun stood still, "what were you going to do, madre?"

"The doctor said to . . ." The nun didn't finish and she turned her back on them.

"I can usually stop her," said Angeles. "She's the one who should be in the institution." There was silence. Then, "I'm married, you know," she said this to Arga hesitantly, and then stepped back and heard the words herself.

"I have this message from your husband," and Galíndez recited the words.

"Again, please." And he said it again more slowly.

Of course the last word of the letter was Paul, and she repeated the name several times.

"There are things he can do to help us. Angeles, he wants to stay here near you but we think he ought to go home and start whatever action he can with the State Department and his senator. He's already getting a lawyer there with whom we can correspond. Hope, hope, I think we can dare to hope, Angeles."

"Will they treat me worse or better because I'm married to an American?"

"It'll depend on the officers. I'll find out all I can about the governor of the women's prison they send you to."

"Alcalá de Henares?"

"Most likely, yes."

"Will they let Isa and me be together? Will they let her see Matai? They must do that. You must tell me everything you can so I can help her." Angeles' voice dropped and the nun turned around. "Well, come and listen, madre," she said with a sigh. "I want to know what Isa can expect. You think they'll carry out the sentences right away? Surely not with the protests coming in."

Galíndez answered, "It doesn't seem likely but these barbarous sentences didn't seem likely either. None of us dreamed the sentences would be increased. If they do carry them out quickly, I think at least they will let a priest come here to Isa. We'll certainly ask for it with great force."

"A priest?" said the nun. "What kind of priest? One of those godless Basque priests? I didn't see the wedding yesterday." Now she spoke in a chatty way. "The madre said the monsignor was very nice and not a Basque." Then she stopped herself with a grunt. "They have to go into their cell now. You've been here long enough."

"Let them at least finish their broth."

"I thought they would leave me the rest of the broth. We suffer from the cold too, you know."

"We have to take the thermos bottle back to the governor," said Galíndez, and he poured what was left of the soup into the cup. Each girl took her turn. This served to get Kristiana to drop her head forward.

Arga went into the cell with them and when she emerged she was without her top sweater but the nun didn't notice because she was absorbed with the soup Angeles had left in the cup.

•

The lawyers had been told they could send only three of their number to the other prison to inform the men of their sentences. Drawn lots made the three Rufino Lares, Sahagún Velarde, and Luzarra, counsels to Luku, Valentín, and Isa's brother Gorka. Two of these prisoners had two death sentences each so the arrangement was fair enough, but the lawyers of the other four with death sentences pressed around the emissaries telling them their prisoners' special needs, strengths, weaknesses, how best to talk to them. The sixteen prisoners belonged to all the lawyers. This hard duty of informing them was the duty of all. Finally Suertegaray spoke loudly above the clamor of anxious conversation. "Better to spend the time in preparing yourselves. We know our friends in the prison are strong. What you three need is your own strength, not our advice. Isn't that right?"

They agreed it was and were silent. That hotel sala which had become the lawyers' meeting room was a warm friendly place which the three hated to leave, and a sad waiting place for the others.

The men also had their patio. The two priests had originally been given better cells than the rest but chose to stay with the young men, unless as sometimes happened the guards forced them into their cells. But this morning the patio contained all the Burgos prisoners and a number of common prisoners. Hardly any of these miscellaneous murderers, thieves, confidence men were Basque.

There was also the band of small boys who had been working the Madrid-Paris train, hiding in toilets or baggage cars between making some valuable hauls.

When the Burgos accused were first brought there, considerable animosity showed up against them. The Basques were accustomed to this in the other prisons they had known during the last year. Sometimes the animosity was not dispelled, but in this case the common prisoners had got caught up in the trial and followed it with increasing interest. Their sources of information were seldom anyone who was witnessing the trial and, since the Burgos accused were not supposed to talk with the others, it was not easy to correct whatever faulty ideas the common prisoners acquired from their wives and friends bringing food and cigarettes.

Apparently the news that came was favorable to the Basques because each day of the trial the goodwill toward them increased. There were surreptitious gifts of cigarettes, a good sweet roll, a fried trout, and, for the priests, each a knitted scarf. The little pickpocket boys, who had certainly led a life of considerable terror in the slums of Sevilla, were nevertheless the least afraid. Two had attached themselves openly to the Basques, doing services like washing a shirt for next day's session, or shifting a blanket from the cell of an informer into a Basque cell.

The informers were having a bad time of it. Nearly everyone had turned his back on them, partly because the Basques, more adept at spotting them since they were seldom Basque, had taught some of their skill to the others.

When the lawyers came in that noonday the patio was divided into two unequal groups. There was a small collection of informers with a few friends, furtively disconsolate and talking very little. There was a large group composed of the Basques and nearly all the rest of the prisoners. No one was talking to the Basques and they were talking only to each other. Under different circumstances the conversation would have been comic. The Basques would tell each other some of the events from the court, then the criminal friends told each other reports they had heard from outside. This included information about strikes and so on, but also local items, which by this time in their habitation of the prison had become the backbone of life, and interested the Basques as well. For example, one of the pickpockets named Hilario was to be allowed to go home to Sevilla because his grandmother was dying. She was a famous prostitute with good connections. He might have to come back after her death but maybe not. God would decide.

The entire patio full of men saw the three lawyers.

The informers made a move to approach the main group. Several common prisoners turned toward them menacingly and they retreated. The guards in their posts on the second gallery shifted their rifles. The lawyers walked toward the Basque prisoners. And then with great good taste the murderers and thieves, having seen the faces of the lawyers, drew away into a group of their own, halfway between the informers and the Basques.

"It's bad news, isn't it, Rufino?" That was Luku talking very softly.

"Why don't you just read the judgment to us. Then we'll hear what the judges said exactly and each man can make his own interpretation." That was Valentín Lizaldi and he too spoke softly but with fatal balance.

"Get it over with. Over with, and then you can read us whatever you choose." Gorka came near to shouting and the man nearest him put his arm around his shoulders.

"It's about what they asked for," Rufino spoke huskily.

"Not worse?"

"A little worse."

"No more deaths?"

"The same except that Matai, Luku, and Sabino are given two sentences."

"Two death sentences . . ." Sabino Etxebe seemed to be exploring a new language.

"Tell me about Isa." Matai's voice was hardly audible.

Rufino couldn't carry it any longer and Luis Luzarra answered the question. "Arga is with her now. They gave her fifty years."

Matai turned away. He left the Basque group altogether, stood with the pickpocket boys for a few minutes.

Hilario took his hand. "Let me help you, señor."

Matai looked down at him and smiled.

"I can get out a paper if you want."

Matai nodded. "You're a friend, Hilario."

"I'm not Basque but yes. Bonavit you know. And that Silva who has persecuted you, you know he tried to kill my grandmother once - very long ago. She got him with a hoe, though. I hear he still has the scar. And you'll get them, you know."

"Thank you, my brave friend. You take care of yourself, do you hear me?"

Luzarra had continued quickly, "Angeles received fifteen years. Kristiana was exonerated but she must return to the manicomio."

"Better that than prison," murmured her husband with tears on his face.

"All right, now read the whole thing."

Matai came back to hear the reading and he had recovered his voice, and his strength. "We have to write an answer."

A committee was chosen and with the lawyers they sat down to do that. The communication was not to the court-martial Board but to the Basque people. Here are the few words they wrote. As the lawyers left, the sixteen prisoners called the gora after them, the Gora Euskadi Askatuta.

"The sentence we have received does not in any way affect our revolutionary morale. We expected this brutality from fascism. We will continue to fight it until the end. We send an appeal to the whole world, to those who have human feelings, that they do everything they humanly can to impede this new crime." The six with death sentences signed it.

Hilario carried out the little piece of paper with him, who knows how because of course he was searched. A Basque met him at the corner of two tenement streets and took the paper. By night it was printed and was being read by many persons.

Two weeks passed. It was almost Christmas. Spanish mayors of Basque towns ordered householders and businessmen to put up holiday decorations. Those who worked for the government or for Spanish establishments did string lights and streamers, but most houses and bars and stores went unadorned. There was little shopping for holiday goods. Celebration could not go on merely by order of the Crusade.

In Madrid, Franco's advisers, confidantes (if any), and loyal opposition talked endlessly. In Burgos, General Maldonado, the district commandant, and a survivor of the Blue Division which fought in Russia, received callers from all factions; still he didn't confirm the sentences. This could hardly mean he was opposed to them; more likely he was waiting for clarification from Franco. Most blues were aggressively loyal to the Supreme Leader.

Arrano and Matilde were staying at San Andrés, she with the nuns, until they knew the end of the matter. No, not end.

The night of December 24 those of the defense lawyers who had not gone home to other towns for Christmas gathered at San Andrés. First they individually attended a rosary said for the prisoners, and then filtered back into the monastery, except Arga, whose credulity was strained by prolonged prayer, and who did not go to the rosary. Instead she came to the nuns' residence and visited Matilde. Now they were all together in the parlor. Eagle and Bachi were also there, and the priests in rotation, taking turns with their church duties.

They came to pool information and exchange hopes and views. The lawyers were getting information from many sources. There was sympathy in high places for the prisoners. There was also self-seeking concern: they heard that two ordinarily unfriendly army factions, Young Captains and the liberals, were both offended by Franco's use of their service to bring in the death penalties and so carry the onus for a political gambit which was not their idea or responsibility; the Spanish army is not supposed to meddle in politics.

That was a nice-sounding reason for resentment. Pragmatically, the army, or at least the Young Captains, hoped to take over after Franco's death and they did not want to be any more unpopular than necessary. Therefore they resented the bland way in which a military court-martial was ordered to bring in verdicts of such severity that the world was protesting them.

The lawyers argued about whether de la Vega, a clever man, had acted on his own - merely doing what was best for his career - or had followed the lead of the Young Captains who, as they knew, came to see de la Vega during the deliberations. The lawyers heard the captains had urged him to respond to government commands by bringing in a verdict of greater severity than even the government wanted. If they were ordered to take revenge let them be more vengeful than God himself - an expression one of the captains had used to Calvo Peralta, who was a friend of the young officer's father.

Strikes and protests had accelerated constantly and there was a deep excoriating new anger among non-ETA Basques. Comparing notes, the lawyers concluded that never under Franco's rule had Euzkadi been as united as now.

One of the two lawyers from Cataluña came in then, late, and brought the bad news that the other, Sahagún Velarde, had been arrested the day before in Barcelona.

"For what?"

"For having attended the Montserrat gathering, of course." That had happened during the trial. Sahagún had flown over for one evening to explain Burgos events to the three hundred catalán intellectuals gathered there. Among the artists were Miró and Tapiés. There were actors, including the great Nuria Espert, writers, musicians, cantantes - Raimón and Serrat, two of the most popular in Spain - and many faculty members of the University school of architects. They went up to the catalán mountain shrine, Montserrat, and stayed there to protest Burgos, until the Civil Guard surrounded the fifteenth-century monastery and threatened to break down its doors. Monsignor Just, the abbot, stood firm with them, in spite of a telephone call from a member of Franco's cabinet, and the group didn't leave until they had written a strong, harsh manifesto; it was published in *L'Osservatore Romano*. Now the punishments were beginning. A professor of philosophy who had attended was put in an insane asylum. Sahagún was arrested.

"We can all expect something the same, I suppose," said Thevet. "My wife has been receiving threatening calls."

"My car receives them daily, placed under the windshield wipers," from Luzarra.

"I'm well off," said Arga. "I'm not married and I have no car."

They laughed a little. Then Suertegaray said, "I must tell you what that son of Calvo's old friend said about the revolution."

"Yes? How'd he come to talk to you?"

Suertegaray shrugged. "He has a sister with polio. Also he's a kurdu of a drinker. Also he thought he was getting information from me. Calvo introduced us."

"What did he say?"

"In effect - mind you, this was after the judgments had been announced - he believes if Matai and the other five are executed there will be a revolution."

"He's right about that, but was his opinion wishful thinking?"

"It sounded like it; he has it figured out that the army will have to take over."

"Risky man to be around. He'll get you arrested."

"Very risky. He said that all police are scared to death to be stationed in Euzkadi. He thinks there'll be a total strike - the first step; then Basques will try to disarm and neutralize the police forces, then establish a separate Basque government. Except, of course, the army would have intervened long before things went that far."

"The real first step may be that they start assassinating each other." Suertegaray spoke softly.

"Mascaró?"

"Oh, much higher than him."

"Let's not spend time waiting for that," said Bachi.

They decided de la Vega had followed the advice of the Young Captains and that General Maldonado too was under pressure from them. No doubt eighty-year-old Franco was annoyed by the intervention of forty-year-old captains which added to the grievous worries the Basques gave him. It seemed to the lawyers that Maldonado was reflecting Franco's angry confusion.

The lawyers had brought a few bottles of wine with them, not to deplete the priests' supply. Now they sat quietly, each one staring into his glass or ahead of him. Suertegaray looked up as if to remove his eyes from that which they all saw: the prisoners in their ten-degrees-below-freezing cells waiting for a cruel Christmas. A small last straw came when the families sent chorizo and Spanish champagne and it was denied the prisoners.

Arga spoke, "What do they care, blues or Young Captains or the old arrotz himself? They don't care." She was very angry. "Nine deaths. Twenty deaths. A hundred Isas tortured and debased . . . To them, our people are sticks and stones and dust. They don't know what a man is."

As if Thevet had taken Calvo's role, he spoke calmly and persuasively. "Dear Arga, dear friend. That's just it, what you've said. They don't know what a man is. They're scrambling around each for his own advantage. We have to hold on. Basque sticks and stones and dust . . ."

Arga was weeping. The other lawyers didn't try to comfort her; perhaps she was expressing their sorrow for them. But Bachi said, "Add the tears to the dust and all that and there's your man . . ." Bachi's voice gave the last word an upward turn that drew not only Arga but all of them out of despair. There was a bustle of movement, refilling glasses.

The Eagle remarked, "Someone's at the door, Bachi."

When Bachi got back he said to Arrano, "No wonder you heard the knocking. It was for you. You have to go to the door yourself. He won't leave the message."

A scruffy man, who kept his face in the dark, told Eagle that if he went to the new hospital on its plaza near the

Begoña church at ten that evening he might be permitted a half hour with Jon Arizeder.

"Who says so?" Arrano demanded but the man slipped away. Bachi, who had stayed out of sight but near enough to help, told Eagle a small boy had come out of shadows and was signaling him anxiously.

Arrano heard, "Eagle, Eagle."

"Who is it?" Eagle asked Bachi.

"Street boy. You better listen to him."

"Let him in then. Let's not keep him standing outside."

"That message came from Bonavit," the boy said.

"How do you know?"

"It's my business to do that." The boy sounded as though he were trying out his two listeners.

"You're one of the pickpocket boys?"

"I'm Hilario."

"He's the one who brought out the letter," Eagle told Bachi.

"I know that. You're probably hungry?" Bachi asked the boy.

"I'm hungry but give me something I can carry in my hand. I have to keep going."

"What's that great roll of cloth you're carrying?" Bachi spoke harshly and that seemed to suit the boy, who answered at once by unrolling a Basque flag which filled the entryway.

Bachi said, "It's our flag, Eagle, but it's not correct. Look, Hilario, it's made wrong."

"Yes, I know. It looks like Mascaró's face, crooked, right? I brought it here so they couldn't fly it anywhere."

"Who couldn't?"

"Oh, the police, you know. Well, I didn't go to my grandmother's. Maybe it was a sin but I didn't go. She's done all her screwing without me to help her. She probably knows how to die without me. She'd know why I didn't come."

"Why didn't you?" Arrano had a hand on the child's shoulder.

"Matai . . . those . . . I couldn't go off until I knew. Isn't that right, Eagle?" The way the boy pronounced the English word enchanted Eagle and he touched the small shoulder.

"Well, you're still here," said the boy.

"Tell us about the flag," Bachi's voice was softer than before.

"The beasts picked me up when I didn't leave Burgos right away. Oh, they didn't treat me badly . . . the way they did before."

"That was Bonavit's special idea. We heard about it."

"Yeh, in Sevilla. He killed my partner. About the flag, they had it made to put up somewhere - there in Burgos I suppose. In connection with their spontaneous demonstration. They were going to fly it and then make a riot and shoot some of you . . . "

"Oiba, they don't think we give them enough trouble so they have to make up some!"

"To make chances to kill you. That's why I came. I've had a lot of time to listen, Eagle. That's just what they're figuring on."

"What do you mean?"

"No more trials, that's what they're saying. Shoot first and you don't have to shoot later. Bonavit, all of them, are getting that word."

"Are you sure, Hilario?"

"I've had a chance to listen, I tell you. They think I'm a cockroach that can't understand Spanish. They don't know that my grandmother" - and he kissed his left thumb and pointed it toward heaven - "made me learn good

Spanish. I hope that poor old vieja verde is dead, not suffering," he said in an undertone. "Anyway, kill's the word now."

"Bachi, get him something to eat, eh? Hilario, how did you get the flag out of the Burgos jail?" Arrano knelt to bring himself down to the boy's height.

The little boy laughed happily. "This sergeant, you know, who had charge of it, he'd already told me I had to carry it for him next day; so I just rolled it up and took it out ahead of time. They let me out because they knew I was the sergeant's helper and I told them I was to meet him . . ."

"When was that?"

"Three days ago."

"And you've been carrying it around ever since?"

"Right."

"Ay, Hilario, hijochu, what a glorioso glorioso you are!"

"Listen, Eagle, that arrangement about going up to the Plaza de Nueva Hospital, it could be a trap."

"It could be but I have to see Arizeder if I can. Will you go along with me and my daughter?"

"Naturally I planned to. You won't see much of me but I'll be around. I can bring word back here if there's any trouble. But I can't carry that wall-eyed flag another step."

"Roll it up and put it just inside the church door. Inside, you understand?"

"I know San Andrés like my grandmother's house. I slept there last night, me and the flag, in a confessional."

"Bachi'll give you a warmer corner tonight."

•

Arrano and Matilde were climbing from San Andrés to the plaza of the new hospital. Arizeder was in this civil

302

establishment because of skin grafts that couldn't be done in the prison infirmary. It was nine o'clock. They walked rapidly up the steps and steep streets. Loitering was unnatural to them both. They reached the plaza.

"Do you want to sit on one of the benches, Papa?"

"I would rather stand. Let's get as near as we can to the hospital windows. I think his room is on the plaza tonight."

"Don't they move him around from room to room? Bachi was telling me that."

"So Basques never know where he is and can't take him away? As if the nurses or an orderly didn't bring out word every time they move him. I've heard he's on the plaza tonight but I'm not sure which room."

"Papa, on the second floor someone is opening the top part of a window, letting the curtain fly out. Now they've closed the window."

"Then he's there. Stand where he can see us."

"With all those bandages how can he see?"

"I see and I'm blind. What are a few bandages?"

Arrano was singing under his breath. Then he said, "Aupa! I'll talk to him right here and now."

"Do you also think he can hear two floors up?" She laughed at her father and he joined her.

But he said, "Yes, I do."

•

The Eagle had made every effort to visit Jon Arizeder because he needed to talk with him. He had been surprised at those who seemed to have tried to help him, not least of all Bonavit.

There were many things Arrano had to tell Jon. His life had started again. He and Matilde had decided to work with ETA, substitutes for ones in prison. Jon's life might have started again too in spite of the swath of bandages. They said he looked like the bulto of a sacred statue being shipped from the stone carvers of Córdoba to Santiago Compostela. Arrano enjoyed thinking of a statue of Jon set up in Franco's church, or even better carried on a pilgrimage, flower-decked, through the streets of Franco's home town, El Ferrol.

He had Matilde to tell Jon about and he wanted to ask Jon how he managed for so many years to keep the secret about the French woman. Had Jon ever talked to her during this time? Had he ever thought about Matilde being Eagle's daughter? From what Eagle had been told there was a resemblance between them.

Above all he wanted to talk to him about the trial - for a half minute he had been able to set aside that load by thinking of Jon's triumphal parade as statue. Jon was sure to have heard the judgments. A nurse with a bedpan could report a part of the verdict on each visit and if necessary Jon could have a diarrhea so she would also have time to tell him about the protests from half the capitals of the world including the Vatican. Arrano kept hearing that if only the other John were still in the Vatican something human would have been said, not the careful siempre y cuando of this pope. He'd told them never mind, if the nine lives of Matai and the five are saved it may well come from Pope Paul's siempres y cuandos. But Eagle wanted Arizeder's ideas on the protests, from everywhere, including Greek intellectuals - those in exile, of course - and certain individuals in the United States, Edward Kennedy and the labor leader Meany, for instance.

Of course all clemency petitions did not signify the same thing; but, for the most part, are these high protestors, the safe people who will never be tortured, only augmenting their own safety by growing eloquent about half measures? Few of the telegrams published (usually in the foreign press) decried the vengeful cynicism of the trial. Now, with the judgments proclaimed, a little of the savagery has been denounced. Let an innocent man, they begged, be allowed to serve fifty years instead of being garroted. Or as if bloody Bonavit were removing, one by one, each member of a young man's body and they urge him to leave the youth his index fingers and right leg. Could these little protests be in truth the permission for the original brutality? What would Jon say? In his suffering these many months since his own Gernika fire, Jon must have found some answers.

In spite of Matilde's discomfort, Arrano began to talk to Jon under his breath. ". . . concerned not with each man but rather with the gains for all men? . . . not a Basque thought . . . anyway I don't like it. What do you think, Jon? . . . I've heard leaders think that way. Then Basques are not leaders . . . may be the case. Nor followers . . . good fighters . . . Each respects himself so they respect each other? And at the end because he is complete he dies a complete death, am I right? Not a fragment of some disgraceful common death, mass death . . . through common deaths a dictator rules . . . he doesn't know about any other kind . . . Every Basque death . . . as important as the creation or destruction of the world. That's too much for any dictator to swallow. He chokes on it.

". . . Matai . . . all of them giving their deaths . . . but I don't know if I could do that . . . for the freedom of the Basques. How is it different from the Christian martyrs in the Colosseum? I know there's a difference but you must help me find it.

". . . Jon, when one Basque is tortured or forced to spend his days in a smelly prison we can't talk about humility and acceptance of God's will, do you agree? Where did Christians get that idea? Their martyrs are part of a sporting event, players, spectators, and the ball. Martyr-ball. He humbly offers himself as God's ball, and his sufferings become a debt God owes him. That's where arrogance enters. Behold their martyr . . . Their hero is a step away . . . even more arrogant, and that topples him over into cruelty. The cruel hero of My Lai or Roncesvalles, take your choice . . . that's what Paule says.

". . . but our young people - and you too, Jon, - are neither humble nor arrogant, not hunter or hunted. The crest of Gernika, Jon, wolves each with a lamb in his jaw, preserving the lamb. God once told man that he was His equal and nearly everybody, except the Basques, has forgotten that Word.

". . . Is that where it comes from - our respect for a farm, a plow, a tree, the place where many hawthorns grow? Our language and our names . . . Yours, beautiful oak, and Suertegaray, a fire on the peaks, and that's what the man is. Of course you know what your name means to you, but I'm asking you: does our respect for each man make us name him after God's creations?

". . . Wasn't it true, Jon, what I witnessed? That every one of our sixteen was himself, neither a manufactured confessing prisoner nor a bleary martyr but a young man or woman who to the end of human days will be that person we knew at the trial and before, himself, herself, and because of this we can't be defeated? Is it really true that man can't be defeated? Imagine if that's true!

". . . one more question and I'll tell you something that will amuse you. Once Colonel de la Vega, furious with the prisoners' self-respect, shouted that his court-martial had nothing at all to do with Vietnam. (Or Mozambique or Andalusia or Uruguay?) No importa, no importa, but it seemed to me he really meant he didn't dare see the connection. And I want to ask you - when you dove off that railing, Jon, what did your fire mean to you? I know what you say in your diary, that you were bringing home to Franco what he had done in Gernika but I don't think that was all that was in your mind. I want to hear the rest . . ."

A nurse came to the second-story window. She lifted her hand in salutation to Arrano but Matilde wasn't there to tell him; she was talking to a little boy behind the statue of El Cano at the end of the square. Arrano walked up and down beneath the window. The nurse leaned out and seemed about to call to him when someone pulled her back.

Arrano spoke again . . . ". . . you want to know what happened, the things no one else can tell you. And how will I tell so no one else hears? Will they let me lean across you to give you a bedpan, or say a prayer over you?

"Here's one thing: that Vizor revolver belonged to Mascaró himself . . .

"That's right. On my way from Anboto with Paule I stopped at the whorehouse which you and I both know. A few days before, I heard the gun was there. The wonderful woman, you know her, Jenara, had taken it when Mascaró came there. She got it without his remembering where he had left it. He had been searching all over Bilbao and she had it put away for the day of his death. She gave it to me. So maybe Mascaró was shot with his own Czech revolver because I fired it at his mouth when he shouted my name. Of course I may have missed him. That death at the top of the stairs was a series of cholas, trolas, drolas. What a way for the Great Inquisitor to die! At least we straightened his face for him - one in the mouth and one in the forehead.

"Mangy Silva was skulking around. Did you know that? Until I saw the French woman the other day, I only knew that someone was on the other landing. I heard the shot just after my shot and I could tell it was from a service revolver.

"Now we can piece it together. That man in the other box in San Andrés - naturally the priest didn't tell me who it was - must have been Silva; so the priest heard two confessions of the execution in ten minutes. To be on the safe side I confessed it myself. But imagine Silva having to tell a Basque priest that he had just killed a Spanish inspector of police and hating himself for trusting the priest! I hear you laugh.

"You understand, Jon, the police knew there was a service revolver used because the bullets had to go somewhere. That's right, so did the bullets from the Vizor. But none of them showed up in court. Which makes you think they dug the Czech bullets out of a wall, not a human body, as they said. Oiba, Jon, wait until you hear the rest of it.

"I wiped off the gun and threw it into a rat hole after I came out of Mascaró's vivienda and I wished the police a pleasant day when they found it. The captain had bullets from it and here was the gun, no matter if those in the corpse were from a service revolver. I wonder if they knew the Czech was Mascaró's own pistol. That may be our private joke. Ujuju!

"I heard Jenara talking to the Belgian woman lawyer. For a whore, Jenara has the youngest voice I've ever heard, but then she's from Eibar . . . She was telling about the celebration the night after Mascaró's death . . .

"Yes, naturally, I went to Suertegaray and told him everything that happened on the stairs. He had heard from a Social Brigade doctor about the two wounds. He said he would use me if it would help Matai. He wanted me to attend every session but you know about the witnesses. The bishop of Donostia was also ready to testify.

"Jon, here's the real gogo. I haven't time to tell you my whole conversation with the señora viuda de Mascaró, but when she told us Silva was on the stairs she said if I wanted to know why he was there I would have to ask the pendejo, and this alarmed Silva very much. I talked about it to Suertegaray. It makes sense. Mascaró was expendable, you know that. The foreign press was onto him. And Zendejas needed that death.

"But Silva was expendable too. He's really too crazy even for a torture squad. Nobody on earth could believe Silva killed the inspector for the love of my old love, that reputa of all time. But on orders from a famous captain and with some money? And that Silva seemed to have: Paule told me about his elegant clothes; you had told me what a chapichusqui he always was before. And a promise that he could leave Spain? What a chain they made between him and the señora! Her addiction and her information were rings fastened right into his nose . . . If it weren't for Matai we could laugh this thing into the blackest part of hell.

". . . I have the story of Angeles and Paule to tell you, Jon. You've never met Paule, who's gone back. There was no trouble at the border. A call came from him in Paris to the young priest at San Andrés. About Paule . . . I know he'll never stop trying to help Angeles. No doubt he'll come back and I'll be very glad to see him. Later I'll tell you how this is, Jon.

"And you must have things to tell me. The doctors are good to you, we hear, two of them Basque but one from the Canary Islands. Suddenly the Canary Islands are coming alive, this doctor, a man who knows more about skin grafts than anyone around, so they say, and of course the remarkable comisario.

"There has been no Paris phone call from him and there's gratifying scandal about his disappearance. There's even speculation he might have committed suicide. That he has, Jon.

"I hear you saying, 'You saw my book?'

"Only part of it, Jon. The priests got hold of the first part and had it read to me - why didn't you tell me you were thinking those things?

"You won't answer. You'll ask if the culetro mushrooms are out in the valley below Anboto.

". . . The matter which we need most to talk about will be spoken in silence, to put it that way: what the young people of the trial have suffered, and will suffer, is it worth what they think it's worth? And, silently, we will both say yes. You, Jon, standing in the middle of the fire, will know about Isa and you might be the only one who would know how to comfort her. God give you a chance to do that, even if it's the way we're talking now . . ."

•

He felt someone touch his arm. He thought it would be Matilde but he realized it was the fat child Bonavit with small gobs of matter in the near corners of his eyes.

Bonavit said, "I'm terribly sorry, Eagle, I didn't mean to deceive you."

"I can't visit him then?"

"You better get away from here. There may be trouble. I'm telling you for the good of yourself and the young lady."

"But what about Arizeder?"

"They're just this minute taking him out of there. They're putting him in an ambulance for a Madrid hospital."

310

"This is a good hospital here."

"There's no use fooling you, Eagle. There's going to be trouble and people are always standing around under his window the way you've been doing for the last hour. What were you doing anyway?"

"Nothing. Waiting. But you police are on the wrong track. Everybody's thinking about Burgos now. Arizeder's no danger to you. I just wanted to see him for a few minutes. Can't you get me in?"

"No, Eagle, I don't want to see you in trouble. I'm your friend."

"Ene, bada, Inspector." Arrano gave him the back of his hand, although he believed Bonavit, in his way, meant what he said about being a friend. It was just as well, though, that he had had the long talk with Jon Arizeder; probably he himself had known all along the other kind of talk wouldn't come off. So now Bonavit hurried away - a small fat man's noise of hurry. Matilde returned when he was gone. The little boy had disappeared with Bonavit's arrival.

Across the plaza and up a side street an old man - it was apparent he was old because he was a master musician - played his flute briefly and once or twice tapped his drum. Then another txistulari was heard on another street, far away. The night city was touched over and over by flute voices.

18

"Matilde, it seems to me there's a lot of motion in the plaza. Describe it to me. Are the benches full? Who's sitting on them?"

"They were full. Some of the chivatos I knew from my mother's time were on the benches when we came."

"No obscenity - you know what I mean, those gestures of theirs?"

"Not yet. They aren't sure how to treat me."

"So where are the chivatos now?"

"Most of them have left the plaza. A few have gone over to the statue of El Cano."

"What are they doing?"

"One's climbing the statue looking up the streets that come into this plaza."

"I can hear people in the streets."

"How far are they?"

"They're still quite a ways off but it sounds as though people are on all the streets of Bilbao, Matilde, listen."

"Yes, Papa, I can just barely hear them. But why aren't they singing?"

"They prefer to be silent."

All the chivatos were hurrying off, some running.

"They're afraid, Papa."

"No wonder. They heard the signal of the txistus. Who wouldn't be afraid to fight a hundred flutes? Ospa, Matilde."

But Matilde looked back. "Papa, wait a minute. They're different men coming into the plaza. Maybe police, but they're not like the ones we're used to."

"How do they look?"

"Well dressed. Some have sideburns. No thready overcoats."

"What are they doing?"

"There's one - they're all young, Papa - who seems to be giving directions."

"Is he on El Cano?"

"No, no, that one ran away. This one is giving directions standing there with the others. They look alike, Papa. Some of them have maps on writing boards."

"It sounds as though they're a special service from Madrid. We could tell by their accents."

"Two are coming this way."

The one who spoke had such an exaggerated Madrid accent it might have been put on. He was polite but nervous. "We're going to need this plaza. We suggest you go home."

Said Eagle, "The plaza will soon be full of people who won't go home."

"Shall we arrest him?"

"No arrests. What makes you think it will be full of people?"

"Because I hear them coming."

The men glanced at one another and laughed. Some kind

313

of Basque eccentric, one laugh was saying; all Basques are crazy eccentrics, the other said. They looked intelligent but that was evidently the way they thought.

The Eagle and Matilde walked away from them. Eagle was very angry. Matilde said, "They look like de la Vega when he wore civilian clothes."

"That's probably what they are."

"Where do you want to go, Papa? What are we doing?" Her voice sounded uneasy. Just then the lights went out all over Bilbao.

"It's dark, Papa," and now Matilde was greatly alarmed.

"I thought it soon would be. ETA has taken the power station. We're going up as far as we can while there's time . . . something for you to see up there. Use the stairs. Hurry, Matilde."

She took his arm. She was trembling. Then the little boy she had talked to was at her other side and took that hand. "Don't be afraid, señorita. Hola, Eagle."

"Kaisio, Hilario."

"I'm not afraid now," said Matilde.

They came to the top of the stairs. Matilde was getting used to the dark. Her father moved in it easily, as always, and Hilario acted as free as if he too were blind. Stairs, streets, plazas above and below were filling with people, but for a moment on the top landing they three were alone.

Eagle heard the dry whisper of a shot at the same time others saw the flash. Hilario and Matilde heard the bullet strike Eagle's chest, heard no cry from him but a scuffle near them, blows and grunts as if a man had been downed and was struggling.

Eagle leaned on Hilario and Matilde. He whispered, "Hold me up. And watch the mountains." And when a sweet voice from the dark asked, "Eagle, are you all right?" he answered, "Yes."

So it was that silence and the dark and the people were

314

ready when the first peak was lighted in the Pyrenees above them. Twenty-seven mountains were long ago elected to wear crowns of fire when Basques climb there to put the crowns in place. This December night, 1970, there was fire on sixteen of the twenty-seven, and if not every flaming peak could have been seen from Bilbao, each one was clear in Eagle's island mind.

When the first fire rose to its feet as a fire does and the crowd drew in its breath, he murmured, "For Matai - it's for him."

"For you too, Eagle." Hilario was crying but he didn't shift under the increasing weight of the arm around his shoulders.

When the next mountain stood aflame the voice of Arrano, like wind in mountain beech trees, whispered, "For you, Luku."

Fire on Aranzazu was for Isa.

Then Mount Itzkorri. Then the peak of Urku. Another. And another. Each time, a name was said by the crowd in noiseless, building passion, ingenerate anger which could be assuaged only by freedom, men and ponies running swiftly down from the caves of Roncesvalles, their strength already drawn for whatever had to happen. Let a man ride once so, from cave to meeting place, and no one on earth can make him forget.

Eagle could no longer stand even with the help of Matilde and Hilario. Before he fell, seven Basques gathered him up. How had Suertegaray on his crutches climbed the stairs? But he was there, standing beside Matilde, and Eagle thought he raised his hand to them.

Someone said, "It was Bonavit. We have him."

It seemed to Eagle that he answered, ". . . you, Bonavit . . . poor, fat, God-pissing hero . . . he's your Roland, Paule . . ."

Mostly he was surprised. Of course he knew he was

mortal, yet he had really thought he would never die; he laughed at that universal joke, remembering the decent words he had spoken about the deaths of others, never his own.

. . . *So now will they let me see again? Can I have my eyes back?* A jubilee of light, demand no less. The mountains had been splendid but not enough. He wanted to see his city blazing up from Barandiaran's heaven under the earth - Bilbao in joyous flames. And although they had not yet given him back all his vision, a first step was the understanding that Jon's Gernika, aflame, consisted of the sun, the sun of truth shouting from Jon's eyes. And he knew he also was going to have that lent help from sun, soon, now.

. . . *Paule, Paule, the raven is made of light.* Who could ever say a raven is somber? Not Mari's raven, with gold, green, blue, opal wings. Arrano held his breath: sight was returning.

Matilde, in a corona of light, was a tiny girl wearing a dark woolen dress and a blue apron, traveling into the sky above the peaceful ocean. She got smaller and smaller; she disappeared. But how fortunate he was to have known her, a daughter. Now the corona became a radiant, terrifying spear through his body, so hot it was melting his shoulder blades and spine. Then Matilde returned from the horizon, older, fourteen he guessed, and she passed him saying nothing. She was on her way to meet Isa and Angeles. And to meet Suertegaray. Or had Eagle seen him there among them? *Ospa, Matilde, you have a long trip wherever you're going.* The corona had become a comet.

He had little to do now. Alive, he had thought a man's death would be stronger than his life. Now he found it was the other way around, although the events of a proper death might be an epic, in their way - about that expectation at least he had been right. But how explain this immortal

316

longing for life stronger than any passion he had ever felt? He could contain it only because he had to.

And for those who were still going to be alive - that grand enthralling anguish - what must he do for them? At last he could see them. His eyes had returned, claiming sweet dimensional vision, and Matilde, Angeles, Ander were more human than he had known from their voices and their handclasps. What word could he say? Kaisio, friends and shining ravens?

Not enough.

He didn't know how to cry the irrintzi because, being a younger child, he had not been taught it. Was there some gifted angelic or demonic thing, up there, down there wherever it was, who would help him? Now Arrano heard and saw an irrintzi, so the others must be hearing it too. It was the spear, comet, crown, the sun.

Sun-fire on the mountains, wind from the Cantabrian sea. At the foot of stairs and streets lay Siete Calles and the police stations hedging it round, and the estuary webbed with loading cranes. Down from the high caves they went, carrying a dead eagle.

AFTERWORD

In December 1970, in the Spanish city of Burgos, in Summary Court Martial number 31/69, the following sentences were given to these sixteen Basques, who are real persons, not fictional:

EDUARDO URIARTE ROMERO, student
Two death sentences and thirty years of prison

JOSÉ MARÍA DORRONSORO CEBERIO, teacher
One death sentence

MARIO ONAINDIA NACHIONDO, bank employee
Two death sentences and fifty-one years of prison

JOAQUÍN GOROSTIDI ARTOLA, mechanic
Two death sentences and thirty years of prison

FRANCISCO JAVIER IZCO DE LA IGLESIA, printer
Two death sentences and twenty-seven years,
six months, and one day of prison

FRANCISCO JAVIER LARENA MARTINEZ, student
One death sentence and thirty years of prison

JOSU ABRISQUETA CORTA, chemist
Sixty-two years and one day of prison

ENRIQUE GUESALAGA LARRETA, agricultural technician
Fifty years of prison

319 (continued)

JON ECHAVE GARITACELAYA, priest
Fifty years of prison

VICTOR ARANA BILBAO, machinist
Sixty years of prison

GREGORIO LOPEZ IRASUEGUI, student
Thirty years of prison

JONE DORRONSORO CEBERIO, teacher of music
Fifty years of prison

ITZIAR AIZPURUA EGENA, teacher of piano
Fifteen years of prison

MARÍA ARRANZAZU ARRUTIODRIOZOLA
Sent to a mental hospital

JOSÉ ANTONIO CARRERA AGUIRREBARRENA, agronomist
Twelve years of prison

JULIÁN CALZADA UGALDE, priest
Twelve years of prison